HOME AT NIGHT

ALSO BY PAULA MUNIER

THE WEDDING PLOT

THE HIDING PLACE

BLIND SEARCH

A BORROWING OF BONES

HOME
AT NIGHT

A MERCY CARR MYSTERY

PAULA MUNIER

MINOTAUR BOOKS
NEW YORK

First published in the United States by Minotaur Books, an imprint of St. Martin's Publishing Group

HOME AT NIGHT. Copyright © 2023 by Paula Munier. All rights reserved.
Printed in the United States of America. For information,
address St. Martin's Publishing Group, 120 Broadway, New York, NY 10271.

www.minotaurbooks.com

Library of Congress Cataloging-in-Publication Data

Names: Munier, Paula, author.
Title: Home at night / Paula Munier.
Description: First Edition. | New York : Minotaur Books, 2023. | Series: A Mercy Carr Mystery ; 5
Identifiers: LCCN 2023024845 | ISBN 9781250887894 (hardcover) | ISBN 9781250887900 (ebook)
Subjects: LCGFT: Detective and mystery fiction. | Thrillers (Fiction) | Novels.
Classification: LCC PS3613.U475 H66 2023 | DDC 813/.6—dc23/eng/20230526
LC record available at https://lccn.loc.gov/2023024845

Our books may be purchased in bulk for promotional, educational, or business use.
Please contact your local bookseller or the Macmillan Corporate and Premium Sales
Department at 1-800-221-7945, extension 5442,
or by email at MacmillanSpecialMarkets@macmillan.com.

First Edition: 2023

10 9 8 7 6 5 4 3 2 1

For my granddaughters
Elektra, Calypso, and Demelza

Where thou art—that—
is Home.

—EMILY DICKINSON

The Ghost Witch of Grackle Tree

Beware the ghost witch in the woods
Where the grackles shriek and cry
The mourning song of her lost bairn
A most bewitching lullaby.
She lies in wait for the children
Who might hold the stolen key
To the poor ghost child she doth grieve
For all cursèd eternity.
Careful, child, when you walk these woods
Lest she cast her sorrow's spell
And you fall, forever locked
In hell where the undead dwell.
Wander not far into the woods
Home at night you'd better be
Beware the blackbirds and beware
The Ghost Witch of Grackle Tree.
Beware the blackbirds and beware
The Ghost Witch of Grackle Tree.

—EUPHEMIA WHITNEY-JONES

HALLOWEEN, 2004

THE MOON SHONE DIMLY THROUGH THE FOG THAT NIGHT. Dusk fell quickly, shrouding the old manor in shadow. The ivy-covered Victorian stood dark and silent under a towering maple, Bear Mountain hulking on the horizon. One hundred and fifty years of history and mystery lurked within the house, and as she crept along the brick path that led to the heavy front door, Mercy Carr cursed the boy who'd dared her to come here and her own reckless curiosity for accepting that dare.

A rapid-fire crackling—*ki ki ki!*

Mercy swallowed a scream as grackles stormed the sky above her, whirring and wheeling and whirling as one until they hurtled into the thick branches of the big maple. A shuddering of leaves. A whistling of beaks. A rustling of feathers.

Silence once again.

There must be a thousand grackles in that tree, thought Mercy. As forbidding as the manor was, she'd rather face a million shrieking specters inside its gloomy walls than spend another minute out here with these yellow-eyed demons. Or maybe she should just go home. Maybe her mother was right, and she was too young to be reading all that gothic literature.

But she loved all those macabre poems and stories—and the opportunity to spend the night in a real-life haunted house was too good to pass up. Especially one whose most celebrated spirit was the subject of one of her favorite poems: "The Ghost Witch of Grackle Tree."

This was the house where the woman who'd written it had lived. Her name was Euphemia Whitney-Jones, and her family still owned this estate. The old Victorian sat empty now, as it had for years, neglected by them and ignored by most everyone else.

Except on Halloween, when local teens and out-of-town ghost hunters tried to catch sight of the witch, who was said to wander the grounds on this night every year. Mercy's classmate Damien—a pain on a good day—had challenged her to come here tonight and meet the ghost. He'd never let her live it down if she chickened out.

She looked for the spare key he'd told her about—and found it under a stone lying at the foot of one of the huge hydrangeas that flanked the entrance. Mercy wouldn't be surprised if Damien was hiding inside somewhere. It would be just like him to lie in wait, hoping to leap out at her and scare her silly.

She didn't frighten that easily. Her big brother, Nick, with his newly minted driver's license, had dropped her off here, thrilled for the opportunity to run the hairpin turns up to the remote property. He'd offered to go inside with her if she wanted. But she'd sent him on his way to join his friends in the nearby woods, where they'd drink beer and do stupid boy stuff. Mercy didn't need a bodyguard. She could take care of herself. And she was armed with a small volume of Euphemia Whitney-Jones's poetry, her talisman against evil spirits.

She unlocked the heavy front door and pulled it, hard. Nothing. She pulled again, harder. And once more. The door creaked so loudly when she finally managed to move it that she had to steel herself not to jump. She stepped into the entry, flicking her flashlight around the hallway and up and down the staircase. All very beautiful, very creepy, very desolate. A Miss Havisham of a house.

Mercy sidled into the formal parlor, a ruin of a room with blotchy red flocked wallpaper. No witch, just dust and grime and spiderwebs. She wondered why no one lived here anymore. Somebody should buy this house and fix it up. That's what she'd do if she were a grown-up. Embrace it, grackles and ghosts and all, and move in to stay. Restore it to its former glory. A place of magic and poetry.

She heard the distant din of voices, and thought she recognized Damien's scornful laugh. She ducked into the kitchen. When the chatter seemed to follow her, growing louder with every step, she stumbled into the pantry, slamming the louvered doors behind her. A tin canister of flour fell from the top shelf, the top falling open, banging her forehead and dousing her in white powder. Sticking to her hair, her cheeks, her lashes, her lips. Even her sweatshirt and her jeans.

She yowled in surprise and clouds of the yeasty stuff slipped into her mouth. She needed to cough, but she didn't dare. She tried to hold her breath to keep from wheezing. She heard footfalls and disembodied voices in the kitchen, saw slivers of faces and bodies through the louvered doors as beams of light bounced around the room.

She switched off her flashlight. Shuffled feet and muffled mutterings headed her way. She blinked away the white powder that fell into her eyes, and more flour fell in. She blinked again.

A jerk of the handle and the door bounced open. A glare of light blinded her; someone screamed. The giggling ghostly figures advanced upon her. A loud boom silenced them—and Mercy realized it was the sound of her own falling, falling, falling to the floor of the pantry. The last thing she heard before she passed out was the clatter of the kitchen visitors scattering like so many blackbirds.

Mercy didn't know how long she was out. Long enough for a chill to set in and goose bumps to appear along her pale arms. Her head ached; she could feel a bump forming on the left side of her brow. She listened for sounds of life outside the slatted doors.

The silence of the old house was overwhelming. She could hear nothing but the pounding in her head. She counted to one hundred and back down to one again, just to make sure that no one was coming back.

She tried to brush off the white stuff clinging to her person from head to toe, but it stuck too fast and took too long. She gave up and slipped out of the pantry, passing though the empty kitchen and leaving by the back door. Forget Damien, forget dares, forget gothic novels.

Mercy ran, crazily, into the dark, her flashlight forgotten, a bouncing strobe on her hip. As she passed under the towering maple full of grackles, she stared up into its elephantine branches, expecting to see hundreds of glowing pairs of yellow eyes.

"Stop!" came a roar from nowhere and everywhere.

Mercy collided with a tall figure in flowing, glowing white garb and screamed, a full-out howl of fright. She tried to push the diaphanous thing away, but it took her by the shoulders with its large white-gloved hands and held her in place. She twisted in its hold, but it held firm.

"Calm yourself." Something about the voice, with its low-pitched Yankee grumble, struck a discordant note. Mercy stared at the creature before her, with its dark eyes gleaming through the veil. Was this the fabled Ghost Witch of Grackle Tree?

The creature looked pretty real to Mercy. In fact, as she peered at the face obscured by the filmy veil, she realized that this was not a ghost or a witch or even a woman. Under the girly dress and the waist-length platinum wig was a man. An honest-to-goodness human male.

"Who are you?" she whispered.

"I'm the witch."

"No, you're not."

The creature laughed—an odd *heh heh heh* staccato—but did not correct her. "You dropped this." He let go of her shoulders and pulled her little book from a hidden pocket in his voluminous skirt. He handed it to her.

"Thank you." Mercy slipped the volume of poetry into her pocket. She was glad to have it back. Proof that what was happening to her was not a figment of what her mother called her overactive imagination.

"Everything you need to know is in her poems." And with that, he retreated into the shadows of the mammoth maple. "Home at night you'd better be."

"Right."

He was gone. She looked around her, but all she could see was darkness.

Mercy withdrew the flashlight from her belt and shone it around the property. She heard shouts from inside the house. Time to go. She ran for the woods and didn't stop to look back until she reached the edge of the forest.

In the dim illumination of the flashlight, the backside of the manor looked as bleak and beautiful as the front. There, on the wide back porch, stood a ghostly figure in a long white gown reaching after her, slender arms and pointed fingers glowing, as if to pull Mercy back to the house. It could have been the same creature that gave her back her book, but she couldn't be sure. This one seemed more ethereal, more feminine, more otherworldly than the so-called ghost witch she'd encountered under the grackle-filled tree.

It was colder now, or maybe that was just the fear talking. For it was only now that she felt truly anxious. Mercy shivered, shoving her hands in her pockets. She felt the book, which seemed bulkier than she remembered. She retrieved it, and that's when she noticed the bulge in the middle. She opened the book, and there lay a stone with a hole in the middle. It had not been there before. The stone was a gift. A gift from a ghost.

Or not.

The eerie caws of the grackles sounded above her, and she looked up at the screeching. A barred owl swooped past her, flapping its enormous brown-and-white feathered wings in a rush of cool night air. A sign, like the poem and the witch and the stone. A sign that this house was meant to be home to more than blackbirds.

Mercy fingered the flat rock in her open palm. Maybe someday . . .

DAY ONE
OCTOBER 27

CHAPTER ONE

Are we not homes? And is not all therein?
—CHARLOTTE ANNA PERKINS GILMAN

T HERE ARE MANY PLACES WE CAN CALL HOME, AND THE LONGER we live, the more places we will call home. This was a lesson that Mercy Carr kept learning over and over again. First in the military, and now in civilian life.

The good news was that she and her new husband Troy had found the perfect house to call home. A mid-century post-and-beam lodge in the woods, big enough for Mercy and Troy, the dogs, the cat, and Amy and Helena, the young teenage mother and child Mercy had met during a case and taken in afterward. The bad news was that the deal had fallen through at the last minute, thanks to squabbling siblings, one of whom pulled out just before closing. And just after Troy had sold his converted fire tower to the State of Vermont.

Now there were three animals, one child, three adults—well, four if you counted Amy's boyfriend Brodie, who practically lived here anyway—all squeezed into Mercy's cozy, if small, cabin in the Green Mountains.

"You need to move." Her mother Grace sat next to her in one of the two rocking chairs on the front porch of the cabin, regarding Mercy with her signature *I'm your mother and your attorney so listen up* look.

"We *bought* a house." Mercy stroked Muse, the sweet little Munchkin kitty she and Elvis had rescued from a crime scene a couple of years ago. Muse was curled up in her lap for her usual post-breakfast nap.

"Breach of contract. Get over it and go find another one."

"Easier said than done."

"Since when do you like easy?"

Mercy laughed. Like most mothers—and this was the only way in which her mother was like most mothers—Grace knew her child too well.

"I have to love it." Like she loved her cabin, where she and Elvis had come to get on with their lives after Afghanistan. Both she and the bomb-sniffing shepherd had been mourning the loss of her fiancé, Martinez, who was also Elvis's handler. He had died in the same battle that left Mercy wounded and Elvis traumatized. This cabin, with its massive fieldstone fireplace and floor-to-ceiling bookshelves and a wall of windows looking out at the woods, had been a comfort to her and to Elvis.

She'd never thought there'd be another man she could love like Martinez—and then she met Troy. Mercy couldn't believe her luck.

She'd never thought there'd be another place she could love like this—and then they found the lodge. Her good luck was holding.

And then they lost the lodge. And now she and Troy had to start all over again. So much for luck. Mercy sighed. "The lodge was the perfect property."

"There is no such thing." Her mother tapped on the front window of the cabin behind them. "It's a nightmare in there. Too many people, too many animals, too many books and moving boxes and clothes and toys and other paraphernalia. Too much stuff. You can't escape outside to this porch forever. Winter is coming."

"I know." Mercy whistled for Elvis, who was making his daily morning patrol of the perimeter. She needed backup, and the former bomb-sniffing Malinois was one of the few sentient beings immune to her mother's imperious charm. Grace neither impressed nor intimidated Elvis. Mercy loved the dog for that—and so much more.

Elvis came racing down from the barn, ears perked. The loyal Belgian shepherd could never ignore her whistle. But he could ignore her mother. He settled into a graceful sit at Mercy's side without so much as a sniff in Grace's direction. Nothing better than a cat in your lap and a dog at your feet, was Mercy's way of thinking. Especially when talking to your mother.

"Then you need to get back out there," Grace went on. "I'd be happy to help."

The very thing Mercy most wished to avoid. She scratched the shepherd's sleek head, trying to buy time.

"The first thing you need is a new Realtor." Grace leaned toward her. "A good one would have seen that family quarrel coming, and steered you to another property. I could sue on your behalf."

"Not necessary." Her mother believed that litigation solved all ills.

"You should use that woman who sold Troy's place."

"Jillian Merrill?" Mercy had known her—or known of her, at least—when she was a teenager. Jillian Rosen then.

"She closed Troy's deal in record time. To the State of Vermont, a government entity, no less."

"I know." Her husband had sold his one-of-a-kind converted fire tower without a second thought before they even found the lodge. And even after they lost the lodge, his faith that they would find a wonderful new home together never wavered. Even as hers was wavering right now.

Her mother waited. Waited for her to admit her loss of faith. Instead, Mercy surveyed the garden in all its glory: black-eyed Susans, purple asters, and pink bee balm against a blaze of orange and gold maples.

"It's a seller's market," Grace finally said. "The best properties are going fast."

"That's why I'm in no hurry to list the cabin. We need a place big enough for all of us. If the cabin sells before we've found something, we could all end up spending the winter in a trailer." She knew this was her chic mother's idea of hell.

"You know it doesn't have to come to that." Grace crossed her legs, careful not to crease her caramel-colored tweed trousers. She'd gone full-on Ralph Lauren for the fall season. "You don't need such a big place. You don't have to sell the cabin. Amy and Helena can stay here, and you and Troy can find something that's right for you. There are a lot more medium-sized properties to choose from."

Mercy didn't say anything. She'd heard this argument before. All her adult life, really.

When she'd found the cabin, her parents had offered to buy it for her, as had her grandmother Patience, but like a good soldier, she'd insisted on purchasing it herself through a VA loan. Likewise, they'd all offered to buy her and Troy a house, too, and God knows they could more than afford it. But Mercy had refused. And she would keep on refusing.

Her mother frowned. "That pride of yours will be the death of you someday. Just like your grandfather."

Mercy's beloved grandfather was a sheriff who died in an arrest gone wrong, because he didn't wait for backup. He was a proud man, and Mercy admired him for it. If she was like him, then she was glad of it.

"You think that to maintain your autonomy, you have to do everything by yourself. But you don't," Grace went on. "It's bad enough that you won't let *us* help you. Don't make that mistake with your husband. You're not a one-woman band anymore—you're a team now."

"I know that." Mercy scratched the shepherd's ears. She knew how to be part of a team. The military was all about esprit de corps. And since she'd come home from the war, she and the shepherd had worked through their troubled past together. When she and Elvis met Troy and his search-and-rescue dog Susie Bear, the four of them became a team in work and in love and in life.

"Then act like it. If you insist on selling the cabin, then list it now. Maybe that will get you off this porch and into 'Open Houses.'"

"Troy's fire tower and my cabin are both very special homes. I don't want to be forced to settle for something mediocre just because we got married."

"According to Lillian Jenkins, you've seen practically every property currently on the market."

This was true. Mercy had no defense other than the expected one. "Nothing I could fall in love with."

"Is that your only criterion? Or are you waiting for a sign?"

Mercy knew her mother didn't believe in signs. But soldiers were a superstitious lot, and signs were as much a part of the military as bad food and battle drills. She thought of signs as synchronicity, little coincidences that could point to larger truths if you were paying attention. Mercy tried to pay attention.

Elvis leapt up and took off, tearing down the garden path, sliding to an elegant stop at the edge of the driveway. He settled into his happy waiting stance, black-tipped tail up and wagging hard. Mercy grinned at the sight of her grandmother's oversized yellow van barreling up her driveway and coming to a stop behind her mother's blue Volvo. Patience was a veterinarian, and the Nana Banana was her fully equipped mobile clinic.

Elvis greeted his favorite vet with a quick yip as she exited the van. The Malinois adored her grandmother, as did most species, domesticated and undomesticated. Patience hurried up to the porch, a Tupperware container in her hand, Elvis on her heels.

Mercy rose to her feet in alarm. Patience was not the sort to rush, especially when transporting baked goods.

"Mother?" Grace remained seated, but Mercy could hear the worry in her voice.

"Is everything all right?" asked Mercy.

"Just fine. But you need to get a move on." She offered up the plastic tub.

"Why?" Mercy pulled up the top of the Tupperware to sneak a peek. Just as she'd hoped: her grandmother's famous cinnamon rolls. "Thank you!"

"Lillian sent me. Grackle Tree Farm is going on the market." Lillian Jenkins was her grandmother's best friend and the grande dame of Northshire. If there was news to know, she'd know it first—and spread it fastest.

"Now, that is a very large property." Her mother glided to her feet. "Let's get those rolls inside."

Mercy ushered her mother and grandmother into the cabin. "Have a seat. I'll get us some coffee. Who wants a roll?"

"No, thank you." Grace never ate any of her mother's amazing desserts. How she resisted, Mercy had no idea.

"They're all yours, love." Patience settled into a chair at the farm table across from Grace. Elvis stretched out at her side, his head on her boots. He adored his vet. "The house itself is a historical gem. One hundred and fifty years of history behind it. And you love old houses."

"True enough." Mercy poured coffee into three mugs, and brought them to the table on a small tray, along with cream and sugar and a roll for herself.

"I've heard it's a mess," warned her mother. "And then there are the grackles." She sipped her coffee, which of course she took black.

"Grackles are fine, intelligent blackbirds." Patience defended the birds with the confident air of the real expert in the room as she added sugar and cream to her coffee. "Their bad reputation is undeserved. They've earned the enmity of farmers because they feed on crops like sorghum, wheat, corn, all the grains. But they're really great for your garden, as they eat lots of insects. Just don't grow corn."

Grace was not impressed. "They're the hyenas of birds. They make a horrendous racket. And they're the bullies of the bird feeders."

"Mercy knows better than to put out bird feeders." Patience looked to Mercy for confirmation.

"Indeed I do." At this time of year, bird feeders attracted bears as well as birds. Which never ended well for the bears. Responsible Vermonters drew birds to their gardens with flora, not bird feeders.

"Go ahead, show off your new knowledge." Patience had encouraged her to go back to school to get her degree in wildlife management more than anyone else in her family, apart from Troy.

"Grackles are an essential link in the food chain." Following her grandmother's example, Mercy added generous amounts of cream and sugar to her coffee. "They eat most anything—plant and animal—and hawks and owls and foxes eat them."

"I stand corrected," said Grace. "Apparently blackbirds are one of this property's biggest assets."

"It's a house full of mystery and drama and poetry." Patience looked at Mercy. "Enough to satisfy even *your* inner Shakespeare."

"Also true." Mercy hadn't been out there in years, but she remembered the place well.

"'The Ghost Witch of Grackle Tree.'"

"Of course!" Her mother laughed. "You were obsessed with that poem as a teenager—and everything else that woman wrote."

"Euphemia Whitney-Jones." Patience gave Mercy a knowing look.

Her grandmother was the only grown-up she'd told about meeting the witch all those years ago. Of course, everyone in middle school knew about it. She'd brought the holey stone to school, regaling her classmates with her encounter with the witch and showing off the present she'd given her. Much to Damien Landry's dismay. She'd left out her discovery that the so-called poltergeist was really a brown-eyed man in a silver-white wig with a weird laugh.

That was then, this is now. Mercy looked out the large windows, staring past the lavender that lined the footpath to the flagpole in the middle of the garden, where the American flag flew night and day, in honor of her fallen comrades. Yes, she believed in ghosts. Not the horror-story kind of demons or the ghost witches of poems, but the spirits of the warriors who visited her in her dreams. "I do believe in ghosts." She stood up. "But I'm not afraid of haunted houses."

"Every house is haunted by something," said Patience.

"It would be perfect for you and Troy. It's large enough for you and your dogs and all your strays and a couple of children of your own, too. Go look at it. Buy it." Grace finished her coffee, and rose to her feet, her trousers falling neatly into line. "I have a luncheon to attend."

"I can't stay, either." Patience gave Elvis a pat. "Got a rabies clinic to run in Rutland. I promised Lillian you'd meet Jillian Merrill at the house in thirty minutes."

"A *real* Realtor." Grace headed toward the door, and the rest of them followed her out to the porch.

"Apparently the owner is anxious to sell," said Patience. "And if you don't buy it first, the poets will want it for a museum, the builders will want it for McMansions, and the developers will want it for God knows what kind of monstrosities."

"That would not be good."

"Go save a historic Vermont landmark. Live among the dead poets. You know you want to."

"Amen." Grace swept past them onto the gravel path toward her Volvo, wiggling her long fingers goodbye.

"Thirty minutes." Her grandmother kissed her on the cheek, stroked Elvis's ears, and started toward the driveway. "I'll tell Lillian you're on the way."

Mercy and Elvis watched as the blue Volvo and the Nana Banana roared off in reckless succession. Speed being the one thing that her mother and her grandmother had in common.

The shepherd nudged her hand with his nose.

"I know, I know." She grabbed a cinnamon roll for the road. "The clock is ticking."

Elvis was ready to go. He wasn't afraid of ghosts, either.

LEVI BEECHER WATCHED THE man in the fancy leather jacket as he examined the low-hanging branches of the big old sugar maple behind the manor house at Grackle Tree Farm. He knew the man's name was Max Vinke, and he knew he was from California. The trustee had told him that Vinke was checking out the place for Maude, the last remaining member of the Whitney-Jones family. But Levi suspected that he'd really been sent by Maude to dig up all her sister Euphemia's secrets. Secrets long buried all these years. And they would stay buried—Levi would see to that.

Vinke couldn't see him behind the thicket of red osier dogwood; the Santa Barbara snoop didn't realize he was under observation. Levi was good at hiding; after fifty years as caretaker here, he knew every inch of this property. And he was good at observing people; he'd much rather watch people than talk to them.

Vinke kicked the thick trunk of the tree. Frustrated, no doubt, by the search that was leading nowhere. At least for now. But Vinke was a good private detective, according to the testimonials on his website. And Yelp. If he persisted, he might figure it out eventually.

Levi knew that Vinke had done his homework. He'd started with the poetry. He'd even gone to the Northshire Alliance of Poets celebration last night. Levi himself usually avoided the pretentious get-togethers, but his sister Adah was up for the Euphemia Whitney-Jones Poetry Prize, and he wanted to be there to support her when they gave it to someone else. Someone writing "stately stanzas of dazzling virtuosity." Which is how that blowhard Horace Boswell had praised the winner's poems when he presented the prize. Not to his sister, but to another self-important academic like himself. Big surprise there.

Levi loved poetry, but he hated poets. In his experience, the greater the poet, the lousier the human being. Except of course for Euphemia Whitney-Jones. And his sister Adah.

The fact that the most illuminating poems were often written by the most unenlightened people always exasperated Levi. At the party, Horace and his hangers-on were in rare form, basking in the attention of the so-called film scout from LA—aka Max Vinke—like starlets soaking up the sun at the Beverly Hills Hotel pool.

Like movie people ever made movies out of poems. Apart from *The Odyssey*. Which he doubted many of those in attendance had actually read the whole way through.

Levi followed Vinke from the old maple to the manor house. Maude must have given the private detective a set of keys, because he let himself into the house. He didn't lock the door behind him.

While Vinke searched the downstairs, Levi remained at the front entrance behind one of the tall cedars that anchored the front façade of the house. He knew for sure the investigator would find nothing there. Eventually, the guy must have reached that same conclusion himself, because he abandoned his exploration of the first floor and climbed the staircase to the second floor. Levi counted to one hundred, then sneaked inside and stole up the stairs quietly, avoiding the creaky spots. Quiet as a bobcat in his rubber-soled duck boots.

The library door, which was always kept locked, was wide open. If there was anything to find in the house itself, Effie's library was the logical place to look. Vinke was right about that.

But Levi wasn't worried. He, not the estate, was the keeper of Effie's secrets. He sneaked back down the stairs and out the door, headed for the barn. As he left, he looked up at the windows of the library on the second floor.

Knock yourself out, California, he thought. There was only one way anyone would ever learn the confidences Euphemia Whitney-Jones had kept so close to her heart.

Over his dead body.

CHAPTER TWO

Turn up the lights. I don't want to go home in the dark.
—O. HENRY

GRACKLE TREE FARM WAS ONLY ABOUT EIGHT MILES NORTHWEST of town as the grackle flies. But getting there if you weren't a blackbird was not that easy. The most reliable route—"reliable" being a relative term in the Taconic Range—was the way to Equinox Mountain, south along Route 7a and then turning north again via Skyline Drive. Mercy decided on the shorter route, which would lead her onto private roads, "private" being Yankee-speak for "unpaved." Eighty percent of the roads in Vermont were unpaved, but her trusty Jeep could handle most of them. The less-traveled back roads were her best bet, especially now, as leaf peepers from all over the world jammed the main throughfares to enjoy Vermont's shining spectacle of fall foliage. She was glad few of them knew that the best views were on these back roads.

Behind her on the back seat, Elvis pressed his paw against the power switch, and his window rolled down. He leaned to the right, nose into the wind, ears blown back.

"I'm glad you're enjoying yourself." Mercy cranked up the heat.

It was a fine crisp and sunny autumn day, but there was an undeniable chill in the air. The cold harbinger of winter to come. But not before the oaks and maples and beeches and birches set the forest ablaze with color. Yellows and reds and oranges, bright against the cerulean-blue sky.

She amused herself by identifying the trees along the road as she drove. *Sugar maple. Paper birch. American beech.* When she was a child, her grandfather had taken her for long walks in the woods, pointing out the trees. She could tell a maple from an oak even then. But now her fieldwork was teaching her how to observe the forest the way she'd once observed the battlefield. The trees she'd thought of only as evergreens revealed themselves as eastern hemlocks and white pines, balsam fir and eastern white cedar. The hard-to-name trees—the various species of ash, maple, cherry—were making themselves clear to her, not only by their leaves but by their bark and buds and bugs.

As she steered the Jeep around the hairpin curves of Skyline Drive, Mercy kept an eye out for Old Sheep Lane. She found it about a quarter mile later, and made a sharp right at the small hand-painted sign. Old Sheep Lane was unkempt, even for a private road. She slowed down, navigating carefully around the deep ruts, fallen limbs, and encroaching ferns.

"Hold on," she told Elvis, whose focus was on something rustling back in the trees. Out of the corner of her eye, she caught a glimpse of a white-tailed deer.

"Stay, Elvis." The shepherd whined but stayed put.

Mercy wondered whether or not the land was posted. In Vermont, the right to hunt, fish, and trap on open, private land had been guaranteed since the 1700s, In Vermont, the right to hunt, fish, and trap on open, private land had been guaranteed since the 1700s, unless the landowner posted the property—which prohibited hunting, fishing, or trapping without written permission—and put up warnings to that effect.

She had seen no such notices, and it was archery deer hunting season right now. Prime time to harvest a white-tailed deer if you were so inclined. Mercy was not. Her grandfather had taught her to shoot a variety of weapons, and she'd gone with him on hunting trips when she was young. But not since he died. And never again since Afghanistan.

As the Jeep approached a wooded rise, the pitted and pocked road narrowed, and the branches of the trees on each side overlapped, creating a canopy of dark gold. They moved through the shadowy tunnel of leaves, and came upon a wooded rise. At the top of the hill, a stand of junipers obscured all but the tall chimneys of the main house and the enormous sugar maple beyond it.

The road looped around a couple of outbuildings and a big barn to the southern side of the rise, leading past the line of trees that fronted the two-and-a-half-story limestone manor. Mercy parked the Jeep in the dandelion-studded gravel lot on the west side of the house. She let Elvis out of the vehicle, and for a moment they stood together, getting a sense of the place.

The air was thick with the musky-sweet smell of dark earth and fallen leaves and rotting wood. The only sounds were the rustle of leaves at their feet and the raucous cry of the grackles perched high in the upper branches of the massive maple. Her mother was right. They were noisy. When she was a girl, that noise had unsettled her. But now it all sounded like good noise to Mercy's ears.

The house itself looked much the same as she remembered it. The Second Empire Victorian was covered in ivy; even the keystone lintels were mostly masked in deep green. A three-story tower anchored the entrance, crowned by a widow's walk. The roof was missing more than a few of its shingles. The paned windows were dull with dirt, even the ones in the arched dormers. The once-dignified entrance, with its massive carved arched door, was showing its age.

Still, the house was a beauty. A faded beauty, but a beauty nonetheless. Mercy couldn't help but admire her handsome lines and long history, which were punctuated by the towering tree that stood like a sentinel at her side. The sugar maple was even more colossal today than it had been the last time she was here.

The sun disappeared behind a cloud, the sky darkened, and the forlorn manor took on a more forbidding look in the gloom. Now, this was the haunted house the locals talked about, the one kids dared each other to enter. The one where the grackles and the ghosts scared the living half to death. The one she'd fallen in love with that foggy night twenty years ago.

Mercy and Elvis walked along a crumbling brick path past a moss-covered stone bench to the front of the manor. The flower beds flanking the entrance were thick with unruly boxwood, leggy hydrangeas, and knee-high weeds. A small white marker to the left side of the door read "c. 1866, Capt. Addison Strong House."

Mercy wondered if that was a sign. Probably not, as so many of the old houses still standing in New England were built by those who'd served in the military. She tried to look inside through the windows, but between the grime and the overgrown ivy, she couldn't see very much. The ungroomed lawn ran right up to an old stone wall behind the stand of junipers.

"Come on, let's see the grounds." They followed the old brick path around to the back, continuing up to the expansive, if sagging, porch.

With its wide planks and graceful columns, the porch would be a lovely spot to sit with a book, thought Mercy. She pictured white wicker furniture with plump blue-and-white-striped cushions and a coffee table set for tea and her grandmother's *dessert du jour*. She laughed at herself for decorating the place before she'd even set foot inside. Elvis perked his ears. "Don't mind me, boy."

She focused her attention on the ornamental garden that stretched out from the porch to the edge of the rise, the thick branches of the massive old maple shading its north corner. Bear Mountain loomed in the background, and the grackles screeched a scratchy song that sounded more like a warning than a welcome.

Nice try, she thought. It would take more than the bawling of blackbirds to scare her off this time. The forgotten green space had good bones; even after years of neglect, the formal beds echoed the symmetry of the home itself, connecting the brick pathway with tangles of boxwood, yew, foxglove, lavender, oleander, rosemary, monkshood. She could only imagine what else gardeners had grown here over the years. It would be fun—if exhausting—to find out.

Nothing that a good pruning wouldn't fix, she thought, then chastised herself for getting carried away. Still, she could dream. This was the gothic manor she'd imagined living in as a girl reading *Jane Eyre* and *Wuthering Heights* and *The Woman in White*. From the first sight of its ivy-covered façade, Mercy had felt like she was born to live in a house just like this one. And that feeling hadn't changed. Something about this old place simply felt like home.

She rambled through the disorderly garden, Elvis at her side. An Italianate fountain graced the circular centerpiece, its tiers harboring all kinds of detritus. Creepy now, yes, but also full of potential.

Mercy wished she could have seen the place 150 years ago, in its prime. And despite the enormity of such an undertaking, part of her longed to restore the place to even a little bit of its former magnificence. It had been forgotten for far too long.

Where the northwest corner of the back garden met the forest, she spotted a six-foot-high limestone wall capped with granite and obscured by tumbles of climbing roses. There were a few pink blooms—*the last rose of summer,* as her grandmother would say—but mostly the foliage was thick with thorns.

"A secret garden?" she asked Elvis, who ignored her, intent on the chipmunk darting under the gate into the hidden space. She didn't remember seeing this when she'd been here as a girl. But then, she'd made a rather quick exit.

A small engraved brass plaque on a medieval-looking gate made of dark oak read "Sweet Sorrow" in a florid font. *Parting is such sweet sorrow.* A literal sign.

Mercy applauded the *Romeo and Juliet* reference, even though now she realized that what lay beyond the gate must be a broken heart. She yanked open the rusty slide-bolt lock and pushed open the heavy gate. Elvis bounded ahead. The square space was paved with granite and brick, and despite the overgrown moss, the labyrinth pattern was still visible. At the center of the labyrinth was Michael the Archangel, head bowed and hands folded around the hilt of his sword as if in prayer.

The pedestal on which the stone angel stood was worn, but Mercy could still make out the epitaph:

MICHAEL EMIL ROBILLARD
MAJ HQ2 BOMB WG
B. MAY 12, 1918
D. AUG 1, 1943

Mercy saluted the fallen B-24 pilot. She thought of herself and Troy and Martinez and all those who'd served with them in Afghanistan. Some of whom never made it home. Also warriors. Also avenging angels. She walked the labyrinth, coming to stand side by side with Michael the Archangel. She looked back across the garden to the old manse.

This was no haunted house. This was hallowed ground. How many signs did she need? She placed her warm hands over the cool stone hands of Michael the Archangel. *Sweet Sorrow.*

Elvis barked once, his signal bark, and raced out of the enclave. Mercy gave the statue one last pat and ran after the shepherd. She found him in a far corner of the ornamental garden, licking the tattooed hand of a woman in black leggings and a colorful hand-knitted poncho. She wore

an orange boonie hat over the thick gray-streaked dark hair that spilled
out over her shoulders and down her back, and carried a myrtle wood
garden trug on one arm, just like the one her grandmother Patience had.

Mercy didn't know the woman, and as far as she knew, Elvis didn't,
either, but the shepherd was treating the trespasser like a long-lost friend.
"Elvis!"

At her approach, the woman straightened. "Hello."

"Hi." Mercy considered the contents in the trug: chives, basil, mint,
rosemary, oregano. "Are you here to see the house, too?"

"I'm not sure what you mean."

"It's for sale."

"About time." The woman extended her hand, exposing the inked
roses that wrapped their way around her wrist, forming a floral Celtic
triple spiral on the back of her hand. "I'm Adah Beecher."

"Mercy Carr. This is Elvis."

Adah pushed her hat back on her head, revealing more of her face. It
was a friendly face, with honey-brown eyes and dimples that deepened
when she smiled. She was smiling now.

"Nice to meet you."

"It is a lovely garden."

"It was, truly, once upon a time, when Levi looked after it full-time. He's
my brother, and the caretaker here. It's getting to be too much for him now."
She turned toward the barn and yelled, "Levi! Come down here!" She turned
back to Mercy. "He's semi-retired now, but he still does what he can."

Within seconds a tall, well-muscled man loped into the garden, carrying huge loppers in his hand. His energetic gait belied the deep lines
that marked his lean, long face. Mercy realized Levi was far older than he
looked. He ignored her but held out a fist for Elvis to sniff. The shepherd
trotted over to him, and allowed him the privilege of scratching his neck.

"This is Levi. Levi, this is Mercy Carr."

"I remember." He fixed his dark eyes on her face.

Mercy could feel herself blush under his scrutiny. "But we've never met."

"You were here before."

She wondered how he knew. "That was a very long time ago."

"On Halloween. Covered in flour." He laughed. *Heh-heh-heh.*

The strange chuckle echoed through Mercy's memory—and there

stood the man she'd met on that Halloween night years before. It wasn't just the laugh—his dark eyes were the same, too.

"You're the ghost witch."

Levi said nothing.

"I still have that holey stone you gave me."

"Mercy's here to look at the house," said Adah.

"You're not the only one."

"What do you mean?" *The man speaks in riddles,* Mercy thought. "I didn't see any other vehicles in the lot. Yours or anyone else's."

"We always park up by the barn," explained Adah.

"Guess he's gone now." Levi held the lopper up toward the house. "Once the 'For Sale' sign goes up, people will line up to see the place."

"Levi's right," said Adah.

He ignored his sister. "You still like her poetry." A statement, not a question.

"Absolutely. I have all her books."

"Good."

Adah lifted a tattooed arm toward the manor. "A nice young couple should buy it, fix it up, and raise a family here." She fixed those honey-brown eyes on Mercy. "You will be very happy here."

"We'll see—"

"You already love it," the older woman interrupted her. "Your husband will love it, too. The back bedroom on the second floor will make a lovely nursery."

"Adah's never wrong. Buy the house." With one last piercing look, he stalked off, loppers bouncing along his leg.

"Don't mind Levi. He's not that good with people. He's better with plants and poems."

"Poems?"

"He's a poet."

"I didn't know."

"Poets are like seeds around here. We may hide underground for years, then we all break out into the sun sooner or later."

Before Mercy could ask her what she meant by that, Elvis cocked his triangular ears, turned on his back legs, and tore down the gravel path, disappearing around the house.

CHAPTER THREE

A home without books is a body without soul.
—MARCUS TULLIUS CICERO

E XCUSE ME."

"Nice dog," the woman called after her, as Mercy huffed along in Elvis's wake to the front of the house. The shepherd stood at the edge of the lawn, by the parking lot.

She heard the spin of gravel as a vehicle squealed to a stop, reaching Elvis just as a petite blonde dressed head-to-toe in Talbots and carrying a Vera Bradley tote climbed out of a red hybrid Porsche. Maybe Realtors liked speed, too. Just like Grace and Patience.

"Hi." Mercy snapped her fingers, and Elvis came to sit at her side, nose at her hip. "I'm Mercy Carr. And this is Elvis."

"Jillian Rosen Merrill." The blonde regarded her with hazel eyes that seemed to be laughing. "I remember you from when we were kids. I never thought you'd grow up to be a soldier. I thought you'd be, like, a professor or something. You were always reading."

"Soldiers read, too."

"If you say so."

"You haven't changed at all." Which was true. Jillian looked just like she had when she was hanging out with Troy and the other older, cooler kids. She had the kind of doll-faced cuteness that never faded. No awkward stage for her; she'd been cute at birth and cute at sixteen and she was cute now and she'd still be cute at sixty. Ninety, even.

"Now you're just being mean." Jillian's hazel eyes were still laughing. "I was so chubby back then."

Mercy stared at her. "You were not."

"It took giving birth to twins to get me to finally lose those seven pounds." Jillian looked Mercy over. "You're as slender as ever, just more muscled. All those military push-ups, maybe?"

"I'm not a soldier anymore." Even if she did still dress like one, she thought, suddenly all too aware of her camo cargo pants and army-green Henley shirt and backpack.

"No, now you're Troy Warner's wife."

At least she didn't say *second wife,* thought Mercy. Troy's first wife Madeline had been one of the older, cooler kids, too.

"Congratulations."

"Thank you."

"You'll be good for Troy." Jillian studied her. "Two crusaders for truth and justice and endangered species. I'm happy for you both."

"Thank you."

"And now that you're married," Jillian went on, "you need a bigger property." She opened her arms wide, and turned toward the house. "This classic Victorian, thirty acres of land, mostly woods and wetlands. A pond, too."

Our own woods. Our own wetlands. Our own pond. Every nature lover's dream come true. As if the poetry connection wasn't enough.

Over its long history, Grackle Tree Farm had been home not only to soldiers and poets but to bears and moose and wild turkeys and beavers and more. The poets and the soldiers may be long gone, but the wildlife was still here—and it needed protection from the poachers and predators of the world. Who better to steward this land than a game warden and a student of wildlife management?

Mercy knew she needed to put on her game face. "It needs a lot of work."

It would take years to get the place back into shape. What Jillian didn't know was that for Mercy, that was part of its charm. She loved that the grand old manor, with its overgrown gardens and sad soldier's memorial, needed saving. She loved that she and Troy could bring it back to life. Just like Adah Beecher and her brother Levi believed they should. She'd made up her mind. She wanted this property. But she didn't want Jillian Rosen Merrill to know it. Not yet.

"Troy's no stranger to hard work. And I suspect you aren't, either."

Mercy considered that. Persuading people to mortgage their lives for their so-called dream homes required more than salesmanship; it required emotional intelligence. Seemed like Jillian Rosen was as smart as ever. Just as well that she didn't know about Adah's prediction.

Jillian escorted her up to the arched front door. Elvis trotted along behind them. She rummaged around in her tote bag, pulling out a tablet and a cell phone, a charger and a makeup bag and sanitary wipes before coming up with a ring of keys and a plastic baggie full of dog treats.

Mercy couldn't help comparing the contents of Jillian's oversized tote to those of her backpack. She bet the Realtor didn't have plastic gloves or duct tape or a compass or trail mix. The one thing that they both carried? Dog treats.

Jillian handed Mercy the bag. "Give one to Elvis."

"Thank you." Mercy slipped the shepherd a goodie, and he chomped it down in one bite.

"A good Realtor always carries dog treats." Jillian unlocked the lockbox, retrieved the key inside, and opened the door. "After you."

Elvis pivoted on his paws and dashed away. Again. *What is up with this dog today?* thought Mercy.

A horn honked. Gravel crunched. Dogs bellowed.

She swiveled around, and beyond the garden, she saw Troy pulling up in his trusty Ford F-150, his search-and-rescue dog Susie Bear hanging her big shaggy black head out the passenger window. Baying for joy.

"Hey, wait up!" Troy leaned over to let out the Newfoundland-retriever mix, then jumped down from the truck himself. The Malinois greeted Troy and the Newfie with cordial restraint, while Susie Bear shook from jowl to tail with delight at the sight of Mercy and Elvis.

They joined her and Jillian at the front door.

"That's a lot of dog." Jillian stood back while Mercy hugged Susie Bear and Troy patted Elvis. Greetings over, the dogs raced off together to explore the grounds. Jillian looked a little relieved.

"You're here," Mercy said to Troy.

"Of course I'm here. Where else would I be?"

"My mother called you."

"She did." Troy gave Mercy a quick kiss and took her hand in his. "I tried to text you."

"Spotty cell service up here," said Jillian. "But after you move in, you can get really good high-speed internet. Wi-Fi calling."

"And so it begins." Troy gave Jillian a quick kiss on the cheek before addressing Mercy. "Grace said you'd found a fixer-upper for us." He looked up at the run-down manor. "It's a fixer-upper, all right."

"Now you listen to me, Troy Warner, we're talking one of a kind here!" Jillian tapped him on his broad chest with her bright-pink fingernails. "Thirty acres of prime real estate. I mean, look at all this! And this historic mansion—built by a hero of the Civil War and home to one of New England's greatest literary heroines. And you haven't even seen the inside yet. It's—"

Troy laughed, raising his hands. "You don't have to sell me, Jilly. It's up to Mercy."

"No, it's not. It's our decision."

He shrugged. "Happy wife, happy life."

"Smart man," said Jillian.

"I do love the literary-heroine part," admitted Mercy.

"Of course you do, seeing as you're such a bookworm." Jillian grinned at them as if they'd already signed the deed. "Wait until you hear the whole history of this house."

Troy laughed again. "Go on."

"The Strongs built the house in 1866, but they lost most of their fortune in the Panic of 1873," Jillian began. "The place changed hands several times until 1918, when Charles Whitney-Jones, heir to the Whitney-Jones fortune, bought the estate as a wedding present for his young wife Cornelia. The Whitney-Joneses were old-money, you know. New York City's famous 'Four Hundred' and all that. Charles and Cornelia raised two daughters, splitting their time between their mansion on Fifth Avenue and Vermont."

"Euphemia Whitney-Jones."

"The one and the same."

"Who?" asked Troy.

Mercy turned to him. "The poet. You know, 'The Ghost Witch of Grackle Tree.'"

"I think we had to memorize that in the third grade."

"It was fifth grade," corrected Jillian.

Troy looked up at the old Victorian. "I do like that tower with the widow's walk."

Mercy looked up, too. "Isn't it great?"

"Think of the view up there," added Jillian. "As good as your fire tower, Troy."

"Maybe." He looked at Mercy. "I'm surprised no one's turned this place into a museum."

"Euphemia already has a museum."

"How's that?"

"She spent most of her life in the South of France," said Mercy. "She's buried there at her estate *L'Heure Bleu*. Which is a museum now, dedicated to her life and work. It's in Languedoc-Roussillon, not far from Pézenas, where Molière lived for part of his life."

"I don't know about the Molière part, but the rest sounds about right," said Jillian. "In the sixties and seventies, she spent her summers here, hosting a literary salon—a smaller version of the one she hosted the rest of the year at her farmhouse in France. Poets came from all over to stay." She grinned. "Although if the rumors are true, there was more sex, drugs, and rock and roll going on than poetry."

"She wrote about her ex-pat days at *L'Heure Bleu* in her journals." Mercy had read some of them. "But they were more about the charms of life in Provence than the sex, drugs, and rock and roll. The journals were big bestsellers back in the day."

"And the house has been in the same family all this time?" asked Troy.

"The house is part of the Whitney-Jones family trust. When Euphemia died, her sister Maude became the sole beneficiary," said Jillian.

"I'm surprised she let it fall into such disrepair."

"She never cared about it. Married a guy in California decades ago and never came back."

"Then why didn't they just sell it?" asked Troy. "To someone who would care about it?"

Like us, thought Mercy.

"According to the terms of the trust, they couldn't sell as long as the sisters were alive." Jillian held up her hands. "Weird, huh?"

"What changed?" asked Troy.

"She just passed."

Mercy stared at her. "But she must have been . . ."

"A hundred and three."

"So now they can sell it," said Troy.

"The trustee is dying to sell it, the sooner the better. The place has been nothing but a tax drag for years." She leaned in toward them, as if she were sharing a secret. "I'm giving you a head start by letting you see it before the 'For Sale' sign has even gone up. You could get a great deal if you move fast."

Troy crossed his arms. "Let's see it first."

"Sure." Jillian swept them into the entryway. "Voilà!"

They stepped into a center hall dominated by a long staircase with a carved handrail and spindle balusters. At their feet, the parquet floors were uneven and scuffed; above them dangled an enormous crystal chandelier caked with dust and spiderwebs.

To the right was a sitting room with faded damask wallpaper, brighter blocks revealing where paintings once hung. What little furniture remained was covered with old sheets.

"I know it needs a good cleaning." Jillian sighed. "But you must remember that it's been sitting empty for years. A caretaker used to live above the garage, caring for the gardens and running off vagrants and teenagers." She smiled at Troy in that way old friends smiled at one another. "You remember old Levi Beecher."

"I ran into him and his sister here on the grounds before you came," said Mercy.

"Levi tries. And his sister helps out a little in the garden, too. But this is a big place. And Levi's getting up there."

"I remember him." Troy turned to Mercy. "We used to sneak in here to drink beer and party back in high school. Mr. Beecher would kick us out. Threaten to tell our folks, call the police. But he never did."

"He told us the ghost would get us first." Jillian giggled. "Scared us silly."

"Not all of us." Troy rolled his eyes.

"Did you ever see any ghosts?" asked Mercy.

"No."

Of course Troy would say no, Mercy thought. "Jillian?"

"That depends. Would you rather buy a house with or without ghosts?" Jillian the Realtor was back.

"I'm surprised Levi is still working here," said Troy.

"He sort of retired, moved back to the family farm about ten miles north of here. He still comes by, but as you can see . . ." Jillian's voice trailed off. "The owner should have hired more help, but she never did."

"Give us the grand tour."

Jillian ushered them through the first floor, starting with the sitting room. Mercy took stock of it: a good-sized space dominated by a falling-down fireplace and what might be more parquet floors under the dirty rugs that covered most of the area. Long south-facing windows with wide sills and crown molding let in a surprising amount of light, considering how dirty the panes were.

"Needs new paint, new windows, maybe new flooring." Troy ran a hand along the sagging mantel. "And the fireplace needs a complete rebuild."

"All of which your father and brothers will help you do for nothing," Jillian reminded him.

"Not nothing, exactly."

"Close to nothing." Jillian turned to Mercy. "And let's not forget Ed."

Ed was Mercy's cousin, the master carpenter who'd built the magnificent floor-to-ceiling bookshelves in her cabin. He was an artist.

"Mercy, what do you think?" Jillian's Spidey sense knew it was all down to Mercy, just like Troy said.

"I see potential here," Mercy said in a neutral tone.

They moved on to the kitchen, which was vintage 1950s. And not in a good way. The paneled walls and cabinets were painted a deep green so dark it looked black in some places, although maybe that was simply grime. A Formica-topped island of very fake brick cut the narrow room in two, leaving no space for dining. Holes where appliances should stand did not include one for a dishwasher. And there in the corner was the door to the pantry where Mercy had been doused in flour.

"You're going to need more than paint here." Troy frowned. "This is plain ugly."

Mercy laughed. "The ugliest kitchen I've ever seen."

"You'll put in a brand-new kitchen," said Jillian. "The twenty-first-century kitchen of your dreams." She embarked on a blow-by-blow remodeling plan.

Mercy stopped listening somewhere around "state-of-the-art Sub-Zero refrigerator." She rolled her eyes at Troy, and put her fingers to her lips. Quietly, they backed out of the hideous room while Jillian chatted on.

Mercy pulled Troy into the guest bath off the hallway—all white marble and pink toile wallpaper—and kissed him.

"I guess you like the place." He kissed her back. "And we haven't even walked the woods and wetlands yet."

"It'll take a lifetime to get it in shape," she warned.

"A lifetime is what we've got."

They heard a scrambling on the hardwood floor, followed by the sound of panting outside the bathroom door. They stepped into the hallway outside to acknowledge Elvis and Susie Bear, back from their romp in the garden.

"There you are." Jillian took one look at the rowdy dogs and stepped back into the kitchen doorway.

"Down," Mercy commanded, and Elvis and Susie Bear dropped to the floor. "Come on out, Jillian."

The petite woman moved slowly toward them. "I know they're well-trained, I know they're working dogs, but they're *so, so* big . . ."

"They won't hurt you, Jilly. Promise."

"We have a Yorkshire terrier. Very small. Eight pounds. Yours must weigh much, much more."

"Elvis and Susie Bear are our housemates," said Mercy. "If they don't like it, we can't buy it."

Jillian looked from Troy to Mercy and back again. She giggled. "You're *serious*."

"Damn straight," said Troy.

"I'm afraid so," added Mercy. "They'll be fine—"

Elvis bolted upright and thundered by Jillian. She clutched her bag to her chest as the shepherd streaked past her, headed for the front of the house, and held on tight when Susie Bear clamored after him. "Wow. They are *fast*."

"We'll be right back," Mercy told Jillian, as she and Troy trailed the dogs. As they rounded the staircase, they heard the clatter of canine nails on the oak treads. They glanced up, and there were Elvis and Susie Bear, topping the stairs. At the landing, the shepherd whipped to the right and out of sight, the Newfie lumbering along behind him.

Mercy took the steps two at a time, beating Troy by a nanosecond. She caught a glimpse of Elvis in his Sphinx pose and Susie Bear stretched out beside him, front paws facing the door of one of the south-facing bedrooms on the second floor.

Unlike the other bedroom doors, this one was shut and locked. Mercy thought about picking the lock, which was relatively easy to do on these old doors. But first she ran her fingers along the lintel for a key. Bingo.

Mercy unlocked the door and the dogs raced past her. She stepped into the room after them. The first thing she saw was the leather-bound books. Hundreds of them, filling the custom mahogany bookshelves that lined every inch of every wall in what had to be the most beautiful home library Mercy had ever seen, outside of her billionaire friend Daniel Feinberg's mansion.

Maybe even more beautiful. Her dream library. Complete with library ladders and what looked like an old desk draped in a sheet in the corner.

The second thing she saw was the dogs. Elvis again in his Sphinx position. Susie Bear again stretched out beside him in her own more casual alert, her plumed tail swirling dust with every thump.

The third thing she saw was the body.

CHAPTER FOUR

*Home is the place where, when you have
to go there, they have to take you in.*
—ROBERT FROST

I N THE MIDDLE OF THE ROOM, A DARK-HAIRED MAN WITH A FULL
salt-and-pepper beard lay sprawled upon a musty red-and-blue Persian
carpet. He was on his back, his jean-clad legs akimbo, his blank eyes staring
up at the coffered ceiling. He was wearing a white T-shirt and a dark-brown
leather jacket and work boots. Even though he did not appear to be injured, at least from this view, Mercy realized there was no point in calling
an ambulance. She knew a dead man when she saw one.

She could sense Troy behind her. He laid his large hand on her shoulder
and squeezed. "Shall we take a closer look?"

She nodded and they approached the corpse.

Troy leaned down and felt for the man's pulse, which they both knew
he would not detect. He straightened up. "It's a beautiful library."

"Apart from the dead guy."

"Not the perfect house, after all."

"It's not the house's fault he's dead." Mercy scrutinized the tableau before her. "But it's somebody's fault."

"Could be natural causes."

"He's a little young for that."

"Heart attack. Stroke. Aneurysm." Troy frowned. "Not to mention
pulmonary embolism, drug overdose—"

"I know, I know, but there's something off here." She pointed at the
man's mouth. A trickle of . . . saliva, vomit, some other kind of drool . . .

glistened on his face. "There's something coming out of his lips. And in his beard."

"I see it."

"And that redness on his forehead could be a rash." A shriek interrupted Mercy's line of thought. Jillian stood at the edge of the room in the doorway, slumped against the frame. "Oh my God." She looked away from the body, focusing on Mercy and Troy. "Is that what I think it is?"

"Yes," said Troy quietly.

"Is he dead?"

"Yes." Mercy turned to Jillian. "Do you know him?"

"I don't know. I don't think so." Jillian inched her way toward the body, one hand across her face, hiding her eyes from the reality of death.

"We need you to take a look." Troy motioned for her to come closer.

"I've never seen a dead person before, except for my grandmother, but that was at the wake, and the Galloway Brothers made her look so, so *fake* that it didn't look like her at all. It was ghoulish. I had nightmares for weeks after."

"Please, Jillian." Mercy went to the woman's side, wrapping her arm around the Realtor's shoulder and walking her a little closer to the body. "Just a quick look."

Jillian sighed, then lowered her fingers from her eyes. She stared at the face of the dead man for a long time. "No. I've never seen him before."

"Okay."

"How did he get in here?" Jillian paled. She shook off Mercy's grip. "I'm going to the ladies' room."

"Sure."

"Downstairs." She turned and ran out of the library.

"I'll go call it in," said Troy.

"Adah and Levi Beecher were in the back garden when I first arrived."

"I'll take a look. Stay here with the dogs. And no snooping."

"It's a crime scene."

"We don't know that for sure yet." Troy paused at the door. "But if you're right, and our friend here *was* the victim of foul play, I know you'll be itching to solve this unexplained death as quickly as possible so we can go ahead and buy the house."

"You want to buy a house with a dead body in it?"

"No, *you* do. Dead guy or no dead guy."

"Maybe it's cursed."

"I don't believe in curses."

"Or ghosts."

"Or ghosts." He smiled at her. "This house is a hundred and fifty years old. Whoever this poor guy is, odds are he's not the first to die here. And he probably won't be the last. Either way, if this is the house you want, then this is the house we'll buy."

Mercy watched him leave. Troy was a man who didn't worry himself over the mysteries of the universe, supernatural or otherwise. He took things as they came. People said that faith was a gift, but faith had a dark side. Not believing could be a gift, too. If you didn't believe in divine goodness, then you didn't have to believe in diabolical evil.

Still.

"Troy's right." She gave each dog a sweet petting and a treat for a job well done. "We can't let curses or ghosts or even bad luck keep us from getting this place."

She told them to stay put as she circled the corpse, keeping far enough away not to annoy the medical examiner and the Crime Scene Search Team. Mercy saw nothing untoward about the victim; he was neatly put together, apart from whatever liquid stained his mouth and beard. She paid special attention to his clothes, but saw no bulges in the pockets of his jeans, where she'd hoped to find a wallet with identification. Probably in one of his back pockets, but she'd have to leave turning him over to the crime scene techs. Maybe they'd find something.

His weathered lambskin jacket looked expensive, with its studs and zippers and pockets. All kinds of pockets: double-snap hand pockets on the side, pleated flap pockets on the chest, even two zippered pockets on the left sleeve. She noted that one of the breast pockets was slightly raised. She looked closer and spotted what appeared to be a folded piece of paper just under the flap.

After retrieving her Swiss Army knife from the side pocket of her cargo pants, she pulled out the tweezer tool. She dropped to her knees by the body and reached over to extract the paper with the tweezers. She placed it on the floor and used the tool to open it and lay it on her knee.

It was a letter handwritten in a florid, old-fashioned script.

Elvis leapt to his feet. Mercy grabbed her cell phone from another pocket and snapped photos of the letter, then folded it back as neatly and quickly as she could and slipped it back into the dead man's jacket where she'd found it.

She heard footfalls on the steps and rose to her feet. Troy poked his head in. "Dr. Darling and the Crime Scene Search Team are on their way. No sign of the Beechers."

"They didn't look like murderers." Not that you could tell a murderer by their outsides. It was their twisted insides that made them murderers. "And Elvis liked them."

"Well, if Elvis liked them." Troy laughed.

"Come on, dogs." Mercy followed them out of the library. Troy closed the door behind her and tossed her a roll of crime scene tape.

"You've got that gleam in your eye."

"What gleam?"

"That puzzle-to-solve gleam. What did you find while I was gone?"

"You still up there?" called Jillian from the bottom of the staircase.

"Later," Mercy whispered to him.

Troy turned toward the stair railing. "Be right down," he yelled to Jillian. Together they quickly secured the scene with the tape as the dogs watched from their *stay* positions. Then they all traipsed down the stairs to join Jillian on the first floor.

"Can I leave now?" Jillian's eyes were no longer laughing. Her bravado seemed to have deserted her.

"Not yet," said Troy. "They'll need to take your statement."

"I've got to get back to the office. Explain this . . . this *nightmare* to my boss."

"It'll be all right," said Mercy.

"No, it won't." Jillian put her fists on her hips and stared down at the floor. "Ghosts are one thing. But real-life dead people are another. Nothing kills a sale faster than a corpse. No one will ever buy this house now." She sniffed, and lifted her head to look at them coyly. "Except maybe you guys."

NORTHSHIRE POLICE OFFICER JOSH Becker and his partner Alma Goodlove were the first to arrive. Troy took Becker into the house to show him the crime scene while Goodlove stayed with Mercy and Jillian and the dogs. The young officer gave Elvis and Susie Bear some petting love, and then pulled out her notebook.

Mercy watched as the officer took Jillian's statement, realizing that the real estate agent was pale under her tennis tan. In a voice that veered from loud to soft and back again, she told Goodlove about showing Mercy and Troy the house, and the dogs leading them all to the dead man in the library.

Goodlove glanced with approval at Elvis and Susie Bear, now splayed out on the unkempt lawn, their work done, at least for now. The officer addressed Jillian again. "Only you have access to the lockbox."

"Well, me and my colleagues at Northshire Royal Real Estate."

"But the dead man was not another agent."

"I don't think so. I mean, I've never seen him before." Jillian still looked shaken.

Becker and Troy joined them outside, closing the front door behind them.

"Crime scene's secure," Becker told Goodlove. "And we walked the perimeter of the house. No evidence of trespassing, at least not recently."

Mercy told them about meeting the Beechers in the back garden.

"Levi's the part-time caretaker. Adah's his sister," explained Jillian. "She's very, uh, creative."

"Creative, how?" asked Becker.

"Very crunchy, tree hugger, alternative medicine, live-off-the-land old hippie—you know the type." Jillian paused. "But she's made it all pay off. Runs a successful organics company out at Beecher's Pasture. About ten miles north of here."

"I've heard about her." Goodlove wrote in her notebook. "My sister swears by her skin-care products."

"Anything else?" Becker looked at Mercy.

"Maybe they didn't come in through the front door."

"No sign of forced entry," said Troy, "from the first floor or the cellar."

"What about keys to the other outside doors?" asked Goodlove.

"Yes," said Jillian. "There's one to the back door, and the kitchen door, and the cellar door."

"And the library door." Mercy told them about finding the key above the doorframe.

"So he was locked into the room." Goodlove chewed on the end of her pen. "Which points to another person on the scene."

"The murderer." Jillian looked scared. "Who's still out there somewhere."

"Not for long, Jilly," said Troy.

"Any other locked doors we should know about?"

"Door to the guesthouse and some of the outbuildings." Jillian waved her arm vaguely in the direction of the barn.

"Guesthouse?" Mercy and Troy exchanged a look. "That would be great."

Jillian brightened. "I never got to show you the rest of the property. There's a sweet guesthouse back behind the barn. Small but nice. You could rent it out—"

Goodlove cut in. "Let's stay focused on the deceased, shall we?"

"Sorry." Jillian flushed. Mercy felt sorry for her; she was just trying to do her job. This was probably the first time her sales pitch had ever been interrupted by murder.

"Who has access to the house?" Goodlove reminded Jillian.

"We have a full set of keys at the office, but we haven't used most of them. No reason to yet."

"And presumably the owner has a set as well."

"Yes, but she lived in California. Santa Barbara. The estate is owned by a family trust. The trustee has keys—but he's out there, too."

"What about Levi?" asked Troy.

"Levi Beecher is mostly retired now, but he still does some work around here," explained Jillian to Goodlove and Becker. "He has a set as well."

Goodlove wrote that down. "How do you conduct business with the trust?"

"On the phone and online. DocuSign. You know. The usual." Jillian frowned. "I suppose I'm going to have to call and tell them about all this, this . . ."

"That's all for now." Goodlove closed her notebook as two new vehicles arrived in the parking lot. She and Becker headed off to greet the medical examiner and the Crime Scene Search Team.

"Now what?" asked Jillian.

"We wait. It shouldn't be much longer," said Troy.

"You should be able to go soon. But while we have you here, let's think this through." Mercy stepped forward. "Either the victim had a key and let himself in or—"

"Or he picked the lock." No doubt Troy was referring to her gift for lock-picking.

"I was going to say, or he remembered where the spare key was."

"What?" asked Jillian.

"Good memory." Troy laughed. "You remember, Jilly—when we snuck in here as kids, we always used the spare key."

"That's right. I totally forgot about that. If we got too drunk, we'd forget to put it back in its hiding place, and Old Man Levi would find it and hide it somewhere else."

"Mr. Beecher kept moving it, and we kept on finding it. It was sort of a game we played." Troy smiled at Mercy. "How did you know about that?"

"I spent a very creepy night here once." Mercy told them about her Halloween visit to the estate when she was a kid. "My gothic Brontë-sisters period."

"Of course."

"We should tell the crime scene techs to check for hiding places under stones here out front. That's where I found it."

"That was a long time ago," said Jillian.

Mercy glanced around her. "Not much else seems to have changed."

"True enough." Troy grinned as Becker and Goodlove accompanied Dr. Darling and the Crime Scene Search Team to the house.

Dr. Darling stopped to greet Mercy and Troy and the dogs. "I heard this place might be going up for sale."

That's what comes of living in a small town, thought Mercy. Although she suspected that even if the cheerful medical examiner lived in New York City, she'd know all the gossip there, too. For a woman who spent most of her time with dead people, she knew as much about the goings-on of the living here in Northshire as Lillian Jenkins did.

"I was giving Mercy and Troy a sneak peek, but then all this happened." Jillian winced at the thought of the dead man in the library.

Jillian's emotions really were all over the place, Mercy thought. The woman really needed to sit down and breathe.

Dr. Darling ignored the agent, addressing Mercy and Troy instead. "She's a grand old dame, isn't she?"

"That, she is," agreed Mercy.

"I'm sure she's seen her fair share of death." Dr. Darling hustled them to the side to make room for the rest of her team. First in line was Bob, the head of the Crime Scene Search Team, a lean and laconic man of so few words that even hello and goodbye were not among them. He wore his Tyvek suit, as did his crime scene techs.

"Hey, Bob," said Mercy.

"Only a fool would buy this dump."

"Shut up." Jillian was obviously regaining her composure.

Bob smirked and went on into the house, and the techs filed after him with their gear.

Dr. Darling laughed as she slipped on her own protective suit and slippers. "This would be a great house for you newlyweds. Of course, we'll have to relieve you of the corpse first."

"The sooner you do that, the better," said Jillian.

"No worries. Nothing as insignificant as a dead body will keep these two from a good deal." The medical examiner tapped Jillian's chest with her gloved index finger. "And you will get them a good deal."

"Of course."

"I suppose in the end it will be up to me just *how* good a deal it will be."

"What do you mean?" asked Jillian.

"Well, it could be natural causes. In which case, the asking price may not change." Dr. Darling cocked her head at Mercy. "But our Mercy here has a gift for discovering wrongful death. If it does turn out to be a homicide, then you may have a fire sale on your hands."

"That's an awful thing to say," sputtered Jillian.

"The poor man is already dead. There's no saving him now." The medical examiner regarded Mercy and Troy with amusement. "So we may as well hope for a good result."

"You can't mean murder." Jillian stared at her.

"It happens." And with that, the doctor disappeared into the house.

CHAPTER FIVE

The past is a dark house . . .
—MAL PEET

"CAN I LEAVE NOW?" JILLIAN GAVE BECKER AND GOODLOVE A pleading look. "I told you what I know. Which is nothing. Really."

Jillian seemed ready to bolt. The real estate agent had gotten a lot more than she'd bargained for when she took on this listing, thought Mercy. She felt badly for Becker and Goodlove, too, who would soon be answering to Detective Kai Harrington, head of the Major Crime Unit. Harrington was a glory hound who only came to crime scenes when the optics were good, but managed to give everyone a hard time regardless. Given the Euphemia Whitney-Jones connection, this was bound to be a high-profile murder case. It would be interesting to see how the detective tried to spin an unknown victim in an unoccupied house into PR gold.

"Let me see what I can do," Becker told Jillian.

"Why don't you come sit with me?" Mercy pointed toward the old stone bench.

Goodlove shot her a look of gratitude as she led Jillian along the brick path. Elvis followed at a discreet distance, then settled himself at Mercy's feet as she sat down on the bench. They waited for Jillian to join them.

"If I must." Jillian yanked her skirt down before lowering herself carefully onto the moss-covered granite. "I just can't believe someone died in one of my listings. I mean, we sell a lot of houses when people die, but they're already dead. We don't have to see the bodies."

"Everything will be fine. We just have to let law enforcement do their job."

Jillian frowned. "As long as they don't take forever to do it. They need to figure out who this guy is and what happened to him. Fast."

"Dr. Darling knows what she's doing. They all do."

They fell silent. The afternoon sun was slipping behind the mountains. Jillian pulled her cardigan more tightly around her and crossed her arms.

"Are you cold?"

"I'm fine."

Jillian didn't look fine. She looked exhausted. Death wore people out, especially those who weren't used to it. But Mercy knew all too well that even for those who were used to it, seeing too much of death would take its toll. It was just a matter of time.

Her perky smile faded, and for the first time, Mercy noticed the fine lines around her mouth.

"I could really use a cigarette." Jillian paused. "I don't suppose you smoke."

She shook her head. "No."

"Of course not." Jillian sighed. "I don't smoke, either—not really— but I have a pack hidden in my underwear drawer for days like this. Not that I've ever had a day quite like this."

Troy and Susie Bear came over. "Jilly, Becker says you can go now if you want to, with the understanding that you may need to answer more questions later on."

"No problem."

"We can have a uniform drive you back."

Jillian jumped to her feet. "That won't be necessary. I'm out of here."

"Are you sure you're up to it?" asked Mercy.

"I'll be in touch." The real estate agent beamed at her, death and cig- arettes forgotten. "Listen, once the word gets out about this dead guy, everyone's going to know the estate is for sale. The doc says that might deter buyers, and I was thinking that, too, but we could be wrong. I know you didn't get to see the guesthouse or the rest of the property."

Mercy smiled. "Guesthouse."

"It's a converted sugar shack." Jillian turned to Troy. "You remember the sugar shack. Everyone used to sneak in there to make out on the bunk beds."

"Love shack, baby." Troy laughed. "I remember."

"I can send you a link to some photos," Jillian told Mercy. "Take a look, because if you want this place, you may not have long to make your move." She cocked her index fingers at them. "Talk it over, you two, and text me."

As Jillian dashed off to her Porsche, Troy joined Mercy on the bench. "Okay, let's hear it."

"What?"

"Whatever it is that you saw up there in the library that I didn't."

"Don't beat yourself up, you weren't there long enough to notice. While you were out, I took a closer look. I noticed one of the victim's pockets had a slight bulge. Under the flap was a piece of paper."

Troy groaned. "You took it out."

"It's fine. I used the tweezer tool on my Swiss Army knife."

"Tell me you put it back."

"You know I did."

"But not before you took a picture of it."

"You know me too well."

Troy laughed. "Show me."

"I haven't had time to study it closely." Mercy scrolled through her phone to the image of the letter and held up the cell so they could read it together:

MAY 31, 1942

Dearest Captain,

By now you are wherever you must be, and I am back at home. You have flown, and are flying still, high in the clouds, and I am grounded here under our Scary Tree.

I know your place is elsewhere, now and forever. Do not worry. I am not alone. I keep a part of you with me always, my love, my solace, my salvation.

Stay aloft.

Yours,

Effie

"What does it mean?"

"I'm not sure. It's not really a love letter."

HOME AT NIGHT   45

"More of a Dear John letter. Between a World War II pilot and the woman he left behind."

"She writes like a woman thrown over."

"Maybe he's a married man."

"Or maybe she's just letting him off the hook."

"What's it got to do with our murder victim?"

"Maybe nothing." Mercy slipped her cell back in her cargo pocket. "But whoever the deceased was, this letter was important enough for him to keep it on his person."

Troy kissed the top of her head. "If there is a connection, I'm sure you'll find it."

"I feel like I'm missing something. Did you see the memorial in the garden?"

"The one for the bomber pilot?"

"Yes. He was a major."

"The date on the letter," began Troy.

"May 31, 1942. According to the gravestone, the major died in the summer of '43."

"He could have been promoted in the time between the writing of the letter and his death. Promotions come fast and furious in wartime."

"It's possible."

"If the captain is our pilot, then who is Effie?"

"You took the words right out of my mouth. I'm guessing Euphemia Whitney-Jones."

"Warner! Over here!" Detective Harrington's clipped command sounded across the lawn.

"Duty calls." Troy rose to his feet.

Mercy watched the elegant detective as he paraded across the parking lot to the house, the picture of law enforcement chic in his bespoke suit and Italian-leather loafers.

"Thrasher's with him."

"Good." Captain Floyd Thrasher was Troy's boss. Not only was he an officer and a gentleman, he was the antithesis of Harrington. With his fierce intelligence, extraordinary good looks, and low-key charisma, Thrasher always overshadowed Harrington without even trying. "That means he won't stay long."

Troy snapped his fingers and Susie Bear lumbered to her feet. Mercy and Elvis stood up, and the four of them walked together over to the entrance of the manor, where Harrington was dressing down Becker and Goodlove while Thrasher stood aside.

The detective spotted them and made a beeline for Mercy. Becker and Goodlove looked relieved to be out of the spotlight.

"You really are a bad penny, Carr." Harrington managed to insult Mercy and ignore Troy at the same time.

"We came to see the house. We didn't expect to find a body," she said evenly.

"Where's the Realtor?"

"Her name is Jillian Merrill."

"I know her. One of Northshire's best. She sold me my loft downtown."

"We took her statement," said Becker.

"And let her go?"

"We told her we'd contact her if we had more questions," added Goodlove.

Harrington was silent, but his disdain was deafening.

"Jillian was too exhausted to be of any more help," said Mercy.

"Not your call to make."

"Mercy's right," said Troy. "Becker and Goodlove weren't going to get anything else out of her. They were right to let her go."

Two techs came out of the house carrying the stretcher with the body bag, Dr. Darling bringing up the rear. She paused when she saw Mercy standing with Troy and Captain Thrasher.

"Who's our victim?" asked Harrington.

"Unknown," said Dr. Darling. "No ID on the body. No wallet. No fobs."

"No vehicle?" Harrington glared at Becker.

"No, sir."

"We did discover something in the deceased's pockets." Dr. Darling smiled at the detective.

"What?" Harrington was not a patient man, and it seemed that the medical examiner liked testing his patience to the limit.

"An old letter," she said sweetly.

"An old letter?"

"Yes. From a woman named Effie to an officer posted somewhere over-seas during World War II."

"What's that got to do with the deceased?"

"No idea."

"Not helpful."

"Agreed." Dr. Darling snapped off her gloves. "At least not as far as I could tell. But I specialize in bones, not letters."

"Cause of death?"

"Unclear. Based on rigor mortis, I'd say he's been dead about twelve hours. The rash and the drool and the bluing around the mouth point to poison. Maybe cyanide. But of course, it's just a theory until I run the labs."

"Poison." Harrington leaned back and crossed his arms. "So we don't know who he is or how he got here or why he came to begin with."

"The autopsy may tell us more."

"Right." Harrington regarded them dismissively. "Looks like you've all got work to do. Keep me informed." The detective strode away without looking back, his phone at his ear.

When he was out of earshot, Dr. Darling turned to Mercy. "Let's hear your theory."

Mercy demurred.

"Come on, I know you've got one."

"I was thinking cyanide, too." Mercy's actual knowledge of poisons was mostly limited to what she'd learned about chemical weapons in the military, but she'd read enough Agatha Christie novels as a kid to hazard a guess.

"So you think it happened here," said Thrasher. "This was the crime scene?"

"No evidence that the body was moved after death."

"Poison can take a long time to kill someone." Mercy wondered how long the dead man had suffered.

Dr. Darling nodded. "That's true. It all depends on the kind of poison and the dosage. But cyanide is one of those poisons that can drop you like a shot."

Like a shot, thought Mercy.

"Cyanide is an interesting poison," explained Dr. Darling, warming to her deadly subject. "They say it smells of bitter almonds, but not everyone can smell it. The ability to detect it is genetic."

"Do you have that ability?"

"Hard to say. Even those who have the ability may not detect the smell if they suffer from olfactory fatigue."

Mercy could imagine fewer professions more conducive to olfactory fatigue than medical examiner. "I hear you."

"Again, all conjecture at this point. If it *is* poison, it's definitely premeditated. My money's on a woman."

"That eliminates half the population of Vermont," Thrasher said dryly.

"Indeed." The doctor grinned at Mercy. "Don't worry—no matter who did it, you're going to get a good deal on this house."

CHAPTER SIX

One need not be a chamber to be haunted;
One need not be a house . . .
—EMILY DICKINSON

B Y THE TIME MERCY AND ELVIS PULLED UP TO THE CABIN, IT
was nearly four o'clock. They'd left Troy and Susie Bear at the crime
scene. It was hunting season, the Vermont Fish & Wildlife Department's
busiest time of year, and Troy and Susie Bear were needed on patrols.

The sun was just beginning its lazy descent behind the mountains, and
the cabin and the front garden were bathed in the magical light of late
afternoon. She'd always love this place, but she couldn't help but wonder
how Grackle Tree Farm looked at sunset. In her mind, the property was
already theirs.

Elvis barked, signaling her to hurry up and let him out of the Jeep.
He'd spotted Amy and her toddler Helena on the porch, blowing bubbles.
Amy's boyfriend Brodie was with them.

Mercy had invited the teenage mother to crash here when she and her
baby needed a place to stay during a tough case nearly two years ago—and
they'd never left. Now they weren't just housemates—they were family.
Brodie, too, since he practically lived here anyway.

Elvis loved playing bubbles, although like with everything else, for him
it was more mission than game. Mercy reached over and opened the door.
The shepherd vaulted for the toddler, who sat on her mom's knee, squealing with every effervescence. When she saw Elvis, the squeals rose to a
crescendo of delight. The dog licked her cheek, an honor bestowed on
very few.

Amy blew out another billowing of bubbles, and to Helena's great gratification, Elvis leapt up into the froth, snapping at the soapy circles. The baby clapped her hands as the bubbles burst in the air. *Like bubbles, in a late-disturbed stream* . . .

"So how was it?" asked Amy, frowning.

"Like all murders." Mercy sat down on the porch step. "Horrible."

"Murder? I thought you went to check out a new listing."

"We did." Mercy filled them in briefly on the events of the past few hours. She left out the part about the letter. The letter was evidence in a murder case, so the fewer people who knew about it, the better. Even she wasn't really supposed to know about it.

"That is horrible." Amy blew more bubbles into the golden haze.

"Guess you're not buying that house." Brodie popped one of the biggest bubbles with his finger, and Helena giggled.

"You'll have to keep on looking." Amy dunked the wand into the bottle.

"Maybe."

"What do you mean, maybe?" Amy wriggled the wand and a ripple of bubbles floated across the garden.

"It's a long story. Let me feed Elvis and pour myself a glass of wine, and I'll tell you all about it."

They all went into the house, Helena wailing, "More bubbles. More bubbles. More bubbles."

"Time for a snack," her mother told her.

Helena stopped crying. "Snack" was one of her favorite words. Elvis's, too. The shepherd licked her tearstained face, and took off for the kitchen. The toddler waddled after him.

"You must be hungry, too," she said to Mercy. "Hors d'oeuvre?"

"That would be wonderful." Mercy realized that she hadn't eaten since that cinnamon roll at breakfast.

Amy couldn't cook, but she was getting very good at putting together charcuterie boards with salami and prosciutto, grapes and strawberries, almonds and olives and hummus, crackers and crudités, and a sampling of Vermont's finest hard and soft cheeses. Easy to make and easy to eat. Helena, at nearly two years old, still preferred finger food. Mercy and Elvis, too.

While Amy prepared the board, Mercy measured Elvis's high-grade kibble into his bowl and freshened his water. He wolfed it down in a matter of seconds, and then stretched out at the foot of Helena's high chair. He knew that all good things come to those dogs who wait.

Brodie settled Helena into the high chair. Mercy poured herself a glass of Big Barn Red and slipped onto one of the dining room chairs at the old oak farm table that separated her kitchen from the rest of the great room. She loved this space, with its high ceilings and exposed beams and wood-burning flagstone fireplace, where the red maple longbow carved by her late grandfather hung over the mantel, reminding her that she was a warrior in a long line of warriors. The Victorian manor boasted many fireplaces; when they moved in, she'd see that the longbow graced the best of them.

Amy placed the charcuterie board on the table, along with a pitcher of iced tea. Brodie passed around plates, silverware, and napkins. Mercy helped herself to some Brie and sliced baguette.

Amy and Brodie sat down on either side of the baby. Amy handed Helena a cracker topped with a slice of cheddar cheese. "Tell us about the house."

"It's not just a house, it's a whole estate." Mercy pictured the place in her mind: the stately old manor, the overrun gardens, the giant maple dominating the grounds. She launched into a litany of its best features, realizing too late that she sounded more like the seller than the buyer. Jillian would be proud.

"It sounds wonderful. Even better than the lodge."

"Old houses are always too much work." Brodie shook his head. "Besides, aren't you forgetting something?"

Mercy sighed as she slathered herbed goat cheese on a water cracker. "You mean the corpse."

"Pretty creepy." Amy shivered.

"Worse than creepy." Brodie leaned across the table. "Mercy, you can't buy a house with a dead guy in it."

Mercy ignored that. "I may have left out the best part. Well, the best part to me, anyway. It's Grackle Tree Farm."

"Seriously?" Amy stared at her as she automatically dipped a celery stick in the hummus and handed it to Helena, who giggled. Helena loved hummus, too.

Brodie stabbed the hummus with a carrot. "That place is haunted, you know. Now that there's been a murder, there'll be even more ghosts stuck there, in between earth and the afterlife."

Mercy ignored him again. She focused on Amy, who was convinced that she and Helena should find a place of their own when Mercy and Troy bought a new house together. "Amy, we're housemates. That won't change. No matter where Troy and I live. You'll be part of our household."

"Newlyweds want to be alone. You *should* be alone." Amy focused on feeding Helena, avoiding Mercy's gaze.

"There's a guesthouse. I haven't checked it out yet, all we saw was the main house. Jillian is sending me a link to some photos. If it's in decent shape, maybe you could have your own space."

Amy considered that. "My own space."

Mercy could tell she liked the sound of that. It would be the ideal solution, really. She hoped the small cottage was in better shape than the main house.

"Your own place." Brodie chomped down on the carrot and helped himself to a breadstick. "With a dead body. And ghosts. You're both crazy."

"Mercy will solve the murder like she always does. Then everything will be fine."

"Everything will *not* be fine. Even if you solve the murder." Brodie tapped the breadstick on the table. "You can't live in a house riddled with ectoplasm."

"Brodie watches a lot of *Ghost Hunters*."

"I'm serious." He broke the breadstick in two and stuffed the short half into his mouth. "You need to get some paranormal investigators in there to check it out."

Mercy nearly laughed. "You mean like Bill Murray in *Ghostbusters*?"

"That's just Hollywood," scoffed Brodie. "This is *real*. I know this guy named Joey Fyfe. He's got all the equipment." His voice rose as he warmed to his subject. "EMF meters, digital thermometers, thermographic cameras, night vision goggles, digital audio recorders, Geiger counters, you name it."

"Impressive," said Mercy aloud. *For pseudoscience,* she thought.

"Joey does ghost tours all around Northshire, but he also does investigations of private homes. I can text him if you want. I know he's really busy this time of year, with all the tourists in town for Halloween, but I'm sure he'd make time to check the property for you. It's like, paranormal on steroids."

"I appreciate that."

"You have no idea what monsters that house could be harboring. We're not just talking ghosts." Brodie popped the other end of the breadstick into his mouth and ticked them off on one hand. "We're taking spirits, haunts, poltergeists. Maybe even evil shape-shifting demons."

As always, Brodie managed to amuse Mercy as much as he annoyed her. "I don't think so. I think it's mostly just poets."

"Weird poets, you mean. That poem totally creeped me out as a kid."

"Euphemia Whitney-Jones was more than just that one poem." Amy made Helena another cheese-and-cracker sandwich. "We've studied her in American Lit. Very dark. Very feminist. Very Sylvia Plath."

"She did have a lighter side, too, like in her dog poems." Mercy loved her dog poems.

"Dog poems?" asked Brodie.

"That's right." Mercy popped a grape into her mouth. "They were little ditties, mostly, that often relied on wordplay. Anagrams, palindromes, homophones, homonyms." She stopped to think for a moment, and then recited:

> *Dog may be god spelled backward*
> *Tail to nose*
> *And deer may be dear indeed*
> *As the homophone shows*
> *But a cat is simply a cat*
> *Regardless of your prose.*

"Dog, god, deer, dear. I bet she would have been good at Wordle." Amy frowned as Helena pushed the cracker off the tray of her high chair. Elvis caught it in midair.

"No doubt."

"The last line is like the punch line of a joke." Brodie grabbed another breadstick. "Cool."

"She kept animals on the farm in Provence," said Mercy. "She always had a pug; she named them all Cherie. Barn cats, too, which came and went as they pleased. And horses in the stables. The only happy poems she ever wrote were about animals."

"I guess you can relate." Brodie hitched a thumb at Elvis, who was licking Helena's stray cracker crumbs off the floor. And again at Muse, who was asleep on one of the armchairs in the living area.

"That I can. Although God knows I'm no poet. I won't be immortalizing Elvis or Muse in rhyme anytime soon. They'll have to settle for treats and belly rubs and lap naps."

"Didn't she commit suicide, too?" Amy gave Helena a celery stick. "Now, you eat this one, please."

"I'm not sure." Much of whatever Mercy had once known about Euphemia Whitney-Jones she'd forgotten. It was time she reacquainted herself with the poet. Reread her poems and her journals, too.

"So many poets commit suicide. Plath and Anne Sexton and Sara Teasdale. What is it about poetry?" asked Amy.

"I'm not sure you can blame poetry." Mercy considered that. "There are poets who lead long lives. Robert Frost, Maya Angelou, Mary Oliver."

"Stanley Kunitz lived to be a hundred years old." Brodie did not look up from his smart phone. "He wrote that great poem about Halley's Comet."

"Is he your favorite poet?"

"I like comets." He finally raised his head. "Did this Euphemia commit suicide here at home?" He didn't wait for an answer before he started googling it.

"I don't think it was suicide." Mercy tried to remember that long-ago report for sixth-grade English class. "I do know that she was buried on her farm in Provence, where she lived with her longtime companion Leontine Bonnet." Surely Jillian would have mentioned it if Euphemia had killed herself at the estate. Then again, maybe not. Suicide was no more a selling point than murder.

"Euphemia and Leontine were like the Gertrude Stein and Alice B. Toklas of Provence." Amy was obviously pleased she knew as much, if not more, about the poet than Mercy did. Mercy was pleased, too. Amy was doing so well with her studies, and that was nothing but good for her and little Helena.

Brodie looked up from his cell phone. "She died here. Of oleander poisoning. Rumored to be self-administered but officially ruled as inconclusive."

"Says who?" asked Amy.

"Wikipedia, of course."

"What an awful way to die." Amy looked at Mercy. "Why wouldn't she just take sleeping pills?"

Oleander poisoning, thought Mercy. She'd seen oleander in one of the overgrown flower beds that fronted the old Victorian.

"Great." Brodie shook his head. "Another ghost. That's all you need. The place is a demon pit."

Amy left the table and went toward the fireplace, past the sofa, and over to Mercy's floor-to-ceiling bookshelves. The shelves ran the length and width of the entire inside wall of the great room. Books by and about Shakespeare predominated, but there were many other fine writers represented as well. Many of whom were poets. Mercy organized her library by genre—plays, poetry, novels, nonfiction—and after living here with her for so long, Amy knew right where to go to find the poems not written by the bard. Amy pulled out a slim, faded blue leather-bound volume of poems from the many works by Euphemia Whitney-Jones. "Here's one."

The book fell open to one of the most admired poems in Whitney-Jones's oeuvre. Mercy remembered marking the page with a dried yellow rose from Patience's garden. Her grandmother had given her the book when she'd joined the army. It was one of her favorites, too.

"You must like this one." Amy carefully removed the pressed bloom and placed it on the bookshelf, turning her attention once again to the book. "Listen to this." Amy cleared her throat and began to read in a strong, clear voice:

ALL THE UNNAMED WOMEN
by Euphemia Whitney-Jones

> *All the unnamed women*
> *Shadows living in the land of men*
> *Who are we?*

We are the warriors of France
We are the witches of Salem
We are the wantons of Amherst
We are the women who burn
And when we burn, we rise
In sacred plumes of bittersweet smoke
To a forgotten heaven
Made of blood and ash and sorrow.
Who are we?
We are the unnamed women
Shadows living in the land of men
Fighting battles already lost
Casting spells already broken
Loving men already untrue
Until we die and are born again
In a fire of naming
Shadows no more
We rise in the land of men.
Who are we now?

"Well done." Mercy applauded, and Helena joined her in the clapping, her little fingers messy with hummus.

"Intense," said Brodie. "No wonder everyone thought she killed herself."

"Sometimes you are such a *guy*." Amy replaced the rose and returned the slim volume of poetry to its rightful spot on the bookshelf and came back to the farm table. "You look tired, Mercy. Why don't you curl up on the couch? Brodie will clean up while I put the baby to bed."

"On it." Brodie slipped on his earbuds.

"Bath, book, bed," Amy said to Helena.

"Bath, book, bed," repeated the toddler with glee.

"Thanks." Mercy took her wine with her to the sofa. Elvis, having licked the floor clean of Helena's droppings, joined her at his end of the couch, laying his head at her hip.

Mercy welcomed the time alone. She had some thinking to do. Sipping her wine in silence, she scratched the sweet spot between the shepherd's ears while she let the incongruous incidents and impressions of this consequential day drift through her mind like clouds across a summer sky. She closed her eyes, the better to see the collage of images forming in her overactive imagination. Grackles squawking in the trees. Pilots burning in their B-24s. Poets penning their angry verses. Maude. Michael. Euphemia. Captain. Effie.

Mercy opened her eyes. *Effie. Euphemia. Sister of Maude. Writer of the letter found on the dead man. Who comes to Grackle Tree Farm just after Maude dies.*

That could not be a coincidence. She grabbed her phone and texted Jillian:

What's the name of the trustee of the Whitney-Jones trust?

She didn't have to wait long for the Realtor to reply.

Ren Barlow, Esq., of Barlow and Rothman.
Also sending link to photos of GTF.

Mercy checked her watch. Eight o'clock here. But just quitting time in California. With any luck, the receptionist at the Barlow & Rothman law offices had gone home and one of the principals would pick up. It was a ploy she sometimes used on her investigations. Sometimes it even worked.

She could wait until tomorrow and ask Jillian to make a formal introduction, but she wanted to get a sense of Ren Barlow, the man behind the curtain, the man who was handling Maude's estate—and protecting its secrets. And she wanted to do it before law enforcement contacted him, if they hadn't already. She punched in the number, hoping her hunch was right.

"Ren Barlow." The voice from the West Coast boomed from Mercy's cell, bright with confidence.

"This is Mercy Carr from Northshire, Vermont. Jillian Merrill gave me your number. I'm calling in reference to Maude Fergus and the Whitney-Jones trust."

"I see. What can I do for you, Ms. Carr?"

She explained who she was and why she was calling. "There's been a suspicious death here, and I believe you may be able to shed some light on it."

"Jillian told me about the situation there. I was sorry to hear about it.

An unfortunate incident, to be sure. But apart from cutting short your visit, I don't see what that has to do with either you or with this office."

"We have a dead man here, as yet unidentified," said Mercy. "But I have reason to believe there's a connection between you and the victim."

"We're talking about an event that happened thousands of miles away, in a place where Maude Fergus, may God rest her soul, hadn't set foot in for decades. I don't see how there could possibly be a connection, as you put it. And even if there were, I wouldn't be discussing it with you."

"The deceased had in his possession a document that would indicate such a connection." She could talk legalese, too. She'd learned it at her mother's knee. And her father's.

There was a moment of silence at the other end of the line. Mercy knew that she'd surprised Barlow. Good attorneys did not speak until they knew exactly what they wanted to say. Words were weapons, and they fired them deliberately. Silence was a strategy meant to buy them time to plan their next move.

"What sort of document?" he finally asked.

Got you, thought Mercy. Barlow didn't know about the letter because Jillian didn't know about the letter; she'd left the crime scene before Mercy had shown it to Troy. While the police would most certainly question Jillian about it eventually, odds were they had yet to do so. Another reason she had called the lawyer herself, before he could find out from Jillian or Harrington about the letter in the dead man's pocket.

"As you yourself admit, Maude Fergus is deceased."

"Even so. You are not law enforcement, and even if you were, I am bound by confidentiality."

Mercy tried another approach, one she used on her mother when Grace refused to discuss something with her. And Grace played the "not up for discussion" card a lot. "Mr. Barlow, please hear me out. You don't have to say anything. Just let me talk and you listen, and then if you still have nothing to say, I'll go away."

"Somehow I doubt that, Ms. Carr. You strike me as a determined young woman." There was a brief pause. "I can give you five minutes."

"Maude Fergus had an older sister. Euphemia Whitney-Jones, the poet. She ran a literary salon here in the summers after the war until her death."

"Public knowledge," said Barlow. "What's your point?"

Mercy ignored that. "The man who died in the library of the main house had nothing on him, no identification of any kind. But in his breast pocket was a faded piece of paper, a short letter written by a party named Effie to a party she addressed as Dearest Captain."

"Effie," repeated Barlow.

"Effie, short for Euphemia. But then, I'm sure you knew that. It's what Maude would have called her sister."

"I will not be confirming or denying any conversations with Maude Fergus."

"The contents of the letter imply that the captain was a pilot in the Second World War. Much like the one to whom the memorial in the back garden is commemorated. And now, seventy-some years later, just as the place goes up for sale, the letter turns up here in the pocket of a dead man."

"I'd like to see that letter."

Mercy ignored that as well. She figured he was very familiar with the contents of the letter, whether he admitted it or not. "I believe you may know who the victim is, and what this letter refers to. And that it might be relevant to the investigation."

"If that's true—and I'm not saying it is—that's a matter for law enforcement."

"As trustee of the Whitney-Jones trust, you are charged with selling Grackle Tree Farm. Buyers may be few and far between now that there's been a murder in the house. The sooner the case is resolved, the better for you."

"I will take it all under advisement, and if I feel that further communication is necessary, I will contact you. Good night, Ms. Carr."

"Good night, Mr. Barlow." Mercy heard the attorney ring up and congratulated herself. Ren Barlow, Esq. knew more than he was saying. One way or another, he would have to come clean. If not with her, then with Harrington.

Barlow knew who the victim was and what he was doing there in the house. And if he wouldn't tell her, she'd just have to figure it out herself. And she had a pretty good idea where to start—with Effie herself.

She swapped her phone for her wine and whistled softly. Elvis sprang from the couch and led the way to the front door. She pulled her duffle coat from the coat tree in the hallway and slipped it on as she followed the shepherd outside. It was a clear and cold night, the sky bright with stars and a nearly full moon. The only other light being the one that illuminated the pole where the flag fluttered in the light breeze. Elvis raced down toward the barn, scattering leaves, off to do his business. Mercy stood at the edge of the porch and stared out across the garden, past the barn toward the dark forest. She thought about Effie and her lost pilot, herself and her lost soldier, all the people who mourned the soldiers who never came home.

But Mercy had come home, and inherited Elvis. And Troy had come home from the war, too, and found Susie Bear. Together they had all moved on. Just as Euphemia had moved on.

You could leave your past behind, but your past never leaves you behind. Whatever had gone before could return to haunt you at any time, even from beyond the grave. Just like Effie's past had come back to haunt the estate. The ghosts that stalk us are the secrets we cannot keep, the trespasses we cannot forgive, the truths we cannot bury.

Grackle Tree Farm had held the poet's confidences close for decades. But after all these years of silence, now her secrets were coming to light.

It all started with the sisters Effie and Maude.

Mercy and Elvis came back into the house, where Amy was saying goodbye to Brodie, who was actually going home to sleep in his own bed for once. Little Helena was already down for the night. Mercy curled up on the sofa, laptop balanced on her knees. Elvis circled the couch pillows a couple of times before settling down on his end. As promised, Jillian had emailed her the link, where she'd posted photos of the property in anticipation of listing it. What Mercy saw there was enough to convince her that she and Troy really should make an offer before this listing went live.

"Amy, you've got to see this."

Amy joined her on the couch, and together they took a photographic tour of the estate, Mercy clicking through from one picture to the next.

The slide show started with a postcard exterior shot of the grand old limestone manor, and then revealed the interiors of the large house. Amy *oohed* and *ahhed* over every room upstairs and down while Mercy began to realize that she'd be in over her head with this place. While she'd decorated her cabin in what she thought of as rustic chic, she'd have to count on her mother's sense of high style to help her take on this faded nineteenth-century lady. It would take a grande dame's sensibility to decorate a grande dame.

The next shots were of the outbuildings: a beauty of a nineteenth-century barn, a collapse of a chicken house, weedy raised beds from some long-ago vegetable garden, a dilapidated greenhouse, a fairly new sugaring shed, an old kennel and dog run.

"Where is this guesthouse?" asked Amy.

"We're getting there." Mercy kept clicking through, and there it was: a guesthouse with traditional board-and-batten siding, tilt-in barn sash windows, and a green metal roof with a cupola. A charming, if run-down, place.

"Cute."

"It's a converted sugar shack."

"Look at this." Amy pointed to a plaque by the door that read SYLVIA BEACH SHANTY.

"Interesting. Sylvia Beach was a patron of the arts. She founded Shakespeare and Company."

"The famous bookstore in Paris."

"That's right. And she was a publisher, too—she published James Joyce's *Ulysses* when no one else would."

"We have to read *Ulysses* this semester. I know I'll never make it through it."

Mercy laughed. "Don't try to understand it. Just let the prose wash over you. You'll get the gist."

"If you say so."

Mercy regarded the photo of the renovated sugar house with curiosity. "Euphemia must have loved this cottage, to name it after Sylvia Beach. She could very well have known her—they both lived in France around the same time—and they could have traveled in the same circle of expats. Although Sylvia Beach was much older."

She clicked through to the interior shots.

The main room of the house seemed to be a fairly good-sized room, with high ceilings and exposed beams. There was no furniture, just a scattering of area rugs covering the wide-planked floor. A fireplace dominated one wall; on the opposite wall, a tiny kitchen was tucked into a corner next to sliding glass doors. The doors opened onto a deck in a narrow strip of yard flanked by forest.

More photos revealed two small bedrooms and a dated bathroom with pink and black tile. "Vintage," said Amy.

The last photo showed a barracks-style addition, which housed built-in bunk beds.

"Weird, right?"

"It is weird. I would have bet money that Euphemia intended this as a writing studio, given its name. But all the beds say otherwise."

"Maybe she did convert this old sugar shanty into a writing studio when they built the new sugar shed. And then they added the bedroom wing and the barracks wing after she died."

"Or after she started the summer literary salons. Maybe she needed the extra beds for her guests. Although the main house has plenty of room for guests."

"Maybe she had lots of guests."

"Well, whatever it may have been used for in the past, the Sylvia Beach Shanty would make a cute place for you and Helena today."

"And Brodie."

"And Brodie."

Amy gave Mercy a big hug. "I can't believe it."

"Well, it's not ours yet."

"But it will be." Amy uncurled herself from the couch. "You still staying up?"

"Research."

"Right." All smiles, Amy said good night and disappeared into her bedroom.

Mercy and Elvis were alone. Now she could get to work. She could feel Elvis's eyes upon her as she did a deep dive on the Whitney-Jones sisters, Ren Barlow, and the property itself. "Go to sleep, boy."

The shepherd continued his vigil for several minutes, and when it was clear to him that she would be at it for a while, he dozed off to sleep, his ears still perked. She stroked his silky ears, and they relaxed under her touch. She knew he'd be alert and action-ready at the slightest botheration. She took comfort in his diligence. It was going to be a long night.

DAY TWO
OCTOBER 28

CHAPTER SEVEN

Home is one's birthplace, ratified by memory.
—HENRY GRUNWALD

T HE NEXT MORNING MERCY SLEPT LATE, AWAKENING TO AN
early-warning signal bark from Elvis. She'd fallen asleep on the
couch, which was where she always slept with Elvis when Troy and Susie
Bear were out on patrol. She stumbled to her feet, smoothing her wrin-
kled clothes and pulling her wild morning hair into a ponytail with the
scrunchie she always kept around her wrist.

Signal barks meant only one thing: visitors.

Visitors rarely came to the cabin this early. The sun was just rising, so
it couldn't be any later than seven o'clock in the morning. She knew it
wasn't Troy and Susie Bear coming off the night shift, as Elvis would greet
them with a tail wag rather than a bark. The only person she could think
of who might show up at dawn was her grandmother. And Elvis wouldn't
bark at her, either.

The shepherd sat at the door, his nose nearly touching the knob.

"Back."

Elvis scooted back an inch. Not giving much ground. Alert and yet not
agitated. Behind door number one was neither friend nor foe. Puzzling.

Mercy swung open the door, and there stood two of the most enig-
matic men she knew: her great-uncle Hugo Fleury and her sometime em-
ployer Daniel Feinberg. "Good call, " she whispered to Elvis.

Uncle Hugo was a retired army colonel, the kind who never really
retired but instead aged out of the military and then founded a security
company known for its elite special ops. Daniel Feinberg was Vermont's

only billionaire. Mercy did investigative work for him from time to time.

The sly octogenarian and the shrewd financier were allies who'd run operations together designed to save the world's art and antiquities from looters, thieves, and terrorists. God knows what they were up to now. Or why they were here at her house. But she'd bet her grandfather's longbow it had something to do with the dead man in the library. And the estate. And that letter.

"Let me guess." She leaned forward to kiss her uncle on the cheek. "You and Ren Barlow go way back."

"I can't imagine what you mean by that."

Mercy sighed. The colonel knew full well that his tendency to keep his cards close to his chest drove her crazy.

"Mercy." Feinberg's dark eyes took in every inch of the place as she ushered them into the great room. "I hope we're not interrupting anything."

"Nothing but sleep." She grinned at her uncle.

"I thought you were an early riser." His implication being that she should be.

"I am, normally. And yes, I know that I can sleep when I'm dead."

"Or when the war is won."

"If we're going to war, I'm going to need coffee." She waved them onto the sofa. "I'll make us a pot."

"That would be just fine." The colonel appreciated the niceties. "Cream, two sugars, please."

"Black for me." Feinberg smiled. "Thank you."

Mercy busied herself in the kitchen, keeping one eye on Elvis and her guests as she got the coffee brewing and puttered around with mugs and milk. The two gentlemen were silent, each taking turns petting the shepherd, who sat between them, straight and sturdy as a fence post.

She placed her grandmother's cinnamon rolls on one of her turquoise stoneware plates. No doubt the men would eat them all, more's the pity, but on the plus side, Patience's rolls would sweeten whatever tricky conversation they were about to have. She couldn't help but be intrigued by the fact that Uncle Hugo and Feinberg were here together to talk to her, but she knew them both well enough to know that whatever they wanted from her, it would be complicated at best and downright dangerous at worst. Not that she minded a little peril from time to time. Trouble kept her—and Elvis—sharp.

Coffee made, she placed the pot on a large teak tray with cups, milk pitcher, sugar bowl, spoons, napkins, and her grandmother's rolls. Elvis lifted his head as she carried the tray across the room and placed it on the coffee table in front of the sofa. He sniffed but restrained himself, focused on Mercy as she told her visitors to help themselves and fetched a doggie treat from the tin on the island that separated the living and dining area from the kitchen.

Mercy tossed Elvis his green goodie and he caught it, munching it down in a single bite. She sat down on the ottoman facing the colonel and Feinberg, retrieved her coffee, and wondered if she should grab one of the cinnamon rolls before her guests devoured them all.

"So to what do we owe this pleasure?"

"All in good time." Uncle Hugo reached for another roll. "My sister Patience made these."

"Best rolls in the county," said Feinberg.

"The world," said the colonel.

There were only three left now. Mercy slipped the smaller one onto her napkin. There was no rushing these guys. Feinberg claimed the second-to-last roll while her uncle finished his coffee.

The colonel replaced his cup on the tray, patted his mouth with his napkin, folded it neatly, and put it next to his cup. "We have a proposition for you."

She looked from her uncle to Feinberg. "What kind of proposition?"

The colonel ignored the question. As did Feinberg.

"Let me tell you a story," began the colonel.

Uncle Hugo loved telling stories. She willed her eyes not to roll.

"It will be relevant to the current situation," promised Feinberg.

Which situation? she thought, but aloud she said, "Go ahead."

"When I was a young soldier, I was stationed in Europe." Uncle Hugo crossed his arms across his narrow chest.

"During the Cold War." Mercy knew that the colonel had never explained what it was he was actually doing over there during that treacherous time. At least, treacherous for spies, and there was little doubt that he was, in fact, a spy.

"I was there with an artillery battalion."

She looked at Feinberg. "You know, Daniel, this was when the war in Vietnam was heating up. You'd think, given Uncle Hugo's special skill set, they would have sent him there straightaway. But instead they kept him in Europe."

"I served in Vietnam," said the colonel stiffly. "With honors."

"Of course you did. But that was later in the conflict." She kept her eyes on Feinberg. "Uncle Hugo speaks fluent German." The better to slip behind the Iron Curtain during the Cold War for the purposes of espionage. Not that he'd ever admit it. Not in this lifetime. "I suppose you already knew that."

"My understanding is that Hugo speaks several languages."

"Thirteen fluently, twenty-four conversationally. But who's counting?" The octogenarian folded his heavily veined hands as if in prayer. "What is pertinent to this conversation is a party I attended in the late sixties. A party held at a large country house in the South of France." He fixed his sharp gaze on Mercy. "Hosted by the poet Euphemia Whitney-Jones."

"*L'Heure Bleu.*" Mercy had refreshed her memory of Effie's Provençal estate last night.

"The perfect name for the place. A two-story stone farmhouse sitting at the top of a small rise overlooking the countryside. Fields of sunflowers that glowed in the light of sunset."

Uncle Hugo really had been everywhere there was to be back then, thought Mercy, and maybe he was everywhere there was to be even now as well. The old man was nothing if not cagey, and he was as cunning and au courant as ever. "Her legendary literary salon. What was it like?"

"It was a scene, as we liked to say back then."

"It means something different these days."

Uncle Hugo pursed his lips as if to say there was no comparing that extraordinary past to this mediocre present. "Euphemia ran a literary salon with a free-love twist. Same house-party style, the usual weird mix of acid and free love and psychedelic rock. But with a more glamorous guest list. Brigitte Bardot was there. Simone de Beauvoir and Jean-Paul Sartre, François Truffaut and Charles Aznavour, Louise Bourgeois and Antoni Clavé, Elizabeth Taylor and Richard Burton. All kinds of people drawn together by Euphemia."

"And her companion Leontine Bonnet," Mercy reminded him.

"Yes," conceded the colonel, "but Euphemia was really the allure."

"She was beautiful." Mercy had seen many images of the poet online, the loveliest being the portrait Leontine had painted of her not long after they first met. She'd painted her lover in the garden, surrounded by flowers, as if Effie were a bloom herself.

"She was beautiful, yes, tall and slim as a willow, shiny waves of dark hair framing her pale face, dark expressive eyes you could lose yourself in if you weren't careful. But it was more than that. She was one of those rare individuals who was completely and thoroughly herself. Alive in a way that few people are." The colonel paused, seemingly distracted by the memory of Effie. "She attracted all sorts—hippies, artists, actors, musicians, poets, revolutionaries. No one was immune to Euphemia. Everyone wanted to bathe in her light."

"Including you." Family lore held that the colonel had been quite the ladies' man. A dashing figure in his prime. Even now he was probably the darling of the elder set.

"She was the *l'heure bleu* herself. I was as smitten as everyone else." The colonel gazed dreamily at the fireplace, as if the past were revealed in its stones. "Of course, I was younger than she was. But that didn't matter."

"To her or to you?" Mercy calculated that the octogenarian must have been in his thirties at the time, Euphemia in her forties.

"To either of us."

"What about Leontine Bonnet?"

"Everybody was sleeping with everybody. She was no different."

"But she was said to be very jealous of Euphemia."

Uncle Hugo turned his gaze back to Mercy. "I suppose she was. But it wouldn't make any difference. It would be like being jealous of the sun. There was nothing she could do about it. She may not have liked it, but she went along with it."

"You had an affair with Euphemia."

"A very strong word for a very casual encounter."

"One you seem to recall quite vividly," teased Feinberg.

The colonel sighed. "Of course I was in love with her, like every other man and woman in the South of France. But I had a job to do."

"Care to elaborate?" Mercy knew the colonel never interacted with anyone by accident. If he went to *L'Heure Bleu*, he had a reason to go there, apart from any romantic pursuit. No doubt related to his espionage activities on the wrong side of the Berlin Wall. Maybe now she'd finally get some answers to the questions she'd had about her uncle's mysterious Cold War past.

"I'll tell you what I can. Need-to-know basis only. I don't have to tell you that bad guys have long memories."

Even longer if those bad guys were KGB or Stasi, thought Mercy. This was the closest the colonel had ever come to confirming that he was an intelligence agent during the Cold War. He would have been up against his rival agents from the GDR and the Soviet Union. Definitely bad guys with long memories.

"Effie wasn't interested in our little spy games. She was a true patron of the arts. She wanted to save the world, one artist at a time."

Mercy was not sure what he meant. Her uncle had a penchant for talking in riddles. "Through poetry?"

"Not only through poetry. In those days, many artists were considered subversives. The powers that be didn't approve of their novels, their songs, their artworks—"

Mercy interrupted. "Their poems."

"Exactly," said Feinberg. "Not so different from now."

"Indeed." The colonel paused. "These artists paid a price for their art. Sometimes the very highest price."

"They weren't safe behind the Iron Curtain." Mercy was beginning to understand. "Euphemia helped them get out."

"She gave them a place to go," said the colonel.

"After *you* helped them get out." Mercy could see it now, her uncle's intrepid younger self sneaking writers and composers and painters and performers over the Berlin Wall and on to the freedom of Euphemia's home in Languedoc-Roussillon.

"And eventually beyond."

"That all sounds very admirable. But what does that have to do with the dead man at Grackle Tree Farm?" Mercy tucked one leg up under her hips, and patted her lap. Elvis scooted over to her, placing his handsome head in her lap for a good scratching between the ears. "It must have something to do with it, or you wouldn't be here at dawn."

"We think we know what he was looking for," Feinberg told her. "Or at least where he was looking for it."

"Mr. Max Vinke, private investigator, of Los Olivos, California." It was a guess, but when she'd checked out Ren Barlow online, Vinke's name had come up in association with some of the Santa Barbara attorney's cases. She could tell by the bemused look on her uncle's face that she'd hit the mark. While the colonel seemed surprised, Feinberg did not.

The billionaire grinned. "She's as good as you are, Hugo."

"I wouldn't go that far. At least not yet."

"She's getting there."

"I'm sitting right here, guys." She put her hands on her knees and leaned forward. "Let's hear it. Starting with Vinke and Barlow."

Uncle Hugo and Feinberg exchanged a glance. The billionaire bowed his head slightly. "Go ahead, Hugo. Tell her everything. There's no real reason not to."

Except for his intrinsic desire for secrecy, thought Mercy.

"Very well." The colonel regarded Mercy with an incongruous combination of intimidation and respect. "As you know, Daniel and I have worked together from time to time on saving antiquities."

"Of course." Mercy understood that more than one country owed the ancient manuscripts, priceless statuary, and other archaeological finds in their museums to these two determined men, who'd tracked them down, rescued them from looters and crooked collectors, and returned them to their rightful homes. Still, she wasn't clear how that applied to the current situation. "What artifacts do you mean to save here?"

"Not artifacts. A literary treasure."

Mercy remembered the paper she'd pulled from Vinke's breast pocket. "The letter."

"If there's one letter, there must be more," predicted Feinberg.

"And maybe more poems as well." The colonel smiled at his friend the billionaire.

For a moment Mercy was speechless at the thought of it. Finally, she found her voice. "It would be like discovering a stash of new Emily Dickinson poems. Or Sylvia Plath. Anne Sexton. Elizabeth Bowen . . ." She lapsed into silence as she considered the impact of such a bonanza on the literary world.

"Amazing," agreed Feinberg. "Although new work could bring to light a side of Euphemia Whitney-Jones that some may not appreciate. Especially if they were written to a man."

"The keepers of the flame."

"She's known for her feminism, her relationship with Leontine Bonnet, her defense of oppressed women throughout the ages."

"But you said she slept with everyone back then. She slept with *you*."

The colonel laughed. "Don't say it like that."

"You know what I mean."

"I do. I think most of the literati view the orgiastic sixties and seventies as a blip in Euphemia's sexual history. As it was for most of us. More reflective of the times than our true selves. An anomaly."

"Either way, any new writings—whether letters or poems or both—would be a revelation." Feinberg rapped his fingers on his thigh. "And worth a fortune."

"Wait a minute." Mercy knew they were holding out on her. "Why are you so sure that there are more letters? The one Vinke had read like a Dear John letter. A final communication. What aren't you telling me?"

"We'd better tell her the rest of it."

The colonel nodded. "Before she died, Maude Fergus confided in Ren Barlow."

"Who just happens to be a friend of yours."

"Actually, he's my friend," said Feinberg. "We do business in Santa Barbara."

"Of course you do." Mercy laughed. "Go on, Uncle Hugo."

The colonel poured himself another cup of coffee and sipped before continuing. "Maude knew she was dying, and although she'd fought off the Grim Reaper many times, once she hit a hundred, she figured her days really were numbered. Like many elderly people, she gave a lot of thought going back over her life and times, tallying up wins and losses and rewards and regrets.

"She told Ren that there was one loose end she wanted to tie up while she still could. She told him that she and her sister had had a falling out over a man when they were young."

"A man?" Mercy flashed on the stone angel in the back garden. She did the math in her head. The math worked. The lost pilot was around the same age as Euphemia and Maude. "Michael Emil Robillard."

Feinberg and the colonel stared at her.

"There's a memorial to Robillard at the estate," she explained. "He was a B-24 pilot. Shot down in the war, according to the epigraph."

"Interesting." The colonel sipped his coffee. "Robillard was Euphemia's lover; they were still engaged when Maude ran off with him to Florida and eloped."

"She stole her sister's fiancé?" Mercy couldn't imagine what could possess a woman to betray her own sister that way. Robillard must have been quite the charmer. "No wonder they had a falling out."

"Hell hath no fury like a sister scorned." Feinberg appeared to be speaking from experience.

Sisters. Mercy had only an older brother, but her mother had a sister with whom she was always at odds. Grace and Verity fought over everything, but as far as she knew they'd never fought over a man. What Maude had done to Effie crossed a line Mercy couldn't imagine Grace and Verity crossing. Ever.

"I didn't find anything about this romantic rivalry in my research on the sisters."

"Apparently they never spoke of it," said Uncle Hugo. "They never spoke again, period."

"Like it never happened."

"Euphemia moved to France. Apparently Maude and Robillard were happy, but that happiness was short-lived. He went off to war, never to return."

Mercy thought about that. "Are you sure they never spoke again? Euphemia must have come back home to Vermont when the war broke out. Maude, too, after Robillard died."

"It's more complicated than that." Feinberg poured himself more coffee. "When Robillard died, they sent his duffle bag back to his widow. In his things Maude found a letter her sister Euphemia had written to him."

"The letter in Vinke's pocket."

"The one and the same," said the colonel. "Maude felt duped by both her sister and her husband. She moved to California, married Wilfred Fergus, and never looked back."

"Ironic, considering what she'd done."

"Sisters," repeated Feinberg.

"Euphemia carried a torch for Robillard." Mercy knew only too well how hard it was to mourn a man lost in battle. "She must have built the memorial. How heartbreaking."

"Barlow says that when their parents set up the Whitney-Jones family trust, they specified that Grackle Tree Farm could not be sold as long as the sisters were alive, in the hope that they'd come home and they'd reconcile. But they never did. Maude never went back again. Effie only returned in the summers to run her poetry retreats."

"Such a sad story." Maybe Brodie was right, and the place was haunted. Not by ghosts, but by remorse. "I still don't understand what that has to do with Vinke's murder. You say he was here looking for more letters. If Maude felt so betrayed, why would she want to find more evidence of that betrayal? And why would she think there were more letters? If there'd been more, wouldn't they have been there with Robillard's things?"

"This is where it gets interesting," said the colonel. "Not long before Effie died, she sent her sister a poem. Something about this huge tree that towered over the garden where they used to play as children."

Mercy pictured the old maple that towered over the house and the garden and remembered the line from Effie's letter: *and I am grounded here under our Scary Tree.* "Scary Tree. It's still there. I've seen it."

"That's right." Uncle Hugo regarded her with pride, as if she were one of his brightest cadets. Somehow managing to acknowledge her accurate analysis and patronize her at the same time. Still, that acknowledgment was an improvement of sorts. "'Scary Tree' was the title of the poem, which was about the tree and the secrets it held. Maude thought it was a peace offering and threw it away. Two weeks later, Effie died."

"Poisoned."

"Yes. The general consensus was by her own hand."

"And Maude believed it. My sister, the crazy poet." Mercy thought about her conversation with Amy and Brodie about poets and suicide.

"Wouldn't be the first time," said the colonel.

"Some people burn so brightly that eventually they go up in smoke." Again, Feinberg seemed to speak from experience.

"And she did burn brightly." The colonel closed his eyes.

"She'd had a run of bad luck." Mercy recalled what she'd discovered the night before about Euphemia's last days. "Leontine died after a long bout with breast cancer. Euphemia took care of her, and by the time Leontine passed, she was suffering from exhaustion as well as grief. She came home to Vermont for the summer, hoping the change of scenery would cheer her. She started a new volume of poetry, dedicated to Leontine, but the work wasn't going well. Her inability to write seemed to be the last straw for Euphemia. They say she took her own life the next day. But that was never proven to be the case. She left no suicide note, and anyone could have doctored the herbal tea that killed her with oleander." Mercy sipped her coffee. "Even her death was a mystery."

The colonel opened his eyes. "Barlow told us that the older Maude got, the less sure she was that her sister committed suicide, after all. She kept a scrapbook documenting Effie's career and had copies of all her books. The more she thought about it, the more she became convinced that Effie was trying to tell her something with that poem, and she wanted to find out what it was. She hired Vinke to investigate. That investigation brought him here."

"To the Scary Tree."

"Exactly." The colonel regarded her expectantly.

Mercy laughed. "That's why you're here. You want me to do the search. Pick up where Vinke left off." She looked from Uncle Hugo to Feinberg. "Why not use your own people?" Between the colonel's security agents and Feinberg's contacts, they certainly didn't need her.

"I thought you were our people." The colonel appeared to be offended.

"As did I." Feinberg seemed dismayed as well.

"So we're keeping it all in the family. May I ask why?"

"We trust you," said her uncle.

Feinberg shrugged. "And you want the house."

"And you want the letters."

"And whatever else you might find."

"What do you mean, whatever else I might find?"

"Beautiful people attract beautiful things," said Feinberg. The billionaire knew about beautiful things. "The world likes to reward beauty with beauty."

"The way a man might dress his lovely mistress in diamonds," added Uncle Hugo.

"You're saying that people gave Euphemia beautiful things, tokens of their affection and gratitude."

"Yes." The colonel leaned forward. "Everyone loved Euphemia, and no one loved her more than the people she helped save from tyranny."

"I can see that. But aren't most of those things at *L'Heure Bleu*?"

"We thought so." Feinberg paused. "Until you found the letter. If Euphemia has hidden one treasure, maybe she has hidden more."

"That's a big *if*," said Mercy.

"There's one *if* I'm sure of." Feinberg smiled at her. "If there's anything to find, you are the one who can find it."

CHAPTER EIGHT

Turtles carry their homes on their backs.
—CHRISTINA BAKER KLINE

TROY CROUCHED IN DEAD WATER AMONG THE ROOTS AND branches and fallen leaves that littered the edge of a waterway somewhere in the Green Mountain National Forest. He was wearing his waders, and he was waiting patiently, along with Susie Bear and his good friend, park ranger Gil Guerrette, for something to happen.

The wiry park ranger was wearing waders over his uniform, too. They both wore blaze orange baseball caps—and Susie Bear her blaze orange vest—as it was hunting season in Vermont. The woods were full of hunters armed with crossbows and muzzleloaders and rifles, the better to take down deer and bear. Among other species, some of which were protected from harvest all year long.

Because hunting season was poaching season. The poachers were hunting the wildlife, and the wardens were hunting the poachers.

Troy hated poachers. Gil, too.

Something *would* happen, eventually, here at this undisclosed location in the riffles and flows of this cool, clear tributary of the White River. At least it had been undisclosed until a clueless out-of-stater took a picture of a rare reptile he'd seen there and posted it on the internet.

Now Troy and Gil were setting up a surveillance operation to catch the poachers who inevitably showed up every time some tourist from away showed off a selfie, senselessly exposing endangered species to risk and ruin. In this case, a colony of wood turtles.

The wood turtle was curious and clever and cute—and at only five to nine inches long, the perfect size for a pet. People loved them, and they were in great demand on the illegal international pet market. Troy didn't even want to think about the black market in Asia, where wood turtles were used in traditional medicine and served up as delicacies at restaurants.

He'd been sitting here with Gil and Susie Bear for about an hour, and they had seen neither man nor turtle. Not even a single bow hunter, usually out in force in the forest, harvesting white-tailed deer this time of year.

Troy's legs were getting stiff; he needed to move—and soon. Susie Bear was getting restless; he could feel her neck muscles tensing under his hand. And if the deep frown on his friend's face was any indication, Gil was getting frustrated, too. He was an intense guy, given to quoting Thoreau when agitated. At this rate, Troy expected to hear wise words from *Walden* any minute now.

"We asked the guy to take down the post." Gil finally broke the silence. "And he did. But I'm still worried. Maybe the bad guys got to the turtles first."

"Or they moved on." This time of year wood turtles were surprisingly active, the males fighting for the right to mate with the females before settling down for their long winter's nap.

"Maybe they got wise to the bad guys and are hiding out."

"They are smart." Troy knew that wood turtles were in fact one of the smartest reptiles on the planet. Another reason people liked them so much. "Why don't you put up a trail camera here, and then we can split up and search along both sides of the river."

Gil rose to his feet. He pulled the trail camera from the pack and secured it to the trunk of a maple tree growing at the water's edge. He used the silky dogwood that crowded this section of the shoreline to hide the camera. "*The question is not what you look at, but what you see.*"

And there it was, thought Troy. *Thoreau.*

"You take that side." Gil pointed to the opposite bank of the river.

"Sure." Troy laughed. "Come on, Susie Bear."

The Newfie flung herself into the river with an enthusiasm neither Troy nor Gil would or could ever duplicate. Susie Bear loved nothing more than a plunge into a pool, anywhere, anytime, anyhow. Troy loved watching her; it was like watching an elephant dance. She may have lumbered around a bit on dry land, but when she swam she was as graceful in the water as she was when she romped in the snow. Liquid or frozen, water was her element.

The black shaggy dog plowed through the river with her webbed feet, her big head nosing toward the other shore. She clambered up the bank, shimmying, streams of water flying from her lustrous wet coat. She shook herself again, and sat down on her haunches and waited for Troy.

He waded into the flow, into the center where the river ran deeper and faster, rushing around his thighs and onto the outside of the curve, where the current was fastest. Even at the deepest section, Troy was only hip-deep in water, so he stayed relatively dry. Still, it was a chilly foray to the bank.

Running hard in this section of the current, the cold water was swirling with the detritus of autumn. Troy noted flashes of silver-scaled minnows and the darting of dragonflies and damselflies as he made his way to land. At the shoreline, he followed the trampled trail left by Susie Bear, through the bluejoint reedgrass and shrubby hedges of black willows and the clumps of wool grass, spike rushes, and cudweed. Susie Bear bounded ahead heedlessly.

Troy called her back, not wanting the Newfie to go too far afield. Even with her orange vest, he worried that, given her size and shape and coloring, she might be mistaken for a bear. Last year a hunter right here in Vermont critically wounded one of his fellow hunters when he mistook the guy for a bear. Too many hunters did not positively identify their targets before they pulled the trigger. They fired first and identified later.

Susie Bear returned to his side, and slowly they walked the border of the river, coming to a logjam flanked by a muddy patch. There Troy spotted tracks in the silt. He waved the Newfie into a *down,* and she plopped onto her belly.

Troy studied the wet ground. These were not the sure-footed tracks of a mammal. They were the rigid impressions left by tanks, marked by a distinct tail drag. They were the tracks of a wood turtle.

He whistled a warbler call across the river to Gil. The park ranger was gazing down at the boundary of water and land, looking for tank tracks himself. He stopped cold, straightened his spine, and turned to face the opposite bank. Gil whistled back. He did a good wood thrush, and he knew it.

Gil quietly stole down his side of the shore, away from Troy and Susie Bear. Then he waded slowly to Troy's side of the embankment, and traced their steps, joining them by the tracks. Together they stared into the water, looking for the wood turtles. They walked along the bank, which slid from mud and muck to cobble bar and gravel bar and sandbar.

Troy noticed it first, from the sandbar. There in the water, resting in the sand like a muddy stone, was a wood turtle about seven inches long. Its carapace was somewhat obscured by silt, but Troy could see pale yellow illuminating some of the brown scutes, reminding him as they always did of carved Inuit art objects. He pointed to the turtle. "You do the honors."

"You found it." Gil slipped his cell phone out of his breast pocket and began snapping photos.

Troy leaned down and scooped up the turtle, washing the sand from its shell, and holding it upright in his large hand. The wood turtle blinked at him with his gold-rimmed pupils.

"*Glyptemys insculpta.*" Gil used the scientific name.

"Sculpted turtle." Troy gently tapped the V-shaped notch at the rear of the carapace, the space where a male turtle could tuck his tail away for safekeeping while mating.

"Male," agreed Gil as he documented every inch of the wood turtle. "Let's see that plastron."

Troy turned the turtle over, revealing its creamy-yellow undershell, marked with the black blotches that always reminded him of Rorschach inkblots. "Looks like Susie Bear's profile."

Gil laughed. "You see big doggy heads, I see the map of France."

"I thought you were going to say family." Family was often Gil's answer to everything. He was a happily married man and father to three little girls, and he never let you forget it. He was a walking encyclopedia when it came to families. He knew more about the mating and parenting habits of humans and every other species on Earth than anyone Troy had ever met.

"France *is* family. *La famille avant tout.*"

"*Family before everything.* I remember." He should, since he'd heard Gil say it almost as often as he'd heard him quote Thoreau. "Maybe there's something to that Rorschach test, after all." He studied the pattern of the plastron's markings, which were as unique as fingerprints. "Do you think this is our Facebook wood turtle?"

"Can't say. The guy only shot the top view." Gil sighed. *"Quelle surprise."*

"Too bad." The trouble with amateurs was that while they often included photos when reporting sightings, they hardly ever shot bottom-view photos, which were critical in identifying the individual specimens.

"Let's see if he's old enough to do the mating dance." Gil counted off the rings on one of the scutes. These were the markings formed by keratin as the turtles grew. Each ring represented a cycle of cold and warm seasons, so roughly a year for every ring. "Fourteen. *Bien, mon ami.*"

"Just the right age." Most wood turtles reached sexual maturity between fourteen and twenty years of age, and could live to be seventy or more— but they had to survive fourteen years of peril first. Between the poachers and the predators (nothing foxes and raccoons and coyotes liked better than turtle eggs and hatchlings) and the cars and the tractors (no meaner death than getting whacked by a mowing machine), only the strongest and the luckiest turtles made it to adulthood. "You're a survivor, bro." Troy gently tapped the turtle's orange leg in a high five.

"Time to go forth and multiply." Gil kept on taking photographs.

Troy held the turtle aloft as he examined the surrounding area, peering into the water and the nooks and crannies of the logjam. "I think he's the only one here. At least for right now."

"If you could help me put a GPS tracker on him, we'll release him and hope he leads us to his kin. He should be looking for a mate about now. Either way, we'll keep an eye on him and this habitat. And if there's any trouble, we'll know where to find him."

"Sure." Troy sat down on a nearby boulder and held the turtle on his knee.

Gil pulled off his pack and retrieved the GPS unit, a cloth, and some specialized putty.

He wiped off the turtle's carapace, and rolled the putty between his hands, flattening it into a scute-sized plate, which he attached to one of the scutes on the front end of the shell. He pressed it into the carapace to secure it, then placed the GPS onto the putty. The antennas rose up from the telemetry unit and back out over the shell like the ribbon of a kite.

"Very aerodynamic."

"With any luck it will stay on." Gil checked his watch. "Give it ten minutes for the putty to harden, and we'll release him to fulfill his romantic destiny."

"Let's name him Poseidon."

"Greek god of the sea. Lots of children. Good choice." Gil grinned at him. "Speaking of children . . ."

"Stop right there. We just got married. And we don't even have a house yet."

"You don't need a house. All you need is Mercy." Gil pronounced her name the French way, as if it were *"merci."* That used to irritate Troy, but not anymore. Now he thought it appropriate, given how thankful he was to have Mercy in his life. Apparently Gil had known that all along, somehow, thanks no doubt to his uncommon knowledge of love and marriage and family.

Troy couldn't believe he was married to Mercy. It had happened so fast—she'd proposed to him out of the blue, and within the hour, they were husband and wife. Luckiest day of his life.

And now that they were married, he was more than ready to get on with it: house, kids, the works.

"Don't be in such a hurry to buy a house," warned Gil. "You're officially a couple now, that's all that matters. The rest will come in time."

"I guess. But the lodge fell through. And I've sold the fire tower. Mercy's cabin is getting a little crowded."

"You'll find another place. For now, carry your house on your back. Like a turtle."

"On my back," repeated Troy.

"I heard about the homicide at Grackle Tree Farm." Gil shook his head. "Just as well. You don't want that place."

"Thirty acres of woods and wetland and wildlife and a big old house to boot. Of course we want it."

"Rien ne pèse tant qu'un secret." Gil frowned at him. *"Nothing weighs more heavily than a secret.* And that place is full of secrets. How well do you know it?"

"We didn't get a chance to walk the acreage. All we saw up-close was the house and garden."

"And the dead guy." Gil checked his watch. "You know, one of the most mysterious corners of the property isn't far from here. You should see it. But first, let's release Poseidon."

Troy handed him the wood turtle. Gil placed Poseidon carefully on the sandbar. Susie Bear wagged her tail.

"Stay." Troy knew she'd want to dive right into the river with the turtle.

Gil clicked a few more pictures and waved at the water. *"Allons-y!"*

They all watched as Poseidon, decked out in his new GPS, steadily made his way across the sand to the water. Once in, he paddled off, the telemetric unit in place and seemingly not a hindrance at all.

"So long, Poseidon," said Troy.

Gil saluted the wood turtle. *"Bon voyage!"*

After Poseidon had disappeared from view, they placed a few more trail cameras up and down the river while Susie Bear dried off in the sun, basking on a boulder near the water's edge. With any luck, the cameras would catch poachers in the act, should any show up in search of wood turtles.

"Follow me," said Gil.

They hiked along an unkempt trail through a dark canopy of gold and red and brown. The ferns that had crowded the forest floor in the summer had died back, with drifts of fallen leaves taking their place. A brisk breeze funneled them into spirals, whipping them around Troy and Gil as they picked their way toward a destination still unclear to Troy. While he'd explored much of the state's wilderness, he didn't recognize this part of the forest. At least not yet. Susie Bear shuffled and snuffled along, happy to play in the puddles of leaves.

Troy spotted a dark hulking form peeking through the tall pines farther up the trail. "What is that thing?"

"We're almost there."

The path narrowed, and Gil and Troy pushed back branches thick with rust-colored leaves, in order to pass through the dense thickets of twelve-foot-high gray dogwood that obscured the entrance to a small clearing.

Gil disappeared into the clearing, the shrubs folding back in on themselves.

"Come on, girl." Susie Bear wagged her agreement, swishing foliage with her plumed tail. Troy parted the leaves and they stepped into the middle of a crescent-shaped space dominated by an odd configuration of granite. Scattered boulders. A set of stone arches that reminded Troy of the bridges built by the Romans he'd seen in Europe. A long camber of stairs leading up to nowhere. Remnants of a stone floor that must have grounded the room a hundred years ago. It all seemed vaguely familiar to him somehow.

"I think I've been here before. When I was very small."

"If you have seen it, it probably was years ago. Not many people know about it, and we'd like to keep it that way. One, because it's an unstable site, and two, because it's situated on a small pocket of private land within the general confines of the national forest."

"Grackle Tree Farm."

"*Exactement.*" Gil sighed. "It's off the beaten path for us all. So we try to discourage visitors."

"It looks like the ruins of a small castle." They walked the crescent, peering at the ruins. Sugar maples towered over the old foundation and stairway. A stone fireplace rose like a Stonehenge monument, tapering up to a freestanding chimney.

"Originally it *was* a castle—or at least it was inspired by one."

Troy studied what was left of the structure and tried to imagine it in its prime. "The castle."

"That's what the Druids call it."

"The Druids?"

"The local Druids love this place. They like to do their rituals here."

"It *is* beautiful. No matter what you call it." Troy ran a gloved hand along the lowest of the three grand arches. This was fine stonework. He considered the inexorable weight of time and wondered how much of these ruins would remain in another hundred years.

Of course, most of Vermont's forests hadn't been here two hundred years ago; much of the land had been cleared for farming and sheep ranching and logging by the 1800s. The woods had come back as the farmers and ranchers moved west and the workers moved to the cities and people turned from wood to coal and oil to heat their homes. This back-to-wilderness reversal was *not* the way most of the rest of the world was going. At least here, for now, Mother Nature was, if not winning, holding her own.

Troy was happy that he spent his days trying to improve her odds.

"Good thing it's surrounded by a designated wilderness area. So far it seems to be working."

"You can only hike in on foot, and only in small groups. No dogs— well, except for Seeing Eye dogs and Susie Bear. There are groups that will make the effort. Photography clubs and architecture buffs and nature lovers."

"And Druids."

"Yes. There's a thriving community of them here in Vermont. Mostly New Agers and hippies and nature freaks into Mother Earth and Celtic wisdom and the like. Mostly harmless, except for this trespassing." Gil walked under the middle arch to a nearby stand of birch trees shivering in the wind. "Around the birches."

Troy and Susie Bear traced the trees and found themselves in a small glade. There under a tall red oak was a marked gravestone. Troy stood before the simple headstone, which read:

WILLA STRONG
1846 TO 1872
BELOVED WIFE AND MOTHER

"Willa Strong. She must be one of the original Strongs, who built the main house at the estate. Jilly told us about them."

"Yes, Augustus Strong built the house for his new bride Willa. He was a decorated hero from the Civil War. She was a great beauty, the catch of the county."

"Then why is she buried way out here?" asked Troy. "The Strongs must have had a family plot."

"They do have a plot, a corner tomb in the old Northshire Cemetery."

"So if they had a family plot, why keep Willa out here?"

"It's a very sad story." Gil fingered the cross around his neck, pulled it up to his lips, and kissed it.

Troy found a granite boulder close to the gravestone and sat down heavily. "One more story and then we go home. Right, girl?" Susie Bear plopped down at his feet, and he scratched her shaggy head.

"This is a haunted place." Gil stood in the center of the clearing. Center stage, as it were. He rocked back and forth on his heels as he spoke, his hands in his pockets. "Bad things happen here—like the dead man in the library—and it all began right here.

"Augustus and Willa Strong married and moved into the house. The locals loved Willa, although they weren't so fond of Augustus, who by all accounts could be cold and aloof even if he was a war hero. But they all tolerated him because they loved her. When their first child was born, everyone in town celebrated. Lottie was a lovely little girl, with long yellow hair. Willa doted on the little girl and wanted to keep her close to her at all times. Augustus insisted that the child sleep in the nursery upstairs—instead of in the room next to their bedroom on the same floor, as was the custom."

"I can see where this is going—and it's not good."

"It happened on Halloween," Gil continued. "Augustus was away on business, and Willa woke up in the middle of the night. She knew something was wrong, and when she went upstairs to check on her, Lottie was gone."

"Gone?"

"Gone. They searched the grounds, of course, with the help of all their neighbors and most of Northshire, under the direction of the High Sheriff."

"No clues?"

"They found the three-year-old child's blanket here, where the middle arch now stands. Willa had made this woolen baby blanket for her daughter, embroidering it with a fairy-tale castle. The little girl loved fairy tales."

"So Lottie's blanket was the only lead?"

"For a while they suspected the maid, an indentured servant from Ireland named Molly. She turned out to have an alibi; she was in the barn with the stable boy, whom she later married.

"The groundskeeper was also a suspect, as he found the blanket. But his devotion to Willa and Augustus seemed sincere; he spent the rest of his days searching through the forest for Lottie, finding nothing of importance."

Troy stood up, and walked back to the middle arch, and pictured the young mother Willa Strong reading fairy tales to her daughter Lottie, the little girl with the long yellow hair. He took some pictures with his cell to show Mercy later. "What do the ruins have to do with this story?"

"Patience, *mon ami*." Gil took Troy's place on the boulder. "The case captured the public's imagination. Augustus had commissioned a portrait of Willa and the baby the year before, and that image was copied and distributed throughout the land. Sightings all over the state raised Willa's hopes and then dashed them over and over again as the leads led nowhere.

"As days became weeks and the weeks became months," Gil went on, "Willa continued to believe that Lottie was alive. At first she thought that her daughter had wandered out of the house somehow and gotten lost in the woods and that she'd find her way home. Or that she'd been kidnapped, and that she would escape her captors and come home. But Willa worried that Lottie was so young when she disappeared that she might not remember the path through the woods back to home. She had this small castle built, just like the one she'd embroidered on her baby daughter's blanket, just like the picture in the books of fairy tales she read to her every night."

"She thought the little girl would somehow recognize the castle?"

"Yes. And find her way home."

"That's a fairy-tale ending." Troy shook his head. "Magical thinking." He'd known parents in similar circumstances, and they either abandoned all hope early on or held on to it far too long. Both coping mechanisms were heartbreaking. And the only thing you could do as law enforcement was solve the case and bring the missing child home, one way or another. Closure was better than no closure, but losing a child was a tragedy that unmoored people, often for good. That must have been what had happened to Willa.

"You're right." Gil sighed. "There is no 'happily ever after' to this story. After Willa had the castle built in the woods, she spent much of her time there waiting for her daughter, roaming the surrounding forest, searching for her, always coming back to the castle."

"And how did she die?"

"Ultimately, she went mad with grief. One Halloween, on the anniversary of her daughter's disappearance, she came here to the castle, got caught in a freak blizzard, and died."

Troy walked back to the gravestone. At the right end of the foundation stone, he spotted a flat gray rock about the size of a compass, with a hole at its center. He picked it up and pocketed it, a small gift for Mercy. "What happened to Augustus?"

"He buried Willa here, and when the Panic of 1873 hit, he sold the property, moved west, and never looked back."

"Left it all behind."

"After Willa died, the rumors began. A woman in a white nightgown was seen haunting the house, wandering the grounds, searching the woods."

This was the part of the story that Troy knew. "The Ghost Witch of Grackle Tree."

"Exactly."

Susie Bear shambled to her feet and dove into a grove of white pine and hemlock, the blaze orange of her vest just a blur in the understory. He heard the crunch of footfalls not his own nor Gil's. *Hikers. Hunters. Poachers.*

Troy called after the Newfie, but he was too late.

CHAPTER NINE

. . . the house shelters daydreaming, the house protects
the dreamer, the house allows one to dream in peace.
—GASTON BACHELARD

I ASSUME YOU'VE ALREADY TOLD HARRINGTON THE IDENTITY OF the victim." Mercy raised her eyebrows at Uncle Hugo. "Otherwise, I'll have to do it."

"We've informed him that there's a good chance that the murdered man's name is Max Vinke." The colonel folded his hands primly on his lap.

"To buy you some time while you have me search for the letters."

"If the letters exist, they shouldn't languish in an evidence locker."

Mercy looked at Feinberg. "Daniel?"

"They'd be safer with us. Of course, we'd allow any documents we find to be examined by police as well as the appropriate experts."

"Experts?"

"Appraisers, linguistics specialists, philologists. Foremost among them, the director of the museum at *L'Heure Bleu*, who knows more about Effie's life and work than anyone on earth. She's coming over to examine the letter you found, and anything else that may be discovered."

"If we find letters or poems or journals or any documents relating to Whitney-Jones at all," said Uncle Hugo, "the interest will be overwhelming, and we'll need to manage that process."

"And whatever else I might find?"

"There's no real evidence that there is anything else." The colonel crossed his legs. With his hands folded and his legs crossed and his imperious look, he reminded Mercy of her mother. Maybe that's where Grace got it. "But at least we have the letter."

"Thanks to you," added Feinberg.

"Thanks to you," conceded the colonel.

"Don't change the subject. Sounds like you didn't tell Harrington."

"We saw no reason to bother Harrington with speculation."

"Which means, what, exactly?"

"It really is just a hunch," said Feinberg.

"You've made billions following your hunches," Mercy pointed out.

"*Imagination is more important than knowledge.*" Uncle Hugo quoted Einstein, for a change. Usually it was famous generals.

She thought about that for a minute. "You're saying that Harrington lacks imagination. But he makes up for it in ambition."

"We're focused on what could be a one-of-a-kind literary treasure." Uncle Hugo tipped his head at her wall of books. "You of all people should understand that."

"Given my overactive imagination."

"Exactly." Feinberg grinned at her.

Kai Harrington may not be the world's greatest visionary, but he was smart. He knew being counted among Feinberg's inner circle would help make his career, and he'd probably do anything to gain the billionaire's favor. Even if he knew he was being played, he might not care. "So Harrington agreed to this search for this fabled treasure. What did you ask for in return?"

"Just a little quid pro quo."

"I bet." Her great-uncle was the king of quid pro quo.

"We convinced him that if anyone could find something worthwhile, it would be you." Feinberg was nothing if not smooth.

"He must have hated that," said Mercy.

"He's a good-enough cop to recognize that you're the best man for the job." The colonel corrected himself. "Uh, woman."

It was unlike her uncle to compliment her. Twice in one day, no less. She nodded in acknowledgment of his flattery and he frowned.

"He's granted you full access to the crime scene." Feinberg saw the question in her eyes. "The CSST techs have all come and gone."

"What's the catch?"

"No catch. You'll be paid your standard hourly fee. The going rate."

"Well, thank you, Daniel, but that's not what I mean." Her going rate for investigative work was dear—but then, Feinberg could afford it. And, unlike some of the ultra-rich people she'd met, he wasn't cheap.

"Thrasher will meet you there and assist you with your search," said Feinberg.

There it was: the catch. Not that it bothered her, but it would gall Captain Thrasher to be reduced to Harrington's errand boy. Harrington must think the odds of finding anything major to be infinitesimal, as he'd never willingly miss the opportunity for a big PR triumph. But he knew, given the murder, he'd have to have someone from law enforcement accompany her, as the perpetrator was still at large.

"Everyone needs backup," said the colonel. "And we know you want that house. The sooner this is all cleared up, the sooner you and Troy can have it."

"You'd better make an offer soon," advised Feinberg. "If you need any assistance, let me know."

"The letter alone will generate new interest in Euphemia."

"Your uncle is right. People will line up to buy the house she grew up in. Anything else we find will just add fuel to the fire."

"We won't let anyone swoop down and turn it into Disneyland for poets." She finished her coffee. "As soon as Troy gets back from patrol, I'll talk to him about making an offer."

"He'll be fine with it," predicted Uncle Hugo. "He loves you."

"Indeed." Feinberg stood up. "Meanwhile, I'll ask Ren to keep me apprised of any other offers. No Disneyland for poets."

"Thank you." Mercy rose from the ottoman. "Elvis, let's go find this mysterious trove of whatever." The shepherd leapt to his feet.

Feinberg laughed. "Why do I get the feeling you already know where to look?"

"We start with the Scary Tree."

"Agreed." Uncle Hugo snatched up the last of the cinnamon rolls and pointed it at her. "Happy hunting."

AN HOUR LATER MERCY stood with Captain Thrasher and Elvis at the base of the imposing maple that rose like a dark tower in a Tolkien novel, casting the house and the garden in shadow. The wind had picked up, and fallen leaves churned around them. The air was cold now, the sun obscured by thunderous clouds. It looked like rain.

There were footprints marking the ground around the tree's burly trunk, but the crime scene techs had obviously processed them already. Not that they would have found much of interest; the pattern in the soil left by the soles of the footwear worn by whoever was here resembled that found on work boots. The same style worn by the victim at the time of his death.

Mercy studied the prints. "Max Vinke."

"Yep. We've already confirmed these prints as his." Thrasher's eyes were on the ground, too.

"Have we learned anything more about Vinke's movements before he died?"

"He flew in from Santa Barbara two days ago. Rented a car in Albany and drove here, stayed at the Northshire Marriott. Nosed around the library, talked to the director of the Northshire Historical Society, met with the Northshire Alliance of Poets."

"Asking about Euphemia Whitney-Jones, I'd imagine." Mercy circled the tree, Elvis on her heels. She squatted down to study the area more closely, swiping away the swirling leaves, but saw only the one set of impressions.

"You got it." Thrasher made his own circle from farther out from the trunk of the massive maple. "Which presumably led him here."

"No evidence of anyone else here." Mercy straightened up. "Seems like Vinke was alone."

"Any other prints elsewhere?" She told the captain about meeting Adah and Levi Beecher on the grounds before discovering the body.

"Their prints are mostly confined to the back garden. But there is evidence that Levi Beecher was in the house."

"He *is* the caretaker."

"Yeah, he said he was setting out mousetraps in the kitchen, the attic, and the cellar. Which seems to be the case."

"Means, opportunity, motive." Mercy frowned. "What possible motive would he have?"

"If Feinberg and your uncle are right about the treasure, well, that becomes a motive for damn near everyone who knows about it." He stared up into the massive horizontal branches of the majestic sugar maple, which stood steady in the face of the wind, even as its bloodred leaves rustled wildly. "How would you hide a stack of letters here?"

"I don't know." Mercy examined the trunk, with its dark brown furrowed bark, looking for hiding places. All she found was a carving of a heart with P + M inside. Carving initials into a tree was once seen as a romantic gesture, but now most people knew that cutting into a tree's bark was wounding the tree, and the resulting carving was simply scarring. At least, she hoped most people knew that now. "I don't see any hollows anywhere, and if someone did stash them in a crook somewhere, how would they survive the elements?"

"Could have buried it."

"True." Mercy grinned at him. "Did you bring a shovel?"

"Got one in the truck." Thrasher put his hands on his hips and leaned back on his heels. "But I'm sure you do, too."

"I do." All smart New Englanders carried a shovel in their vehicle; you never knew when you'd have to dig yourself out of the snow or the mud or the sand. "But I don't think either of us are going to have to break a sweat. Vinke didn't find anything here, and I don't think we will, either."

Thrasher considered that. "He died in the house."

"In the library."

"No evidence of a search there, by Vinke or his assailant." The captain paused. "Maybe his murder had nothing to do with this presumed treasure. It could have been a robbery. His wallet and ID and fob were missing. They're still missing. We found his rental car abandoned in a field on the outskirts of Northshire. Wiped clean."

"Who even knew he was here at the house?"

"This time of year, you get teenagers and ghost hunters and poetry fans, all looking for the witch. What some people think of as Halloween fun. Someone could have seen an opportunity and went for Vinke. Maybe they didn't mean to kill him."

"I thought he was poisoned."

"Dr. Darling is still running tests. We should know later today."

Mercy had every confidence that the autopsy would prove her and Dr. Darling's first instincts correct. Poison killed Max Vinke.

"I can see you're set on poison."

"If I'm right, then we'll need to know how and when the poison was administered."

"If that's the case, Dr. Darling may be able to shed light on those questions as well."

"Let's check out the room where he died. Maybe he went there to look for the letters, and someone followed him."

"I can see the wheels in that brain of yours turning." Thrasher held out his arm. "After you."

Elvis raised his head in expectation, ears perked.

"Excuse me." Thrasher apologized to the shepherd. "After *you*."

They trailed after Elvis as he bounded back toward the house.

"It *is* a nice piece of property. I can see you and Troy here."

"I can, too." She gazed around at the grounds, which were once again in the light, the sun peeking through a break in the clouds.

Elvis twisted around, waiting for instruction, and Mercy waved him onto the porch. "Front door."

Thrasher let them in, and they stepped into the hallway of the old manor. Thanks to the comings and goings of the forensics team, the place was even more of a mess than it had been before. Not that it mattered. Standing at the bottom of the lovely staircase, gazing up to the second floor, where the light flooded in through the multipaned window that graced the landing, she wanted the place more than ever.

Mercy took the stairs to the library two at a time. Thrasher followed at a normal pace, but Elvis raced past her, turning at the landing as if to say, "Come on, slowpoke!"

"Show-off."

Together they all entered the library. The crime scene techs had gone over the room for fingerprints and other evidence, but they'd focused on the floor where the body was found. Apart from the volumes lining the shelves and the bare writing desk in the far corner, the room was empty.

"Doesn't seem like much to search." Thrasher glanced around the room. "They've already gone through the books."

"True." At least they'd gone through them perfunctorily; Mercy could tell by the streaks of dust they'd disturbed when the forensics team had added their own black fingerprint dust to the spines of the books. She pulled a pair of plastic gloves from her backpack and slipped them on.

Elvis parked himself at the right of the doorway in sentry mode. Thrasher stood to the left. "Go ahead, do your thing."

Mercy took her time examining the books. In truth, there was nothing she liked better than snooping in a stranger's library. You could tell a lot about a person by the books they read. Or pretended to read.

In addition to the usual leather-bound classics—Charles Dickens, Mark Twain, Jane Austen, and the Brontë sisters, tomes on mythology and philosophy and religion, essays and plays—there was a whole section of poetry, from volumes by the most celebrated of poets of the ages to chap-books by local poets, including several Northshire Alliance of Poets collections. She looked at the contents pages in the anthologies and found poems by Levi Beecher and Adah Beecher there. And, of course, Euphemia Whitney-Jones's own volumes of poetry—including *A Fire of Naming, Animals and Other Conundrums,* and *Home at Night: Poems for Children.* The latter featured "The Ghost Witch of Grackle Tree."

Mercy also found a surprising number of books on the occult, witches and spells, ghosts, the tarot, the *I Ching,* runes, goddesses and angels and demons, all manner of paranormal and supernatural literature. There was an entire shelf devoted to the ancient Celts, Druids, and their sacred groves. An entire spirituality inspired by trees.

Sacred tree, thought Mercy. *Scary Tree. Dog. God.* Euphemia loved anagrams. *Sacred tree* was almost an anagram of *Scary Tree.* But not quite. In her mind, Mercy pictured the words and the letters composing the words. She arranged them and rearranged them. "Secretary."

"What?" Thrasher crossed the room to join her.

"Secretary," she repeated. "It's an anagram of *Scary Tree.* Poets like to play with words. They like obscure metaphors and literary clues and anagrams. Certainly Euphemia Whitney-Jones did." She quickly recited the "Dog Is God" poem for him.

"I'll take your word for it."

"So maybe the secret lies with Leontine Bonnet."

Thrasher gave her a blank look.

"Bonnet was a painter, but she's better known as Euphemia Whitney-Jones's secretary and companion. Euphemia's Alice B. Toklas, as it were."

"Right. And how does that help us here?"

"I don't know." Mercy felt like she was missing something, something obvious. She returned to the section of the library where she'd noted novels by Djuna Barnes, Radclyffe Hall, and Nella Larsen, among other works considered part of the lesbian literary cannon. She pulled each off the shelf, one by one, and flipped through them. No handwritten dedications, no notes in the margins. Nothing.

"Anything?" asked Thrasher from his post by the door.

"No. Maybe the answer lies in France with Leontine. Daniel Feinberg says that the director of the Whitney-Jones museum in France is coming over to check out the letter we found. Maybe she can shed some light on it." Mercy had done all she could with the books, short of going through every single one of the hundreds of volumes here. It might come to that, if she came up empty everywhere else. There was always the floor, but the crime techs had surely covered that ground. Still. "You didn't notice any loose floorboards, did you?"

Thrasher grinned back. "I'll look."

Before she could protest, the captain was down on his knees, examining the wide pine planks. Elvis accompanied him, sniffing the floor. The shepherd could sniff out anything, but his experience finding lost letters was minimal.

Mercy left them to it and went over to the far side of the room, where the lone piece of furniture sat tucked in the corner. When she'd first seen the old desk, it was draped in an old sheet. The crime scene techs had removed it to dust for prints. Unlikely that they would have found any, given the covering, but it did speak to the thoroughness of the forensics team.

Now that she got a good look at the piece, she realized that it might be a very valuable antique. What the French called an escritoire—a tall, heavy, single piece of furniture designed in the French Empire style, with a base of deep drawers on lion-paw feet. The lower section was topped by a bookcase enclosed by cabinet doors and crowned with marble.

This one was beautifully carved from mahogany, with intricate floral inlays on the doors and brass pulls and locks. The keys were in the locks, so Mercy turned them and opened the doors, revealing a fitted interior with several pigeonholes and small drawers. The dark-green leather writing surface was made to pull out. Mercy pulled it out, picturing Euphemia Whitney-Jones at this desk, composing her poems.

She wondered if the piece had belonged to the Strong family, who'd built the house after the Civil War and had been passed it down from one resident to the next. Or maybe Effie had brought the antique home from France after the war.

Either way, Mercy couldn't understand why such a fine piece was still here. Of course, the books were still here, too; maybe since this room was kept locked, trespassers had contented themselves with trashing the first floor. Or maybe the witch protected Effie's library, and scared the riffraff away.

Thrasher joined her at the desk. "The floor's clean." He slapped the dust from his uniform. "But I am not." The captain was one of the most stylish, impeccably groomed men in the state; even in his standard-issue uniform, he gave their well-dressed friend the billionaire a run for his money. Although Troy had told her he suspected Thrasher had all his uniforms custom-tailored.

"Sorry." Mercy stared at the escritoire.

"Now what?"

"This escritoire."

"Escritoire," repeated Thrasher.

"Writing desk. The English would call it a—" She slapped her forehead.

"What?"

"A *secretary*."

"Back to the anagram, I see."

Carefully, Mercy opened and closed each drawer and explored every pigeonhole. Nada.

"What are you looking for?"

"These antique desks were built to hold secrets." She ran her gloved fingers under every inch of the desk. "There's got to be a hidden compartment here somewhere."

"Hidden compartments? Like in the *National Treasure* movie?"

"Yes. Exactly." Mercy pulled out the drawers again, each in turn, searching for a mechanism that would reveal a secret hiding place. "It has to be here."

"You're usually right about these things."

She tugged on the last of the brass lion's-head knobs. The drawer was stuck. She tugged harder, and it sprang open. She groped the underside, hitting upon something, ripping her plastic glove. And releasing a rectangular-shaped cedar casket. Letter-shaped. About three inches wide and nine inches long and two inches deep. With a slide-top.

"I'll be damned."

Gingerly, Mercy slid the top from the wooden box. "Sweet."

"Let me see."

She held the small crate up to the captain. Nestled inside was a stack of faded letters, tied with a pale-blue silk ribbon.

"Unbelievable." For a moment they just stood there together, gazing at their find.

Finally, Mercy plucked the potentially priceless papers from the crate, letters in one hand, box in the other. "Maybe they're not Effie's. Anyone could have written them."

"Maybe. But I'm beginning to believe in this fairy tale of yours."

She flipped through them, noting that among the notes on creamy linen stationery were the legendary papers marked with the "V for Victory" symbol. "Some of these are V-mail."

V-mail was the system put into place to process all the letters to and from the military during World War II. When the U.S. had entered the conflict, the postal service was overwhelmed with mail. That mail took up valuable storage space on transports needed for vital war supplies.

So the government collected the letters, censored them, and then copied them onto microfilm, which took up a fraction of the space of paper correspondence. Upon arrival at its destination, the film was printed onto paper again and distributed to the recipients. Mercy started to explain, but Thrasher cut her short.

"I know what V-mail is. My great-uncle served in World War II. Ninety-second Infantry."

"A buffalo soldier?" Mercy knew that these African American soldiers were celebrated for their extraordinary courage and honor and sacrifice.

"I've seen the letters that passed between him and the family during the war. They're part of our family legacy."

"I'm sure." No surprise that the fearless Thrasher was descended from warriors.

Thrasher pointed to one of the papers. "The first letter was written in May 1942, on regular stationery."

"Before they started using V-mail. This means that they continued their correspondence throughout the war."

"Well, the timing is right," agreed the captain. "This could very well be the biggest literary discovery in Vermont in years."

Mercy realized she was holding her breath. Slowly she exhaled, and turned to the captain. "Shall we?"

"Sure."

She put the box down on the writing surface so she could examine the letters more closely. But she was distracted by a flash of something at the bottom of the cedar casket. There lay a Victorian-era key, the old-fashioned brass skeleton kind that some people like to collect. She placed the stack of correspondence by the box, and removed it. She held it up to the light, the old brass glinting dully in the sun.

"Another mystery for you to solve, Mercy. No pressure."

She laughed. "One at time, please, one at a time." This place was full of mysteries to solve, she thought. One hundred and fifty years' worth.

Elvis barked and barreled out of the room.

Thrasher looked at Mercy. "Good sign or bad sign?"

"Could be either, this time of year. Perp or wild turkey."

"Who knows we're here? Besides Harrington."

"Just Uncle Hugo and Daniel Feinberg. As far as I know, even the real estate agent doesn't know we're here." She glanced at her phone. "I sent Troy a text when I left the cabin, but he didn't reply. He's probably out of range."

"Are you armed?"

"No." Her Beretta was at home in its safety box in her dresser drawer. "But I've got my Swiss Army knife."

"It shouldn't come to that. You stay here with the letters. I'll go see what your dog is up to."

Mercy registered his exit, and part of her was aware of the faint sound of his footsteps as he stole down the staircase. But she remained focused on the letters. She was stunned by their presence, and what it could mean. For literature, for the estate, for Vermont at large. She was desperate to read them, but she held back, waiting for Thrasher. She supposed she should contact Uncle Hugo and Feinberg, too. And Troy. They would want to witness the unveiling.

Still, it wouldn't hurt to open one of them. To make sure they were the real thing.

She still held the old key, so she slipped it into one of her side pockets. Cautiously and deliberately, she untied the neat bow that held the small stack of letters together. The ribbon fell to the sides of the box in graceful pools of pale blue. Mercy picked up the first letter, the one on top, one of the creamy notes she guessed were written by Effie. *If only.*

She balanced the fragile linen-finish paper on her palm, as if she were holding a holy relic from a famous letter-writing saint. St. Paul. St. Catherine of Siena. St. Jerome. She didn't know if she believed in saints, but she believed in the power of poetry. Her saints were Shakespeare and Dickinson and Frost. And now, maybe Effie.

Another deeper, angrier bark outside brought her back to the present—*uh-oh,* not good—and she pulled her Swiss Army knife from her back pocket. She looked out the windows but saw nothing and no one.

Where was Thrasher? Where was Elvis?

Thrasher would tell her to stay put, let the guy with the gun handle it.

She couldn't do that. Something was wrong. And she should have known it the minute Elvis left the room.

Always trust your dog.

CHAPTER TEN

The ruins of time build mansions in eternity.
—WILLIAM BLAKE

A BAM! ECHOED THROUGH THE FOREST. BIRDS SKITTERED TO higher ground. The foul-smelling smoke of gunpowder drifted toward Troy and Gil.

Troy barreled off the trail through the brush and brambles, into the trees. He could hear Gil jogging behind him. "Susie Bear!"

He couldn't see her anywhere. What he did see were three hunters dressed like Daniel Boone, standing at the base of a towering pine. Woolen pullover shirts, coonskin caps, and all. One was old enough to be the father to the two burly young men, who looked enough alike to be brothers. Tweedledee and Tweedledum with guns.

Great, he thought, *long hunter wannabes.* He announced himself firmly. "Game Warden Troy Warner."

"Your dog's fine." The older hunter stood as if posing for a photograph, holding his muzzleloader upright in his right hand and resting his other hand on his leather ammo pouch.

"I missed." He pointed to the splintering of the pine's trunk right about the same height as Susie Bear.

So much for the one-shot challenge, thought Troy as he desperately scanned the area for signs of the Newfie.

"Be thankful that you missed." Gil glared at the hunters as he joined them. "I got this," he told Troy quietly.

Troy nodded at his friend, and went on looking and calling for Susie Bear, one eye on Gil and the hunters, the other on the woods.

"Ranger Gil Guerrette. Let's see those hunting licenses. And your early-season bear tag."

The older man handed the ranger his license. "I'm Dr. Horace Boswell." As if that should mean something to them.

"The poet," said one of his companions. As if that would explain everything.

Gil ignored that. "And you are?"

"Quaid Miller." The taller of the young men pulled his license from the pocket of his camo pants, the only modern piece of clothing he wore. He jerked his thumb at his look-alike. "This is my cousin Braden."

"We haven't done anything wrong," said Boswell. "I have a permanent license, so I don't need a bear tag."

Permanent licenses were issued to resident hunters over the age of sixty-six in Vermont, allowing them to hunt without buying the tags. The older man looked to be in his early seventies.

"You shot at a search-and-rescue dog. That is, by definition, wrong."

"We thought it was a bear. An honest mistake."

"She's wearing a blaze orange vest. Hard to miss."

"We didn't see it."

"With a muzzleloader, you only get one shot. If you'd waited until you could see the target well enough to positively ID it, you would have known it was not a bear."

"I told him that." Quaid Miller shook his head.

"Shut up." Boswell was not pleased.

"Where's your early bear season tag, Miller? You're no senior."

"I'm just out for deer."

"Right," Gil scoffed, and turned to Troy. "Any sign of her?"

"Not yet." The forest floor was so matted with dead leaves and decayed wood and a profusion of prints Troy was having trouble finding Susie Bear's tracks.

Gil turned back to the long hunters. "Did you see where the dog went when you shot at her?"

"No," said Boswell pridefully.

Troy knew he was lying. In his experience, conceit was often a mask that liars wore to hide their untruths. Pomposity was just a particularly annoying form of conceit.

"I think she's hiding in that snag over there." Braden Miller raised an arm at a circle of standing dead trees anchored by a huge cavity tree and a pile of deadwood. His face was red, and Troy figured he was embarrassed—whether because of what he'd done or being caught or both, he wasn't sure.

Troy made his way to the snag while Gil checked their licenses. He could hear the park ranger launch into a lecture on the importance of hunting safety as he finally spotted the telltale orange of Susie Bear's vest. The Newfie was crouched in the mess of rotting wood, trying to squeeze her large bulk into the largest of the fallen logs.

"I'm here, girl." He squatted down to the dog's level. "It's all right, come on out."

Her tail thumped, sending dead leaves and detritus flying. She scrambled to her feet, nearly knocking him over as she swept in for a hug. He rubbed her belly while carefully examining her thick glossy fur for any possible injury. He didn't find any welts or wounds, but he did find a sticky white substance sticking to the flews along her jowls and the shaggy ruff around her neck. *Donuts.*

Susie Bear gave him a big lick on each cheek. Newfie for *I'm fine, you're fine, we're all fine.*

"How is she?" yelled Gil over his shoulder.

"She seems okay." Troy rose to his feet, helping the Newfie up to a standing position. Susie Bear shuffled along beside him as they picked their way across the snag to Gil and the hunters. "Move away from the tree."

Boswell and Quaid Miller stared at Troy, who returned the stare with a glare of his own.

"You heard the warden. Move away from the tree."

The two men slouched away from the pine. Quaid Miller looked ready to bolt. Boswell just looked bored.

"That's good. Stay right there by that boulder." Gil leaned over to whisper to Troy. "What are we looking for?"

"Donuts." Troy told Susie Bear to stay, and walked over to the base of the pine that had taken the shot. He dropped into a squat and used his gloved hand to sort through the fallen leaves and broken twigs and small stones for evidence of sweets, notably pastries and donuts and cinnamon rolls. All favorite foods of the black bear—and cheap and easy bait for poachers.

Gil stepped between Troy and the hunters, addressing the men in a stern voice. "Bear baiting is illegal in the state of Vermont."

"We didn't use any bait," said Boswell.

"Better just to tell us the truth now," ordered Gil.

"We didn't bait the bear." Quaid Miller hooked a thumb at his cousin. "But Braden here may have had a Dunkin' Boston cream or two for breakfast."

"Seriously?"

"Tell them, *cuz*."

Braden's face reddened. "We did stop at Dunkin' on the way. But not for bait. I swear."

Troy listened to the hunters' lame story. Susie Bear loved donuts as much as the next dog, but she'd never eat human food she found on the trail unless given permission. She knew a bait pile when she saw one, and normally, she'd simply alert to the bait. Not eat it.

These long hunters must have encouraged her to eat the bait. Troy kept digging through the flotsam and jetsam of the forest floor, but he couldn't find anything.

He wasn't surprised; if presented with donuts as a gift, Susie Bear was not a dog who would ever leave a donut behind. Whatever evidence there had been here—and he knew there had been evidence here—it was lost somewhere in the Newfie's digestive system. He rose slowly to his feet.

Gil looked at him, and he shook his head.

"We know you put out bear bait," said Gil, "and we know you tried to shoot what you thought was a bear while using bait."

"The only thing you can prove that we did was hit that tree." Boswell squared his shoulders. "We're leaving."

"This is private land." Troy glared at them.

"It's not posted." Quaid Miller glared right back.

"It will be. Don't come back."

"You got lucky today. Nobody died." Gil handed each man his respective hunting license. "Next time, you may not be so lucky."

Boswell tucked his license under his coonskin cap and sauntered off without another word.

"Sorry," whispered Braden Miller.

Quaid Miller gave his cousin a push. "Come on. We're out of here."

Troy and Gil watched the younger men huff after Boswell. Susie Bear played in the leaves, back to her jolly old self now that the morons with the muzzleloaders were gone.

"We'll get them next time," promised Gil.

"Yes, we will. What is it with poachers?"

"What is it with poets? This place is overrun with them."

"What's wrong with poets?"

"*Poetry is the mysticism of mankind,*" intoned Gil.

Thoreau again, thought Troy. "That doesn't sound so bad."

Gil leaned back and crossed his arms. "Be careful what you wish for."

LEVI BEECHER TRAILED THE long hunters as silently as the grave. He didn't trust them, especially Horace Boswell. Horace had always been arrogant, in the way of arrogance of youth, but he'd been an earnest student of poetry and a decent human being once upon a time. But all his subsequent success seemed to have spoiled him. He was so busy playing the part of the Warrior Poet that he'd forgotten how to be an artist.

Levi had admired him, back when they were all Effie's young protégées. Horace's early poems were rough, but all their poetry was rough back then. He'd gotten better, good enough to win the Pulitzer, not that Levi had ever read the later work. He'd given up poetry by then, except for Effie and Adah and his own secret scribbling.

Over the years, he'd watched Horace go Hollywood. He'd beaten the hunter archetype into the ground. Becoming a long hunter and roaming the woods with a muzzleloader and writing slick, violent poems about what it meant to be a man. They'd even made one into a very bad video game—and an even worse movie. Rambo meets Kipling.

Cynical bastard.

Levi had never caught Horace poaching here on the estate. Although it would not surprise him; he'd always wondered how the man had managed to harvest all those moose and bear and bucks he wrote his poems about. Poets and poachers both preyed on the lives of others.

The Miller boys were another story. He'd seen them at the castle ruins, hanging out with the Druids. Quaid struck him as shifty, but he liked Braden enough to hire him to help out on the farm.

Levi didn't approve of the Druids' or anyone else's so-called events at the castle, but Effie had allowed it and even hosted poetry readings there during her summer literary salons. So he'd turned a blind eye.

But no more.

He pursued Horace and the cousins through the woods and along a narrow ridge. They were easy to shadow; Horace wasn't moving that fast these days. Decades of sitting behind a desk had slowed him down. At least Levi could still hold his own, although the Miller boys were big guys. And most of it was muscle, not fat. If they came to blows, he'd have to outsmart them, which wouldn't be that hard, as they weren't the sharpest tools in the box.

The long hunters followed the trail across the ridge to the point where the rise sloped down into a meadow. They descended slowly, traipsing through the wildflowers and grasses, crossing over the property line that bordered the field, and heading into national forestland once again.

There was a little-used trailhead at the edge of the meadow. They'd probably left their vehicle there in the small nook off the side of the road provided for parking. Levi stayed back among the maples bordering the meadow and watched them leave. He listened, waiting for the sound of the engine as they drove away.

Good riddance, he thought. At least for now.

Levi walked out into the meadow, then stood among the goldenrod and milkweed and asters. He surveyed the area around him. He loved Grackle Tree Farm. And he had protected her secrets as well as he could all these years. For the sake of Effie and the wildlife and the land itself.

But he was getting old. He wasn't going to be around forever. Effie's place needed new stewards. Strong young people of principle, who appreciated poetry and valued wildlife and could keep a secret.

Like Mercy Carr and Troy Warner.

CHAPTER ELEVEN

Charity begins at home, and justice begins next door.
—CHARLES DICKENS

WHAT TO DO WITH THE LETTERS? Mercy didn't want to take the time to put them back in the box and hide them in the secretary again. She'd never done it before, and she wasn't even sure the mechanism would work after all these years anyway. She couldn't afford any delay. She had to assist Thrasher and Elvis.

But she couldn't leave the letters out in the open, either. She cut the stack like a deck of cards, pulled open the big thigh pockets on her cargo pants, and pushed half of the letters in one pocket and the other half in the other. She ripped off her plastic gloves, snapped the pockets closed, and slipped her backpack onto her shoulders. She opened her Swiss Army knife and held it in her right hand.

A sharp yelping from outside, followed by a burst of gunfire.

In her mind, she could hear her late grandfather say, *Never bring a knife to a gunfight.*

But she had no choice. She abandoned the desk and ran for the doorway of the library, stopping just long enough to scan the space before she went downstairs.

All clear. She slipped across the landing, creeping down the steps as quickly as she could, cringing at each creak in the old stairs.

Still no sign of anyone, two-legged or four-legged. Mercy listened hard, but all she could hear was the rattle of the branches against the windows as the wind picked up again. No more yelping. She didn't want to think about what that could mean.

She came to the bottom of the steps. The front door stood open. She was tempted to whistle for Elvis, but she didn't want to reveal her position or his. She leapt across the hall, flattening herself against the wall by the door. She pulled out her cell to call for help.

No signal.

Mercy cursed and shoved her phone back into her side pocket. She peered through the sidelight window. She saw a figure lying askew in one of the unkempt flower beds, framed by tall weeds and partially hidden by overgrown shrubs. She wasn't sure but she thought he was wearing green. The color of a game warden's uniform. *Thrasher.*

She tore across the porch, cleared the brick pathway, and crashed through the boxwood and hydrangeas. She crouched by the man lying on his back. It was the captain.

"Thrasher." There were two punctures in his forest-green dress shirt. She wrenched it open, and saw the battered bulletproof vest that covered his chest. Mercy swore with relief.

"Mercy."

"You're going to be fine. We'll get you some help."

Thrasher tried to sit up, leaning on his elbows. His face creased with pain, and he fell back again against the crushed bushes.

"Stay down." She glanced around but saw no one.

"Where's the shooter?"

He jerked his head to the right. "Around the house." The captain's voice was thin, and his breathing was labored. "Looking . . ."

Looking for her. Both the captain's vehicle and her own were in the lot. The shooter would know Thrasher wasn't here alone. "And Elvis?"

"Don't know." The captain closed his eyes. His handsome face glistened with sweat despite the chill in the air. "Ran off."

"Was he hit?"

"Don't know."

She tried her cell again. No signal. "Where's your radio?"

Thrasher didn't answer. She felt for his radio on his belt. She pulled it out of the case on his belt. That's when she saw it—the blood seeping from the captain's left shoulder.

"Oh no." She shrugged off her backpack and retrieved the duct tape and a pack of cleansing wipes. Placing the cloth on the wound, she tore her scarf from her neck, folded it into a square, placed it over the cloth, pressing firmly. With her other hand, she punched on the radio.

At first all she heard was static. More static. Finally, the dispatcher Delphine Dupree answered, her words just barely intelligible through the white noise.

"Delphine. Mercy Carr here. Officer down, Grackle Tree Farm." She tucked the radio under her chin and rattled off the address as she staunched the captain's wound. "It's Thrasher."

"Thrasher?" Delphine was a dispatcher known for her calm, but a note of alarm colored her voice.

"Affirmative."

"Hang on," said Delphine. "Twenty minutes out."

"Over and out." Mercy nudged the radio down to her lap and turned it off. Thrasher moaned, opening his eyes again.

"Help is on the way," she told him, and he passed out again. She used the duct tape to secure the makeshift bandage. It would have to do until the EMTs arrived.

TROY WAS FOLLOWING GIL back to town for a quick lunch before heading home to the cabin when both his warden service radio and his police radio crackled on at the same time: *10-32. Shots fired. Officer down. Grackle Tree Farm.*

He answered the police radio first: "In the vicinity. On the way."

Then he checked in with Delphine, the game warden dispatcher.

"It's Mercy and Thrasher. Get over there."

Troy switched on his lights and sirens, and gunned the Ford F-150, overtaking Gil in a burst of speed. He could hear Susie Bear rousing herself in the back seat, straining at her harness. She knew something was wrong.

"Sit tight, girl." Troy swerved around the ranger's truck, passing him at eighty miles an hour, which was way too fast on this winding two-lane road. He flicked his hazard lights at Gil, waving his arm from his car window, indicating that he should follow him.

Gil honked in response, and flipped on his own lights and sirens.

Troy kept his eyes on the road and his foot on the gas, focused on his driving even as his gut knotted and his mind flitted all over the place: Why were Mercy and Thrasher there? Who was after them? Why? *What the hell was going on?*

MERCY NEEDED TO FIND Elvis, but she couldn't leave the captain. She could try a bird call, which Elvis would recognize and maybe the assailant would not, but she risked his following the shepherd right back to Thrasher and finishing him off—along with her and Elvis. There was always the possibility that he'd already gotten to Elvis. But she couldn't think about that right now.

She continued to press against the captain's shoulder with her right palm. She needed to stop the bleeding. But she also needed to keep them safe from the guy who'd shot him until help got here. Mercy reached for his gun, but the holster was empty. She searched him gently, but the weapon was not on his person. Desperate, she clawed through the vegetation with her spare hand, but found nothing. She'd have to try and switch sides and search again.

A terrific yowling interrupted her search. *Elvis.* He was alive. The barking was coming from the back of the house. She looked up, and there he was, blasting toward her, a rocket with fur. She was overwhelmed with relief; she could feel the tears forming at the edge of her eyelids and blinked them back.

The shepherd slid into a *down* at the captain's feet and whined.

"It'll be okay. Good boy." Mercy checked him out, and he seemed to be fine. She gave him a hug as best she could, and focused again on Thrasher. He didn't look good. She figured help was still at least fifteen minutes out. "Hold on, Captain."

Thrasher whispered something, but she missed it. She leaned over, her ear at his lips. "What?"

"Six o'clock."

At least, that's what she thought he said. That didn't make any sense. It wasn't near six o'clock. And even if it were, she didn't know what was supposed to happen at that time. She asked the captain to repeat himself, but before he could answer, a low rumbling distracted her. An aggressive growl, meant to alert her to possible danger. Elvis was focused on the porch, his long nose pointing to trouble.

A man stood there, dressed all in black. A black-and-red ski mask was pulled over his head and face. He was around six feet tall, with the broad shoulders and slim waist of a guy into fitness. He looked like a pro.

Which was not as unlikely as it might have been, given the fact that this house could hold far more secrets—priceless secrets—than anyone had imagined. The fact that Euphemia's mysteries may finally be coming to light now, so long after her death, might seem surprising, but not necessarily to the colonel and Feinberg, who always knew the possibility was there. And if they knew, others knew. This guy could be one of the others.

The masked man stepped off the porch, and as he stepped forward, Mercy could see that he held a pistol, aimed right at Elvis. It looked like a 9mm Glock. He held himself so securely in the shooter's stance that she figured that he knew how to use it.

The shepherd leapt to his feet.

"Control your dog, or he dies first."

His voice rang out with the cold confidence of a man who killed for a living.

"Down." Elvis whined his objection, but he did obey her. "Stay." She wrapped her fingers around his collar to make sure he continued to do so.

The man approached them, prepared to fire. As he grew nearer, Mercy realized the balaclava he wore was a Spider-Man mask. Which was an odd choice for a professional, who'd usually prefer something more discreet. Maybe he wasn't that seasoned a warrior, after all—or maybe he was so sure of himself that he took unnecessary risks. Either way, it didn't bode well.

"Give it to me."

"I don't know what you're talking about." She held the dog collar tightly as Elvis squirmed his disapproval. She knew the shepherd wanted to get this guy as much as she did. But she didn't dare react, or he could kill all three of them. And no doubt he would.

"I know you've got it. I saw the desk." He waved the gun at her. "That was smart. How you found that secret hiding place."

She had nothing to say to that. She hoped against hope that Uncle Hugo and Feinberg had sent people to surveil her and Thrasher, and that they'd come to the rescue any minute now.

"You need to keep on being smart. Give it to me."

Mercy could only stall him for so long. Sooner or later he was bound to notice the bulges in her cargo pockets, now partially hidden from his view by Elvis. *Where was that backup?*

The man moved closer toward them. Elvis snarled and lunged forward. Mercy gripped his collar and pulled the shepherd back just as a bullet whizzed by his long muzzle.

"Down!" she ordered so fiercely the dog dropped to the ground. She looked up at Spider-Man. "You didn't have to do that."

"I hate dogs."

Of course you do, thought Mercy. Aloud, she said, "He won't hurt you."

"No, he won't. You don't bring a dog to a gunfight." He laughed, a weird choking sound, as if laughter were a rare form of expression for him.

Or a knife, thought Mercy. Little good that Swiss Army blade would do her now.

"I'm not going to tell you again. Control your dog."

"I've got him." She could hear the pleading in her voice, and she hated herself for it.

He shifted the barrel of the gun, aiming it now directly at Thrasher. "Give it to me. Or the next bullet hits your fish cop right between the eyes."

"Okay, okay." Mercy had to do something, and fast. She didn't trust this guy not to eliminate them all. He'd already shot an officer of the law, perhaps mortally wounding him, and didn't seem troubled by that at all. And he'd tried to kill her dog; only luck had saved Elvis.

With Thrasher down, this guy had little left to lose, and wouldn't hesitate to blow them all away, if only to tie up any loose ends. He looked like the kind of guy who hated loose ends. Just like he hated dogs.

Out of the corner of her eye, she looked down at Thrasher's wound. The bleeding seemed to have stopped, but the captain remained unconscious. She remembered his last words to her before he passed out. *Six o'clock.* Not the time. A message.

Mercy had a decision to make. And that decision could have devastating effects if it went sideways. Still, she had no choice. *Do or die.*

She pulled Elvis close to her, and softly kicked her backpack toward Spider-Man. "In there."

CHAPTER TWELVE

The devils enter uninvited when the house stands empty.
—DAG HAMMARSKJÖLD

SIX O'CLOCK. MERCY HELD HER BREATH AS SHE WATCHED THE man in black consider the backpack and his next move. The backpack lay in a gangly clump of yarrow about a couple of yards away from her and Thrasher and Elvis. About ten feet from the guy with the Glock.

"Don't do anything stupid," the man warned as he strode over to the backpack. As he leaned down to pick it up, she lifted her hand quickly from the captain's wound, and reached her arm over behind him and fingered the grass for his gun. *Six o'clock.* As soon as she felt the cold metal of the firearm, she seized the weapon.

The man in black didn't notice. He smiled as he tucked his gun into his belt and crouched down, unzipping the bag.

"Attack!" she whispered fiercely to Elvis, releasing his collar. The shepherd leapt, lunging for the assailant. Clamping his Maligator jaws around the guy's right wrist. Mercy heard the crunch as she jumped up, armed now with Thrasher's pistol.

The man did not scream out the way most would in his circumstances. He simply rose quickly to his feet, Elvis still hanging on to his forearm.

"Don't move," she told him.

He ignored her, pulling his gun from his belt with his left hand, and raising his firearm at Elvis.

Mercy fired, aiming for the left side of his body, away from Elvis. "Release," she yelled, and Elvis sprinted away.

The man did not go down. But a growing circle of blood stained his black T-shirt at the shoulder. He swore, and fired wildly at Mercy, and missed. The bullet hit the stone edge of the raised bed, and she felt a fiery stabbing in her right foot. *Ricochet.*

She fired again at the man in black, and this time Spider-Man went down, dropping his gun.

Mercy realized she'd been shot in the foot, but she didn't think it was too bad. Her steel-toe Timberland boots had protected her from the worst. Or at least she hoped they had. Still, it hurt.

She limped over to the shooter and pocketed his Glock. She'd winged him again. He was laid out flat, eyes closed.

Thrasher moaned, a sickening gasping sound. He was trying to get up. She needed to get back to the captain.

The perp was bleeding in three places now, two bullet wounds and one dog bite. He wasn't dead—not yet, anyway. But it didn't look like he was going anywhere. She checked him for more weapons and pocketed a knife from his boot.

She whistled for Elvis and he appeared at her side.

"Guard."

The shepherd sat down on his haunches, eyes on the perpetrator. She knew he'd stay right there until she called him off.

"Good boy." Mercy lumbered over to Thrasher. He was chilled now, in shock, and shaking. His wound was seeping again. She took off her hoodie and wrapped it around him, then pressed her palm against his wound.

The sound of sirens echoed through the crisp autumn air. Mercy exhaled. The cavalry had arrived.

Elvis barked. His *friends have arrived* bark. She didn't know which officers were coming to their aid, but the shepherd did. His ability to recall and identify the particular sounds of a given vehicle was only one of his extraordinary talents.

"Go get them." She smiled as Elvis streaked off to show their rescuers the way.

The singsong wailing of the law enforcement vehicles roused the man in black. Mercy looked over at him, but she didn't move. Thrasher came first. She didn't dare release the pressure on the wound again.

She kept her eyes on the perp, watching as he realized the shepherd was gone, and she was more concerned about tending to the captain than shooting him one more time. He crawled to the edge of the garden, grabbing her backpack along the way. He pulled himself up to a standing position, and careened around the house to the back garden. Out of sight.

Mercy let him go. She didn't know how well or how far she could chase him, anyway. Her foot was throbbing. She had his weapons. Backup was here.

Spider-Man wouldn't get very far.

And even if he did, he'd soon realize that his was a Pyrrhic victory. The letters were safe in her cargo-pants pockets.

"You're going to be all right, Captain. Help is here."

Thrasher's eyelids fluttered. "Roger that."

Mercy heard the *rat-a-tat-tat* of nails on stone. Elvis and Susie Bear rocketed down the brick path toward her and the captain.

Which meant only one thing: Troy was here. There was no one on earth she'd rather see right now than her husband. But Thrasher was his boss, his mentor, his friend. Seeing the captain like this would be so difficult for him.

If he was here, it was because Delphine the dispatcher had sent him. Troy must know that Thrasher had been hit. Mercy hoped that would help prepare him for what he was about to see.

Troy came running after the dogs. Gil Guerrette was on his heels. She was so glad the park ranger was with Troy.

They both shouldered first-aid packs and held pistols down at their sides as they huffed over to Mercy.

"Are you all right?" asked Troy.

"Fine. It's the captain we need to focus on right now."

"How is he?" Troy dropped to his knees and pulled off his pack. He opened the first-aid kit. Mercy showed him the wound.

"Warner," said the captain in a shaky rasp.

"Here, sir. EMTs five minutes out."

Mercy knew Troy so well that she could detect the faint trace of worry in his voice. She hoped the captain could not.

"Where's the shooter?" Gil was still standing and surveilling the area, gun drawn.

"Gone." Mercy pointed toward the back of the house. "He went that way. The back garden. He's got a bullet in his left shoulder and another in his upper chest on the same side. His right wrist may be broken."

"*Mon dieu.*"

"I shot him and Elvis bit him."

"That'll do it," said Gil. "Is he still armed?"

"I relieved him of what he had on him. A Glock and a blade. I don't know what else he brought with him."

"He shouldn't be too hard to track."

"How did he get here? The only vehicles out front are yours and Thrasher's."

"He got here somehow. I'm going after him before he gets away from us." He looked at Troy.

"We'll be fine. Go on."

"Take Elvis with you." At the sound of his name, the shepherd stopped wrestling with Susie Bear. "Go on, boy. Go with Gil."

"Stay, Susie Bear." The Newfie whined but did as she was told, settling down at Troy's feet. Gil jogged off toward the back garden, Elvis at his side.

"I think we should let the EMTs handle this, provided they show up in the next sixty seconds." Troy covered Thrasher with a foil blanket from the first-aid kit. The captain was breathing unevenly. "I'm surprised you didn't go after the perp yourself."

"I didn't want to leave the captain. And I knew help was on the way."

Troy frowned. "You're leaving something out."

More sirens announced the arrival of the ambulance. Mercy wasn't sure who was more grateful to see the EMTs—her or Troy. Or Thrasher.

"Go meet them. I'll stay with the captain." She didn't want Troy to know she'd suffered an injury, however minor, until Thrasher was safely in the hands of the paramedics. And as soon as she stood up, he'd know. So she stayed right where she was.

"Be right back."

She waited for Troy to return with the EMTs. More waiting. She hated waiting. She'd been waiting for someone to save the captain for what seemed like hours. She couldn't do it alone. And she hated that.

Troy ushered the EMTs down the brick pathway. They rushed into the garden and took over. Mercy tried to stand up, and stumbled.

Her husband caught her. "Whoa." He held her gently in his arms. "What's wrong with you?"

"I may have been shot in the foot."

Troy stared at her. "When were you going to tell me?"

"When were you going to tell *us*?" An EMT named Parker looked at her with a combination of dismay and disapproval. "You're next. As soon as we get the captain stabilized, we'll check you out."

"I'm fine, really. I don't think the bullet even penetrated my boot." She tapped her good boot. "Steel toes."

The EMT rolled his eyes and went back to work on Thrasher.

Troy slowly lowered himself onto one knee, steadied Mercy on the other. Together they watched as Parker and his colleague put a drip on Thrasher, injected him with what Mercy truly hoped were painkillers, and lifted him onto a stretcher.

"You need to get the captain to the hospital. Troy can bring me in to the ER."

Parker looked at Troy. Troy looked at Mercy.

She raised her chin. "I'm not leaving without my dog."

Troy sighed. "Get the captain to the hospital, guys. I'll bring my wife in to the ER, even if I have to carry her in kicking and screaming."

"Your *wife*?"

"I'm a lucky man."

"I can see that." He gave Troy a quick salute. "I'll leave her in your capable hands. We'll be on our way now."

The EMTs carried the captain out to the ambulance. Mercy and Troy sat in silence until they heard the ambulance drive away.

"You should go after Gil and Elvis. It's been a while. They may need your help." She patted his thigh, the one upon which she sat. "Besides, your leg must be falling asleep about now."

Troy ignored that remark. "Becker and Goodlove should be here any minute, and Gil and Elvis can help them. We're going."

"Not without Elvis."

As if the shepherd had heard her—and he probably had—Elvis came tearing around the house. Gil loped along behind him, with Levi Beecher at his side, a kindling bag slung over one shoulder. Elvis greeted Mercy with caution, sniffing her carefully. As if he knew she was hurt—and he probably did.

"I followed the perp to that row of trees outside the wall. The trail stopped there. There were motorcycle tracks. He's long gone now."

"And you?" Troy asked Levi.

"I was just passing by." Levi stuck his calloused hands in his pockets and stood there, steadfast as an oak.

"I found him in the back garden," said Gil.

"I was in the woods, collecting kindling. I heard the shots, and came back."

"Right." Troy looked at Gil. "Wouldn't we have heard a motorcycle?"

"Not if it's one of those electric models."

"He may have been here before you and Thrasher got here. Lying in wait." Troy stood up, still carrying Mercy in his arms. "We'll get the crime scene techs on those tracks."

"Get a room," teased Gil.

"We need to get her to the hospital. Gunshot to the foot."

"Ouch." Levi shook his head.

Gil glanced at Mercy's boot-shod feet. "Steel toe?"

"Yep."

"Then you probably won't die."

CHAPTER THIRTEEN

There is nothing like staying at home, for real comfort.
—JANE AUSTEN

A T THE HOSPITAL, MERCY SAT ON THE EDGE OF AN EXAMINATION table in a curtained-off space in the emergency room. The nurse, an earnest young man named Dwayne, had put Mercy through the usual preliminary tests and was now ushering in the doctor. It was not Dr. Sharma, who knew Mercy and indulged her unusual requests, like allowing Elvis in the examination room.

"This is Dr. Chen," Dwayne told Mercy. "She's new."

"What is that dog doing in here?" Dr. Chen stopped short at the sight of the shepherd curled up in the corner, his eyes on Mercy. Ignoring the physician. "Dogs are not allowed in the ER."

"The dog stays." Mercy used her MP voice. "And I need to keep my pants on."

"He's her emotional support dog," explained Dwayne.

"I was *shot*."

Dr. Chen sighed. "Okay." She folded up the right leg of Mercy's pants to her knee and then proceeded to cut off her right boot. "Nice boots."

"Well, they were." She tightened her lips against the throbbing of her disabled foot.

The ER physician was young and confident, but she seemed more world-weary than a woman her age should be. Mercy imagined that hers was an occupation that matured a person quickly, given the things she'd seen and done on the front lines of medicine. Like being a soldier had matured Mercy, given the things she'd seen and done on the front lines of the war in Afghanistan.

Dr. Chen removed the boot, and placed it aside. It was evidence now. What was left of it.

Next she cut off Mercy's bloody Darn Tough sock, one half of the pair with the purple-and-green-bear design she liked so much.

"I loved those socks," she said evenly, instead of screaming at the touch of the doctor's gloved hand on her battered toes.

Dr. Chen ignored her and focused on her foot. "Severe contusions but not much bleeding." She shook her head, apparently at the wonder of it. "You were very lucky. The bullet did not pierce the steel toe. I would have bet against that."

Mercy laughed. "Me, too." Luck, fate, divine will, whatever you wanted to call it, it was on her side today. She suspected the good doctor was familiar with that concept as well.

"There don't appear to be any fractures." Dr. Chen consulted her tablet. "Normally, we'd do an X-ray to confirm that, but given your condition, we could skip that."

Mercy looked at her. "What condition?"

"Maybe you haven't noticed yet." Dr. Chen smiled at her. "You're pregnant. Congratulations."

"What?" This was simply not possible, thought Mercy. Well, it was possible—pregnancy was always possible.

"About twelve weeks."

Mercy and Troy had been married about twelve weeks. And they tied the knot so unexpectedly that they'd never even talked about having children. Of course she wanted to have kids someday, and she assumed that Troy wanted them someday, too. She just didn't think someday would come so soon. She bet he didn't, either. "How did you know?"

"We always test for pregnancy before giving any woman of child-bearing age an X-ray."

"Is the baby okay?" Surely getting shot while you were pregnant was not a good thing.

"The baby should be fine. You just need to take it easy." Dr. Chen was still smiling. "Your first?"

"Yes."

"Rest is critical, for you and baby," said the doctor.

"Right." Mercy hated being sidelined, and she couldn't imagine being sidelined for months. It was bad enough getting shot; once people found out she was pregnant, everyone in her world—from health-care professionals to friends and family—was going to try to sideline her.

"Step aside." Her mother Grace flung aside the curtain, flanked by a nurse.

Starting with my mother, thought Mercy.

"I couldn't stop her," the nurse told Dr. Chen. "She's a lawyer. She said she'd sue."

"And she would." Mercy could see her mother's maternal instinct had kicked in, big-time. "Mom, what are you doing here?"

"I heard you were the victim of a shooting." Grace looked from Mercy's foot to her abandoned work boot and back to her foot again, finally finding her daughter's face. "What has happened here?"

"I'm fine. My steel-toe boot stopped the bullet."

Grace blanched. She turned to Dr. Chen. "Is this true?"

"It is true. Your daughter will be fine."

"I said I was fine."

"We'll clean and bandage the toes, more for comfort than anything else," said Dr. Chen. "I'll prescribe an antibiotic ointment to prevent infection. We'll get you a medical walking boot. But you should keep off of the foot as best you can for at least a couple of days." She cleansed the wound, bandaged and taped Mercy's toes while Grace watched the doctor like the mother raptor she was. "The limping should subside as your toes heal. In the meantime, you should use crutches."

Mercy breathed through the pain. She was relieved when Dr. Chen finally slipped a white hospital sock on over her bandaged foot.

The fact that she was hurting did not escape the doctor. "You will experience some discomfort. I can—"

"Don't bother with painkillers," interrupted Grace. "She won't take them."

The doctor looked from Grace to Mercy. "You can take Tylenol, only as directed."

"Okay, but nothing stronger." Mercy shook her head slightly, hoping she wouldn't say anything about the baby. She didn't think the doctor was allowed to, even to her mother.

"Ice packs for the first forty-eight hours, heating pads thereafter. That along with the Tylenol should alleviate any pain you are feeling. And be sure to follow up with your primary care physician right away."

Grace crossed the room, past Dr. Chen and around Elvis, and came to stand next to Mercy. Her mother kissed her cheek and squeezed her shoulder. "I'm so glad you're okay, darling girl."

"I'll be fine. No reason to worry, right, Doc?"

"Correct," said Dr. Chen, writing on her tablet.

"How did you know I was here, Mom?"

"Lillian heard it on the police scanner. She texted your grandmother, and your grandmother texted me."

"I thought you hated texting."

"Necessary evil these days. Vile but useful."

Mercy was surprised that her grandmother wasn't here.

"Your grandmother is stuck up in Danby, delivering a colt," said her mother, whose maternal instinct primarily manifested itself in an uncanny ability to read Mercy's mind. "Otherwise, you know she'd be here. Where's Troy?"

"He's with Thrasher. The captain's injuries are more serious. Third floor." Mercy's voice cracked.

"I see. I'm so sorry."

Dr. Chen stopped typing and raised her head. "We're doing everything we can for Captain Thrasher. He should be out of surgery in a couple of hours."

"Let's get you home."

"I can't leave while Thrasher is . . ." Mercy's voice trailed off. It didn't bear talking about.

"You can't do anything for him. The best thing you can do for Thrasher is to heal and get back on your feet and catch the creep who wounded him and nearly crippled you." Her mother spoke in the very clipped manner she usually reserved for her closing statements in the courtroom.

The nurse returned to the examination room carrying a walking boot and crutches. She handed the boot to Dr. Chen, who eased Mercy's sore foot into the footbed, securing it firmly with the Velcro bindings.

"Your mother is right. Time to go home and put your foot up. Doctor's orders." The ER physician said goodbye and left the room.

Grace looked around. "Where are your things?"

"I don't have anything. The perp took my backpack." Mercy rolled her pants leg back down over the walking boot.

"The nice Topo Designs bag that Troy gave you?"

"Yes."

"We'll get you another one. Did he get anything else?"

"I had my wallet and my cell in my pants pockets. So he didn't get those." *Or the letters,* she thought, but did not say aloud. No one had thought to ask her about the letters yet, and she wanted to get a good look at them before Feinberg and the colonel showed up to claim them. The shooter had been willing to kill to obtain them, and she wanted to know why. The answer could help reveal his identity. Her mother was right; they needed to find this guy and bring him to justice.

"That doesn't make much sense, if it were a robbery. Maybe he assumed your wallet was in the backpack."

"Maybe." Mercy looked down at her mismatched footwear and changed the subject. "Those were my favorite boots."

"We'll get you another pair of those, too."

"I thought you hated those boots."

"They stopped a bullet. They're growing on me."

Elvis jumped to his feet just as Troy pulled aside the curtain and strode up to the examination table. He kissed her mother on the cheek and Mercy on the lips. "You look much better." She could hear the relief in his voice.

"I'm fine."

"You always say that."

"That's because it's almost always true. How's the captain?"

Troy frowned. "Still in surgery."

"Thrasher's strong, he'll make it," she said with more confidence than she felt.

"I hope you're right." There were shadows of worry under his warm brown eyes. "I should take you home."

Mercy shook her head. "You need to stay here. For the captain." She was desperate to talk to her husband alone, tell him about the baby. But now was not the time. She could see that he was torn between his love for her and his loyalty to his friend and mentor—and if he knew she was pregnant, he'd never stay.

"You can't drive with that foot."

"I'll take her home," said her mother. "You stay here with your captain."

"Go on," Mercy told him. "Get back up to the third floor."

GRACE DROVE HER BLUE Volvo fast, the way she always did, regardless of the circumstances or the conditions of the road. Mercy sat in the passenger seat, pushed back so far it nearly touched the back seat behind her to accommodate her injury.

Elvis stood on the back seat, paws planted on the navy leather on the driver's side, his head resting on her mother's shoulder, eyes on the road. It was as if the shepherd didn't trust Grace to take them straight home. He was her navigator, whether she liked it or not.

Mercy fought to stay awake. The day's adrenaline rush had long since dissipated, and she was exhausted. But she'd never been able to sleep while her mother was driving, even when she was a child. She sure couldn't do it now. Whenever her mother put the pedal to the metal, Mercy's instinct was to plant her foot on the car floor, as if she could slam on the brakes and slow her mother down. This pantomime was a default reaction—but with an injured foot, it was a reaction to be avoided. She focused on her breathing, inhaling and exhaling, a strategy that kept her mind off her mother's driving but made dozing off even more likely.

She was just about to drift into dreamland when her mother's voice cut though her drowsiness.

"What are you hiding in the pockets of your cargo pants?"

"My pockets?"

"Don't play dumb with me, Mercy Fleury Carr. It's beneath you."

Leave it to the chicest woman I know to be the only one to notice the unsightly bulges on my thighs, thought Mercy. It was just a matter of time before her mother noticed she was pregnant. Although she didn't think she was showing yet. She couldn't believe she was pregnant.

She felt fine—well, tired, but she'd chalked that up to crowded quarters at home and staying up too late with her new husband. Not pregnancy. If she were going to keep the news about the baby to herself long enough to share it with Troy, she needed to keep her sharp-eyed mother focused on something else. Like the letters. Mercy sighed. "It's a long story."

"Start at the beginning."

CHAPTER FOURTEEN

*Home is where the heart is, we say, rubbing the flint of
one abstraction against another.*
—DIANE ACKERMAN

IN A GLOOMY, GRAY-WALLED HOSPITAL ROOM ON THE SECOND
floor, Troy sat on a hard, blue plastic chair, staring out the window at
the parking lot below. Susie Bear was curled up at his feet, thumping her
plumed tail listlessly, her big shaggy head resting on his foot. She sensed
that the captain was hurting. And that Troy was troubled by it.

This understanding was what made her such a good search-and-rescue
dog: she could follow the human scents of fear and anxiety and pain. But
she was not in search mode here. The big furry lump of love was all comfort and compassion now.

Thrasher was stretched out along a hospital bed. They'd just moved
him down from post-op to a private room, and Troy supposed that was a
good sign. At least he wasn't in the ICU.

Still, lying there with all those tubes, hooked up to all those machines,
the captain looked more vulnerable than Troy had ever seen him. Which
was why he was studying the parking lot as if he'd never seen one before.
It was easier than seeing his captain like this.

He wished Mercy were here. She'd know what to do, she'd know what
to say to the captain when he woke up. She'd make him feel better—hell,
she'd make him laugh. The human version of Susie Bear.

Troy was good at his job—he was good *outdoors*, protecting the flora
and fauna of Vermont for present and future generations and chasing
down the bad guys who tried to ruin it for everyone else. He was less good
indoors, where social skills and emotional intelligence were more useful

than the physical and mental strength that served him so well in the wilderness. If only Susie Bear could talk.

Thrasher groaned in his sleep. Maybe the meds were wearing off. Troy did not want to be the only person here when the captain woke up. Thrasher was a widower with no children. Troy knew the captain's mother was still alive, in a nursing home somewhere down south. That was all the family he'd ever heard the very private man talk about.

But there was Wyetta Wright. The captain had been the subject of much feminine attention after his wife Carol died of cancer a few years back. He'd resisted it all, telling Troy to get over Madeline leaving him even as he refused to consider dating himself.

And then the captain met the beautiful and accomplished Wyetta. An acclaimed textile artist, she also ran her family's popular soul food café up in Lamoille County. She'd be up there now, as this was peak tourist season. Although the locals were as crazy about her pecan pie as the peepers.

Troy wondered if anyone had called Wyetta. Surely Delphine would have let her know. Troy texted the dispatcher, who called him back within seconds.

"She's not his emergency contact," said Delphine. "You are."

"I think he'd want her here."

"So do I."

"I'll call her."

"Keep me informed. I want to know everything." As if Delphine didn't know more about what went on in Northshire than anyone else in the county. Still, she must be itching to be here at the hospital herself.

"You got it." He rang up. He tried Wyetta's cell, but it went straight to voice mail. He dialed the number of the café, and she picked up.

"Wyetta's Café," she answered in a singsong voice.

"Wyetta, it's Troy Warner."

Thrasher grunted, a surly rumbling that told Troy he was rousing himself despite the pain.

"Hold on a sec."

He could hear the chatter and platter noise in the background fade. The captain's grumbling faded, too, to Troy's enormous relief.

"Go ahead, I'm in the office. What's happened? Is he . . ." Her voice trailed off.

"He's out of surgery now and stable." Troy explained the captain's injuries. "But you might want to come down here. I'm sure your face is the one he'll want to see when he wakes up."

"I'm on my way."

He heard her choke back a sob. "Do you have someone who can come with you?"

"I'll be fine." She sniffed. "Thank you, Troy, for calling. You'll stay with him till I get there." It was a statement, not a question.

"Yes, ma'am."

"Good. I'm on my way."

"Drive carefully." It would take Wyetta two and a half hours to make the drive from Lamoille County to Northshire, although Troy suspected she'd make the trip in record time.

"Warner." The captain's voice was commanding, if rasping.

Troy slipped his cell into his pocket and stepped toward Thrasher. Susie Bear clambered to her feet, joining him at the bedside. She nosed her muzzle through the bars of the guardrail and licked the patient's arm.

"Susie Bear." Thrasher smiled weakly. "Good girl."

"Captain." Troy was nearly moved to tears at that smile.

"No waterworks, Warner."

"Sir." Troy smiled back at the man who'd had his back ever since the day he reported to duty as a game warden.

Thrasher crawled his fingers across the blanket that covered his lap. Feeling for the bed's remote control. When he found it, he raised the back of the bed so he was sitting up.

"I don't know if you're supposed to do that."

The captain shot him one of his *shut up, soldier* looks. He was back in charge, should Troy ever forget it. As if he ever would. "How's Mercy?"

Troy welcomed the change of subject. "She's fine."

"And Elvis?"

"All good." Troy briefed him on the events that had transpired since he was wounded.

"So the shooter got away."

"Not for long. Gil found his motorcycle tracks. And two sets of footprints."

"So he may have had an accomplice."

"Right. Common sneaker brands, so not much help there. But we've got a good set of the tire treads. A late-model Zero. Becker and Goodlove are running all the vehicles of that description right now."

"Any other witnesses?" Thrasher spoke with effort.

"Gil found the caretaker Levi Beecher in the back garden. He says he was in the woods collecting kindling when he heard the shots. He came back to the house, but he says he didn't see anything."

"You believe him?"

"I don't know. We can talk about this later."

"You are neither my nurse nor my nursemaid," said Thrasher through gritted teeth—whether due to his pain or his subordinate's insolence, Troy wasn't sure.

"Understood, sir."

"And the letters? The key?"

"Letters?" Troy wondered if the captain was hallucinating. "I'm not sure what you mean."

"You don't know." The captain leaned forward, and pain creased his face. He fell back against the headboard.

Troy waited while the captain breathed through his discomfort. As the pain eased, Thrasher's drawn face relaxed, settling into his usual neutral expression, the one that saw everything and gave away nothing.

"You did the night shift and then you went straight there."

"Yes, sir. Gil Guerrette and I had finished up a surveillance op, and we heard the call over the radio."

"And when you got there, I was down, and Mercy was injured."

"She saved your life."

"That's not how it's supposed to work."

"I felt the same way when she saved my life."

Thrasher ignored that. "How much did Mercy tell you about what she found in the library?"

"I don't follow." Troy was perplexed. "She didn't say anything about the library. But we haven't really had the chance to talk about what happened. I drove her here, but she didn't say much. I think she was in more pain than she was willing to admit. And I was focused on getting to the hospital as quickly as possible."

A tall nurse whose name tag read "Mary" came into the room to take the captain's vital signs and check his bandages. "It's good to see you up, but you mustn't overdo it." Mary regarded Troy and Susie Bear with misgiving. "We can't risk overtiring our patient." She turned back to Thrasher. "The medications you're on to help prevent infection and relieve discomfort should make you sleepy. And you need your sleep."

"Yes, ma'am." The captain bowed slightly, a polite gesture so genuine it transformed Mary from severe taskmaster to luminous healer. She beamed at him.

Troy was always amused at the effect his movie star–handsome boss had on women without even trying. Few were immune, including his nurse. The good news was that Thrasher would be well-cared-for by Mary— and every other female health-care worker on the floor.

Still, the best medicine for the captain would be Wyetta Wright. Mary finished her ministrations and left the room, and the captain dozed off. Troy and Susie Bear settled down to wait for Wyetta. Troy hoped it wouldn't be too long.

After what seemed like forever but wasn't really, Wyetta herself strode in. About ninety minutes sooner than he'd expected her. Susie Bear thumped her tail in a discreet greeting.

"That was fast."

"Feinberg sent his private jet."

Good for Feinberg. Troy watched as Wyetta went straight to the captain's side. She kissed his forehead, and held his hand.

"Wyetta." Thrasher gazed up at her with such naked tenderness and affection—matched only by her own—that Troy knew the couple was far more serious about one another than either had ever let on. He brought the blue plastic chair over to the bed for Wyetta, and she sank into it.

"Thank you. I'll take it from here."

"You called her," said Thrasher.

"I did." He hoped the captain would not think he'd overstepped.

"Thank you." Thrasher looked better already, just as Troy knew he would.

He snapped his fingers and Susie Bear shuffled to her feet. "Let's go, girl."

"You don't have to leave," said the captain.

"Sure, we do." Troy grinned at them. "Wyetta's in charge now."

"Don't I know it," he quipped, but Troy could tell he liked it that way.

He was leaving his captain in good hands, so he could leave with a clear conscience. He ached for a good night's sleep, but he couldn't hit the sack quite yet. Troy had to check on Mercy and find out what letters Thrasher was talking about—and what Feinberg had to do with it.

CHAPTER FIFTEEN

*. . . I shall try to make my life like an open fireplace, so
that people may be warmed and cheered by it and so go
out themselves to warm and cheer.*
—GEORGE MATTHEW ADAMS

GRACE STEERED THE BLUE VOLVO UP THE DRIVEWAY TO THE cabin, where Amy and Helena were waiting on the porch. Mercy struggled with the crutches, and her mother helped her make her way to the house. Elvis did not fly ahead as he would usually do but hung back to oversee their awkward journey.

"What happened?" Amy balanced Helena on her hip as she extended a hand to assist them. Grace waved her away.

Amy was undeterred. "We heard about the shooting. Are you all right?"

"I'm fine."

"She's not fine," Grace said to Amy. "Let's get her into the house and onto the couch. She needs to elevate that foot."

Amy held open the door with her free hand. "Of course."

Elvis streaked past them into the house. *The poor dog must be hungry,* thought Mercy. She was pretty hungry herself, although she didn't know if she could stay awake long enough to eat anything. She clunked into the hallway and was greeted by the heavenly smell of lasagna. Her grandmother's lasagna. "Is Patience here?"

"No, not yet." Amy smiled. "But she texted me and told me to take the lasagna out of the freezer and put it in the oven for you. She's coming by with garlic bread and more cinnamon rolls as soon as she delivers that colt."

"Leave it to your grandmother to find a way to feed you all the way from Danby."

"As always." Nobody made comfort food like Patience, and no one was more comforted by it than Mercy was. She could only imagine the culinary delights that awaited her once her grandmother found out that she was eating for two.

"You need to get out of those clothes, pronto."

Her mother was right. Mercy looked down at her Henley shirt, which was blotched with the captain's blood. And her grass-stained cargo pants, with their bulging pockets of secrets. As exhausting as the thought of changing clothes was, staying in them was not an option. She had to find a safe place for the letters and clean up a bit. She'd have to wait for a bath, given her bandaged foot, but she could do her "toilette," as her mother called it.

"Come on, I'll help you." Grace led the way to the bathroom.

Mercy struggled along behind her on the crutches, Elvis at her side. "These crutches are more trouble than they're worth," she told the shepherd, who did not disagree. She was relieved when she reached her mother, who stood by the open bathroom door. Elvis went in first and curled up under the window.

"Undressing may be difficult," her mother warned.

"I'm good, Mom."

"I'll be here if you need me. I'll bring you some pajamas."

Mercy closed the door. She looked with longing at her deep soaking tub with the whirlpool jets—one of her cabin's few extravagances—where she loved to escape from the world for a soothing soak, book in one hand and loofah in the other. No way she could get in and out of there gracefully or even ineptly right now. Not without getting her bandaged foot wet.

She'd have to settle for a sponge bath at the sink. She placed the wretched crutches against the wall, and slipped off her shirt, then her pants, careful not to disturb the pockets. And the extraordinary contents therein. She still hadn't had the time to get a good look at those contents, but the fact that Spider-Man had been willing to kill for them more or less proved they were extraordinary.

She cleaned herself as well as she could, weight on her good foot. Elvis kept his eyes on Mercy. There was no way he'd leave her side now that she was injured.

The lavender soap revived her a bit; it felt good to wash away the grit of a day gone very wrong. And very right. Bad and good, this had been a day to remember.

A knock on the door foretold its opening. Grace handed her a long nightgown of navy satin with white piping and a matching robe—as always, she'd chosen something she'd given Mercy herself—and one of the toile-patterned decorative tins Mercy kept in her closet for sundries, along with a pair of plastic gloves. "For your treasures."

"Thank you." When Grace had asked about the bulges in Mercy's pockets on the way home from the hospital, she'd told her mother about the letters, knowing that, as her mother and her lawyer, Grace was honor-bound and legally bound to keep Mercy's confidences.

After closing the door, she pulled the nightgown over her head and smoothed it down over her hips, and wrapped the robe around her waist and tied the long sash. She put on the gloves, and carefully removed the letters from her cargo pants pockets and placed them into the toile tin, securing the lid. She emptied the rest of her pockets—cell phone, wallet, Swiss Army knife—along with the key she'd found with the letters, which she slipped into the side pocket of her robe. She pulled off the gloves, irritated by the feel of them against her fingers in a way she had never been before. Could pregnancy make your skin more sensitive? She had a lot to learn, and she'd better learn it fast.

For her mother's sake, she ran a brush through her tangle of red hair. Not that it did much good. She looked like an extra in a 1930s drawing room comedy on a bad hair day.

Another discreet knock. Grace poked her sleek blond head in, handing Mercy a paper bag. "For those dirty clothes, in case forensics needs them." She looked at the box and the cell and the wallet and the knife. "Shall I carry those for you?"

"Sure." Elvis jumped up and waited patiently while Mercy gathered up the crutches, then accompanied her as she clomped back to the living room after her mother.

Grace placed her stuff on the coffee table and took away her crutches while Mercy eased herself down onto the sofa. Her mother stacked up the throw pillows at the other end.

"Stretch out," Grace ordered. "You need to place your foot up there."

"That's Elvis's side of the couch."

"He's a dog. He'll get over it."

Mercy sighed. As much as she hated to admit it, for once her mother was right. Her foot was throbbing rather fiercely after the very uncomfortable trek from Grace's car to the cabin and then again to the bathroom and back.

If she didn't lie down here, her mother would insist that she go into her bedroom and lie down there, and she wanted to be here in her great room, with her fireplace and her books and her grandmother's lasagna. She made herself comfortable, extending her legs as her mother advised. Grace helped lift her legs onto the soft pile of pillows.

"Now stay right there, and we'll get you some of that lasagna." Grace leaned over and kissed Mercy's forehead. "Then you can go through what's in that tin. Which I know you're dying to do."

"Thanks, Mom."

As soon as her mother walked away, Elvis positioned himself on the floor right by Mercy, placing his sleek head at her elbow. She stroked his triangular ears and closed her eyes. She'd just rest a minute while she waited for that lasagna.

MERCY DREAMED OF POETS *and ghosts and Spider-Man, all chasing a woman in white through overgrown thickets of chokecherry. Thunder rolled and lightning blazed and rain drenched the woman. She ran for the shelter of the Scary Tree, which loomed in the darkness, illuminated by flashes of light as the storm raged on. But as she huddled in the crook of the monster maple, the branches curled around her, and the leaves turned into letters, and the shroud of foliage smothered her screams . . .*

IT WAS DARK OUTSIDE by the time Mercy woke up. She bolted upright, relieved to find herself on her own sofa, safe in her own home. The lights were on low, and flames flickered in the fireplace. Her cozy cabin was filled with people, all speaking in hushed voices. Elvis was still at her feet, on guard.

Troy was on Elvis's end of the couch, her legs supported by the pillows on his lap, Susie Bear's head on his knee. Her mother Grace and her grandmother Patience occupied the easy chairs opposite her, talking to Uncle

Hugo and Feinberg, who perched stiffly on the dining room chairs they'd brought over to the living room area. Amy and Brodie were seated at the dining room table; baby Helena was undoubtedly asleep in her crib in her mother's bedroom.

The toile-patterned tin was still on the coffee table; Effie's key was still in her pocket. Mercy hoped that meant she hadn't missed too much. "What's going on?"

"You were dreaming. A bad dream, I think." Troy squeezed her good foot. "How are you feeling?"

Mercy shook away the vague memory of the unsettling nightmare. "Much better," she answered automatically, but she realized it was true. She was feeling much better. The throbbing in her foot seemed to be subsiding. "How's the captain?"

"He's hanging in there."

"You should be with him."

"Wyetta's there." Troy lifted her bare, unbandaged foot and kissed it. "My place is with my wife."

Mercy still got a kick out of hearing him say "my wife," just as she still got a kick out of saying "my husband." She wondered when the little thrill of it would wear off. She hoped the time never came when it did. She needed to tell him about the baby. "We have to talk."

"Shoot."

One by one, everyone else stopped talking as they realized Mercy was awake.

"Later," she said.

The colonel and Feinberg rose to their feet, along with Grace. Amy and Brodie left the table, moving toward the couch. Only Troy and Patience kept their seats.

Elvis raised his head and growled softly, flattening his ears and curling his flews. It wouldn't surprise Mercy if the dog had already sniffed out that she was pregnant and was even more protective because of it.

"We're all friends here," Patience reminded the shepherd, always the good veterinarian. She turned to the assembly. "Let's not rush our patient. Give Mercy some room—or Elvis might do it for you."

Everyone sat back down, except for Grace, who would never deign to accommodate a dog, even a dog as vigilant as Elvis.

"It's okay, boy." Mercy scratched that sweet spot between the Malinois's ears.

"Let me get you some of that lasagna."

"That would be wonderful. I'm surprised there's any left." Everyone loved her grandmother's lasagna.

"And there's garlic bread and more cinnamon rolls for dessert." Patience regarded her with the practiced eye of a veterinarian. Mercy felt like a poodle.

"Great. Daniel and Uncle Hugo finished the other batch off already."

"I made sure we saved you some." Amy jumped back up. "I'll get it, Mrs. Carr."

"Thank you, dear." Grace sank back down into her chair and crossed her legs. "Your father's in New York on business, but he's flying home."

"He doesn't have to do that."

"Yes, he does." Her mother pointed to the carafe of water, empty glass, and bottle of Tylenol on the coffee table. "Take your meds."

"Not necessary." Mercy waved her arm to include them all. "This is not necessary. Although I suspect you're here as much to ask me about my version of today's events as to make sure I'm all right."

"You know we all have your best interests at heart. And we promise not to eat any more rolls." Uncle Hugo crossed his heart.

"Right." She poured herself a glass of water, suddenly wildly thirsty. "But before you ask me any questions, I have some for you and Daniel."

"Ask away," said Feinberg.

"I can't believe you didn't send some of your guys out there for backup. Why didn't you?"

To his credit, the billionaire looked abashed. The colonel frowned— whether in irritation or in self-reproach, Mercy couldn't say. Either way, her usually unflappable great-uncle was uncomfortable.

"I'd like to know the answer to that myself, Hugo." From the tone of her voice, Patience wasn't cutting her brother any slack.

"We didn't want to involve anyone else if we didn't have to." Feinberg fiddled with his gold cuff links. "It was a matter of discretion."

"That worked out well." Brodie rolled his eyes. Mercy had to give the young man credit; he wasn't the least bit intimidated by anyone here, including the colonel and Feinberg. He had a kind of youthful bravado that she couldn't help but admire.

"Who are you again?" asked the colonel, although he knew very well who Brodie was.

"That's harsh, dude."

"Your obsession with secrecy has always been your Achilles' heel," Patience told her brother. "And now others are paying the price for it."

Uncle Hugo ignored his sister and addressed Mercy. "I told you to be careful."

"They were ambushed." Troy spoke with such a quiet force both Elvis and Susie Bear sat up and took notice. "You must have suspected that they could be in danger."

Feinberg leaned forward. "I swear we didn't see this coming."

"You were wrong," said Grace.

"We were wrong." Feinberg looked at Mercy. "We couldn't be sorrier about what happened."

"Who was the shooter?" Mercy addressed the colonel.

"We don't know," said Uncle Hugo.

"You must have some idea." Troy's indignation made it clear he didn't believe him.

"We've got a team on it."

"That's only so reassuring, Daniel." There was frustration in Patience's voice, too.

The wagons are circling, thought Mercy. She hoped Feinberg and her uncle were paying attention.

Her grandmother went on. "We've got a man poisoned and Captain Thrasher in the hospital and Mercy on crutches. And your suspect has gone to ground."

"We're doing everything we can to find him," said the colonel.

"So are we." Troy straightened, his broad shoulders wider now. "If there's anything you know, or even suspect, you'd better tell us now."

"We talked to Harrington," said Feinberg. "We're cooperating fully in the investigation."

"Harrington." Troy punched the arm of the sofa. "If you had any faith in him, you wouldn't be here."

"We're here for Mercy."

"It's okay, Troy." Mercy understood that her uncle and her friend were concerned for her. She didn't doubt that. Any more than she doubted there was more to the story. Both things could be true at the same time.

"No, it's not. He'll be back, you know." Troy glared at Feinberg and Uncle Hugo. "He didn't get what he wanted."

"What do you mean?" The colonel stared at Mercy. "Becker told Harrington your backpack was stolen."

"It was," said Mercy.

"Oh ye of little faith." Patience looked at Feinberg and Uncle Hugo with pity.

"Congratulations, Mercy." Feinberg smiled at her. "You did find something. And somehow you held on to it."

"Outstanding." The colonel favored her with a big smile. The cat who swallowed the canary.

"Are these the letters Thrasher was talking about at the hospital? I thought he was hallucinating."

"No, he wasn't hallucinating."

Troy frowned. "You don't have to tell these guys anything. But Harrington will be after you for a statement sooner or later. I'm surprised he hasn't sent Becker around to take one already."

"Becker did come by," said Grace. "While Mercy was sleeping. I told him to come back later."

Say what you wanted about Grace—and Mercy herself said plenty—but she was one heck of a mama bear when she wanted to be. And an even better lawyer.

"Go ahead," advised her mother. "Tell them your side of the story. Tell it *your* way."

Which Mercy knew was lawyer-speak for *Don't say anything you might regret later*. She sighed, and tried to collect her thoughts before she began. She was still tired, weary to the bone, and her mind was a little muddled.

Everyone was waiting for her. She could feel their impatience growing. Her foot was throbbing again. She looked longingly at the bottle of Tylenol, but she was reluctant to take it despite Dr. Chen's permission. Maybe she'd try an ice pack.

"If you're not going to take that Tylenol, I'm getting you an ice pack," said Grace, rising from her seat and heading for the kitchen. "Don't say anything until I get back."

Mindful of her mother's directive, everyone sat in taut silence. Amy interrupted them, breaking the tension as she handed Mercy a plate of steaming-hot lasagna, along with a fork, a napkin, and a glass of Big Barn Red. She looked at the wine, and realized that she wouldn't be drinking it. There was no red wine in her foreseeable future.

She moved her good leg and tucked it into her pelvis, yoga style, leaving her impaired foot on Troy's lap. She balanced her plate on her good thigh, holding her glass of water in her left hand while she raised a forkful of lasagna to her lips with the other. She chewed. She swallowed. She sighed. "This is so good."

"You're welcome." Her grandmother beamed at her.

Her mother returned with a package of frozen peas and placed it gingerly on Mercy's battered toes.

"Thank you. That feels so good." Mercy sipped her water. "Lucky for you all that I can eat and talk at the same time."

CHAPTER SIXTEEN

Keep the home fires burning,
while your hearts are yearning.
—LENA GUILBERT FORD

MERCY STARTED AT THE BEGINNING. SHE TOLD THEM ABOUT
the Scary Tree, and the prints she and Thrasher found that most
probably belonged to the victim.

"Harrington confirmed that," said Feinberg.

She explained that they'd gone back to the library where the body was
found, as that seemed the next logical step. And how she figured out the
anagram for Scary Tree.

"Secretary," guessed the colonel, whose proficiency with crossword
puzzles was a source of familial pride.

"Exactly."

"You mean Leontine Bonnet?" Amy turned to the others. "She was
Euphemia Whitney-Jones's secretary."

"I thought she was, like, her lover." Brodie looked confused.

"That, too."

"Cool."

"She was a painter, and a pretty good one." Mercy paused for a big bite
of lasagna. "But her success was overshadowed by Euphemia's."

"She must have hated that," said Brodie.

"Maybe. You know, Amy, I thought it must mean Leontine Bonnet,
too, at first, but then I realized that right in the library was Euphemia's
other secretary."

"The writing desk." Feinberg looked at Mercy. "Becker found it in the
library. Someone had taken it apart. Was that you?"

HOME AT NIGHT   141

Mercy took another sip of water, pretending it was wine. "I didn't take it apart. I found the hidden compartment."

"Hidden compartment?" asked Brodie. "Like in the *National Treasure* movie?"

"That's what Captain Thrasher said. Yes, just like in that film."

"Dude. Well done."

Uncle Hugo cleared his throat. "Can we get to the point, please? What did you find in the hidden compartment?"

Mercy could feel her mother's eyes upon her. "I found letters. Letters that Euphemia Whitney-Jones wrote to Michael Emil Robillard during the war. And apparently he wrote back."

"As we theorized." The colonel looked very pleased with himself.

"So they did renew their affection for one another." Feinberg steepled his fingers, the tips touching his chin. "Interesting."

"I'm confused." Patience looked to Mercy for clarification.

She told the story of the Whitney-Jones sisters and their love for the same man. And the rift between them that continued years after that man was gone.

"What a waste." Amy shook her head.

"You found the letters, but then the perp showed up," theorized Troy. "He shot Thrasher and you to get the letters. When Gil and I showed up, he'd taken off with your backpack. There were no letters."

They all looked at her, waiting for an explanation.

Mercy finished her lasagna and drank the last of her water. "That's true. I gave him the backpack."

"Misdirection." Patience clapped her hands. "The letters were never in the backpack."

Mercy grinned at her grandmother. "No, they weren't."

"Bravo Zulu." Military-speak for "well done." Maybe the highest compliment the colonel was capable of paying her or anyone.

"But then where were they?" asked Troy. "Gil and I never saw any letters. And Becker and Goodlove never found any at the crime scene later, either. Neither did the forensics team."

"Why don't you tell them, Mom?" Mercy laughed. "Since you're the only one who figured it out."

Grace laughed along with her. "Mercy hid the letters where she's hidden all kinds of things, ever since she was a child. Rocks, golf balls, beef jerky, seashells, marbles, acorns, even a dead lizard once. I nearly fainted."

"In your pockets," guessed Troy. "You hid them in your pockets."

"You killed a lizard?" asked Brodie. "Not cool."

"Of course not. It was already dead. I brought it home to give it a proper burial."

Uncle Hugo pointed his index finger at Brodie. "Not another word from you, young man."

"Calm down, Hugo." Patience grinned at Brodie.

"This could possibly be one of the most important literary discoveries of the decade, and you're talking about dead lizards."

"Maybe, maybe not. I haven't had time to read them yet."

"Seriously?"

"I got shot."

"Then let's see them," ordered the colonel.

"Technically, they're evidence," said Troy. "They belong in police custody."

"They belong to academia," said Amy.

"They belong to the Whitney-Jones trust," said Grace.

"They belong to the world," said Feinberg.

Mercy could appreciate each point of view, but who got the letters wasn't ultimately up to her. Still, she wasn't handing them over to anyone just yet. "We don't even know what we've got here. Let's take a look."

"We have to call Barlow." Feinberg pulled his cell from his suit pocket.

"We have to call Becker." Troy fished his phone from his belt.

"Put your phones away. Nobody's calling anybody." Mercy pulled her leg from Troy's lap and tried to sit up, but fell back on the couch.

"Whoa." Troy tried to help her get comfortable again. "My mistake. You talk and we'll listen."

"Thank you." She smiled at him. "I found the letters, and I want to read them before I hand them over to anyone. I'm responsible for them, and I want to make sure that wherever they end up, they're in good hands. Hands that Euphemia Whitney-Jones and Michael Emil Robillard would approve of.

"All we know right now is that Effie wanted her sister to see them. She sent that 'Scary Tree' poem to Maude as a clue of sorts, hoping it would lead her sister to the letters. And that Maude would decide for herself what to do next. We owe it to the sisters and to the man they both loved to do the right thing. And we won't know what that is until we read them. I'm not turning them over to Barlow, or Becker, or anyone else until I read them."

They all started talking at once. Mercy and Troy exchanged a look of equal parts amusement and exasperation. She knew that he would wait out the chaos with her.

Finally, the colonel stood up. He was not a particularly tall or sturdily built man, but his ramrod-straight posture and commanding carriage gave the old man an authority that transcended his physical presence. When he talked, soldiers listened. Along with everyone else.

Uncle Hugo turned to her. "Hear me out. I understand that having discovered this treasure, you want to protect it. And you should. You've saved these letters from obscurity, and you want to make sure they survive posterity." He paused.

"Go on."

"This is what I propose. We all read the letters, right here, in your house, under your watchful eye." He looked at Troy. "And under the watchful eye of law enforcement. Daniel and I can help ensure that the papers are not abused, for the sake of academia and forensics and the world at large. Although it is my understanding that the only person who has touched the letters since you found them is you, Mercy, correct?"

"Correct. Any possible contamination comes from me."

"Or your pockets," added Troy.

"Or my pockets."

"Where are they?" asked the colonel.

"There." Mercy pointed to the tin on the coffee table.

"Hidden in plain sight." Uncle Hugo smiled. "Of course."

Troy pulled several pairs of plastic gloves from his uniform vest. "Everyone wears these."

"We don't need everyone here," said the colonel, in an obvious reference to Amy and Brodie.

"They stay." Mercy's voice was firm.

"They probably can't even read them." At their puzzled looks, Uncle Hugo explained. "Many of the Gen Z generation never learned to read or write cursive handwriting. The perils of a twenty-first-century public school education."

"That's terrible, if it's true." Mercy looked at Amy and Brodie. "Is that true?"

"I can read cursive." Brodie grinned. "Montessori school."

"My grandmother taught me." Amy looked out the front windows, as if picturing her grandmother in the garden. "She taught me calligraphy, too."

"They stay," repeated Mercy.

"As you wish." The colonel sighed.

"We need to come up with a system that ensures the documents are disturbed as little as possible," said Feinberg, prompting a flurry of suggestions.

After several minutes of debate, Mercy approved a system they could all live with, even if none were completely satisfied, other than she. Her mother turned the lights up, brightening the room as if it were day, even as the silver moon rose in the dark sky above the forest. Mercy stayed on the couch with Troy, the dogs at their feet. Her grandmother handed her a piece of cardboard on which she'd taped a piece of white computer paper, while the others found seats around the long farm table, where they would take turns reading each letter.

Amy lifted the tin into Mercy's gloved fingers as if she were bestowing upon her a holy relic from a medieval saint or an artifact from an ancient civilization.

Or maybe simply a toile-patterned tin filled with the defining mysteries behind a twentieth-century American poet's oeuvre. Everyone drew closer to Mercy to witness the unveiling.

"Here goes." She removed the lid, revealing the two small piles of letters, one from each of her cargo pants' thigh pockets. Mercy removed the stack on the left, and balanced it on the white poster board, which sat on her good leg. She took the letter that was on top and opened the faded creamy linen page, then used her cell phone camera to photograph both sides. No flashes.

"No envelope." She looked at Troy. "Do you think that means it was never mailed?"

"Or the envelope was lost."

"If it was mailed before the introduction of V-mail, then the envelope could have been lost. Otherwise it was never mailed."

"Or perhaps this is the first draft of a letter the writer later transcribed onto official V-mail," said Feinberg.

"It's dated October 31, 1942, after V-mail was introduced." Mercy scanned the letter. "It's written in the same handwriting on the same stationery as the original letter we found on Max Vinke after he was poisoned."

"Written by Euphemia Whitney-Jones?" asked Amy.

"Yes."

"Maybe it was just a draft," said Troy.

"Perhaps we should read the letters in chronological order." Leave it to Grace the attorney to advise that.

Feinberg shook his head. "We'd have to sort through them first to do that. And we need to avoid all unnecessary handling."

"Right." Now that Mercy finally held Effie's lost correspondence in her hand, she was suddenly apprehensive at the thought of what she might find.

"Read it to us." Troy seemed to sense her apprehension. "Go on."

OCTOBER 31, 1942

Dearest Captain,

Autumn has come to Vermont. Scary Tree is ablaze in her rich golden cloak, as are all her neighboring oaks and maples and sycamores dressed in reds and oranges and yellows.

Thanks to rationing there are fewer sweets for the children this year, but we can still partake in that special New England treat, apple cider donuts. If only we could send some to you, but you'll have to settle for the Tootsie Rolls that the War Dept. has decreed better suited for such a lengthy and unpredictable journey.

In this lovely season, I take Cherie on long hikes out to the ruins, where I wrote this homegrown Halloween ditty for you:

THE GHOST WITCH OF GRACKLE TREE
Beware the ghost witch in the woods
Where the grackles shriek and cry
The mourning song of her lost bairn

A most bewitching lullaby.
She lies in wait for the children
Who might hold the stolen key
To the poor ghost child she doth grieve
For all cursèd eternity.
Careful, child, when you walk these woods
Lest she cast her sorrow's spell
And you fall, forever locked
In hell where the undead dwell.
Wander not far into the woods
Home at night you'd better be
Beware the blackbirds and beware
The Ghost Witch of Grackle Tree.
Beware the blackbirds and beware
The Ghost Witch of Grackle Tree.

Happy Halloween!
Fly safe.
Effie

When Mercy reached the last verse, everyone in the room recited it with her. They all remembered it from childhood. From Halloweens past and present.

"I guess we all learned that one in school." Brodie bobbed his head. "Cool."

"This may be the original draft of her most famous poem." Mercy gazed at it in wonder.

"If it is, that letter alone is priceless," said Feinberg.

Everyone fell silent for a moment.

"Proceed," said Grace.

"The next one is from Robillard." Mercy began to read.

FEBRUARY 2, 1942

Dear Pug,

Thank you for your letter. I'm sorry that the war has sent you back home, as I know you were so happy in France. But I'm glad you got out in time. So many did not.

We spend most of our time waiting and drinking and flying, flying and waiting and drinking. We are as leery of the weather as we are of the enemy. Nothing is as it seems, not even the clouds in the sky.

In my dreams I picture you under the Scary Tree, your diary in your lap, writing your verses. I hope you can find it in your heart to write of the light even during this time of darkness. We need the light, now more than ever.

Your devoted brother-in-law,

Michael

Not a very romantic letter, Mercy thought.

"That doesn't sound like a love letter to me." Brodie echoed her own conviction. "Who calls their girlfriend Pug?"

"You'd better never call me Pug," teased Amy.

"Pug used to be a term of endearment, back in the day," said Patience. "For people who love their pugs, I suspect it still is."

"Euphemia had more than one pug named Cherie," Mercy told them. "Maybe it was a reference to that."

"'Cherie' is way better than 'Pug.'" Brodie turned to Amy. "He should have called her that."

"There's no hint of anything more than friendship between them in that letter."

Her mother was right. Mercy had to admit she was surprised by the lack of emotion on the page. She thought about it. "This was written early in the war, months before that first letter we found from Effie."

Mercy knew firsthand that you didn't say much about the war when you wrote to your loved ones, and not just because of the censors. You didn't want to worry the folks back home, and the act of writing itself became a kind of meditation that let you escape the battlefront for a brief while, if only in your mind. But there was usually an undercurrent of emotion that colored your words, no matter what you said or how you said it. You might try to bury your deepest, dearest, even most defeatist feelings in easy endearments or breezy innuendo but the emotion was there, all the same. "Let's keep reading."

"I think we should form an assembly line," advised the colonel. "You document each letter, Mercy, and then pass it down. We can take turns reading it so as few hands touch it as possible."

"Good idea." Mercy looked at them all. "Ready to read?"

CHAPTER SEVENTEEN

To feel at home, stay at home.
—CLIFTON FADIMAN

TROY MOVED DOWN CLOSER TO MERCY, AND THEY SAT NEXT to one other on the sofa, reading each letter together, her aching leg still elevated on his lap. She could feel his soft breath on her neck, his warm hand on her thigh, as they photographed each letter and then read it silently, together but apart. She was grateful that they'd each survived their own war and come home and found one another. Unlike poor Effie and her Robillard. Or her sister Maude and Robillard, for that matter. But the majority of her sympathy she reserved for the jilted poet.

Mercy imagined Effie at her escritoire in the library in the main house, writing to her lost love. And Captain Michael Emil Robillard, on his bunk in the crowded barracks by the airfield somewhere in Libya, stealing time before his next flight to write the woman he'd thrown over for her sister. Mercy wondered if he'd lived—and died—regretting the decision that had divided two sisters forever. When his B-24 cartwheeled into that riverbed in Romania in a blaze of fire on Black Sunday, which sister's name had been on his lips?

As they finished one letter, they passed it to Amy, who carried it to the farm table and placed it on another sheet of white computer paper that Patience had taped to another piece of cardboard. The cardboard sat in the center of the farm table, where the rest of the party took turns reading the letter.

The next few letters were from Effie to Robillard. She seemed to write to him much more often than he wrote to her, or maybe fewer of his letters survived the tumultuous times in which they were written. Her words to him were bright and cheerful on the surface, focusing on daily life at the estate, the only trace of melancholy visible in the short poems she penned at the end of each letter, all telling stories of dark enchantments and witches' curses, doomed princesses and exiled princes and children lost in the woods. Mercy recognized many of the poems from Euphemia's collection of children's poetry.

It was possible that these bleak fairy-tale rhymes were inspired not by their relationship but by the war itself, one of the deadliest the world had ever seen. But Mercy thought not. And in the second V-mail from the pilot to his sister-in-law, her guess proved correct. This was the change of heart that Mercy knew Robillard must have suffered before he died; otherwise, Euphemia would not have his letters at all. And she wouldn't have written so many, either.

JUNE 28, 1942

My dearest Effie,

I read and reread your letters so often that I worry they shall turn to dust in my hands before I can come home to you. The same hands that long to reach out across the mountains and deserts and oceans that separate us and touch you. For now I can only thank you for your forgiveness, a generosity that I have been unable or unwilling to return. A terrible pride has possessed me as a young man—but here in hell there is no room for hubris. Hubris can get you killed.

I am determined to stay alive, to survive this war and come back to you and make right the many wrongs I have committed against you and yours, both wittingly and un-wittingly.

Knowing you are with me is everything. The memory of us together in our little sugar shack and the promise of more memories to come are what keep me going. Keep writing; your letters are the balm that soothes the bane of this miserable part of the world.

Yours,

Michael

Troy nudged her shoulder with his own. "So he did come to his senses."

"And then he died." Mercy sighed. "A year later, in August 1943."

Uncle Hugo left the farm table, and the others drifted along behind him. "What have you found?"

Mercy read the letter aloud to them, marveling again at the pilot's about-face. That was the thing about love—it could make you change your mind when you least expected it—or least wanted it. Your heart was a far more stubborn organ than your brain.

"What about the sister?" asked Amy. "Did she know before he died?"

"I'm not sure. I don't think so. The falling-out between the sisters came after he was shot down, when the military finally returned his belongings to his wife Maude. That first letter from Effie was in his things."

"What about the rest of them? How did they end up with Effie?"

"Good question. She obviously saved all *his* letters to her. But there are many of her letters to him here, written on stationery, not V-mail forms. She must have written these as drafts and saved them."

"Why do drafts?" asked Feinberg.

"When you wrote V-mail, you only got one page." The colonel pointed to the government-issued stationery on the table. "Maybe she wrote drafts to edit them down to fit."

"Or maybe she saved them just because she was a writer. For posterity." Amy looked at Mercy for confirmation. "Lots of writers save all their drafts."

"True enough."

"Like with 'The Ghost Witch of Grackle Tree.'" Brodie grinned at Amy. "Even I knew that one."

"Yeah." Amy frowned. "Her feminist poems have mostly fallen out of fashion. Mostly just students in Women's Studies reading them now."

"Like you," teased Brodie.

"Like me."

"Certainly it's her most famous poem," Mercy said. "Her poems for children were far more popular than her more serious work. Those volumes sold millions of copies."

"Still do. The royalties keep the Euphemia Whitney-Jones museum in France afloat," added Feinberg.

"What happened to the V-mail versions they delivered to the pilot?" asked Brodie.

"Maybe they were destroyed in theater." The colonel's face fell for just a second, and Mercy wondered how much her uncle had lost during his long years of service.

"Or Maude received those as well and she destroyed them." Leave it to her mother to come up with the most devious scenario.

"A terrible thought, Mom."

Grace frowned. "Don't look at me like that. From what I understand, these were sisters who hated each other. Maude stole Effie's man—she wouldn't stop at a little thing like destroying her work."

"I get that. But nothing we've read so far explains why anyone would be willing to kill for these letters." Patience turned to Feinberg. "How much is all this really worth?"

"Hard to say until we've seen them all. But finding the early drafts of Whitney-Jones's work is significant."

"Let's see what else is here." Mercy pointed to the piles on the table. "And we'll regroup when we're finished."

Everyone went back to their stations, and the reading resumed. As the correspondence between the former sweethearts continued, the intimacy of the letters grew. Both Effie and Michael reminisced about their time together as lovers and spoke about happy reunions to come. Effie poured her affection and her ardor into love poems that would please some of her legions of fans and appall others. The room grew quieter and quieter as the amorous nature of the letters revealed themselves.

"Wow," whispered Troy.

"*In black ink my love may still shine bright,*" she whispered back. Mercy was beginning to understand why someone—surely it was Effie herself—had hidden the letters away. After the pilot died, there would have been no need to show her sister the letters and risk driving the wedge between them even deeper. Maude had seen the "Scary Tree" poem Effie had sent her as an attempt at reconciliation. But if it had led her to this discovery, as it had led Mercy, then she wondered what Effie's true motive had been.

"I believe we have all read the entirety of the correspondence," announced the colonel.

Amy replaced the letters in the tin, and brought it back to Mercy. The rest of the company followed her, gathering around the sofa.

"And I've documented it all. I'll send you copies of the photos, Daniel."

"Thank you."

"Thank you all for your help."

"Everyone needs to go home," said Troy.

Everyone ignored him.

"What do we think of the value now?" Patience slipped back into one of the easy chairs as Grace commandeered the other. Her mother and her grandmother wouldn't leave before they felt the time was right, no matter what Troy said. Mercy hoped that would change when they had their new place together. They'd have to enforce some boundaries.

"The love triangle gives the story a salacious angle." Uncle Hugo smiled.

"Not to mention the subject matter of some of these poems." Grace clearly did not approve.

"Don't be a prude," Patience told her daughter. "I thought they were rather splendid."

"Sex sells," said Brodie.

"I think it is safe to say that the value of this collection may be even greater than we first imagined," said Feinberg.

That said something, thought Mercy, coming from the person in the room most qualified to put a price on their find.

"Time to hand the letters over to Becker." Troy texted the officer.

Uncle Hugo looked at Feinberg.

The billionaire smiled. "We will persuade Harrington to announce the discovery together on behalf of law enforcement and the estate at a joint press conference."

"That shouldn't be hard, Daniel." Between Feinberg's powers of persuasion and Harrington's love of a good photo op, Mercy figured this was a done deal.

"All I care about is finding the guy who killed Vinke and shot Thrasher and Mercy." Troy's tone indicated that was all they should care about, too.

"Understood," said the colonel.

"When the announcement is made, people will come out of the

woodwork," warned Feinberg. "Academics, museum curators, collectors. They could prove an impediment to your investigation."

"Let them try." Troy had that look, the look that Mercy had come to recognize as the bulldog in her husband.

"Poets and other crackpots," said Brodie.

"Not all poets are crackpots," said Amy. "They're mostly geniuses."

"Like I said. Geniuses, poets, they're all crackpots."

Uncle Hugo and Feinberg said their goodbyes, and Brodie went home to his own place. Amy disappeared into her room to check on Helena, and Mercy doubted she'd see her again before morning.

Her grandmother brought her a cinnamon roll and a cup of tea, and she and her mother hovered as Mercy indulged herself in one last bit of comfort food. "You can both go home now."

"Troy will stay with you," said Grace. "No night patrol."

"No night patrol," Troy said cheerfully. He rarely, if ever, let Grace get under his skin. He was very disciplined that way; it was one of the many things Mercy loved about him.

Elvis and Susie Bear sat up, tails wagging.

"Becker." Troy got up to let in the police officer.

"How's the captain?" Mercy immediately asked him.

"Better. But he'll be out of commission for a while."

"And the suspect?" Troy's voice was tight. Mercy hoped Becker found him before her husband did.

Becker grinned. "Thought you'd never ask. He didn't get very far. Blew a tire on Skyline. Local trucker saw him pull off the road, didn't stop, but he called it in. Suspect was trying to hitch into town when the state troopers picked him up. All thanks to Ranger Guerrette's superior knowledge of electric motorcycles."

"Well done, Gil."

"He'll never let us forget it." Troy paused. "What about his accomplice?"

At their blank looks, Troy told them about the two sets of footprints Gil had seen by the motorcycle tracks.

"No report of any other suspect."

"Then who did the second set of footprints belong to?" asked Mercy.

"Unclear," said Becker. "Although crime scene techs did say that the blowout was the result of a small hole in the front tire of the perp's motorcycle."

"They suspect tampering?" asked Mercy.

"Very likely."

"So somebody wanted our perp caught or worse," said Troy. "I.D. on the guy?"

Becker checked his notebook. "One Andrei Russo out of Las Vegas. Arrested for armed robbery, aggravated assault, even murder, but nothing's ever stuck. Always lawyers up with the best. Nickname of Spider-Man."

"Spider-Man," repeated Mercy. "That's him. The guy in the Spider-Man mask who nearly killed Thrasher. And tried to kill Elvis."

"And shot you in the foot," added her mother.

"A pro," said Troy. "When he saw that empty backpack, he must have figured that the letters were out of his reach and he may as well get the hell out of Dodge."

"Anything to tie him to the Max Vinke poisoning?" asked Mercy.

"Not yet." Becker checked his notebook again. "We've got his phone. A burner. We'll see what our IT people can do with it."

"I assume Russo's not talking." Troy frowned.

"No. Not yet."

"If he is a pro, odds are he won't talk," predicted Mercy. "Ever."

"We'll see." Becker put his notebook back in his breast pocket. "The evidence, please."

Grace and Patience watched as Mercy handed the tin to Troy, who in turn handed it to Becker.

The officer told Mercy he was glad she was feeling better, and left.

"Our turn." Patience patted Mercy's cheek. "Come on, Grace."

"Sleep well." Her mother kissed her on the forehead. "And if you still want that place, you'd better call that Realtor first thing tomorrow and put in an offer. Before all those so-called crackpots beat you to it."

Troy escorted the ladies to their cars. Mercy heard him lock the door behind him as he came back into the cabin. He gathered her up into his arms and carried her to the master bedroom. Elvis and Susie Bear followed them, each claiming a corner for their own, Susie Bear settling in for the night, Elvis alert, his eyes still on Mercy.

"It's okay, boy, go to sleep." But she knew the shepherd wouldn't close his eyes until she fell asleep.

Troy kissed her nose, and deposited her gently onto the four-poster bed, plumping her pillows and elevating her bandaged foot per doctor's orders. One more kiss, and he turned to leave.

"Where are you going?"

"I thought I'd sleep on the couch. I don't want you to risk further injury."

"You're not going anywhere." Mercy patted the bed beside her. "You're my security blanket."

"Okay, Linus." Troy stripped down to his boxers, folded his clothes, and placed them on the wingback chair next to the highboy. He was neat that way. No clothes on the floor for her husband.

"Come on back in." She crooked her finger at him, and he crawled back into the four-poster bed next to her. She lay her head in the nook of his neck.

"At least the perp's in custody."

"If he's the only one."

"You don't think so?"

"Cyanide vs. Glock. Such different weapons."

"What about Levi? He was there when we found Max, and he was there when you and Thrasher were attacked."

"I don't know." Mercy yawned. "He's a protector, not a murderer."

"Maybe he did it to safeguard Effie."

"That means he'd have to have known about the letters." Mercy yawned again. "And if he knew, why leave them there? Why not move them to a safer place?"

"They'd been safe enough until you found them."

"True. But I still can't see him as a murderer."

"You like him."

"Yes, I like them both. Levi and Adah."

Troy kissed her shoulder. "Now go to sleep."

Mercy couldn't go to sleep, not yet. "We have to talk."

CHAPTER EIGHTEEN

Buy land, they're not making it anymore.
—MARK TWAIN

I T'S ABOUT TIME." TROY REALIZED IT HAD BEEN A LONG DAY FOR his wife, but she needed to come clean. "Tell me about that key."

"What?" Mercy seemed startled.

"Please don't play coy. It doesn't suit you."

"You're mad at me." Her pale freckled skin reddened. A sure sign she was upset.

"I'm not mad, not really." Troy sighed. "A little disappointed."

Mercy reached into the pocket of her robe and pulled out the old-fashioned brass instrument. She held it up for him to see. "I guess Thrasher told you about it."

"He mentioned it, along with the letters. He was in pain, on a lot of meds, I didn't press him on the details. I wasn't even sure he knew what he was saying."

"Why didn't you say anything to the others?"

"They didn't mention it, you didn't mention it—only my boss mentioned it. So I figured I should err on the side of discretion. I hoped that you would tell me about it. But you didn't." He took her hand in his and lifted it to his lips. "Of course, it would have been nice if I didn't have to ask. If you'd told me about it."

"I would have, eventually."

"Eventually." He lowered her hand and released it. "You need to trust me."

"It's not that I don't trust you. I couldn't tell you in front of everyone else."

"Why didn't you want anyone to know about it? Thrasher knew, so you must have known we'd all find out sooner or later anyway. I just don't get it."

"Everyone knows about the letters, including the assailant. And soon the whole world will know about them. Feinberg's right. As soon as Harrington has his press conference, it's going to be a circus."

"Harrington loves a good circus, as long as he's the ringleader."

Mercy held the key in her open palm. "I don't think the perp knows it exists—or maybe he does know it exists and he just doesn't know I found it. I don't know what it goes to, what new mystery it will unlock. I wanted some time to think about it. To talk it through with you and Thrasher before the word got out about it. I just haven't had the chance."

"Okay." He wrapped his strong arms around her and hugged her, tight. "We can't afford secrets." Deception was a deal breaker for Troy. His first wife Madeline had deceived him. It destroyed his marriage. He'd always prided himself on honesty, and he prized honesty in others—now more than ever. He couldn't bear the thought of secrets between him and Mercy. "Just promise me there will be no secrets between us."

"No secrets." She kissed her husband. "Promise."

"Good." He released his beautiful wife and leaned back against the headboard, smiling at her. "And the house? This house full of secrets? Do you still want it?"

"More than ever." Mercy flushed again. "If you do."

"I do. But there's something you should know first." Troy told her about Gil's theory. "He doesn't think it's a good place to raise a family."

"What do you think?"

"I think that anyplace with you would be a good place to raise a family."

"Speaking of—"

Troy interrupted her. "Oh, that reminds me, I brought you a souvenir from the Little Witch House." He got out of bed and picked up his pants, removing the stone with the hole in it from his pocket. He handed it to Mercy.

She held it in the palm of her hand. "Where did you get this?"

Troy described Willa Strong's grave marker, where he'd discovered the stone. "What's the big deal? It's just a rock with a hole in it."

"Not really." Mercy curved her fingers around the stone like a C and placed the little finger of her other hand through the hole. "It's a holey stone."

"A what?"

"They go by other names as well. Fairy stones, hag stones, eye stones, adder stones, serpent eggs, hex stones."

"Come on."

"The Druids wore them as a kind of badge. They believed that holey stones were made of the hardened saliva of slithering serpents roiling and secreting together. The holes are the perforations that occurred when the serpents sliced through the saliva with their pointed tongues."

"Nice."

She held the stone up to her eye and looked through the hole at him. "Some people believe that when you look through the hole, you can see the invisible spirits and creatures from other dimensions."

"Right."

"And if you're a witch and you look through the hole, you'll lose your magic powers."

Troy laughed. "Then you'd better give that back to me."

"Very funny." Mercy handed him the hag stone. "Keep it in your pocket, or I can make you a necklace to wear. It will protect you from evil spirits and dark energies and ghost witches."

"So you do believe in ghosts."

"I believe in Levi Beecher. No way he's a murderer."

"Do you think he left this stone on the marker?"

"Maybe. Or maybe it was a Druid."

"Ghosts, witches, Druids, victims, perps—and we still want to buy the place." Troy placed the hag stone in her palm, and closed her fingers around it, wrapping his own fingers around hers. "I guess that proves we were made for each other."

MERCY KNEW SHE SHOULD tell him about the baby. *Now.* He'd forgiven her for not telling him about the key, and she'd promised him no more secrets. And he'd consider this a big one.

Here goes, she thought. She wouldn't let him sidetrack her announcement with talk of holey stones this time.

"It's a big house," she started. "Plenty of bedrooms. Because we're going to need—"

Troy interrupted her again. "I've been thinking about that. We only need the one bedroom, you know, for us."

"But—"

"I know we haven't even seen the guesthouse yet, but it doesn't matter. Between my dad and my brothers and your cousin Ed—"

"I don't think—" Mercy tried again.

"Don't worry. They'll be glad to do it. With their help, we can make it right for Amy and Helena." He went on and on about what they'd need, and Mercy focused on her breathing, the better to curb her impatience.

Her husband was not usually such a big talker. That was one of the things she liked best about him. He was comfortable with silence. But now he simply would not shut up long enough for her to tell him about the baby. No more breathing. Time to take control of the situation.

"Stop talking!" Mercy reached up and clamped her hand over her husband's mouth. The dogs both raised their heads, awake and alert now.

"What's wrong?" Troy's warm brown eyes searched her face. She hoped the baby had his eyes.

"I need you to be quiet." Mercy removed her hand.

"I'm sorry. I just—"

She placed her hand back over his mouth.

He laughed, and kissed her fingers. "Okay, okay," he said, his voice muffled.

"Do you promise not to speak?"

He nodded.

"I'm going to remove my hand now, because I have something important to say."

Elvis leapt onto the bed, and nosed Mercy's hand with his muzzle. The shepherd's way of telling Troy that it was time to listen to Mercy. Not to be outdone, Susie Bear scrambled onto Troy's side. The double bed was a little crowded now.

"Everybody paying attention?"

One husband and two dogs regarded her with complete concentration.

"We're going to need more than one bedroom. We're going to need a nursery."

"What?"

Mercy inhaled, then exhaled the words that scared her as much as they thrilled her. "We're having a baby."

"We're having a baby," Troy repeated.

"We're having a baby," they said in unison. The dogs barked.

"We're going to need a bigger bed." Troy gave her that smile—that smile that told her she was the only woman in the world for him, that smile that told her he'd always be there for her, that smile that told her she should ask him to marry her.

Only three months ago.

IT HAD BEEN A hell of a day. The day her grandmother Patience and her longtime beau Claude were supposed to tie the knot at the posh Lady's Slipper Inn in a posh ceremony followed by a posh reception planned by Mercy's posh mother Grace. But from the very beginning, the destination-wedding weekend to end all destination-wedding weekends had been a disaster. A missing spa director, the groom's feuding family, unwelcome surprise guests, murder, and an attempt to kidnap the bride had postponed the nuptials long enough to give the bride pause. Patience demurred.

And suddenly, the wedding was off. But the guests and the flowers and the wedding cake were all still there.

What a shame to waste the perfect wedding setup, Patience and Grace told Mercy. Maybe it was that obvious hint, or all the champagne, or the sheer exhaustion from taking down a murderer, or some combination thereof. But for once in her life, the always prepared, always deliberate, always analytical Mercy did something wildly impulsive without thinking twice.

She found Troy in the reception area, hanging out with his parents and his brothers. Susie Bear was there at his side, just as Elvis was by hers.

She smiled at his family, and they smiled back. "Could I borrow Troy for a minute?"

Troy didn't wait for any of them to answer. "Sure."

He placed his large hand at her back and guided her through the weary guests, who were still waiting around for the wedding that wasn't going to happen. They went out to the back garden, where the lights shone in the mist. The rain had finally stopped, and the air was warm and humid.

"Is everything all right?" Troy's warm brown eyes were filled with worry.

"Fine." Mercy closed her eyes. *Screw your courage to the sticking-place.* She opened her eyes again, and took Troy's hands in her own. "Let's get married."

"You want to get married." Troy stared at her. "To me."

She waved at the French doors, beyond which the guests were drinking champagne and waiting for something wedding-like to happen. "Someone should get married here, don't you think?"

Troy smiled. "Your grandmother called it off."

"Yeah."

"Good for her."

"You don't like Claude?"

Troy shrugged. "I like Claude. But I like Patience more."

Mercy waited for him to address the real elephant in the room. She held her breath. This was what you get for acting on impulse, she thought. What every soldier knows. Humiliation and defeat.

Troy smiled at her. "I'll go tell them."

"Tell who what?"

"Tell them all that Patience and Claude will not be getting married today." He drew her to him and kissed her lightly on the lips. "But we will."

"What about your family?"

"The people I love most are all here. And even if they weren't, it wouldn't matter. All that matters is you and me."

Elvis barked, as if he knew he were being left out.

Mercy laughed. "And the dogs."

"And the dogs." Troy wrapped his long arm around her shoulders and whistled for the dogs. He walked her through the French doors. "Go do whatever it is you need to do before you walk down that aisle. I'll inform the troops."

Mercy made her way through the ballroom and down to the room where the Carr and Fleury women waited for her to return with what they all assumed would be good news. Her mother took one look at Mercy's flushed face and said, "Let's do this."

Her grandmother and her sister-in-law Paige and her aunt Verity joined her mother in the huddle around Mercy.

"What are we going to do about the dress?" asked Grace.

"I love this dress," said Mercy of her bridesmaid dress, a simple, sleeveless, mauve, satin, tea-length dress with a V-neck, twirly skirt, and side pockets.

"It's not white," said her mother.

"White is so last century," said Aunt Verity.

"I suppose it will have to do."

"The dress is your something new," said Paige. "And you look radiant in it."

"All you need is a veil." Patience placed her own lovely champagne-colored vintage beaded blusher wedding veil, the veil she was supposed to wear, on Mercy's head. She arranged Mercy's red curls around it as artfully as she could. "Something borrowed."

"I'm borrowing your whole wedding."

Her grandmother laughed. "And I couldn't be more pleased."

"You need something old." Aunt Verity pulled a red heart-shaped stone from the pocket of her bridesmaid dress. "This is carnelian from India. I've carried it for decades."

"Aunt Verity, I couldn't."

"Root chakra. Shakti goddess energy. Just like you."

"But—"

"I have plenty more crystals and healing stones at home. This was meant to be yours."

"Thank you." Her aunt placed the red stone in Mercy's open palm, and she tucked the talisman into her own pocket.

"That just leaves something blue." Her mother held out her left hand, and removed her engagement ring, the 1920s square-cut deep-blue sapphire that she'd worn every day of her married life, the ring Mercy had never seen her without. The elegant ring had been in the Carr family for more than a hundred years, and her father had given it to Grace when he proposed.

"Mom." Mercy's eyes filled with tears. "No."

"Your father and I always planned to pass this down to you when the time came. And that time is now." Her mother took her hand and slid the jewel onto Mercy's ring finger. She smiled at her. "A perfect fit. You did get your lovely hands from me, you know."

"Thank you." She gave her mother a hug.

"One more thing." Her sister-in-law Paige swapped out Mercy's brides-maid flowers for the bridal bouquet.

"Ready?" asked her mother.

"As ready as I'll ever be."

Grace kissed her on the cheek. "That's my girl."

All the favorite women in Mercy's life escorted her down the hallway to the ballroom, where the wedding party was waiting for her. The bride.

Her father was there, along with Troy's brothers and Mercy's brother Nick, the newly appointed groomsmen, and the flower girl and the ring bearer. And of course, the dogs.

Mercy looked out into the ballroom that Grace and Wyetta had turned into a wedding wonderland of candlelight and mauve-and-white cymbidium orchids. Gold and silver pedestal candelabra and flower stands stood among the skirted tables like so many jewels in a crown, the china and crystal glinting like diamonds in the glow. A deep lady's slipper–pink carpet led up to the head table, elegantly laid out for the bride and groom and the rest of the wedding party. The wedding guests had lined up along each side of the carpet in anticipation of seeing Patience and Claude exchange their vows. But that was not what they were going to see.

Mercy spotted Troy on the raised stage behind the head table, standing next to the arch of woven grapevine and mauve-and-white cymbidium orchids where the ceremony would take place. He looked very handsome, his tall figure silhouetted against the floor-to-ceiling windows that flanked the stage. He held a microphone in his hand and tapped it loudly.

"Ladies and gentlemen," he began. "If I could have your attention, please."

The crowd turned toward him, murmuring amongst themselves. Some of the guests clearly didn't even know who he was. *Poor Troy,* thought Mercy.

"What we do for love," whispered her grandmother in her ear.

Troy cleared his throat, and plunged in. "I'm sorry to tell you that Patience and Claude will not be getting married here today."

Everyone started talking at once, and several moved as if to leave.

"Hold on," said Troy in his *don't move, you're under arrest* voice. "Stay right where you are." He grinned at them. "You came here today expecting a wedding. And you're going to get a wedding."

The guests gaped at him. Troy had stunned them into silence. And immobility.

"There will be a wedding, with a slightly different cast of characters. The bride will be the magnificent Mercy Fleury Carr. And yours truly here will be the humble groom."

A couple of loud whoops from the audience. Thrasher and Gil Guer-rette, no doubt. That prompted a round of applause.

"I know today's ceremony has been a long time coming." Troy held out his arms. "But turn your eyes up the aisle. Because here, finally, comes the bride."

The string quartet began to play Pachelbel's *Canon in D*. Mercy and her parents looked on as the groomsmen marched down the aisle with brides-maids Patience, Paige, and her aunt Verity.

"You're not the bride," said Mercy's nephew Toby. "Grandma Patience is the bride."

"Change of plans. But you and Elvis still get to deliver the rings." Elvis appeared beside the little boy, and nudged him in the side with his long nuzzle. Toby giggled.

"Go," Mercy told Elvis, and the shepherd, handsome in his bow-tie collar, started down the aisle, Toby trotting along next to him.

Next up was little Helena. Amy placed the flower girl and her basket of mauve, pink, and cream rose petals in the small beribboned white cart hitched to an orchid-laden Susie Bear. The Newfie pranced down the aisle as Helena hurled petals at the guests lining the aisle, squealing with de-light. The place erupted in laughter.

Mercy laughed, too. The wedding was on.

"You look beautiful." Her father took her arm. "But I'm not sure I'm ready for this."

Her mother took her other arm. "We were never going to be ready for this, Duncan."

Mercy wasn't sure she was ready for this, either. But when she stepped onto the lady's slipper–pink carpet that would lead her to Troy and their new life together, all she could see was the way the groom was looking at her.

He smiled. The music swelled. The dogs barked.

And down the aisle she went.

"GRACKLE TREE FARM IT is," said Troy. "Let's make an offer."

"Absolutely." Mercy looked at Troy. "Asking price?"

"Five percent below." His voice was firm. "I'll text Jilly, you text Grace and Patience. They'll want to know."

"That, they will." Mercy pulled out her phone from the other pocket of her robe.

Troy laughed. "Let's see how long it takes for them to text back."

They cuddled together on the bed, the holey stone on Mercy's pillow, Elvis and Susie Bear still on the bed with them. Troy began counting backward from a hundred aloud, and Mercy, laughing, joined him. "Ninety-nine, ninety-eight, ninety-seven . . ."

Elvis raised his head, perking his ears. He knew a countdown when he heard one. Susie Bear slept on.

They kept on counting and counting . . .

". . . twenty-nine, twenty-eight, twenty-seven . . ."

Mercy's and Troy's phones dinged in rapid succession.

"You go first."

"I've got a text from Mom." Mercy rattled off the messages. "She says: 'Well done.' How about you?"

"Jilly likes nothing better than closing a deal. She says: 'Offer accepted. Meet me at the office at nine a.m. to do the paperwork. Mercy, too.'" He squeezed Mercy's shoulder.

Mercy's phone pinged again. She looked down at her cell. "It's from my grandmother."

"What does Patience say?"

"'Congratulations.'" Of course it was her grandmother who remembered to congratulate them.

Another text, this time a group chat from her mother to her and her grandmother. She couldn't believe Grace was doing group chats. And she couldn't believe what the text said. Mercy laughed.

"What?" asked Troy.

"I don't think they're congratulating us on the house. Or at least, not *just* on the house." She read the group text aloud to her husband. "'First comes love, then comes marriage . . .'"

DAY THREE
OCTOBER 29

CHAPTER NINETEEN

Old houses are steeped in history. They have a soul.
—CAROLINE BRÉZA

MERCY AND TROY WERE UP EARLY WITH THE DOGS THE next morning. Her Jeep was still up at the estate; her cousin Ed had agreed to drop by with Troy's father to check out the manor house, pick up her vehicle, and return it to her that afternoon.

They had a busy morning ahead, between visiting Thrasher in the hospital and meeting Jillian to sign the paperwork for the sale. "I think I might need some serious fortification to get through the next couple of hours."

"Eating for two." Troy smiled. "Breakfast at Eggs Over Easy?"

"Sounds good."

Elvis and Susie Bear dashed for the front door. They loved Eggs Over Easy—and they knew the place by name.

There was a distinctly late-autumn chill in the air, and yesterday's winds had tossed layers of leaves from the trees and scattered clouds of their fallen brethren above and along the dying grass. A light fog had settled in overnight, lending a ghostly air, as if even the weather was in cahoots with the witch.

Grounded by her bad foot, Mercy was forced to forgo driving and instead be driven, a beyond-her-control circumstance that drove her more than a little crazy. Troy helped her into his truck, the dogs piled in the back seat, and she forced herself to relax, reminding herself that her husband the game warden was one of the few people in the world she considered as proficient behind the wheel as she.

As they headed toward town, winding down Route 7 through a mist-laden kaleidoscope of fall color, Mercy allowed herself a frisson of excitement at the prospect of owning such a wonderful property. "I can't believe it will be ours."

Troy reached over for her hand and held it tight. "Ours."

"I'll have to put the cabin up for sale as soon as possible."

"Another sweet commission for Jilly."

"Let's hope so."

He glanced over at her. "I know this is a big step for you, giving up the cabin."

"It was, at first. But not anymore. Now we *really* need a bigger place." Mercy couldn't believe how those two little words—"you're pregnant"— had changed her worldview so thoroughly and significantly from the moment she'd heard them. A seismic change that was literally transforming her from the inside out, and would continue to do so, most likely for the rest of her life. *If every of your wishes had a womb. And fertile every wish, a million.*

Any doubt she had about selling the cabin was long gone, replaced by the certainty that the baby's needs eclipsed hers, now and forevermore. The enormity of this realization was just beginning to hit her. She wiped away a tear.

"Yes, we do." Troy removed his right hand from the steering wheel and placed it over hers. "You know, we never really talked about having a family."

"And now we're having one." She'd proposed to Troy out of the blue, and now she was pregnant out of the blue. "We've only been married like a minute."

"Perfect timing. I was actually kind of worried you'd want to wait a couple of years or more to have kids."

"I did want to wait. But here we are."

"It'll be great. You'll see."

"We have to tell your parents, now that the word is out."

"How did Grace and Patience know?" asked Troy. "You didn't even know."

"I don't know. Maybe it's some kind of mom radar."

"Another superpower for you. Just what you need."

"What I need is coffee." Mercy sighed. "I bet I have to limit caffeine."

"Decaf for you."

"I'll google it as soon as I can get a signal." Mercy sighed again. "The Big Barn Red. That must be how they knew."

"What do you mean?"

"Last night I didn't drink the wine Amy poured for me."

"And your eagle-eyed mother noticed."

"And my eagle-eyed grandmother." Mercy shook her head. "And if they can figure it out, other people will, too."

The traffic increased as they approached the village outskirts. Soon the vehicles were lined up bumper to bumper all the way into town. The leaf peepers were out in full force, driving in from all over the continent to see the splashy show that Mother Nature put on in New England every autumn. Northshire was a favorite destination this time of year, with its cute shops and good restaurants and eighteenth- and nineteenth-century bed-and-breakfast inns and Halloween festivities. Not to mention the legend of the Ghost Witch of Grackle Tree.

Troy maneuvered the truck through the roundabouts that bookended the downtown area and came back around on a side street to try to find a parking place. But every space was taken.

"I'm going to drop you off, and go park at the police station. We'll meet you there."

"What about Harrington?"

"We'll stay out of his sight, if he's even around yet. He's more night owl than early bird." Troy pulled up in front of an old nineteenth-century mill building. Once famous for its textiles, the four-storied redbrick building now housed shops and cafés and apartments, including every local's favorite breakfast joint, Eggs Over Easy. The dogs whined with pleasure, heads out the window, sniffing the air, which was no doubt imbued with the irresistible scents of the meat-lover's breakfasts wafting down from the restaurant on the second floor.

There was already a line forming up the stairs to the entrance of the café, which didn't open for another ten minutes. Troy double-parked, put on his lights, and leashed the dogs. Mercy waited as patiently as she could while he half-lifted her out of the truck and onto the crutches.

"I'm not an invalid, you know."

Troy ignored that. "Stay right there. I'll be back to help you with the stairs."

"No worries." Mercy bit back a smart-ass reply, which he didn't deserve, as he was just trying to help. She hated his trying to help. She hated everyone's trying to help. She watched him get back into his vehicle and drive off with something close to relief.

She couldn't wait to get off these crutches and out of this medical boot, which surely would be possible for her soon. Of course, by the time she was off the crutches, she could be showing a baby bump—and people would be even more solicitous. Maybe she wouldn't mind by then. But somehow she doubted it.

Elvis and Susie Bear were attracting a lot of attention at the bottom of the stairs. The friendly Newfie was greeting her fellow diners with licks and wags, while Elvis stood by at attention, waiting for word from Mercy.

"Mercy Carr!"

She looked up, and spotted Monique, the brusque brunette who served as hostess, lead server, and all-around ringleader here. Mercy liked Monique; cranky was part of her New England charm. She waved at Monique, who was already halfway down the steps, yelling at the customers as she descended.

"Move aside, people!" Monique gave Mercy a quick hug, then pet Susie Bear but obviously thinking better of touching Elvis without his express permission. "I heard about the shootings," she whispered so loudly everyone up and down the queue could no doubt hear her perfectly well. "Are you okay?"

"I'm fine."

"And the captain?" Monique was inordinately fond of Thrasher and had been one of the most disappointed of the countless disappointed women in the state who were dismayed to hear of his relationship with Wyetta.

"We think he's okay. We'll be dropping by to visit him after breakfast."

"I'll pack up all his favorites for you to take with you. You know how gross that hospital food is."

"That would be great. Thank you." Mercy wished she'd thought of it herself.

Monique leaned in as if to tell her a secret. "They say you're buying that old place. You know it's haunted, right?"

CHAPTER TWENTY

Home is where my habits have a habitat.
–FIONA APPLE

TROY PARKED AT THE POLICE STATION, AS FAR AWAY FROM Harrington's Lincoln as possible. He was surprised the detective was here at the office this early; usually he stormed in not long before the lunch hour, barking orders at people. The fact that he was here now could only mean that he was prepping big-time for his press conference at the Town Hall at eleven o'clock.

Troy did not want to run into him, especially with Mercy so close by. Harrington would want to question him, and maybe Mercy, too; the ambitious detective could wait for what would undoubtedly be a thinly veiled interrogation until after they'd had breakfast and visited Thrasher and finalized the offer on the house.

He locked up his truck and was halfway to the street when he heard his name called.

"Warner!" Harrington's autocratic tenor was unmistakable.

Troy could pretend he hadn't heard the detective and keep on walking, but then Harrington would just send Becker or Goodlove after him. Not fair to any of them. He sighed, and turned around, then walked back to join Harrington. "Detective Harrington."

"How's your bride?"

Just the sleazy way the guy said the word "bride" made Troy want to punch him.

"Better."

"Glad to hear it." Harrington tapped his foot—whether in impatience or simply to show off his black Chelsea boots, Troy wasn't sure. "And Thrasher?"

"We'll be dropping by the hospital shortly."

"Good." Harrington paused. "You're coming to the press conference."

"I'll be there."

"Mercy should be there, too. And the dogs."

Troy wondered why Harrington would want them there. Whatever the reason was, it couldn't be good.

"Town Hall. Eleven hundred hours. Be on time." Harrington turned on one of his Italian-made heels and strode away.

Troy jogged down Main Street several blocks to Eggs Over Easy, where he joined Mercy and the dogs at the bottom of the stairs.

Monique was there, too. "Won't be an easy climb for her with those crutches, Warden."

"I can do it." Mercy's pale freckled face began to redden.

He knew she was embarrassed, but she'd have to bite the bullet and accept his assistance whether she liked it or not. And not just for now, but for the rest of their lives. He knew that would be a major adjustment for her. As if marriage and parenthood weren't enough. He was more than ready for it, but he wasn't sure Mercy was.

He reached out for the crutches, and when she turned them over to him, he passed them along to Monique. He scooped up Mercy in his arms.

"Follow me." The hostess sashayed past the line of customers, calling, "Coming through!" as she made room for Troy and Mercy.

Troy carried Mercy up the stairs, the dogs in step behind them. At the landing, Monique propped open the door for them.

"Newlyweds," she announced to the crowd with a wink as she waved Troy and Mercy on into the café. "Aren't they precious?"

Troy headed toward a corner table at the back of the dining area, the spot Monique usually reserved for Thrasher and his guests. The place was empty at the moment, but soon every seat would be taken—and crunch time at Eggs Over Easy would be in full swing.

He released Mercy and she slipped into her seat, back to the wall with a view of the room like a good cop. Elvis sat by her side, licking his lips. Troy sat next to Mercy, so he, too, had a good cop's view. Susie Bear panted at his hip, already drooling in anticipation of the glorious meal to come.

"Shall I bring you guys the usual, with Captain Thrasher's to go?" Monique put a bowl of water down for the dogs and poured coffee into Mercy's and Troy's cups.

Troy looked at Mercy, who nodded. "Sounds good."

Monique flounced off.

"I get one cup of real coffee a day. Then it's decaf."

"I'm sorry."

"I'll live. But I may sleep through the next six months."

"Fine by me. Whatever you and the little guy need."

"Little guy?"

"Little guy, little girl. No preference. As long as it's got red hair just like yours."

"And brown eyes just like yours." Mercy took another sip of her coffee.

Troy told Mercy about his encounter with Harrington and their upcoming command performance at the Town Hall.

"Weird. He never shares the limelight voluntarily."

"Exactly. But he does like having other people around to blame when things go south."

"What's gone south?"

Troy shook his head. "I'm not sure. But we should be ready for anything."

The noise level in the restaurant rose as customers streamed in and secured their places. Monique returned with a tray holding four plates. She served the two heaped with the café's signature venison-blueberry sausage, wild turkey hash, and cornbread to Troy and Mercy. The other two, which held egg-and-sausage scrambles, she set on the floor before the happy dogs.

"Enjoy."

"Thank you." Mercy wasted no time digging into her breakfast.

"You bet." Monique jerked her head toward the front of the restaurant as she left. "Incoming."

A bookish-looking woman wearing wire-rimmed glasses and Birkenstocks approached their table. She wore jeans and a white T-shirt with inky black calligraphy that read POETRY IS MY FIRST LANGUAGE. Troy didn't recognize her, but he knew the man who pushed ahead of her. The long hunter Horace Boswell, dressed in twenty-first-century clothes. No coonskin cap.

"*Yonder comes a poet* . . ." Mercy said quietly.

"Great." Troy put down his fork and rose to his feet.

Susie Bear shuffled to her feet as they neared them. Elvis didn't move a muscle; only the perk of his triangular ears revealed his interest in the newcomers.

"We need to talk to you," Boswell said to Mercy.

"And you are?" she asked politely, but Troy could see that Mercy knew very well who the man was—and she didn't like him, either. This was getting interesting.

"Dr. Horace Boswell," boomed the man as if he were addressing the entire restaurant. Maybe he was. "Poet and Classics chair at Northshire Valley College."

"And winner of the Pulitzer Prize for *Song of Ares*," added his companion.

Boswell twirled his hand with a flourish at his companion. "My colleague, Dr. Elisabeth Bardin."

"Elisabeth with an s," said the woman with an air of importance. As if *Elisabeth with an s* trumped *Elizabeth with a z* every time.

Troy wondered if she were an academic *and* a poet. Which he figured would be twice the fun. Like Boswell, who was not only a poet and an academic, but a poacher as well.

"Elisabeth is the Women's Studies chair at Northshire Valley College and this year's poet laureate of Northshire. She's just been awarded a Pushcart Prize for *The Shires*."

"Got it." Mercy finished off her hash. "Congratulations to you both. What can I do for you?"

"We represent the Northshire Alliance of Poets," said Boswell. "We understand you've found lost correspondence written by our founder and mentor Euphemia Whitney-Jones."

Mercy looked up at Troy, and he shook his head just enough to make his point. He wondered how they'd found out about the letters so quickly.

"No comment," she said dutifully, before popping a bite of sausage into her mouth.

"'No comment is not an acceptable answer.'" Boswell raised his voice. "We have a right to know."

"We have a right to see that correspondence, and preserve it," said *Elisabeth with an s.*

An eye-catching trio of gray-cloaked personages in white tunics and trousers came up behind her. Mercy leaned over and whispered in Troy's ear, "Enter the three witches."

Two women and a man. They all wore pendants around their necks.

"Druids, my mistake," Mercy whispered again, reaching for the cornbread. Troy could see that neither poets nor Druids were going to ruin his pregnant wife's breakfast.

She was actually enjoying this odd encounter, but he wasn't. Neither were the dogs.

Elvis leaned forward, ears back. Susie Bear tilted her big head, as if she were deciding whether this was a situation that truly demanded her attention.

That didn't stop the man in the cloak with the carved maple staff in his right hand. Tall and thin and stooped, he wore a long white beard worthy of a pagan priest. He marched right on up to the table, stopping next to the academics. "Hail and welcome." He pulled the hood off his brow, and the gray wool settled in soft rolls around his neck. "I'm Oisin, Arch-Druid of the Cosmic Ash Grove, Order of the Bards, Ovates, and Druids."

His voice was rich and sonorous, and Troy imagined that when he gave sermons—if Arch-Druids gave sermons—he might hypnotize his listeners with that voice. Troy didn't say anything because he had nothing to say, and he wasn't sure who the man was addressing: Mercy or Boswell or Bardin. But he figured the man wasn't talking to him.

Mercy didn't say anything, either. Even the poets were quiet.

The silence did not deter the Arch-Druid. He held out his hands, indicating each of his companions in turn with long, elegant fingers. "This is Liath the Bard and Muirne the Ovate."

Troy had a vague idea what Druids and bards were—he'd played Dungeons & Dragons as a kid and watched a million King Arthur and Merlin movies—but he was drawing a blank at ovates. Mercy would know—didn't they call her man Shakespeare 'the bard'?—and she'd brief him later.

She had a gift for arcane knowledge that proved surprisingly useful at times.

"You have no place here." Boswell launched into a rant about poetry and pagans and Philistines.

Oisin ignored the poet. "You have no right to those letters or anything else at Grackle Tree Farm. It's a sacred place."

"We're not Philistines, we're Druids," said Liath, the smaller and younger of the women wearing gray cloaks. She, too, pulled her hood down. Her hair was pulled straight back off her moon-shaped face, and gathered into a bright-pink ponytail tied with a black scrunchie. She tapped her narrow chest, and her pendant bounced.

It was a hag stone, strung with black cord through its hole. Much like the one Troy had found on Willa Strong's headstone. He knew Mercy must have seen it and made the connection; she never missed anything. He glanced over at her and she smiled.

"It's not funny," insisted *Elisabeth with an s.*

"You're making a mockery of our religion." Muirne spoke for the first time. She was a striking, sophisticated-looking woman who seemed an unlikely Druid, despite the gray cloak and the white tunic and the hag stone. She left her hood in place, as if she knew the dramatic look suited her.

"We mean no disrespect," said Mercy.

Oisin regarded them with an impassive intelligence that reminded Troy of Thrasher. Here was a worthy adversary. If he were an adversary. "We understand the estate is for sale. And that you intend to buy it."

"No comment."

Monique appeared, Thrasher's takeout in one hand and a frying pan in the other. "Back to your seats, people. This is a café, not a Town Hall meeting."

The poets and the Druids all started talking at once, yelling at each other and at Mercy and Troy. Two guys in gray cloaks joined them. Troy recognized Quaid Miller and his cousin Braden, the brawny long hunters who'd accompanied Boswell. The young men folded their ham-sized hands in front of them, watching and waiting, ready for a fight.

Monique handed Troy a to-go bag. "You'd better get out of here."

"We're going," said Troy.

"Wait. We just want to do right by Euphemia Whitney-Jones." Bardin gave Mercy a flyer. "Please come to our poetry reading tonight. We can talk privately afterward. There are things you need to know."

Elvis barked. Susie Bear bellowed. The table crashers took note of the dogs' displeasure, and they all retreated a few feet, still arguing. The bodyguard Druids didn't move a muscle.

Troy helped Mercy to her feet while the dogs kept the poets and the Druids at bay.

"Go out the back door," Monique advised. "Nobody ever uses it. And give Captain Thrasher my love."

While the hostess brandished her frying pan and threatened to call the police, Troy and Mercy escaped through the back door with the dogs. They could still hear the ruckus as they navigated the rickety fire escape. Troy couldn't carry her, as the structure was too unstable, so he half lifted her as they progressed down the metal staircase step by step.

By the time they made it the ground, they could hear sirens.

"Poor Becker," Troy said.

"And Goodlove."

"Between Harrington and the Major Crime Unit, the poets and the peepers and the Druids, they're going to have their hands full." Troy wondered what other surprises lay in wait, for all of them.

BY THE TIME THEY made it to the hospital, Troy could tell from the flush on Mercy's face that she was hurting.

"You should stay in the truck and put that foot up."

"No way," she said sharply.

Troy frowned. "I think you just proved my point."

"I'm sorry." She grimaced as she let herself out of the vehicle on her own. "But nothing I'm feeling can begin to compare to what the captain is suffering. I'm going in."

"You know that argument won't hold up."

"I know, but I'm sticking to it."

"Okay." He knew there was no arguing the point. "Stay right there." He jogged to the entrance of the hospital and flagged down a wheelchair. He rolled it up to the Ford F-150 and guided Mercy into the seat. The dogs whined, but he left them in the truck, anyway. Windows cracked for fresh air.

"Elvis is going to be very unhappy."

"No unhappier than Susie Bear." He wheeled her toward the hospital. "They'll be fine. The weather is good, and we're not staying long."

Mercy was silent as they moved through the hospital lobby and into the elevator. He wondered what she was thinking and hoped it was more positive than his own dark thoughts, a tangled thicket of murders and poets and witches. He was relieved when they finally got to Thrasher's room.

The captain was sitting up, and Wyetta, a vision in a bright-yellow dress, sat on the hard blue plastic chair next to him. You would never guess she'd pulled an all-nighter at the patient's side.

"We brought you breakfast." Mercy hopped over to hug Wyetta and give the captain his takeout from Eggs Over Easy.

"I'd know the smell of that venison-blueberry sausage and wild turkey hash anywhere. Thank you."

"You're welcome."

Thrasher smiled, and while it wasn't the thousand-watt smile that could charm every man, woman, and child in the state into lifetime support of the Vermont Fish & Wildlife Department, it was a more genuine smile than his pain-laced grimaces of yesterday. This comforted Troy far more than he liked to admit. The captain was the reason he was a game warden, and he couldn't imagine the service without him.

"Relax, Troy." The man always seemed to know what he was thinking. "I'm fine."

"Sir."

"I'll eat and you talk." The captain opened his to-go package and dug in. "What's new?"

They told him what they knew about the letters and the investigation, the hag stones and the poets and the Druids.

"I don't understand how they knew about the letters," said Wyetta.

"We don't, either."

"Somebody talked," said Troy.

"It was bound to happen." Thrasher pronged a piece of sausage. "But we'd better keep the cone of silence firmly in place going forward, where we can."

"Roger that," said Troy.

"And the key?" Thrasher stared at Mercy. "Who knows about it?"

"Nobody."

"You told Troy."

"Yes," said Troy. "But we haven't told Harrington yet."

"He dropped by to see me this morning, but I was sleeping. Next time I won't be so lucky. And I'll have to tell him about it." Thrasher spooned a mouthful of hash into his mouth and chewed, washing it down with the hospital-issued orange juice. "I understand your reluctance. Odds are, Harrington won't know what to do with it, and even if he does, he may ignore it altogether rather than give you the opportunity to make another splash in the press."

"I think the only reason he let us go back to the house to discover the letters without him was because he didn't think we'd find anything."

"Agreed." As the captain chowed down on the hash, he was looking more like himself.

Thank you, Monique, thought Troy.

"It must mean something," said Mercy.

"Something that may have nothing whatsoever to do with the investigation."

"But if it does, and I'm betting it does, you're talking obstruction if you don't turn that key over to Harrington." Thrasher looked at Troy. "You need to do that."

"We will. First thing." He changed the subject. "Speaking of Harrington, he's ordered Mercy and me and the dogs to come to his press conference."

"Has he indeed?" Thrasher finished off the cornbread. "Interesting."

"Maybe he's expecting a scene," said Wyetta. "Like at Eggs Over Easy. They may all show up at the press conference."

"Poets and Druids and God knows who else," said Mercy. "At this rate, there could be a riot."

Wyetta laughed. "I do love Halloween."

"I hate Halloween," answered Troy and Thrasher in unison. Northshire was already crowded with leaf peepers this time of year, and the spooky holiday drew even more visitors, thanks to the town's full schedule of fun events, from the Northshire Psychic Fair and the Vampire Ball to the Great Pumpkin Carving Contest and the HOWLoween Puppy

Parade and Party. Thousands of costumed revelers swarmed the streets, staying out late, drinking too much, pranking too much, and more. Your basic law enforcement nightmare.

"All cops hate Halloween," said Mercy. "And the cop in me hates it, too. But the rest of me loves Halloween. Especially here in Northshire. The magic, the mystery, the ghost stories."

"'The Ghost Witch of Grackle Tree,'" said Wyetta approvingly.

"That's our cue." Troy turned to Mercy. "We've got to get down to Jillian's office to sign the papers."

He wheeled her back to the truck, where the dogs were waiting.

"We can turn the key over to Harrington whenever you want." Mercy patted the right-side pocket of her cargo pants. "I've got it right here."

"Thanks. I don't want Harrington hounding the captain."

"Of course." Mercy grinned. "If only we knew someone who could pick a lock."

CHAPTER TWENTY-ONE

*A man complained that [on] his way home
to dinner he had every day to pass through that long
field of his neighbor's. I advised him to buy it,
and it would never seem long again.*
—RALPH WALDO EMERSON

NORTHSHIRE ROYAL REAL ESTATE WAS LOCATED RIGHT ON
Main Street, a couple of blocks down from Eggs Over Easy, in a
cupcake of a house called Bennett Cottage, painted in cream and white and
many, many shades of pink, from blush to raspberry, and flanked by mature
maples ablaze in color. "Cottage" was a misnomer, as the large house was
three stories high; the real estate office took up the bottom floor, and the
two upper floors had been converted into apartments. Mercy had had her fill
of sharing close quarters in the military, but if she were ever forced to live
in a village (hopefully never) or in an apartment (hopefully never squared),
Mercy would want to live in a place just like this.

Although maybe not at Halloween. In the spirit of the season, the pink-
and-white house was draped in bright-orange lights, its wraparound porch
punctuated with bright-orange pumpkins and lit by the golden glowing
maples on either side, giving the already cheerful place a slightly mania-
cal air. Even the wispy fog that obscured the other decorated storefronts
couldn't dampen this house's festive gaudiness.

Troy parked the Ford F-150 in the small lot beside the real estate office.
He helped her out of the truck, taking her elbow and guiding her carefully up to the porch. Elvis and Susie Bear followed a few feet behind
them, somehow knowing that Mercy needed the space.

She hopped up the stairs on her good foot, using her husband as a prop.
Mercy realized that the pain was easing up now, at least it was better than it
had been before. The throbbing was subsiding, which gratified and reassured

her. She needed to regain full mobility as quickly as possible. She had a bad feeling about the press conference, and she wanted to be mentally and physically prepared for whatever might transpire.

The door to the real estate office opened, and there stood Jillian in another one of her lively dresses, this one a pink-and-orange floral. Mercy understood now why the Realtor wore such bright colors: she had to compete with the cupcake house for attention.

Jillian led them into the office, which was a very modern take on Victorian, with walls papered with turquoise peacocks and magenta flowers and emerald vines, and framed with bright-white elaborate trim and moldings. The furniture was all glass and chrome and plastic and pleather; the refinished hardwood flooring a glowing maple.

"I've had seven offers come in since yours." Jillian led them to a long glass conference table with ghost chairs and waved them into their seats. The dogs curled up in opposite corners.

Jillian leaned across the table toward them. A pink folder and a crystal pen holder with a burgundy Montblanc pen were the table's only ornaments. "All for more money. One for literally twice as much money. *Twice as much.*"

"Are you saying the deal is off?" asked Troy.

"Nah. I kicked them all to the curb." She straightened up to address them officially. "The trust accepted your offer, and the agreement stands."

"Grackle Tree Farm is still ours." Mercy reached for her husband's hand. He clasped hers in his.

"You two are so adorable." Jillian giggled. "Let's get this signed right now." She removed a stack of papers from the pink folder, and pushed it across the table, handing Mercy the burgundy ballpoint pen. "The truth is, I'm glad that the place will be yours. You care about it, and it's been neglected for too long. And you're locals. And newlyweds."

Mercy and Troy each signed where instructed in turn.

"Congratulations." Jillian plucked her Montblanc from Troy's open palm and placed it carefully on its crystal stand. "Now, that's done." She folded her hands together as if in prayer, and smiled at Mercy. "Time to list that cabin of yours. Do you have an asking price in mind?"

NINETY MINUTES LATER, MERCY and Troy stepped outside onto the porch of the Northshire Royal Real Estate office.

"We have a house," she said.

"We have *the* house." He took her hand in his.

"*Our* house." She squeezed his hand.

In the time they'd been inside with Jillian, the entire town of North-shire had gone even more Halloween crazy. Main Street was significantly busier, cars honking as they shuttled down the thoroughfare from round-about to roundabout, people crowding the sidewalks and overflowing into the street. The streetlights, now festooned with witches and ghosts and bats and black cats, gave off an eerie glow in the patchy fog. The store-fronts had upped their game, competing with the cupcake house, decked out with purple and green and orange lights, skeletons and spiders and jack-o'-lanterns, broomsticks and skulls and haunted houses.

Many of the tourists and townspeople alike were already in costume. Mercy spotted princesses and cowboys and superheroes and all manner of ghouls and goblins. She wondered when Halloween had gone from little kids trick-or-treating up and down the streets where they lived one night a year to this 24/7 party that lasted all month.

"We'd better get over to the Town Hall." Troy glanced at his watch. "Are you sure you're up for that walk?"

"I'm sure." She checked Elvis's lead. Crowds made the shepherd hyper-vigilant; she wasn't crazy about them, either. People behaved badly in hordes; like the serpents that slinked together as one, spitting and sluic-ing and stabbing holes in stones, humans in a huddle took on a darker, meaner shape capable of far more destruction than the odd man out. All the wrong crowd needed was a righteous spark, and all hell would break loose.

"Backstreets."

"Backstreets." Mercy grasped the crutches together and pushed the pair toward Troy. "I'm done with these. They're just slowing me down."

"All right." Troy balanced them on his shoulder.

"We can just leave them here and pick them up later. Jillian won't care."

"I've got them. Just in case you change your mind."

"I won't. But keep your eye out for a good walking stick."

"Will do." Troy glanced around, and pointed to the maples that bor-dered the house. He placed the crutches up against the streetlight. "Be right back."

Mercy watched as he strode past the trees to the back of the yard, where someone had gathered a pile of fallen branches and fallen leaves. Fall cleanup. Practically every house had one tucked in a corner of the back garden this time of year.

He pulled out a five-foot-long branch about two-and-a-half inches in diameter, then tested its strength by poking it into the ground and leaning on it. Apparently satisfied, he slipped his hunting knife from its sheath on his work belt and sliced several slanted cuts at one end to a sharp point. Then he rid the branch of its remaining twigs, replaced his knife on his belt, and jogged back to her, bearing his gift.

"Madame, your walking stick. Made of the finest sugar maple, if not the finest carving."

"Thank you." She tried out the stick by taking a few steps. "Perfect." And it was.

They were off. Troy held both leashes in one hand, hoisting the crutches on his other shoulder. Mercy trudged along at a decent pace with far less discomfort than before. She was thrilled to be rid of the crutches.

They turned left at the first side street, the dogs heeling sweetly at their hips. It was only a short walk to village common.

Where Harrington was waiting.

CHAPTER TWENTY-TWO

Home isn't where you're from, it's where
you find light when all grows dark.
—PIERCE BROWN

WITH ITS FOUR IMPRESSIVE COLUMNS DOMINATING THE façade, the Northshire Town Hall was one of the most striking historic structures on the village green. The Greek Revival building had been built in 1832 as a private residence by a rich cattle-broker and presented to the town upon his death by his Parisian widow as a parting gift before she abandoned Vermont forever for Europe.

Despite its ostentation, Mercy had always admired the Town Hall, especially the view from the grand Palladian windows in the huge meeting room on the top floor, which overlooked the common, one of the loveliest green spaces in New England.

Certainly it was clear to Mercy that Detective Kai Harrington loved the Town Hall, too. She thought it was no accident that he'd chosen to conduct this press conference here rather than at the station, which was housed in a handsome, if humbler, structure. In a village mostly made up of Colonial and Federal-style buildings, the more ostentatious Town Hall stood out—a much better fit for the bombastic detective.

Harrington stood at a podium in the middle of the narrow porch that ran the length of the building, flanked by the towering columns. As instructed, Mercy waited with Troy and the dogs behind and to the left of the detective. With reluctant admiration, she observed the detective as he commanded center stage at the entrance of the celebrated Town Hall.

There was a huge crowd gathered on the green in front of the hall, whether to hear Harrington speak or pause as they enjoyed the common's many activities—pumpkin carving, bobbing for apples, face painting, apple cider and apple cider doughnuts, beer and burger booths, wine and cheese booths, even a haunted house—it was hard to know. But the palpable sense of excitement running through the swarms of people was real enough.

A line of police officers stood at the foot of the porch, protecting the detective and other town notables—the mayor, the fire commissioner, Feinberg, Lillian Jenkins, and others Mercy did not recognize—from the crush of locals, tourists, kids, hangers-on, and journalists. The press gathered closest to that police border, not only the Vermont media but some national television news crews as well. Someone—maybe Harrington himself—must have leaked the discovery of the letters to the press. Surely the murder of a private investigator from California was not sufficient on its own to attract such major media.

Mercy spotted the poets contingent, easily identified with their matching POETRY IS MY FIRST LANGUAGE T-shirts, some two dozen strong, led by Dr. Horace Boswell and Dr. Elisabeth Bardin.

They were quiet and respectful—at least, so far.

Troy nudged her, sliding his eyes in the direction of a large group of men and women in long gray cloaks and white tunics and trousers. They outnumbered the poets by at least two to one. Who knew there were so many Druids in Northshire? They were out in force, among them the trio that had approached them at the café. A grove of Druids, thought Mercy, although she couldn't help but think next of a murder of crows.

Another cluster of interested parties wore river vests and fedoras, like Indiana Jones going fly-fishing. Treasure hunters, maybe. Or a bachelor's party on a Halloween pub crawl, she wasn't sure.

A Brownie troop was there, aided by their older Girl Scout sisters and several troop leaders. A loose confluence of teenagers in NORTHSHIRE HIGH SCHOOL WARRIORS sweatshirts wore hawker trays full of Halloween candy, which they were apparently meant to be selling to support the football team. But most of the kids were on their phones.

A fright of ghosts haunted the edges of the crowd, along with the usual zombies and scarecrows and skeletons. Freddy Kruegers and Screams and Batmans and Supermans. She scanned the crowd for men in Spider-Man masks, but she didn't see any.

The clock on the Church on the Green struck eleven, and the bell began to chime the hour. As if on cue, the fog lifted and the sun shone bright on Harrington. The patron saint of PR.

The detective, always a stickler for promptness, tapped the standing microphone to capture the attention of the gathering horde. He began by giving the public an update on the state of the investigation into the murder of Max Vinke and the assault on Thrasher and Mercy. He reassured everyone that the captain was recuperating and that Mercy was fine. He didn't introduce her, which pleased her, although his failure to do so meant he must have some other, perhaps more unfortunate, reason for requesting her presence here.

Harrington went on to say that there was no threat to public safety and that law enforcement was doing everything possible to apprehend the perpetrators. The detective then invited the mayor, Daniel Feinberg, and Lillian Jenkins to join him at the podium. Lillian Jenkins was Mercy's grandmother's best friend and arguably Northshire's fiercest citizen.

Every commission, charity, and nonprofit in town counted on the support of the industrious and indefatigable Lillian, who knew everything about everybody in town. Partly because she was by nature nosy; partly because, as a justice of the peace, she'd married half the county; and partly because she was the owner and proprietor of the Vermonter Drive-In, home of the best burger in the state. Sooner or later, no matter who you were, you crossed paths with Lillian, and she remembered you, and before you knew it, you'd volunteered to help do something for somebody somewhere in the county.

Mercy had known Lillian all her life, as had Troy, and they were mostly better for it. They had her to thank for the early viewing of the estate—and no doubt they'd be volunteering for some worthy project or other not long after closing.

The mayor greeted his audience and invited Lillian to speak. The tiny brunette with the big personality stepped forward, the picture of a well-dressed patron of the arts in a burnt-orange knit dress and knee-high black boots.

"Happy Halloween," she called out merrily, and the crowd cheered. "We of the Northshire Arts Commission welcome you to our lovely village during this loveliest time of year. We have exciting news: thanks to the remarkable efforts of Mercy Carr, Floyd Thrasher, Troy Warner, Gil Guerrette, and everybody's favorite working dogs, Elvis and Susie Bear, a heretofore unknown literary treasure has come to light after nearly eighty years."

She clapped, waiting for Mercy and Troy and the dogs to step forward and be acknowledged. They did the do-si-do quickly, and the crowd applauded along with Lillian. They stepped back, and Lillian resumed her speech.

"On behalf of the town and the commission, we are thrilled to announce the discovery of letters written by the legendary poet, Northshire's own Euphemia Whitney-Jones. You all know her children's poems, especially her most famous poem, 'The Ghost Witch of Grackle Tree.' I learned it at school—and I'm sure you did, too. Whitney-Jones's poems are still popular with children today. But she also wrote volumes of poems for adults, classic verses about women and men and nature and society that stand the test of time.

"This correspondence is a wonderful addition to the literary canon. The letters are being examined by experts in the field as we speak. More to come, but we wanted you to know about this. And how appropriate that we renew our acquaintance with Euphemia Whitney-Jones at Halloween, the time of year when so much of her work was set."

Lillian introduced Feinberg, who spoke briefly about the appraisal process and the plans to display the letters at a special reception at a later date.

Feinberg then ceded the podium to Harrington as the press and the poets and the Druids and the treasure hunters clamored for more information. They were all throwing out questions as they jockeyed for position.

"We got off easy," Mercy whispered to Troy. She was relieved that they'd played such a limited role in the proceedings.

"It's not over till it's over," warned Troy.

"We will have a short Q&A period," Harrington promised the increasingly restless crowd. "But first, I want to congratulate the newly named king and queen of this year's HOWLoween Puppy Parade and Party. The hero dogs we've honored today, Elvis and Susie Bear, will be accompanied by their humans, Mercy Carr and Troy Warner, at this wonderful event. Let's give these K-9 warriors and their handlers a big hand."

"Oh no," said Mercy. "No, no, no."

"I knew he was up to something. Don't worry, no way we're doing this. Not with your foot. Easy out."

"Come on, guys, don't be shy," said Harrington. "Step on up here."

Mercy didn't move.

"Smile." Troy gently looped his arm in hers. "We'll fight this battle later."

She smiled through gritted teeth and stumped over to the podium with her husband, Elvis and Susie Bear at their respective hips. She brought the proud Malinois around in front of her and nudged him to strike a pose, handsome head raised, ears up, a profile in canine courage if there ever was one. Oblivious to the fact that he would soon be subjected to the indignities of a costume.

And for what? For HOWLoween—seriously, HOWLoween?—leading Chihuahua piñatas and hot-dogging dachshunds and lionized golden retrievers up and down Main Street and around the common to the cheers and jeers of onlookers. The thought of it was almost too much to bear.

Elvis was handling the unwanted attention far better than she. He held his nose and his tail high, and the crowd went wild. Susie Bear plopped down next to him, and the crowd went wilder. Mercy envied the Newfie her happy-go-lucky poise. Of course the Miss Congeniality of Dogs would love being queen; she'd actually enjoy the parade. Out of the four of them, Susie Bear alone would thrive in the spotlight, while Mercy and Troy and Elvis would blister in shame.

Harrington made way for Lillian, who returned to the microphone, pausing to scratch Susie Bear's big shaggy head.

"You won't want to miss this fabulous opportunity to showcase your furry four-legged friends," said Lillian. "There will be lots of prizes for the best costumes. Pet parents are eligible for prizes as well, so be sure to dress up along with your dogs. And if you don't have a dog, or you're thinking of getting your pooch a pal, be sure to come to our pet-adoption fair. We'll have wonderful companions waiting to be your new best friend. All proceeds benefit local animal rescues and our K-9 working dogs, who risk their lives to keep us safe. Just like Elvis and Susie Bear here—who'll be available for photo ops. I'm just saying. So sign up now!"

Mercy kept on smiling, but inside she was cursing. And Harrington was laughing. She could see him gloating out of the corner of her eye.

She glanced up at Troy, who kept his gaze on some distant point on the horizon. A trick she knew he used to maintain his composure when he was tempted to overreact.

"Thank you, Lillian." Harrington was back at the podium. He checked his Rolex and cleared his throat. "We have just enough time for a few quick questions before we move on to the main stage in the center of the common, where the Zombie Spells will kick off the start of our all-day-long musical entertainment."

Mercy had to admit Harrington was at his best with a microphone in his hand. "He should have been a game show host," she whispered to Troy as they moved away from the detective and the other local dignitaries. "He missed his calling."

"Come on down!" teased Troy.

"Not."

They retreated slowly, hoping to escape before the detective or the mayor or Lillian or Feinberg noticed—and before the shouting started. Members of the press were haranguing Harrington about the murder, speaking over one another in a barrage of pointed questions for the detective. The poets were closing in on the journalists, trying to shoulder their way through the wave of reporters to the microphone they'd set up for questions from the local citizenry—as opposed to the press, who carried their own mics. The Druids were close on the poets' heels, as were the treasure hunters.

Everyone was talking at once, just as they had at Eggs Over Easy, but here the naysayers were far more numerous and the protestations were far more forceful. Individual cries of "Poets Have Rights, Too!" and "Save the Trees!" and "X Never, Ever Marks the Spot!" became chants.

The Brownies got restless, breaking ranks, and the Girl Scouts began chasing them down. The high schoolers abandoned their candy-sales mission altogether and started filming the ruckus with their cell phones.

All the passersby stopped to watch and listen and chime in if moved to do so. Most just stood and gawked, but lots of little kids ran wild while their parents and grandparents tried to pull them all away, no doubt resorting to bribes of fried dough and cotton candy and candied apples. Not to mention the Zombie Spells, who were due to appear on the bandstand shortly.

The wind picked up, scattering a cascade of autumn leaves on the crowd like rice at a wedding. *Elisabeth with an s* was at the mic, trying to make herself heard. She kept raising her voice, but all anyone could hear was the screech of feedback. Boswell tried to help her, but people were pushing and shoving, trying to get to the microphone. The poets faltered, and fell. One of the Druids—the tall stooped guy with the beard—reached out to help them. They all stumbled, and went down in the crush of people. The Druids and the poets scrambled to pull their fallen comrades to their feet.

"It's like a mosh pit out there."

"We need to get you out of here before you get hurt again."

The line of police officers wavered a little in the face of the surging mass of people. The mayor pushed Harrington aside, and called for order. The journalists scattered to the sides, having figured out that the story was now the people, not the politicians.

"What about Lillian?" Mercy tried to find her in the chaos, but there was no sign of her at the entrance.

"Feinberg will take care of her. She'll be fine."

Troy was right. Feinberg had bodyguards who shadowed him during his public appearances; they'd probably already ushered Lillian and Daniel off the village green and into his massive extended Audi A8L. Odds were Lillian was drinking champagne about now. The good stuff.

The dogs were getting nervous. Elvis whined and pulled on the leash. His way of telling her it was time to go. Even the usually chill Susie Bear was bouncing up and down on her large paws, a sure sign that she was agitated, too.

"Lean on me."

"No need. I still have my walking stick."

"I'll take the leashes, then."

"What about the crutches?"

"I'd leave them if I were sure none of these numbskulls wouldn't use them inappropriately. But I'm not, so I'm taking them."

Mercy nodded. "Better safe than sorry."

Troy let out a low whistle, a signal to the dogs that it was time to move and stay alert. Together they reached the far end of the Town Hall's temple front. There was a two-foot drop at the edge, which was bordered by a raised bed of huge hydrangeas. Troy hopped down after the dogs and dropped the crutches he carried over one shoulder. He told the dogs to stay and let the leashes slip to the ground. He placed his large hands around Mercy's waist and lifted her up and over the bushes, resting her lightly onto the grass.

"Thank you." She smiled up at him, and he leaned down to give her a kiss.

Troy shouldered the crutches, and took the leads in one hand and her arm in the other. He led her and the dogs away from the crowds on the common and down a little-used marble walkway along the side of the Town Hall. A kind of alley, really, although a beautifully landscaped one, with tall sugar maples on the outside and the same kind of large hydrangeas that bordered the porch of the Town Hall on the building side.

It was still windy, and with the quickening breeze came an increasing chill. They weren't moving very fast down the path, but nobody seemed to mind. As they walked along, Elvis and Susie Bear stopped to sniff and mark most every one of the huge bushes, which grew so very close together they served as a long and deep hedge, the alley obviously having served as a favorite destination for other dogs in town.

"Are we there yet?" Mercy was glad that they were going home.

"I'd be happy to carry you the rest of the way."

Elvis whined again, stopping short and sinking into his classic Sphinx position in front of one of the largest of the hydrangeas along the marble walk.

"Now what?" asked Troy.

Susie Bear barked, and shuffled over to Elvis. She shimmied, her thick wavy coat shining, and stretched out beside the Malinois, plumed tail thumping, fallen leaves flying.

"Always trust your dog." Mercy stepped forward, separating the branches of the bushes with her walking stick. "There's a little hidden nook in here with a bench. Somebody's sleeping there."

Troy dropped the crutches, and crashed through the branches to take a look.

"I'm not sure he's sleeping."

CHAPTER TWENTY-THREE

*Go where he will, the wise man is at home, His hearth
the earth, his hall the azure dome.*
—RALPH WALDO EMERSON

I CAN'T TELL FROM HERE IF HE'S DEAD OR ALIVE," SAID TROY.
"He might just be passed out."

"In the bushes?"

"It wouldn't be the first time."

That was true enough, thought Mercy, remembering all the inebriated soldiers she'd arrested and hauled back to base when she was with the military police. Drunks had an uncanny knack for finding any safe harbor—toolshed, picnic table, laundry room, she'd even found one guy in a casket—where they could sleep it off in relative peace.

Mercy held the hydrangea branches back with her walking stick, and Troy shouldered through the narrow break in the bushes to the back. She could see that the shrubs had been sheared back away from the building here, leaving a space about three feet deep for the bench.

"It's a weird place for a bench. How would he even know it's here?"

"He must know this property. Or maybe the bushes have grown together over the summer, hiding the bench." Troy squatted down to get a better look. "I think it's one of the Druids. He's alive. But he doesn't look very good. And there's some evidence here that he's been sick to his stomach."

"Under the influence?" *A drunken Druid.*

"I can't tell. But he needs help. His breathing is shallow."

"What can I do?"

"Not sure yet. Let me get him out of here."

Through the branches, Mercy watched Troy slip his hands under the guy's arms, pull him up, and carry him through the bushes to the path. She helped Troy lay the man out on the path, using her jacket as a pillow. "How'd he even get back there?"

"In his state, it's hard to say. Luck and determination, I'm guessing." Troy pointed to the broken branches and disturbed leaves on the ground. "Here's where he went in."

"It's a good place to hide. Maybe he was hiding."

"From what?"

"I don't know." She looked harder at the ground. "There's a partial print here." Mercy stabbed her stick near an impression of what appeared to be half a boot. "A lot of the treasure hunters were wearing boots."

"And the Druids?"

"I didn't notice." Mercy studied the man while Troy took his pulse. He was a fairly young man, with even features and an attempt at a circle beard that was more like a wispy pale-brown mustache and stubbled chin patch than bona fide beard. His brown hair hung to his shoulders in lank clumps.

"Pulse is weak, but it could be worse."

"No alcohol on his breath."

The man was dressed in the signature Druid costume of white tunic and pants and gray cloak. Mercy unbuttoned the top buttons of his tunic to make him more comfortable, revealing a small black Celtic oak tree tattoo between his sternum and the hollow of his throat. "Definitely one of the Druids."

The man tried to sit up but fell back again, closing his eyes. He pulled his legs up to his chest, as if his stomach hurt.

"We need to get him some help."

"Steady, guy. We'll call an ambulance."

"No," whispered the man, eyes still closed, his face pale under the wannabe beard. "No."

"They must have an emergency tent somewhere on the common." Mercy pulled out her phone and checked the town website. "There's a first aid station on the south side of the common, not far from the First Congregational Church. There should be an ambulance on call, too, given the size of the event."

"Right. I'll take him there to get checked out. You can stay here with the dogs."

"No way. I'm coming with you."

The man touched his own face with thick fingers. "Tingling."

"Let's go." Mercy looked at Troy. "I'm worried about . . ." Her voice trailed off, and she mouthed the last word to Troy so the man wouldn't hear her. *Poison*.

"What's your name?" Troy asked the man.

"Varden Lind," the man said, with some effort. "My chest hurts."

"Okay, Varden, let's get you up." Troy tried to help Varden to his feet, but the man's legs gave way, and he collapsed against her husband's broad chest.

"Numb."

"No worries, I've got you." Troy heaved him onto his shoulder, and the man moaned in pain.

"Stomach pains and chest pain." To Mercy's mind, this was more evidence that he could have been poisoned.

"Understood."

"Go on ahead. Don't worry about me and the dogs. We'll be right behind you, and if we fall back, we'll catch up."

Troy frowned.

"I've got Elvis and Susie Bear with me. I'll be fine."

"Leave the crutches here. Unless you need them."

"I don't need them." Mercy pushed them under the hedge with her good foot. "Go."

Troy strode off, and Mercy, armed with the walking stick and the dogs, followed him down the path along the Town Hall and onto the wide trail that led, as all the main pathways did, to the center of the common.

"Coming through," warned Troy, and those strolling down the gravel pathway parted, some more quickly than others. Several asked if he needed help, and one tall, thin handlebar-mustached man dressed in lederhosen and a Tyrolean hat—as if he were at Oktoberfest in Bavaria rather than a Halloween festival in Vermont—took it upon himself to clear the crowd, yelling out, "Make way!" in a booming voice worthy of an Alpine horn.

A very effective strategy, of which Elvis and Susie Bear clearly approved. The dogs pulled Mercy along, mostly ignoring her admonitions to *"heel!"* and to walk *"with me!"* They passed the high school students still (not) selling their Halloween candy and the Brownies chasing one another up and down the green, all attempts at order forgotten. Other cliques of teenagers dressed like goths were hanging out on the grass, while their elders watched the commotion from the safety of park benches. At the center of the common rose the restored *Fountain of the Muses*, marking the fulcrum of the wheel where all the pathways on the common converged. Vendors sold popcorn and balloons, and parents helped their children make wishes and flip coins into one of the three tiers of the flowing fountain.

Troy took the third path off the pedestrian roundabout, the one that angled off toward the old church that anchored the other end of the common. With relief, Mercy spotted the red-and-white first aid tent to the left of the small church graveyard. She quickened her pace as much as she dared, much to the delight of the dogs, who were desperate to catch up to Troy. Thanks to the walking stick, she was feeling only slight pain, although she was sure that adrenaline was part of the amelioration. No doubt she'd be sorry later.

Herr Lederhosen held the tent flap open, and Troy disappeared into the station with Varden Lind. Mercy followed.

"You plan on taking those dogs in there?" asked the Oktoberfest guy.

"Yes, unless you're volunteering to stay with them."

The tall man stared at Susie Bear, who wagged her tail at him, and Elvis, who regarded him with indifference. "Are they friendly?"

"More or less. The shaggy one, yes; the shepherd, not so much. But they won't hurt you."

"Okay."

"Stay," she told the dogs, holding her palm down toward the ground for extra emphasis, and then addressed the man. "I'm Mercy Carr."

"Marcus Renner."

She handed Renner the leads. "Be right back."

In the tent, she found Troy talking to one of the medics manning the station. Varden Lind was lying on a stretcher, with a couple of EMTs at his side. He still looked unwell.

Troy introduced her to Jacob Moreno, lead medic.

"How is he?" she asked.

"His blood pressure is low, and his heart rate is two hundred beats per minute. Very elevated."

"Do you think it could be poison?"

"Why do you say that?"

"Vomit at the scene. And we've already had one poisoning this week."

"I thought that was cyanide." Jacob raised his eyebrows.

"That's right, but it may have been cyanide made from cherry pits or pits of cherry leaves. Served in an herbal tea or salad or something."

"That seems unlikely."

"I know. But there's a poisoner out there somewhere, and there are all kinds of poisons they could be using. And he has experienced gastrointestinal distress, so you should check him for poison."

Jacob turned to Varden, who was at least still conscious. "What have you eaten in the past twenty-four hours? Any herbal teas, wild mushrooms?"

"Vegetable stew," said Varden. "For dinner last night. Oatmeal for breakfast. Herbal tea, all day, every day."

"If it is poison, the fact that you vomited could be a good sign. But we need to get you to the hospital for a full tox screen."

Mercy and Troy watched as they prepared to take their patient off to Northshire Medical Center.

"Thank you," said Varden, as two of the EMTs lifted the stretcher.

Mercy nodded. "Take care of yourself."

The EMTs headed for the ambulance, and Mercy and Troy followed in their wake. Outside, they found Renner with two very impatient dogs. Mercy introduced him to Troy and thanked him for watching Elvis and Susie Bear.

"They weren't very happy here with me."

"Don't take it personally," said Mercy. "They just like to be where the action is."

"I can see that." Renner handed Troy the leads. "Is that guy going to be all right?"

"We hope so."

"Thanks again for your help." Mercy smiled at him. "We'll let you get back to the festivities."

"No problem."

He bounced off toward the beer tent, his Tyrolean hat slipping a bit.

Troy looked at Mercy. "Now what?"

"We start with the Druids."

"You think whatever happened to Varden Lind is connected to what happened to Max Vinke and you and Thrasher? Seems like a stretch."

"I know." Mercy scanned the village green for cloaks. "But two poisonings in as many days? That can't be a coincidence. I don't know what Lind has to do with any of this, but I think we should try to find out."

"Starting with who he is and why anyone would want to poison him."

"Exactly. Let's go talk to Oisin, if we can find him. He may know Varden Lind."

"The Arch-Druid," said Troy.

"He is their leader." The common was even more packed with people now, most of whom were in costume. Lots of cloaks and capes and sweeping coats muddying Mercy's search for Druids.

"All the more reason for him to lie to protect his flock. Or whatever you call a bunch of Druids."

"A grove," said Mercy automatically.

"What?"

"It's a grove of Druids. Because they worship trees."

Troy, too, was on the lookout, studying the crowd. "Any particular trees?"

"Oaks, ashes, elders—"

"Apples. Merlin liked apple trees."

"Tree of fruitfulness, tree of transformation, tree of true love."

"True love didn't work out too well for Merlin."

"You're right." Mercy laughed. "He did better with transformation."

Troy stared across the green, focusing on one spot, and Mercy followed his gaze.

A cluster of people were dancing in the grass by the bandstand, where the Zombie Spells' version of the Talking Heads' "Psycho Killer" was echoing across the common.

"I think I see some Druids over there. Who knew they liked Halloween tribute bands?"

"Is there such a thing?"

He laughed as the Zombie Spells launched into "Vampire" by Dominic Fike. "There is now."

"Then let's go dance with the Druids."

CHAPTER TWENTY-FOUR

There is a magic in that little world, home; it is
a mystic circle that surrounds comforts and virtues
never know beyond its hallowed limits.
—ROBERT SOUTHEY

T HE BANDSTAND WAS ONE OF THOSE VICTORIAN-ERA GAZEBOS
made of wood and iron that anchored so many of the commons
in Vermont. Mercy believed that Northshire's white octagonal pavilion
bandstand, with its cupola and wrought-iron fencing, was one of the
prettiest in New England. She doubted the town's forefathers would have
condoned today's Halloween festivities, much less appreciated the music
of the Zombie Spells.

They headed toward the bandstand, but Elvis and Susie Bear did not
stay to the gravel pathways. Which was fine by Mercy. With Troy at her
side, she tromped along in her boot with her walking stick across the wide
expanse of lawn, maneuvering around the people lying about on blankets
and beach chairs with their ice chests and picnic baskets.

Mercy felt as if she were already in a costume of sorts. All she needed
was a cloak, and she might be taken for a Druid herself. She wondered
what god-awful costumes Harrington and Lillian would insist they wear
as king and queen of the dog parade. However humiliated she might
feel, she was sure that Elvis would be even more mortified. But maybe it
wouldn't come to that.

"Do you really think you can get us out of HOWLoween?"

"Even Harrington can't argue with doctor's orders."

The music—a screaming cover of "Bat Out of Hell" that would do
Meat Loaf proud—pulsed louder and louder as they approached the left
side of the bandstand. The sun had come out and the wind had died down,

and now in midafternoon, the chilly fog of the morning had given way to a splendid sunny autumn day, the kind tourists flock to Vermont to enjoy.

Mercy spotted Oisin perched on a walk-stool under an old Northern red oak. "There he is, Troy."

"Holding court."

"Sort of." Oisin was indeed surrounded by his fellow Druids, scattered around their leader in radiating semicircles around him. But he did not appear to be addressing his congregation. This was a casual grouping; some of the Druids were dancing to the music, some were eating and drinking, some were playing with their becaped children. Some were simply napping.

As she stood there with Troy and the dogs at the edge of Oisin's crescent, she thought they seemed more like a family on an outing in the park than a religious people practicing some sort of ancient ritual. Although, given the Druids' reverence for nature and the changing of the seasons, maybe being outside on a village green dotted with maples and oaks and beeches aglow with color during one of Mother Nature's most dramatic annual transitions was in fact a very Druidic thing to do. She'd have to look it up.

"I see Liath, the one with the pink hair, sitting to Oisin's right."

"And Muirne, the elegant Druid."

"She is elegant. If my mother were a Druid, she'd look like that."

Troy made a stricken face, and she laughed. "I know, I know, it's a terrifying thought. Human sacrifice and all that."

"I love your mother. But let's not give her any ideas." Troy kept his eyes on the Druids. "I don't see the bodyguards."

"I don't, either. But if their job is to protect the Arch-Druid, they should be here somewhere."

"Let's go find out."

"You go ahead. You may get more out of him if we don't all rush him at once."

"Good point."

"We'll stay close, but not too close."

Mercy skirted the edge of the curve of recreating Druids, heading for Oisin. Troy and the dogs followed at a discreet distance. When he saw her coming, the tall Arch-Druid slowly rose to his full height, his long white beard rippling in the light breeze. He was seemingly rooted as firmly in the earth as the magnificent oak that towered over him. Liath and Muirne hovered nearby.

"Mercy Carr."

"Oisin."

Out here on the common in the dappled sunlight, Oisin appeared older and more distinguished than he had at Eggs Over Easy. Like the other Druids, he wore a hag stone around his neck on a black cord. His cloak was drawn closely around his narrow chest, and for the first time, she noticed the clasp that held the two sides of the long cape together. The beautifully fashioned bronze fastener was made of twin Trinity Celtic knots. The Celtic knot represented the power of three and meant many things to many people: *Life, death, and rebirth. Father, Son, and Holy Ghost. Past, present, and future.* Mercy wondered which most resonated with the Arch-Druid.

"How are you?" He looked her over. "Are you okay?"

"I hurt my foot yesterday. But I've got my walking stick."

"I heard about that. I'm so sorry."

Seemed like everyone in Northshire knew about the shooting, Mercy thought. She soldiered on. "We need to ask you about one of your fellow Druids."

"Who is that?" His light gray eyes seemed kind but guarded.

"Varden Lind."

Oisin frowned. "I don't think I know a Varden Lind."

He held up a noble hand in the direction of Liath and Muirne. The women had kept a low profile during Mercy and Oisin's conversation but had obviously been eavesdropping. They both stepped forward, one on each side of the pagan priest, like two Beefeaters protecting their king. "Do we know a Varden Lind?"

Mercy described the long-haired young man with the straggly mustache and beard. "Dressed like a Druid, with a Celtic oak tree tattoo at the top of his sternum."

Liath bobbed forward, her pink ponytail bouncing up and down. "I don't think so."

"No," said Muirne. "I think I'd remember someone with a name like that."

Oisin turned to Liath and Muirne. "Let's spread the word. Maybe someone knows who this man is." He dug into one of his cloak's deep pockets, pulling out a cell phone.

A *twenty-first-century Druid,* thought Mercy. They exchanged phone numbers, and the Arch-Druid promised to let her know if they found out anything about the man.

"I understand someone else has been poisoned." He folded his hands over his staff, a tall and imposing Druidic Moses. "Could this be your Varden Lind?"

Mercy couldn't believe how quickly and efficiently the grapevine in this village worked. She didn't say anything.

"I understand the need for discretion. But you might want to talk to Adah Beecher."

Adah was the woman she'd met in the garden at the estate that first day. The day Elvis had found Max Vinke dead in the library. She started to ask Oisin about her, but as she began to speak, he swept away, disappearing into the throng of people milling about on the common. Liath and Muirne hurried after him.

Mercy was tired and hungry, and her foot was aching again. Elvis nosed her hand with his long dark muzzle. The clever shepherd always knew when she was hurting.

So did Troy. "Let's go home."

"We need to talk to Adah Beecher."

"We have to get on the road first. Let's get you back across the common to the Town Hall. You can wait there with the dogs, and I'll go get the truck."

"I am perfectly capable of walking back to Jillian's office. It's not far."

"You are a very stubborn woman." He took her arm, and between his support and her walking stick, the jaunt was doable.

Still, the cupcake real estate office was a sight for sore eyes—and feet. Troy snapped off their leashes, and the dogs darted ahead through the parking lot. As they approached the Ford F-150, Troy clicked open the lock.

"Hey!"

Troy spun around, and Mercy pivoted more slowly, surprised to see Becker and Goodlove jogging up to them.

"Where are you going?" demanded Becker.

"I'm taking Mercy and the dogs home," said Troy.

"You need to stay here."

"We're leaving, Becker."

"We can't let you do that," said Goodlove.

A bold statement. Troy gave her a look that would intimidate all but the toughest cops, and she stepped back.

Becker held up his hand. "Troy, Harrington is on his way. He wants to talk to you both."

Troy regarded Mercy with concern. "We should gave gotten out of here while the getting was good."

"What does he want?" asked Mercy, always skeptical of the detective's motives.

"Something about a key," said Becker. "He's not very happy."

Oh no, thought Mercy. She'd forgotten all about it. She and Troy exchanged a look. One of those looks that Becker and Goodlove could see meant trouble.

"What did you do, Mercy?" asked Becker. "I mean, besides turn up front and center to every major crime scene in the county this week. And then leaving some apparently important information out of your statements."

"It's a long story."

"Talk fast." The young officer hooked his thumbs in his belt and leaned back, attempting to look as authoritative as he could, or at least as authoritative as Troy. Which was never going to happen, no matter how long Becker was in law enforcement. Her husband had the solid strength and commanding presence of a mature oak, while Becker was more like a young birch. But Mercy gave him points for trying.

"Okay." She told them about the old brass key she'd found with the letters.

"Let me get this straight." Becker cleared his throat. "You have something that may lead to another literary treasure."

"That's about it."

"No wonder Harrington is so pissed off," said Goodlove.

"What does it unlock?" asked Becker.

"I don't know," said Mercy.

Becker regarded her balefully. "Come on."

"I don't. Maybe it opens a safe or something."

"And you haven't looked for it."

"No."

Becker crossed his arms. "I'm not an idiot."

"I haven't had time to figure out what it fits."

"Why didn't you turn it in right away?"

"Honestly, in all the chaos, I forgot all about it."

"Seriously."

"I did get shot, you know." She pointed to the orthopedic boot she wore to protect her foot.

"Harrington is going to want it. And whatever it goes to."

"Honestly, I do *not* know." Mercy shook her head. "So much of what has happened these last few days doesn't make any sense."

"You think they're all connected?" asked Goodlove. "The Vinke murder and the attack on you and Thrasher and the letters and now this?"

"Probably."

"You left out the poisoned Druid." Troy bit back a grin.

"Sweet Mother of God," said Goodlove.

"Seems like a stretch to me." Becker gave her a confounded look. "Could just be a coincidence."

"I don't trust coincidences," said Mercy.

"Me, either," said Troy.

"This time of year, there are so many people *from away*." Becker sighed. "Most of them are all right, I guess, but all it takes is a few lunatics and look what happens. Halloween brings out the worst in people."

"Greed brings out the worst in people. Greed and envy and vengeance." The way this week was going, Mercy could count all of these as triggers for violence. Greed for a treasure, found or unfound. Envy over a beloved, favored or forsaken. Vengeance for a betrayal, past or present.

The sound of a vehicle reached them, rich with the growl of a luxury SUV. Harrington's Lincoln Navigator, no doubt. The detective steered his shiny black SUV into the parking lot, roaring up to within a stone's throw of Troy's truck.

Elvis leapt, tail up.

"Here he comes," said Troy.

They all stood silent as the detective advanced on them like a one-man avenging army. Thrasher was on his flank, looking a little worse for the wear and moving none too quickly.

"Thrasher. That can't be good," whispered Goodlove, saying out loud what the rest of them were thinking.

"I have a terrible feeling this isn't going to go well." Becker hooked his thumbs in his belt. "At all."

No doubt Becker was correct, thought Mercy. "Let me do all the talking. That way it's all on me."

"No way." Troy put his arm around her. "We're in this together."

"No, we're not. I'm the only one here Harrington can't fire."

"Or *get* fired," pointed out Becker.

Becker was right. As head of the Criminal Division's Major Crime Unit, part of the Department of Public Safety's Vermont State Police, Harrington could fire Becker and Goodlove easily. It would be harder for him to get Troy fired, as he reported to Thrasher in the Fish & Wildlife Department, which fell under Vermont's Agency of Natural Resources. Still, there was no denying Harrington's influence. He was the king of managing up, and the darling of the powers that be in Vermont. Given this, maybe it was time to call a truce, thought Mercy, for everyone's sake. Especially her husband's.

But first she'd have to defuse Harrington's arguably justifiable anger. She felt the metal piece in her pocket, and pulled it out, hiding it in her closed fist. *The best defense is a good offense.*

Harrington angled toward them, coming to an abrupt halt only inches from Mercy's booted foot. Elvis growled.

"It's okay, Elvis." She smiled warmly. "It's our friend, Detective Harrington." Before the detective could say anything, Mercy held out her fist and uncurled her fingers, revealing the old brass key. "I think this may be what you're looking for."

Harrington stared at her. They all did.

"I'm so sorry," Mercy went on. "Between the letters and the poisonings and the shootings, I totally forgot about it. It's been in my pocket the whole time. Can you imagine?"

The detective gave her a sideways glance. "You failed to turn over vital evidence in a murder case."

"And I'm so sorry about that." Mercy could tell he wasn't quite buying her act. She leaned forward, still smiling warmly. "You know, we just found out that we're going to have a baby. Chalk it up to pregnancy brain."

Harrington cleared his throat. "Congratulations," he managed to say before plucking the key from her palm with the silk handkerchief from the breast pocket of his custom-tailored jacket.

"Mercy's had a long day." Troy was playing along nicely. "We really need to get her home. Doctor's orders."

"Just one thing." Harrington slipped the handkerchief holding the key into his breast pocket. Order restored. "You will still be in attendance at the K-9 events?"

"We wouldn't miss it for the world," said Mercy, the warm smile still plastered on her face. It was beginning to hurt. "Right, Elvis?"

The shepherd barked on cue.

"Right. See you at HOWLoween—and *not* before." The detective stalked off without a backward glance, Becker and Goodlove huffing after him.

Leaving Mercy, Troy, the dogs, and Thrasher standing there.

"You should still be in the hospital," said Mercy.

"Look who's talking."

"Mercy is right, Captain. How are you feeling?"

"Better than I look."

"Good. I mean—"

"I know what you mean." Thrasher's voice was kind.

"Yes, sir."

"Stop *sir*-ing me, I'm fine. Besides, look what happens when I'm not around. I had to get out of that hospital so I could save your ass. Both your asses." He grinned. "Although, after that little performance, maybe you can get along just as well without me."

"Never," said Mercy. "Where's Wyetta?"

"I sent her home. Like I'm sending you home. Right now." Thrasher looked at Troy. "No patrols for you for the foreseeable future. Stay with your wife."

"Thank you, sir." Troy took Mercy's hand. "We're on our way. Do you need a ride, Captain?"

"I'm good." He gave Mercy a quick hug. "Thank you for saving my life. And congratulations on the baby."

"Thank you."

"Try to stay out of trouble. Promise me."

"I promise."

Thrasher laughed, sounding more like himself. "I had no idea you were such a good liar."

CHAPTER TWENTY-FIVE

Home interprets heaven. Home is heaven for beginners.
—CHARLES HENRY PARKHURST

"W E REALLY SHOULD GO HOME." TROY KEPT HIS EYES ON THE
road as he maneuvered the truck around the rotary at the end of
Main Street.

"What I really need is a little refreshment." Mercy reached over and
placed her hand on Troy's shoulder.

"Your wish is my command."

Mercy laughed. "At least for the next six months."

They headed down Route 7. She was thrilled when Troy pulled over at
the Vermonter Drive-In. "Good call."

"I know that you're going to be doing the real work here. But what I
can do is keep you well-rested and well-fed and well-hydrated." He parked
at the edge of the crowded lot, by the vintage neon theater sign that read
DRIVE-IN in bright white letters. "Stay right there." After jumping out of
the Ford F-150, he jogged around to her side of the vehicle. He opened the
door for her, and lifted her out, depositing her gently onto the ground.

"Thank you." Mercy appreciated his chivalry, now more than ever.
She searched for a place to sit, but every picnic table, bench, and boulder
appeared to be taken. People were everywhere, all hungry for Lillian Jenkins's famous burgers and milkshakes.

"I'll check the back."

There was a table in the potager garden behind the lean-to style restaurant where Lillian grew the herbs and vegetables that helped make her

food stand out. It was usually reserved for Lillian's own guests. "I really could use something to eat."

"It has been a long time since breakfast."

And a very eventful time, she thought.

"I'll be right back." Troy huffed toward the Vermonter, bypassing the lines of customers waiting to order and pick up their food, and disappeared around the back.

Mercy leaned back against the door of the truck. The dogs were still in the back seat, their heads out the window, their tongues hanging out in anticipation of the beef to come. Mercy looked past their glistening muzzles to the old theater sign. Lillian liked to run quotations where the titles of films had once appeared.

Today it read:

> MAGIC IS REALLY VERY SIMPLE,
> ALL YOU'VE GOT TO DO IS WANT SOMETHING
> AND THEN LET YOURSELF HAVE IT.
> —AGGIE CROMWELL

Lillian Jenkins knew that what tourists and locals alike wanted was a burger and a shake, Mercy thought.

Troy was back. "The VIP table is all ours." He reached down and clicked the leashes on Elvis and Susie Bear. They took the long way around the restaurant to the back, where a high privacy fence enclosed a back garden. A white wrought-iron table and chairs topped with blue-and-white-striped cushions graced the small patio.

Mercy sat down, and breathed in the sweet smell of burgers and fries.

"I'll go check on the food."

"Sounds good." She closed her eyes and gave her face up to the afternoon autumn sun. Elvis scrambled up and laid his handsome head in her lap. Not to be outdone, Susie Bear lumbered up as well, and placed her big shaggy head next to the shepherd's sleek muzzle. Where on earth would she put the baby once it was born? She closed her eyes again and indulged in a little daydreaming. Baby names. Baby clothes. Baby paraphernalia.

They really did need that big house.

"Sleep while you can, love, sleep while you can."

Mercy opened her eyes to see Lillian Jenkins and Troy standing before her, arms full of burgers and shakes and fries and apple cider cookies. "I thought you'd still be off hobnobbing with the mayor and Feinberg and Harrington."

"Gotta be here. Busiest time of year." Lillian handed her a milkshake while Troy gave the dogs their plain burger patties. "Made with pasteurized yogurt and nonfat milk and banana."

"Does *everybody* know?"

"It's written all over your face, love. Troy's, too. And your grandmother may have mentioned something to me . . ." She placed a wrapped sandwich on Mercy's lap. "Congratulations."

"Thank you," they said in unison.

Mercy eyed the wrap on her lap. "Please tell me that's your regular cheeseburger."

"Yes, minus the blue cheese dressing."

"Of course." Mercy had the feeling that she was going to spend the next several months—maybe even years—of her life surrounded by mother hens.

"Eat up. You need your protein."

"Right." Mercy focused on eating her cheeseburger, which may be the best she'd ever had in her life. She couldn't remember being this famished since her military police training at Fort Leonard Wood. Maybe pregnancy would prove the longest march of all.

"We need your help. There's no way Mercy can walk the dog parade with her wounded foot."

"Well, of course not," said Lillian. "We'd never ask her to do that. Don't you worry. We've arranged a very special form of transport for our queen. And her king."

Uh-oh, thought Mercy.

"What kind of transport?" asked Troy.

"A bicycle taxi! Just like in Boston or New York City."

Mercy sighed. "Let me guess. Feinberg."

"He's donating a brand-new one to the town. For this and other events. You and Troy will be the first to ride in it." Lillian beamed. "So exciting."

Troy started to protest, but Mercy shook her head. There was no denying Feinberg. "That *is* exciting." She focused on her cheeseburger.

"Troy tells me you're off to see Adah Beecher."

"What I said was that *you* want to see Adah Beecher, but I think we should go home."

Mercy ignored that, focused on Lillian. "Do you know her?"

"For years and years. She's a kind of genius, really. Knows all the native and nonnative species of plants, grows all her own food on her farm in Mount Holly, makes all sorts of herbal remedies, teas, supplements, creams, and the like. Mount Holly Organics. Sold all over the state and beyond."

"Very impressive."

"She's Northshire's wise woman. Well-schooled in the old ways. She helps out at our psychic fair tent on the village green. You can get your tarot cards read."

"I'd much rather see her farm."

"You and every kid in Vermont. She has a great corn maze there this time of year."

"Sounds great." Mercy sighed with contentment as she slurped up the last of the smoothie that Lillian had made especially for her. She was feeling 100 percent better. "Can I eat here every day until the baby is born?"

"I'm sure your mother and grandmother will have something to say about that."

"I'm sure you're right. It's going to be a long six months."

Lillian kissed her on the cheek. "Everything will be fine. Tell Adah hello for me. And ask her to show you her poison garden."

CHAPTER TWENTY-SIX

A house without a garden or orchard is
unfurnished and incomplete.
—A. BRONSON ALCOTT

BEECHER'S PASTURE WAS ABOUT TEN MILES NORTH OF THE estate, on fifty acres of open meadow and woodland. Mercy could see the nineteenth-century farmhouse, with its old white clapboard and shiny new red metal roof glinting in the sun, as Troy turned the Ford F-150 down the long dead-end road that led to the property. The home sat on a slight rise overlooking a field of wildflowers bordered by stands of birch and maple. To its left, farther up the rise about a quarter mile, a big, sturdy red barn stood amid a clutter of outbuildings and a clamor of tourists. *There for the corn maze,* Mercy thought, gazing at the tips of the stalks just visible beyond the barn.

It was a different world down here. A lovely orchard of apple, plum, and pear trees graced the land between the house and the barn; behind the house was a very large potager garden with a greenhouse and potting shed.

"Beautiful place."

"And well-maintained, from the looks of it." Troy turned onto the gravel driveway and drove up to the house, parking by a new metal-roofed shed built to match. They watched as Adah Beecher opened the garden gate and two howling Jack Russell terriers hurtled toward them. Adah followed in their noisy wake. She was wearing the same brightly colored poncho as before, this time over dun-colored pants and shirt. With her wide-brimmed straw hat and Birkenstocks, she looked more the wild hippie than the wise crone.

Mercy and Troy got out of the truck to meet her. Elvis and Susie Bear stayed in the vehicle, and they were not happy about it.

"I'm Mercy Carr. We met at Grackle Tree Farm."

"I remember."

"And this is my husband, Troy Warner."

"Lovely to meet you," Adah said warmly. "Your father and brothers built our new shop up by the barn. You should go check it out. That's where the corn maze is, too."

"We will, but we're not here for the corn maze."

Adah nodded her head, and the broad brim of her hat bounced. "I've been expecting you."

Of course you have, thought Mercy. "We'd love to check out the corn maze, but we'd like to talk to you first."

"You're here about the terrible goings-on at the estate." Adah pulled off her dirty gardening gloves and stuffed them into a pants pocket. "You don't have to worry about all that. You'll be happy there. All of you." She glanced up at the truck, where Elvis and Susie Bear were regarding the rowdy terriers with interest through the open window. "Quiet, Yin. Quiet, Yang."

"Yin and Yang." Mercy laughed. These were not the names that first came to mind for tough, stubborn-minded Jacks. "That's great."

"You can't have Jack Russells if you don't have a sense of humor. We love them, but they're working dogs, first and foremost. They keep the rodents out of the garden."

"I bet," said Troy.

"You can let your dogs out, as long as they're terrier-friendly and stay down here with us. We don't want them scaring off the tourists up at the corn maze."

"Thanks." Troy let Elvis and Susie Bear out of the truck, and the two tough little dogs and the two tough big dogs began the lengthy canine getting-to-know-you process. Sniffing and snorting and advancing and retreating.

"Lillian Jenkins says you know everything there is to know about plants and their properties."

"You're talking about plants and their toxicity."

"Yes."

"Dr. Darling called me about Varden Lind. Or whatever his name really is."

"You're going to have to break that down for us," said Troy.

"As I'm sure Lillian told you, I know my plants."

"Including poisonous plants," said Mercy.

"Yes."

Mercy sensed a hesitation on the woman's part. "Can you tell us what you talked about?"

"I try to keep the poison thing low profile. No one wants to buy organic herbal supplements and creams from a witch who's into poisons."

"Understood." Mercy smiled at her. "You can count on our discretion."

Adah considered that. "Since it's a matter of public record—or will be soon enough—and you saved the man's life, I don't see why not. Besides, Dr. Darling and Lillian Jenkins speak well of you. And your dogs."

She held out a tattooed arm toward the gate. "We can sit out here and chat."

"Sure."

Mercy and Troy accompanied her into the enclosed vegetable garden, whose raised beds ran out like the spokes of a wheel from a circle of pea gravel in the middle. In the center was a small seating area with a carved teak bench and two chairs grouped around a low table.

"Have a seat." Adah sat down in one of the chairs.

Mercy and Troy settled onto the bench, dogs at their feet. Mercy took in the beds, full of the remains of the harvest—the last of the tomatoes, bolted lettuce and radishes, eggplant, cauliflower, okra, asparagus, peas, and beans. The smell was earthy and savory and sweet all at once.

"I leave most of the plants in place over the winter for the birds and insects," Adah said. "I cut it down in spring for mulch." She pointed out the solar-heated greenhouse beyond the garden. "In there I've got more tomatoes, salad greens, herbs, kale, cabbage, spinach, broccoli, carrots, and leeks." She folded her hands in her lap, still as a Buddha. "But you're not here to talk about my vegetables. What would you like to know?"

"Max Vinke died of poisoning at the manor house."

"Cyanide, according to Dr. Darling. Terrible way to die."

"You were there that morning."

"Yes, you saw me. But I left before you went into the house." Adah sighed and looked down at her hands. "As I told that nice Officer Good-love, I never saw Mr. Vinke. I didn't go into the house, I never do. I find it such a sad place." She raised her head and looked at Mercy. "Now that you and your husband are moving in, that will change."

Mercy flushed and changed the subject. "We believe Vinke was there looking for the letters."

"The letters you found. You think he was poisoned so he couldn't find them?"

"Maybe."

"But you found them anyway." Adah twisted her hands in her lap. "Euphemia Whitney-Jones was a wonder." She looked off toward the woods at a memory only she could see. "Everyone wanted a piece of her. Then and now."

"Who around here would know enough about poison to kill him?"

"You mean besides me," Adah said amicably, her hands still once again. "Practically anyone, thanks to the internet. Cyanide was a common rat poison back in the day, but it's illegal now. You could probably still get it off the dark web. But you could also make your own."

"From poisonous plants."

"Easier to show you. Would you like to see my poison garden?"

"I thought you'd never ask."

They all rose and made their way through the rest of the vegetable garden, exiting via the back gate. Adah led them along a gravel path past the greenhouse toward the meadow that served as the gateway to the woods beyond. They quickly came upon another garden space enclosed by a privacy fence. A hand-painted sign over the gated arbor read BEWARE OF PLANTS.

"I modeled it after the Potent Plant Garden at the Torre Abbey not far from Agatha Christie's house in Devon. She used a lot of poisons in her novels. She was a gardener, too, you know."

"Right." Mercy had devoured all of Agatha Christie when she was twelve, before she became a teenager and discovered Shakespeare and Jane Austen and the Brontë sisters.

Adah stopped at the gate, and told Yin and Yang to stay. "You'll have to leave your dogs outside. Some of the plants in this garden are too toxic for them to come into contact with."

"Go ahead," Troy told Mercy. "I'll keep the canines company while you talk poison."

"We won't be long," Adah assured Troy.

"Right."

Inside the poison garden, Mercy and Adah walked slowly along the gravel path that wound around the rectangular space. In the center was a large fountain made of stacked boulders surrounded by a dwarf yew hedge. Raised beds ringed in stone held flowers and shrubs and small trees. It was a lovely, if deadly, garden, even now at the end of the growing season.

"Poison has been used as a murder weapon for millennia." Adah leaned down to pull a weed from one of the beds. "Of course, many of the toxic plants used by poisoners are medicinal in smaller doses. To paraphrase Paracelsus, the father of toxicology, it's the dose that makes the poison."

"Yes." That was true for so many things, not just plants, thought Mercy. A little could be good, but too much could destroy you in the end.

"Many of the flowers are past their blooming by this time of year, but all of the plots are marked." Adah called out poisons and plants as they walked. "The yew gives us taxine, which can be fatal, but you'll also find it in medications used to treat cancer. Foxglove and digitalis, which, depending upon the state of your heart and the dose, can save you or kill you. Plum tree, one of the prunus family, whose seeds contain cyanide compounds. Deadly nightshade, with its deadly black berries."

"That's a hawthorn hedge, isn't it?" Mercy pointed to the thorny shrubs with the bright red berries.

"Very good. The berries have been used in herbal remedies to treat digestive problems, heart issues, and high blood pressure for thousands of years. But eat the seeds, and you'll die."

"Lots of cyanide possibilities."

"I'm sure you'll figure out who killed him." Adah stopped at a stand of tall, stately purple-blue flowers still in boom.

"Monkshood." Mercy knew that monkshood grew wild in New England. And many gardeners loved the autumn-blooming perennial, with its spikes of purple-blue helmet-shaped flowers.

"Yes, beautiful but very toxic," said Adah.

"Is that what made Varden Lind so ill?"

"Yes. Dr. Darling told me the man you found on the village green was suffering from aconite poisoning. Interesting plant, monkshood. It was used by the Romans to poison wells where wolves came to drink. That's why one of its common names is wolfsbane.

"But it has beneficial qualities as well. It's widely used in Ayurveda and traditional Chinese medicine and even some culinary practices."

"Too much of a good thing will kill you."

Adah nodded. "Tricky stuff. There's not much difference between a therapeutic dose and a toxic one. He was lucky that you came along when you did."

"Elvis found him."

"Elvis the Wonder Dog." Adah paused. "You know, you got to Varden Lind just in time. Dr. Darling said that when they got him to the emergency room, the patient exhibited an abnormal heart rhythm. It took Dr. Chen four hours of drugs and electrical shocks to his heart to bring his heart rhythm back to normal."

"I'm so glad he's okay."

The tour was over, and they were back at the garden gate, where Troy and all the dogs were waiting for them.

Mercy filled Troy in on Varden Lind's condition.

"Lucky guy."

"Did she say how Max Vinke ingested the cyanide?" Mercy asked Adah. "Or how Varden Lind ingested the aconite?"

"That's why she called me. The contents of their stomachs. Varden Lind's stomach revealed that he'd eaten a vegetable stew, in which tubers from the monkshood plant were detected. He's lucky they were dried first, as that lowered their toxicity. Raw tubers can be much deadlier."

"And Vinke?" asked Troy.

"Cyanide dissolved in ethyl alcohol and injected into his neck. She found the injection site above his left clavicle."

"How horrible." An unenviable way to die.

"Yes," said Adah. "Nasty."

"Where could they get the cyanide?" asked Troy.

"Look around. Toxicity everywhere, if you know where to look." Adah pointed her trug up toward the orchard that stood beyond the gardens between the house and the barn. "Cherries and plums and apples.

Crush cherries with the pits and the seeds, and the cherry juice will test positive for cyanide. It would take some doing, though. My guess is the murderer just bought some online."

"Two different poisoners?" asked Mercy. "One do-it-yourselfer and one digital native?"

Adah shrugged. "Maybe. But maybe not. The common denominator here is the poison."

"Homicide by poison is relatively rare compared to other forms of violence." Troy knew his violent-crime stats.

"And by definition, premeditated," added Mercy.

"True," agreed Adah. "Especially today. Death by poison was fairly common in the nineteenth century, when all kinds of poisons were readily available. More than one wife stuck with a husband she couldn't divorce turned to poison instead. Many of those deadly substances are illegal now, and advances in toxicology have made it easier to detect poisoning."

"So it's true poison is a woman's weapon." Mercy didn't want to believe it.

"Not exactly. Sixty percent of poisoners are men. But people in the medical field are overrepresented. Maybe simply because they are more familiar with toxic substances."

"Just like Agatha Christie."

"Indeed."

"Profilers say money is the primary motive in most poisonings. Followed by revenge."

"Nothing new there," said Troy. "Robbery, jealousy, vengeance are often the motives for murder."

"Poisoning is usually a personal crime." Adah gave Mercy a penetrating look. "Nine out of ten poisoners kill someone they know."

Mercy thought about this. Who here in Vermont knew Max Vinke? Or Varden Lind? She needed to know more about the victims. "Earlier, when we were talking about Varden Lind, you implied that might not be his real name. What did you mean by that?"

"I know most of the Druids around here. And I never heard of a Varden Lind." Adah pushed her long hair off her shoulders. "'Lind' means linden tree, and 'Varden' means green hill. It seems contrived. Like a name a civilian would make up to sound like a Druid."

Mercy was amused by her use of the word "civilian." "We'll keep that in mind."

Adah led the way back past the greenhouse and the potager garden to the front of the farmhouse. "Congratulations again on your new home."

"Thank you. We may need your help with the garden."

"Sure. I know you will take good care of the place. I'm happy it will be in such good hands. Levi will be, too." Adah pushed her straw hat back off her forehead. "Levi knows the estate like the back of his hand. If you have any questions about it, you should ask him."

"Thank you. We're certainly going to need his help, too."

Adah pointed up the pastured slope to the barn, then turned to Troy. "Now, go on up there and check out your father and brothers' good handiwork."

"Yes, ma'am."

"Levi should be up there, too. He's usually around by the barn. Or playing the scarecrow in the cornfield. If you want to talk to him, just ask one of the teenagers running the maze where he's hiding out."

Mercy thanked her again, and they all piled into Troy's truck. "She wants us to talk to Levi. Let's go find out why."

CHAPTER TWENTY-SEVEN

Houses are not haunted. We are haunted . . .
—DEAN KOONTZ

T ROY DROVE THEM UP TO THE BARN, STOPPING BEHIND THE
long line of vehicles parked under the sun-dappled shade of the
blazing red oaks that fronted the old stone wall running along the side of
the road. On the other side of the wall was elephant eye–high corn, corn,
and more corn.

"Popular place." Troy clipped the leashes on the dogs.

"Looks like fun." Mercy grabbed her walking stick, and together they
all walked up the long rise to the barn and the Mount Holly Organics
Shoppe. There was an antique hay wagon, presumably for hayrides, although she could see no sign of horses, and a pop-up food truck, too,
selling hot dogs and apple cider and pumpkin whoopie pies. People were
everywhere, young families with small children, grandparents and teenagers and lots of tourists from away.

Mercy peeked into the shop, whose rustic architecture belied the clean
lines of the store, with its lavender walls and gleaming white display cases
filled with glass bottles of creams and pots of dried herbs. "It's as lovely as
Adah said. Your father and brothers did a great job."

"Our place will be next. Need anything to eat or drink?"

"I'm good. Let's go find Levi Beecher."

Mercy approached the mummy manning the ticket booth. All she could
see of the teenager—who was swathed from head to foot in white strips of
cloth—were his eyes and mouth. Incongruously, a walkie-talkie hung on a
belt around his waist.

"I'm looking for Levi Beecher."

"He doesn't like people." The young mummy looked at Troy in his game warden uniform. "Cool costume."

"It's not a costume." Troy patted the badge above his breast pocket. "And we'd really like to see Levi."

"Okay." The mummy raised a loosely wrapped arm, pointing toward the barn. "He's done with the maze for the day. He's probably at his place up behind the barn, by the chicken coop. He usually bunks back there. Go through that gate."

"Thank you."

They all wound their way through the crowd. For once, Elvis and Susie Bear did not forge ahead, the Newfie, distracted by the smell of hot dogs and fried dough, and Elvis by the most sinister-looking villains among the costumed visitors.

"It's okay," Mercy told the shepherd as they maneuvered beyond the throng.

"I'm with you, Elvis." Troy opened the gate. "Some of these characters definitely look suspicious."

A gravel path led past the chicken coop, which was surrounded by an electric fence powered by a solar panel. A couple dozen brown, black, buff, and white-feathered hens scratched and pecked at the grass, ignoring Elvis and Susie Bear, both of whom were inordinately interested in the chickens. Mercy and Troy steered the dogs clear of the fence and veered left along the path, coming to a small log cabin with a narrow porch, green metal roof, and a stone chimney. Blue drapes had been pulled across the paned front windows. Mercy knocked on the wooden door with her walking stick.

No response, but the drapes on the window nearest the front door parted, then fell back into place.

She knocked again, harder this time. "It's Mercy Carr, Mr. Beecher. I'm here with Troy Warner."

"And the dogs?" The voice was loud and tough but unmistakably Beecher's.

"And the dogs, yes." The door flew open, and there stood Levi Beecher. He wore blue jeans and a green plaid flannel shirt with work boots. A walkie-talkie attached to his weathered brown leather belt hugged his hip.

Elvis wagged his tail, and Levi leaned down to pet him. Susie Bear nosed past Elvis for her share of the attention. "I like dogs." The implication being he didn't care much for humans.

Mercy laughed. "Sometimes I like dogs better than people, too."

Troy stepped up. "Game Warden Warner here. We'd really like to talk to you."

"We won't take up much of your time," promised Mercy.

Levi moved back to allow them entry. "Come on in."

The cabin was one large room, with built-in Murphy bed cabinetry on one wall and a galley kitchen on another. In front of the fireplace was a small navy corduroy sofa and two comfortable-looking red leather armchairs grouped around an industrial-style coffee table. A flat-screen TV topped a custom-made entertainment center of reclaimed wood in one corner, and an antique oak armoire graced another corner. To the right of the Murphy bed was a door that Mercy assumed led to a bathroom. Maps of Vermont covered the remaining wall space. A bachelor's man cave with a rugged charm that surprised Mercy.

She and Troy stood on a thick red-and-blue-striped woolen rug in the middle of the room with the dogs seated at their hips.

"This is lovely." Mercy admired the handiwork. "Did you make the built-ins?"

"Yeah." His voice was casual, but she thought she detected a hint of pride.

"Beautiful workmanship," said Troy.

"You may as well take a seat." Levi leaned against the fieldstone of the fireplace and pointed at the chairs.

"Thank you." Mercy walked over to the chair closest to the TV cabinet. Several photographs graced its shelves, most of Levi and Adah, some when they were children, with an older couple who must have been their parents, and some documenting their lives over the years. In one silver-framed photo, the teenage siblings stood with other young people clustered around a striking older woman Mercy recognized as Euphemia Whitney-Jones. "May I?"

Levi nodded and she reached for the picture. "She really was beautiful."

"Yes, she was."

"So were you and Adah."

Levi laughed. "Well, Adah at least."

Mercy handed the photo to Troy, and sank into the supple leather cushioning of the armchair. Elvis settled by her side, his head on her lap. The shepherd liked it here, too.

"Who are these other people?" asked Troy, perching on the broad arm of Mercy's chair, Susie Bear at his feet.

"You know them. Horace Boswell. Elisabeth Bardin. Oisin. Of course, he went by his given name back then."

"His given name?" asked Mercy.

"Peter Gilder. This was before he got into the Druid thing."

"And the other two?" Troy held up the photo and Levi peered at it.

"Doug Smith and Harry Halford."

"Where are they now?"

Levi retrieved the photo and replaced it carefully on the shelf with what seemed like reverence. "In the Northshire Cemetery. Vietnam."

"I'm so sorry," said Troy, and Mercy echoed his sentiments.

"It was all a long time ago."

They all fell silent for a moment.

Levi broke the silence abruptly. "You're buying the estate."

"Yes, and we'll take good care of it." Troy smiled at him. "But we'll need your help. We're hoping you'll stay on as caretaker. If you want to."

"Happy to."

Mercy studied the map to the right of the fireplace, which was labeled "Grackle Tree Farm" and marked with brightly colored pushpins. She wondered what the pins signified. "We know you've worked there a long time. We'd like to know more about the history of the place, whatever you can tell us."

Levi sat down in the other armchair, stretching his long legs out before him. Susie Bear left Troy's side and curled up at the man's feet, her big pumpkin head resting on his crossed ankles. "I started working there in high school. Summer of 1968. As you know, Miss Effie spent her summers here. Said nothing beat summers in Vermont."

Levi's craggy features softened when he spoke of Euphemia Whitney-Jones. Mercy wondered if he had been in love with her like everyone else. Like Leontine Bonnet and Michael Robillard and Uncle Hugo.

"It was my understanding that she held a literary salon here in the summers."

"Poets." He spit out the word as if it were an obscenity.

"You don't like poets. But you're a poet yourself. As is your sister."

"Not anymore. Adah still writes, though. And she's very good, no matter what the rest of them say."

"The rest of them?"

"Look, I liked Miss Effie. She was the real deal. But those friends, so-called." Levi paused, leaning toward them. "I wasn't immune. I wanted to be a poet at first, too. Because Miss Effie was a poet. But the rest of them. Bloodsuckers. Liars. Cheats."

"Why do you say that?"

"They were all so jealous of her beauty. Her talent. Her success." He grinned unexpectedly, and Mercy could see the young man who'd wanted to be a poet. "Most poets don't make diddly, you know. But Miss Effie made a fortune. Left them all in the dust."

"She came from money."

"Yeah, plus she made a bunch more writing her poems. Come summer, every poet in Vermont showed up with their hand out. People from away, too. Boston. California. Europe."

"And she helped them."

"She was a soft touch. Not just with the poets. She gave money to the soup kitchen, the homeless shelter, the daycare center. Wrote letters and sent care packages to lots of soldiers overseas. Peter. Doug. Horace. Harry. My cousin Jack, too. He got several letters from her. Candy and magazines and paperback novels, too."

"How did you come to work for her full-time?"

"Heart murmur, so no Vietnam for me. When I graduated from high school, Miss Effie took me on full-time. I lived on the property, kept it safe while she was away. Handyman, gardener, whatever. Helped get the house ready for the summer when she came home."

"Were you here when she died?"

Levi looked down at the plaid rug covering the wide-planked pine floors. "I found her. In the library. Bad day."

"They say she died of oleander poisoning. Self-administered."

His head jerked up. "Another lie. Miss Effie would never kill herself. She was too tough for that."

"Then who killed her?"

"I've been trying to figure that out for years. She was the kind of person who attracted attention without meaning to. Moth to a flame. She was the flame." He smiled, a tight smear of his thin lips. "Maybe you can succeed where I failed. Figure out who did it. Adah says you're smart that way."

"I can try," promised Mercy, knowing that he would hold her to it. "What happened after she died?"

Levi crossed his arms. "Nothing. Moronic sheriff chalked it up to suicide." He looked at Troy. "No offense."

"None taken."

"That no-good sister of hers kept me on to watch over the place."

"Why was she no good?"

"Two sisters don't speak for years, you know it's over a man. Miss Effie told me she wanted to make amends. Sister refused. I reckon she was as jealous of Miss Effie as everyone else." He shook his head. "Didn't even bother to come to the funeral. Shameful, is my thinking."

Mercy gazed up at the map by the fireplace again. "What are those pins in the map?"

Levi smiled, a genuine, if sad, smile this time. "Miss Effie believed that the witch would never rest until her baby was found. And that she was buried somewhere out there in the woods."

"Why would she think that?"

"Miss Effie did a lot of research on the family. She didn't trust the husband. Believed that he was jealous of Willa's devotion to the child. She thought he had something to do with the little girl's disappearance. And that he fed his wife's grief until she went completely mad. We searched the forest for evidence for years, and after Miss Effie died, I kept on looking. Those pins mark all the places I've looked."

"But you never found anything," said Troy.

"No. It's a lot of woods."

"True enough."

"And now?" asked Mercy. "What do you make of what's been happening at the estate?"

"Every house has its secrets." Levi cleared this throat. "Looks like now they might finally be coming to light."

"Did Effie ever confide in you?" asked Mercy.

Levi stuffed his weathered hands into the pockets of his jeans and closed his eyes, leaning back against the chair.

Mercy and Troy waited in silence. Elvis sat up very tall, ears perked. Like all good soldiers, they were good at waiting.

Susie Bear nudged Levi's hip, pushing her muzzle into his pocket to lick his fingers. The Newfie was all about comfort, and she knew that Levi was uncomfortable. Mercy suspected that he was coming to a difficult decision, and that was what was making him uncomfortable.

Finally, he opened his eyes. He blinked a couple of times, staring at Mercy. "Adah says we should trust you. We have to trust you."

"Whatever you have to say will go no further. Unless you want it to."

"I've done my best to protect the estate, Effie's legacy, and her reputation. But now it's up to you." Levi stood and walked over to the old oak armoire. He opened the carved door, revealing a small area to hang clothes on one side and shelves for shirts and shoes on the other. On the top shelf lay a thick Irish fisherman's sweater. He rested his hands upon the sweater and paused. "She gave me this sweater." He lifted the sweater and put it aside gently, revealing a box beneath it. He removed it from the armoire, and closed the door, walking over to Mercy. He placed it gingerly on her lap. "Effie gave this to me for safekeeping."

It was a lovely old writing box made of burled walnut with an antique lock.

"What's inside?"

"I don't know."

"You never opened it?"

"She didn't ask me to open it, she asked me to keep it safe."

"Safe from what?"

"Prying eyes, is my guess." The man tapped the tarnished brass plate on the lid of the box. A monogram plate engraved with the initials EWJ.

Euphemia Whitney-Jones, thought Mercy.

"But she's long buried now, and maybe what's in here will help you figure all this mess out. So I reckon I'll let you take a look."

"Do you have the key?"

"No."

"Did you ever have it?"

"No. I think Effie was coming back to get the box, eventually. But then she died."

Troy looked at Mercy. She knew he was thinking what she was thinking. Maybe the key to this writing box was the one she'd found in the secretary with the letters. The one she'd just turned over to Harrington.

Troy pulled his Leatherman from his pocket and held it up. "Want this?"

"No, thank you. No decent lock-picking tool on that thing." Mercy reached into her cargo pants pocket and retrieved her Swiss Army knife. She turned to Levi. "May I?"

"Go ahead. I like the Swiss Army knife myself."

She opened the knife and selected the lock-picking tool. Slowly, she worked it into the keyhole on the front side of the burled walnut box. "It's old. Rusted." She looked up at Troy and Levi. "This could take a while."

"You can do it," said Troy.

She could feel their eyes upon her—and not just theirs. It was as if Effie herself were watching. Mercy dropped the knife and she cursed.

Levi returned it to her. "Steady on."

She tinkered with the lock, but no luck. She tried another pick, the half diamond, and then the 5-rake.

Better, she thought, and wriggled the tool into the lock, tripping the mechanism. That did the trick.

"You got it," said Levi with admiration.

"Here goes." At the click of the unlocking, she lifted the lid. "More letters."

She tipped her knees toward Troy and Levi so they could see the contents.

"Now what?" asked Troy.

"May as well read them," said Levi.

Troy tossed Mercy a pair of plastic gloves. She slipped them on and removed the folded papers, unfolding the one on top and reading it before placing it on the coffee table for them to see.

"It's from Doug Smith."

"The guy in the photo."

"Yeah." Levi blinked.

Troy scanned the paper. "It's not a letter, it's a poem."

"This poem is good." Levi closed his eyes as if the darkness were a portal to the past. "I didn't know Doug was this good."

"They all seem to be poems." Even though they were addressed *Dear Miss Whitney-Jones*, they were all poems, hastily handwritten verses exploring the nature of life and death and literature. Dated 1968 to 1970. Mercy didn't know what to think. "Why would Euphemia hide them in this box and give them to you for safekeeping?"

Levi opened his eyes. "I don't know."

"Do you mind if I take photographs of the poems? That way I can leave the box and the letters here with you."

"Go ahead."

Levi, Troy, and the dogs sat in silence while Mercy snapped pics on her cell. When she was finished, she turned to Levi. "We don't know what this means yet, but we do know that someone was prepared to kill for the last set of letters. You could be in danger."

"No." Levi shook his head. "I don't think so. Effie is a famous poet. Those letters you found in the library were part of her legacy. Poor Doug is long dead. Forgotten by all but his loved ones." He gathered the poems together and placed them back in the box.

Mercy locked it for him. "I still think—"

The walkie-talkie on Levi's hip crackled with static. "Excuse me." He pulled the two-way radio off his belt. They all listened as a panicked male voice said, "Boss, we got us some irate customers here."

"On my way." Levi snapped the walkie-talkie back onto his belt. He carried the box back to the armoire and put it under the sweater once more. After closing the armoire and locking it once again, he looked at Mercy and Troy. "Gotta go."

"Of course." They all piled out of the cabin. While Levi was locking up, Elvis yanked the leash out of her hand and took off around the barn.

"Sorry," said Mercy.

"Looking for trouble?" asked Levi.

"That's his job.

"Better not be my chickens."

"He won't hurt your chickens."

They all huffed after the shepherd. They passed the chicken coop. No sign of Elvis.

"See? Your chickens are fine."

Susie Bear pulled at her lead. Troy unhooked the Newfie, and she scampered off in search of the shepherd, slipping into the crowd of visitors in front of the barn. Mercy caught sight of Elvis crashing into the bank of corn, the maze trails be damned. The Newfie barreled after him, plumed tail dark against the faded yellow-brown stalks. A screech of grackles and ravens and other blackbirds filled the sky above the maze.

The mummy abandoned his post at the ticket booth and hustled to Levi. He raised a cloth-bound arm and shook it toward the far end of the farm. "Northwest corner. Customer complaining about the scarecrow being too scary for his kids."

"It's supposed to be scary."

The mummy shrugged.

"Where's he now?"

"I gave him his money back and he left."

"People." Levi shook his head. "I better check it out." He turned to Mercy. "Better get those dogs of yours before they scare away what customers we got left." He jogged through the entrance of the maze and down the narrow mowed path that led through the puzzle of eight-foot-high corn.

"I'll find the dogs. You go with Levi," Mercy told Troy, knowing she couldn't move that fast with her bum foot. "Don't worry about me."

"I'll be right back." Troy ran off down the path to catch up with Levi.

Mercy decided to follow the trail left by Elvis and Susie Bear rather than using the mowed path. Troy probably wouldn't approve of her navigating a crush of corn on her own, but she knew the dogs were onto something, something they were investigating directly by scent. The smell of something very, very wrong.

CHAPTER TWENTY-EIGHT

If you have a garden and a library,
you have everything you need.
—MARCUS TULLIUS CICERO

THE CORNSTALKS WERE BRITTLE THIS LATE IN THE SEASON, easily disturbed and dismembered. Elvis and Susie Bear had left a line of broken stalks in their wake. Mercy picked her way through the fallen corn stems, using her walking stick for leverage and support. The corn leaves rustled as she tramped after the dogs; she could hear the shouts and shrieks of the people in the maze.

The chilly air smelled of dead leaves and chimney smoke and moist earth. She crossed the mowed path that wound through the maze for the visitors at least twice as she kept off the grid and in the corn itself. She stomped along as quickly as she dared, unwilling to abuse her foot any further, swearing at her contused toes as she kept her eye on the mangled stalks ahead. She felt like a doomed character in a Stephen King novel.

Where is Elvis? Mercy had a bad feeling about this. Growing weary, she whistled for Elvis, and after a few minutes she could hear him racing through the field of corn. She whistled again and there he was, ears perked, panting. He licked her hand and then trotted off again, more slowly this time, so she could keep him in sight. Another twenty yards and she trudged into a small clearing, just a broadening, really, of one of the paths that led through the maze.

A stack of hay bales anchored the tiny space of open ground. A tall T-shaped post seemed to sweep up out of the bales, a scarecrow support minus the scarecrow. Some blackbirds perched on the wooden arms and others gathered at the bottom of the bales.

The ravens and grackles were picking away at the fallen strawman. Susie Bear yowled, bouncing on her large paws. Elvis growled and lunged at the birds.

The blackbirds scattered.

And revealed the true nature of the scarecrow. This figure was not made of old clothes stuffed with hay. This scarecrow was made of flesh and bone. But he did have one thing in common with a strawman. He was not moving.

Elvis moved to the scarecrow's feet, and sank into his Sphinx position.

"Good boy, Elvis." Mercy moved in for a closer look at the scarecrow sprawled on the dirt, his legs akimbo, his hay-stuffed sleeves sweeping out from his sides like the arms of a corn-husk doll.

The man wore a peaked hat, which had fallen over his brow, obscuring his eyes. But even with his scarecrow face makeup, he seemed vaguely familiar to Mercy. She leaned over to check the man's pulse, even though she was pretty sure he was dead. As she did so, she was able to see the man's face more clearly. He was one of the bodyguard Druids who'd been with Oisin that morning at Eggs Over Easy.

No pulse. Mercy gently released the man's wrist and straightened up. There was no sign of injury that she could see. No indication of a poisoning, either. No saliva, no vomit, no drool of any kind. No rash on his forehead. None of the signs of cyanide that had marked Max Vinke's corpse.

She wondered where Levi and Troy were. They'd followed the mowed paths, which wound through the maze, rather than taking Elvis and Susie Bear's shortcut directly through the cornfield. Still, they should be here by now.

Two teenagers dressed like Katniss Everdeen from *The Hunger Games* stumbled into the clearing, out of breath. Two hooded young men with scythes trailed the girls. They all came to a sudden halt when they saw the dead scarecrow on the ground.

"What's going on?" asked the taller of the Reapers. "What happened to the scarecrow?"

"I'm afraid he's gone."

"Gone?" asked one of the Katnisses. "You mean dead?"

"OMG," said the other Katniss. "Did he have a heart attack or what?"

"I don't know. But this may be a crime scene. We're waiting for law enforcement." Elvis came to her side, in full guard mode.

"The scarecrow is supposed to be up there." The taller Grim Reaper raised his scythe at the T-shaped post rising from the stack of hay bales. "He's supposed to jump out at you when you pass by and chase you around." He leaned forward, peering at the dead man. "But this isn't the usual guy. He's a lot younger."

"How do you know that?" asked his fellow Reaper.

"I come here every year. This is one of my favorite parts. *Was*." He turned to Mercy. "Maybe he burst a blood vessel in his brain and fell down and died."

"You don't have to be old to die," said the first Katniss Everdeen. "My cousin dropped dead at the gym a week before her thirtieth birthday. She was on the elliptical."

There was nothing Mercy could say to that. She was relieved when Levi and Troy loped into the space.

"Game Warden Troy Warner," he announced to them all. "If you could all stay right where you are for the moment, we're going to need to talk to you." He nodded at Mercy, and she joined him and Levi.

"I believe the victim is one of the Druids," she told Troy and Levi quietly.

Levi nodded. "Braden Miller. He works here part-time."

"Right." Troy lowered his voice, too, so the teenagers couldn't hear. "Braden Miller was one of the long hunters Gil and I came across in the woods on the day you were attacked."

"What's going on?" The taller Reaper edged forward.

"Stay where you are," ordered Troy. "We will need statements from each of you."

"I can stay here with the dogs."

"Great, thanks. I'll take Levi and his customers back to the barn. Levi can help keep the onlookers away while I call it in. Backup should be here shortly."

"Right," said Levi.

Mercy waited until they all went off with Troy to take a closer look at the scene and the victim. Braden Miller was no longer the Druid in a white tunic and pants under a gray cloak. He was a scarecrow now—and the only hint to his Druidic leanings was a thick hag stone on the woven tan leather cord slung around his neck. She used her cell camera to record the scene and the corpse in situ.

She studied the area around the dead Druid. No blood on the ground that she could see, no blood on the body, either, at least not from this angle. The body was positioned at the foot of the bales, in effect serving as its outer wall. She leaned forward to examine the hay more closely and thought she spotted blood and hair. Maybe he'd fallen and struck his head on the bale on the way down. But she wasn't sure.

She'd have to wait for Dr. Darling and the Crime Scene Search Team to see how Braden Miller had died.

Two hours later Mercy was sitting in Levi's hay wagon with the dogs. Becker and Goodlove had roped off the clearing, closed down the corn maze, and ordered any and all rubberneckers back to the barn. Whereupon uniforms took their contact information and Levi Beecher and the mummy passed out tickets for rain checks and sent everyone home.

Dr. Darling and her forensics techs were up in the cornfield, examining the corpse and the crime scene. Becker and Goodlove were taking statements from the Katnisses and the Grim Reapers, who were sufficiently impressed by all the experts and uniforms to cooperate fully. As the taller Reaper told her with a fan-boy intensity that surprised her, it was just like "being in a real-life episode of *CSI*."

All the teenagers insisted they'd seen nothing, heard nothing, and they didn't know the victim. But they'd be happy to form an online armchair detective group and help solve the crime. Becker and Goodlove let them go on home, with the understanding that they would do no such thing.

Troy came up to the hay wagon. "We can go home now, too."

"What about the customer who complained about the scary scarecrow?"

"Apparently he paid cash, so no credit card receipt, but I'm sure Becker and Goodlove will track him down one way or another. Maybe he saw something. If he did, they'll let us know." Troy smiled at her. "Let's go, sweetheart."

"I'd like to hear what Dr. Darling has to say first."

"If you insist."

"I do."

"Then move over." Troy and the dogs climbed back up into the hay wagon to sit with her. She laid her head on her husband's strong shoulder and closed her eyes. She was dozing off when he whispered in her ear, "Here she comes."

Mercy opened her eyes to see the crime scene techs bringing the body bag containing Braden Miller out of the maze. Dr. Darling followed, but waved the techs on when she saw Mercy and Troy and the dogs in the hay wagon waiting for her.

"You really are everywhere," said the ever-cheerful medical examiner. "Did you buy that grand old house yet?"

"We did. It's ours!"

"Good. You'll be happy there."

"That's what people keep telling us. But from what we've learned so far, it doesn't seem like anyone else has been."

"You're the exception to every rule, Mercy Carr. You'll be the exception to this one, too." She smiled at Troy. "You and your handsome new husband."

"How did the victim die?" asked Troy, changing the subject.

"Twenty-five-year-old Braden Miller of Northshire, part-time IT, part-time scarecrow, and full-time bard." Dr. Darling snapped off her plastic gloves and stepped out of her suit. "Died of blunt impact."

"I didn't see any blood on him."

"Neither did I until I turned him over. I found a scalp abrasion on the back of his head and a fracture at the base of his skull. I suspect the autopsy will reveal bleeding and bruising of the brain as well."

"I did see what I thought might be blood on the hay behind him."

"Good eye," said Dr. Darling. "We've taken samples for the lab."

"He didn't just fall?" asked Troy.

"No. He fell and hit some kind of heavy object. No sign of any such object at the scene, at least not yet. Can't say much about the nature of the object yet, either. Of course, that's just my educated guess. The autopsy will tell us more."

"Time of death?"

"Hard to say right now. Under two hours is my guess. But the real question is, how long did it take him to die? That will depend on the nature of his traumatic brain injury."

"So he could have been lying up there awhile before he passed," said Troy.

"I don't think so," said Mercy. "Someone would have seen him. There were so many people going through the corn maze at the time."

"So he died fast?"

Dr. Darling shrugged. "Could have been fast, could have been slow."

"I'm hoping fast, for his sake," said Mercy.

"Sometimes with these kinds of injuries, the victims don't think they've been hurt that badly. By the time they realize they need help, it's too late."

"Like with Bob Saget," said Troy. "Our Druid may not have even known what was happening to him. He could have been walking around here or elsewhere, a little confused, and wandered up here, and collapsed."

"So you think it was an accident?" asked Mercy.

"I didn't say that." Dr. Darling looked from Mercy to Troy. "Did I say that?"

"We're listening."

"There's some bruising on his knuckles that could indicate a struggle."

"So he could have been pushed, and that's why he fell," theorized Mercy.

"Which would make it murder." Troy shook his head. "Not another one."

"It's possible. Hopefully, the autopsy will tell us more."

"One more question, if I may," said Mercy. "Did you find anything of interest on his person?"

"Just the usual. Wallet, car fob, hallucinogens."

"What kind of hallucinogens?" asked Troy.

"Psilocybin powder."

"Magic mushrooms." Troy crossed his arms. "Maybe that's why he fell. He was high."

"Maybe." Dr. Darling paused. "But it is my understanding that Druids collect psychoactive mushrooms to use in their rituals. They should know what they're doing."

"A hundred people die from mushroom poisoning every year," said Troy. "Thousands more end up in the emergency room."

Some people have a knack for remembering names, thought Mercy. Troy had a knack for remembering statistics related to law and order and crime and death. It was one of his superpowers.

"It's possible. We'll do a thorough tox screen. Thrasher will let you know if I find anything interesting."

"He should still be in the hospital." Mercy was worried about the captain. "We saw him earlier, and he did not look well."

"He's a terrible patient," agreed Dr. Darling. "Like someone else we know."

"Very funny."

"The captain doesn't like being sidelined any more than you do," said Troy.

"Who can blame him? He's missing all the action." Dr. Darling flitted her fingers in a merry farewell. "I can't wait to see what happens next."

CHAPTER TWENTY-NINE

My home . . . It is my retreat and resting place from
wars, I try to keep this corner as a haven against the
tempest outside, as I do another corner in my soul.
—MICHEL DE MONTAIGNE

BACK HOME, TROY AND SUSIE BEAR SETTLED ONTO THE four-poster to watch a football game on the TV in the bedroom. Mercy knew they'd both be asleep in minutes. Her husband and his dog had the enviable ability to sleep anywhere, anytime. "Power napping," Troy called it.

Mercy herself was too wound up to sleep. Besides, it was still early evening. Within minutes she heard the comforting sound of Troy and Susie Bear snoring, and she headed straight for the shower. Elvis curled up in the corner on the bathroom rug while she wrapped her sore foot in a plastic bag, securing it with tape, and stepped into heaven. After a very blissful interlude of hot, steaming water, Mercy pulled off the bag, and put on her favorite pair of red satin pajamas—a gift from her mother, of course, and the one addition to her wardrobe of which she could thoroughly approve.

The shepherd followed Mercy down the hall and into the great room, where she slipped him a peanut-butter doggie treat and pointed to his side of the sofa. He chomped down the treat and settled onto the couch, eyes closed but ears still perked. Mercy gave him a quick belly rub before joining Amy and Brodie at the farm table. Given the hour, she figured baby Helena was already in bed.

Amy pointed to the table's offerings: another pan of Patience's cinnamon rolls, homemade apple cider from the farm down the road, and a copy of *What to Expect When You're Expecting*.

"Really? How did you know?"

"Momdar," said Amy, smiling. "I'm so happy for you."

"Ditto." Brodie grinned at them both.

Mercy sat at the head of the table, her injured foot elevated on another one of the chairs. Dr. Chen would be proud.

"Patience dropped by with these rolls this afternoon. She was worried about you." Amy tucked another pillow under Mercy's foot.

"I am surrounded by worriers." Mercy poured herself a generous glass of apple cider, and helped herself to a cinnamon roll. Grandmothers were the best, and her grandmother was the best of the best.

"We heard about the death at the corn maze," said Amy. "Tell us everything."

Mercy filled them in on the day's events between bites. "We'll know more after the autopsy."

"But you think it's murder." Amy joined her in a glass of cider.

"It wouldn't surprise me, not the way things are going this week."

"But if the guy who shot you and Thrasher was in custody, he couldn't have killed the scarecrow." Brodie reached for a cinnamon roll, and Amy slapped his hand away.

"Go ahead, Brodie. You know my grandmother will just make more." Mercy finished off her own roll. "You make a good point. Russo's a pro who has managed to stay one step ahead of the law for years. But no history of poisoning. And if Braden Miller was murdered, it doesn't seem like the work of a pro."

"What do you mean?"

"I get it," said Brodie. "It seems like a weird place to kill someone, what with all those people around."

"Exactly. It seems like an act of desperation. The killer just shows up in that part of the maze, gets into an altercation with the scarecrow, pushes him down, and then leaves, quick before someone comes along to see him."

Mercy's cell phone dinged, and she reached into the pocket of her PJs to pull it out. It was a text from Jillian Rosen Merrill:

Good news! Eager buyer for cabin—7% over asking price.
Cash offer, closing in 30 days.

"Someone's made a substantial offer for the cabin. We're closing in thirty days."

"That means we have to move, like, now," said Amy.

"It is fast," admitted Mercy.

"If you're really going to live in that demon pit, I'd better get Joey Fyfe out there to do his thing for you," Brodie said.

"Joey Fyfe?"

"You know, the paranormal investigator I told you about."

"Sure, why not?" Mercy figured it couldn't hurt.

"Awesome. I'll text him right now."

Amy was right. They were going to have to move. *Fast*. The wheels were in motion to sell the cabin and take over the grand old manor. The train was moving down the track—no stopping it.

Elvis leapt off the couch and headed for the front door, tail wagging. Obviously, these were welcome visitors. Brodie followed the shepherd and opened the door before whoever was there could knock, and in strode Thrasher, Feinberg, and Uncle Hugo. An intimidating trio for most, if not for Elvis, who loved the captain and indulged the colonel and tolerated the billionaire.

"To what do we owe this unexpected pleasure?" Mercy knew something was up, as these men rarely arrived together as a united front.

"I thought you'd want this back." Thrasher handed her a large brown paper bag.

She looked inside and pulled out the nice Topo Designs backpack Troy had given her. The one Russo had run off with. "Thank you."

"There's been a development," continued the captain, as Troy and Susie Bear emerged from the bedroom.

A development that had all three of them in her living room and Troy and Susie Bear cutting short their nap. This was going to be interesting. She waved them into the living area. "Come sit down and tell us all about it."

Uncle Hugo and Feinberg took the easy chairs across from her, and Thrasher sat down on the ottoman parked at Elvis's end of the couch. Happily ensconced in his place, the shepherd allowed the captain to pet him.

Brodie and Amy joined them, sitting cross-legged on the large throw rug by the coffee table.

Thank goodness we're getting a bigger house, Mercy thought, imagining all these people seated comfortably in the large living room in their Victorian mansion. No ottomans needed.

"You know we found a burner phone on Russo when we arrested him," began Thrasher.

"Right." Troy planted himself on the arm of the sofa next to Mercy, Susie Bear at his feet.

"Well, all the calls went to other burner phones, from New York to California, but we can tell you Russo's burner phone came from a convenience store in Las Vegas."

"Las Vegas. Which is no surprise since Russo was from Vegas." Troy stroked Susie Bear's big pumpkin head.

Thrasher nodded. "But even more interesting were the photos we found on the phone."

Feinberg cut in. "Photos of the manor house and you and Thrasher, on the day you were assaulted."

"So no doubt he's our man. I knew it." Troy high-fived Mercy.

"No doubt."

"Anything else revealing?" High fives aside, Mercy got the feeling they were burying the lede.

"Yes." The colonel smiled at her. "One that will prove of particular interest to you."

"And that we're hoping you can shed some light on," added Feinberg.

Thrasher pulled a sheet of paper from his pocket. He unfolded it and spread it out on the coffee table for everyone to see. "This is a copy of a photo we found on Russo's phone."

"Of course. Another poem." She read it aloud.

Scary tree, scary tree
Looming large over me
Hiding stories long untold
Of people and places long grown cold
Treasure in seeds and roots bound tight
'Til all her secrets come to light.

"What does it mean?" Amy seemed confused.

"I'm betting this is the poem that Maude received from her sister Effie, the one that she thought was meant to tell her something." Mercy frowned. "This means that Maude never threw it away, as she claimed. And that she told someone about it." She looked at Feinberg. "Like Ren Barlow."

"I spoke to Ren," said Feinberg. "He says he never saw this, that he believed Maude when she told him that she'd disposed of it. He had no reason or evidence to think otherwise. But he also said she was a bit muddled the last years of her life. Obsessed with her sister, certainly. But she also had problems with memory and confusion and even mild paranoia. When she died, they found cash hidden all over the house."

"And you believe him?" At the incredulity in Troy's voice, Susie Bear raised her head.

"I do."

The colonel folded his hands together prayer-style and held them at his lips. "Which means someone else in her orbit gave this to Russo."

"The usual suspects." Thrasher listed them. "Family, friends, employees . . ."

"What about the step-grandson?" asked Mercy.

"I talked to Ren about him," Feinberg went on. "Maude's late husband Wilfred's son, Gerard Fergus. He was close to Maude. Ren describes him as lazy and spoiled but very devoted to his step-grandmother. He went to see her every Sunday. Apparently they'd have lunch, and then they'd do the *New York Times* Sunday crossword together."

"We're running background checks on him and everyone else in Maude's inner circle." Thrasher crossed one long leg over the other and leaned toward Elvis, the better to rub the dog's belly.

"We're continuing to investigate at our end as well," said the colonel. "We'll keep you informed."

"Why would this guy Russo have the poem on him?" asked Amy.

"Why indeed," said Feinberg.

They all looked at Mercy, and she laughed. "Effie and her poems. They're road maps to all kinds of secrets. Treasure included."

"Russo's primarily a thief by trade. Violence is typically a last resort for him. Means to an end." Thrasher rapped his knuckles on the poem lying on the coffee table. "He was drawn by the prospect of something worth stealing."

"But you and Mercy beat him to it," said Troy.

"Is there anything else?" Mercy asked the captain.

"Dr. Darling has confirmed that Braden Miller's death was not an accident. Although who killed him and why is still very much a mystery."

"From all accounts, he was a harmless young man," said Feinberg.

"He didn't always keep the best company." Troy told them about his and Gil's encounter with Braden Miller and his cousin Quaid Miller and Horace Boswell in the woods—and the telltale sugary substance on Susie Bear's jowls.

"There's no record of Braden Miller being arrested for poaching." Thrasher frowned. "Or anything else. We'll check out the cousin and Boswell."

"They claimed to be legitimate long hunters." But Mercy could tell Troy didn't believe that for a minute.

"That's what they always say," said Uncle Hugo.

"Poems, poets, poetry." Mercy uncurled herself from the couch. "Thank you for coming. If you'll excuse me, I've got to get dressed."

"Where are we going?" asked Troy, rising to his feet.

"To a poetry reading." Mercy smiled.

At Troy's blank look, she explained. "Dr. Elisabeth Bardin invited us to a reading tonight, remember? She said we should come, that there were things we needed to know. I think we should go."

"Good idea." Feinberg sighed. "I begged off this gala, but now I think we should go. Come on, Hugo." Feinberg and Uncle Hugo headed for the door.

"So I guess we're all going." Thrasher grinned. "See you there."

CHAPTER THIRTY

A man travels the world over in search of what
he needs and returns home to find it.
—GEORGE MOORE

T HE FESTIVITIES WERE IN FULL SWING DOWN ON THE VILLAGE
green. Troy dropped Mercy off at the far end on the common, and
drove off, looking for a place to park. They'd left the dogs at home, not
knowing how welcome canines would be among a league of poets. Mercy
stood in front of the First Congregational Church, walking stick in hand,
admiring its handsome façade and classic New England spire. One of the
oldest buildings in Northshire, the church still operated as a place of worship, but also served as a venue for important civic and cultural events.

She walked into the nave and took a seat in one of the pews nearest
the back. The members of the society were gathered at the front of the
church. She saw Adah Beecher sitting in the section reserved for the poets.

Dr. Horace Boswell and Dr. Bardin—*Elisabeth with an s*—stood near
the pulpit, speaking to a slender young woman with shiny brown hair and
the kind of simple, chic dress her mother Grace would appreciate. The
kind of dress you rarely saw in Northshire.

The pews were full of people; it seemed like everyone in town who
wasn't out on the common was here in the church. Lillian Jenkins, of
course, and the usual local dignitaries. Oisin was here, flanked by Liath
and Muirne, along with their fellow Druids. Monique from Eggs Over
Easy was here, and Wyetta and Thrasher, and even Pizza Bob and his family. Who knew there were so many poetry fans in southwestern Vermont?

Troy slipped into the spot next to her just as Boswell stepped behind the pulpit and tapped on the microphone. With him was Jillian, who sat on the other side of Mercy.

"I didn't know you liked poetry."

"I like poets. I especially like selling their houses."

"So you know most of the members."

"Sure do."

"You'll have to fill me in."

"Of course." Jillian regarded Mercy with those laughing eyes of hers. "I knew you weren't just here for the poetry. Don't you ever stop snooping?"

"She can't help herself." Troy smiled at her.

They all turned their attention to the pulpit. Boswell introduced himself as the president of the Northshire Alliance of Poets, welcomed one and all, and informed the audience that his new volume of poetry was available for sale "wherever good books are sold," including the alliance's booth on the common.

"Such a show-off," whispered Jillian. "They say he's been milking that Pulitzer Prize for decades. Lives up on Grand Avenue in a mansion he can barely afford."

Boswell moved aside and let his colleague take the lead.

"And Elisabeth Bardin?"

"Cheap. Took me nearly a year to find her a house she'd actually pay good money for."

"We're here to honor the life and work of Northshire's own Euphemia Whitney-Jones," the professor began. "One of the most celebrated poets of her generation. You all know her as the author of 'The Ghost Witch of Grackle Tree,' but she was so much more than that. To tell us more, we're thrilled to have with us tonight the great-granddaughter of Leontine Bonnet, Effie's beloved companion, and director of the Euphemia Whitney-Jones museum at *L'Heure Bleu*, Effie's home in Provence—Dr. Sandrine Samara Saint-Yves."

Of course, she was French, chic in that way French women seem to be without even trying. Although Mercy knew from her mother—the closest thing you could get to French chic in New England—that it took a lot of effort to look so carelessly perfect.

The elegant young woman Mercy had seen talking to Boswell and Bardin earlier thanked the professor and swapped places at the pulpit. In her smart Parisian accent, Dr. Saint-Yves thanked the Northshire Alliance of Poets, and proceeded to sing the praises of Euphemia Whitney-Jones.

"She's really here to see those letters you found. And Feinberg says she'd like a tour of the estate." Jillian made a face. "Do you think it's safe?"

"The guy who shot Captain Thrasher is now in custody," Troy reminded her. "And the attention seems to have shifted away from the estate."

"You mean poor Braden Miller up at the old Beecher place?"

"Yes."

"I can't imagine why anyone would want to kill him," said Jillian. "Such a sweet guy."

Mercy had been wondering about motive herself. Who kills a scarecrow at a corn maze? Unless Troy and Gil's instincts were right and he was somehow involved with poaching. Some of those poaching gangs played rough. If fall-out among poachers had prompted the assault on Braden, that would have nothing to do with Effie or the estate.

"Well, if you don't think it's dangerous, I'll arrange for Dr. Saint-Yves to get her tour."

"I'll talk to Thrasher about backup," said Troy in an effort to reassure her.

"And Feinberg will have his bodyguards with him," Mercy reminded her. "It should be okay."

"*Shush,*" warned the lady to Jillian's right.

"Sorry."

They listened as Dr. Saint-Yves talked for nearly twenty minutes about Euphemia Whitney-Jones's time in France, which she claimed was the most prolific period of her career.

Not if she wrote all those poems during the war in her letters to the pilot Robillard, thought Mercy. Troy squeezed her hand, and she knew he was thinking the same thing. Effie's and Robillard's letters were inspired by their love, and written at the estate. Of course, Dr. Saint-Yves had yet to see the letters; once she did, she'd have to change her spiel.

The director wrapped up her speech, and the audience applauded with enthusiasm. Mercy did, too; Dr. Saint-Yves had impressed her with her intelligence and charm and her obvious knowledge of Euphemia Whitney-Jones. Dr. Saint-Yves kept her remarks pretty basic, so nothing she said came as a surprise to Mercy, but she was left nonetheless with the impression that what the director told them was only the tip of the iceberg of her scholarship.

The professor came back to the mic, and announced a series of readings of Effie's poems. One by one, the members of the Northshire Alliance of Poets came up, spoke to how Euphemia Whitney-Jones had been such an inspiration and influence on their lives as poets, and read one of her poems. Elisabeth read "All the Unnamed Women." Oisin, of all people, read "Dog Is God." Many chose the dark fairy-tale poems, including one about a bewitched castle in the woods read by Adah Beecher.

"Sounds like the castle ruins where Willa Strong died," whispered Troy in her ear.

"I want to see those ruins," Mercy whispered back.

The readings ended with Boswell thanking Effie for giving a young poet "hope and good editing" before launching into a rousing recitation of "The Ghost Witch of Grackle Tree." Practically everyone in the audience joined in on this one—Mercy and Troy and Jillian included.

Boswell took the pulpit one last time to thank everyone.

"You're coming to the poets reception at the Historical Society, right?" asked Jillian. "It's after this."

"We weren't invited."

"Your friend Feinberg is sponsoring it. I'm sure they'll let you in. If not, tell them you're my guests. See you there." Jillian waggled her fingers in a goodbye and went off to talk poets into listing their homes and buying new ones. The church emptied out, and Mercy and Troy made their way through the throngs of tourists and early trick-or-treaters and across the common to the Historical Society, a plainly built nineteenth-century structure with a small cupola that had originally served as the first Town Hall in Northshire.

The reception was by invitation only, and greeters were checking at the door, but Thrasher and Wyetta were waiting for them with invitations courtesy of Feinberg.

"Daniel could have told us he was the sponsor," complained Mercy, as the greeters swept them through the white-painted double doors without incident.

Thrasher laughed. "I don't know why you're surprised. He's always the sponsor."

"True enough."

The inside was decorated in what Mercy thought of as high-brow Halloween: black and white and orange-gold balloons, strings of white and orange lights, and large poster-size sepia-colored photos of Euphemia Whitney-Jones throughout her life on the walls. While Troy fetched her some ginger ale, she made a study of the photos.

Several featured Effie and Leontine in Provence; others were taken here. The estate was still grand in those days, and the pictures of the house in the green of summer and the white of winter snow cheered Mercy. She couldn't wait to restore the home to its former glory—and she could use some of these photographs as a guide.

There were images of Effie as a child at the estate, too, playing with her dog and blowing out candles on a birthday cake and holding hands in the garden with a girl Mercy thought must be Maude. Happy sisters—before the handsome pilot Michael Robillard came into their lives and separated them forever.

Some of the pictures documented Effie's literary salon. Mercy peered at one in particular, in which Euphemia and Leontine posed with a group of very young poets in what must be the castle ruins. Looking closer, she thought she recognized Boswell and Bardin, Levi, maybe even Oisin. Doug Smith and Harry Halford were not there. Adah was off to one side; she couldn't have been more than twelve, but she had that thick wavy hair and the same hippie vibe.

There was another photo of the same group in front of the sugar shack, photographed after its transformation into the Sylvia Beach Shanty. Soon it would undergo another transformation, thought Mercy, becoming Amy and Helena's new home—and she was so very glad of that.

The most striking of the photos was a portrait of Euphemia, standing in dappled summer light under the Scary Tree. Looking very alive and very beautiful. Mercy could see why everyone fell in love with her.

Troy found her again, and they rejoined Thrasher and Wyetta, content to sip apple cider and watch the people. Servers with trays of champagne circulated among the guests. Poets and their supporters apparently liked to drink, as there were two open bars as well. An expansive buffet table stood along one of the long walls, offering up an enticing display of appetizers and desserts, including a chocolate fondue waterfall. Mercy could smell the chocolate and had to restrain herself from heading right for it. If this was what they meant by pregnancy cravings, it beat the heck out of pickles urges.

She saw Adah talking to Lillian. "I'll be right back," she told Troy, and headed for them.

"Great party," she told Lillian.

Lillian smiled. "Poets love a good gala."

"Yes, we do." Adah was dressed in her hippie best, having traded her colorful poncho for a sparkly tunic and long black skirt.

"I've got to mingle. You two talk poetry and poison."

Mercy and Adah watched as their hostess plucked a glass of champagne from a passing server and disappeared into the happy crowd of poetry lovers. Across the room Boswell and Bardin were surrounded by what appeared to be young poets, taking turns pontificating on the power of poetry. Dr. Saint-Yves was with Feinberg—and why not? Feinberg was a true patron of the arts and one of the most eligible bachelors in Vermont, now that Captain Thrasher was with Wyetta. She didn't see her uncle Hugo, but she knew he was there somewhere, taking it all in.

"I was so sorry to hear about Braden." Adah fingered the jeweled dragonfly pendant she wore around her neck. "What a terrible accident. And at Beecher's Pasture."

"It wasn't an accident. He didn't just fall. Someone pushed him."

Adah frowned. "I don't understand. Who would hurt Braden?"

"That's what everyone keeps asking me. A sweetheart of a guy, apparently, just like the scarecrow he was playing. Straight out of *The Wizard of Oz*."

"That's true. Braden was a gentle soul."

"Though there is reason to believe he may have been a poacher."

"I wouldn't have thought him capable of that." Adah caught herself playing with her necklace and pulled her hand away. "But he is gullible. Maybe he fell in with a bad crowd."

The cousin, thought Mercy. "Do you know Quaid Miller?"

"Not really. Levi didn't like him. Quaid worked at the corn maze, too, for a few weeks, but Levi caught the guy stealing his prize chickens."

"Did he report it?"

"I don't think so. Just let him go and told him to stay off our land."

Mercy knew that Thrasher had run background checks on Quaid Miller and Boswell. Boswell's record came up clean, but Quaid had a record of petty theft. Maybe he was into more serious crime these days. And maybe he'd dragged Braden along with him. Right to his death.

Those were pretty big maybes.

She flashed on the conversations she'd had with Levi earlier that day. Something didn't add up. "Levi said Braden only worked at the corn maze part-time."

"That's right. Two or three days a week. Weekends, mostly. He had a day job, in IT, I think. Levi could tell you more."

"Then who plays the scarecrow the rest of the time? You said something about scarecrows when we asked where to find your brother."

"Levi plays the scarecrow when Braden is off." Adah raised her hand to her lips and closed her eyes briefly before opening them again. "You think Levi was the target."

"I don't know. Does Levi wear the scarecrow-face makeup like Braden did?"

"Yes." Adah folded her fingers together as if in prayer. "It's possible one could be mistaken for the other. With the makeup. They have the same build." She pulled her cell from her pocket. "I'm warning him."

Adah's face was pale under the white and orange lights. "If Levi was the target, they could still be after him."

"Who is *they*?" Troy appeared at Mercy's side.

He had a habit of always showing up when she needed him most. A good habit in a husband. She explained the possibility that Levi had been the target. She didn't say anything about the letters in Levi's box because she didn't know if Adah knew about them or not.

"Why would anyone want to hurt my brother?"

"We can't rule it out," said Troy.

"So much has happened these past few days." Adah made a slow circle, gazing up at the walls filled with photos of Euphemia Whitney-Jones. "Something evil is at work here."

She was right about that, thought Mercy.

Adah's cell pinged and she read the text. "Levi says he'll be careful. He says you should be careful, too. Especially in the woods."

DAY FOUR
OCTOBER 30

———————

CHAPTER THIRTY-ONE

You don't have a home until you leave it and then,
when you have left it, you never can go back.
—JAMES BALDWIN

THE NEXT MORNING, OVER AN EARLY BREAKFAST, MERCY ASKED Troy to take her to see the castle ruins.

"Levi said to stay out of the woods," Troy reminded her.

"Elvis needs the exercise. And I need the fresh air."

"Honesty, remember?" He popped a piece of bacon into his mouth.

"I want to see where so much has happened. Willa and Lottie. Effie and her poets. Even the Druids and the long hunters."

"Don't forget the witch."

"And the witch."

"And the fact that Levi warned you against going in the woods has nothing to do with your wanting to go." He finished off his eggs, tossing the last of the bacon to Elvis and Susie Bear.

She sipped her one cup of regular coffee for the day. "Aren't you curious?"

"Curiosity killed the cat."

"We'll be perfectly safe, won't we, Elvis?" She smiled at her husband. "After all, we'll be with Vermont's most handsome game warden."

"Well, when you put it that way." Troy took their plates to the kitchen sink. "If you're sure you're up to it."

"I'll be fine. I've got the boot and I'll take my walking stick. I need to hang out with some trees."

"I know the feeling."

"Walk." At her command, the dogs scrambled to their feet and ran for the front door. You never had to tell them twice.

It was one of those spectacular autumn days that shimmered with sunlight and golden leaves and bright-blue sky. Troy insisted on driving, and Mercy let him. Her foot was feeling much better, but there was no point in pushing her luck.

The back roads were a riot of color. All the maples and beeches and birches, oaks and ashes and sycamores that lined the route were ablaze in oranges and reds and yellows. Neither she nor Troy spoke; they simply sat in silent appreciation as the truck carried them through the beautiful woodlands and forests of Vermont. They traveled south down Route 7a toward Equinox Mountain, veering north on Skyline Drive, through the scenic rolling hills of the Taconic Range.

Troy maneuvered the winding road—hairpin turn after hairpin turn— with the ease of a race car driver, driving past the turn at Old Sheep Lane for about a mile before turning onto an unmarked, unpaved road. He slowed down, the better to navigate the leaves and logs and ruts that cluttered the narrow lane.

"I can't believe that this will be our way home soon. It's like another world up here."

"A world out of time."

"You should ask me what time o' day; there is no clock in the forest."

"Shakespeare got that right." Troy pulled his truck over to the side of the road and parked near a trailhead so well-hidden by the trees Mercy would never have noticed it if he hadn't pointed it out to her. He helped her down to the ground and the dogs leapt out to join them, and they were off into the woods. Susie Bear and Elvis bounded ahead with the surefootedness of four-legged creatures born to run.

The Newfie took the lead, presumably because she'd been to the castle ruins before, not that Elvis seemed to mind. He was no doubt following his own nose, anyway. Either way, both dogs were headed in the same direction. The same direction Mercy and Troy were going.

They tramped along through the forest after the dogs for another twenty minutes, Mercy testing her burgeoning knowledge of Vermont's flora and fauna against Troy's years of study and experience in the field working with botanists and biologists and foresters and rangers and environmental engineers.

When she correctly identified a cluster of Pholiota—poisonous mushrooms—clinging to the bark of an old beech tree, her husband rewarded her with a kiss. "Well done."

Eventually, the Newfie slowed down, indulging herself in a little happy dance before a dense dogwood hedge. Elvis plunged right through it.

"This is the entrance to the castle ruins."

"What's that sound?"

They stopped to listen. The moaning sound was emanating from the clearing that lay beyond the thickets of dogwood. Mercy recognized the chanting. "Druids."

"Our lucky day."

Troy slipped Susie Bear a peanut butter treat. "Good job, girl." The Newfie chomped down the tasty reward in a single bite. "Go on."

She tilted her shaggy head at him before turning back to the dogwood thicket and crashing through the tangled branches, scattering rust-colored leaves as she went.

"After you." Troy held back the branches so Mercy could follow after Susie Bear and Elvis.

When she stepped into the crescent-shaped clearing, she felt like she'd traveled back in time to the first century. Or before. There, under three massive stone arches, Oisin and his fellow Druids were gathered in a half-circle, some standing along a flight of stairs that seemed to lead to nowhere.

"What a place," she whispered to Troy. "It looks like a film set." They moved into the shadows so they could observe the proceedings undetected. Troy waved Susie Bear down into a *sit*.

Elvis was nowhere to be seen.

Oisin commanded the center of the crescent, dressed in a white velvet robe embroidered with elaborate gold Celtic knot designs. He wore a hammered brass torque around his neck. Quaid Miller stood to his left and Liath and Muirne to his right, like Celtic bookends.

They heard a rustling behind them. There was Elvis, leading Gil Guerrette right to their hiding spot at the far edge of the gloomy glade.

"What are you doing here?" asked Gil quietly.

"Mercy wanted to see the castle ruins. And we came upon this. What are you doing here?"

"I tracked Poseidon's GPS here. Where it's gone silent."

"Someone here took the turtle?" asked Mercy.

"Looks like it."

"No more images on the trail camera?" asked Troy.

"No. We need to locate that turtle. Our friends at Fish & Wildlife intercepted a package at the international mail facility at JFK Airport. Turtles stuffed in socks and taped up and on the way to Hong Kong under false shipping labels."

"Wood turtles?"

"Mostly eastern box turtles and Florida box turtles, but spotted turtles and wood turtles, too but it's harder to, find them. They think these guys have smuggled out hundreds of turtles from New England and the South over the past couple of years. Over a million bucks' worth."

Oisin raised his arms. "We have gathered here together today to celebrate the life and death and rebirth of our brother Braden Miller."

"It's a memorial service for Braden." Mercy found herself moved by the ceremony.

"For a poacher," said Gil darkly.

"We don't know that for sure," said Troy.

"I'd bet on it. Your Boswell, too. I'm thinking they're part of the network of suppliers, smugglers, and buyers shipping our wildlife to China." Gil shook his head in disgust.

"If you're right, maybe Boswell is here." Mercy studied the Bards, Ovates, and Druids in the grove as the Arch-Druid continued his oration. She didn't see the poet, although a few of them wore the hoods of their cloaks pulled so far over their brows that she couldn't see their faces properly.

She wondered if there was a poacher or a poisoner or a murderer among them. If one of them had killed one of their own. Or if someone else had killed Braden, thinking he was Levi.

Oisin stepped forward. "*Turtar* is the gatekeeper to the realm of the spirits. We call upon *Turtar* to keep our brother Braden Miller safe on his journey home to the spirit world and that he may one day return to us in his next life."

He turned and said something unintelligible to Quaid. He slipped behind one of the large boulders and pulled a green plastic tub on wheels up to the Arch-Druid. After pulling off the lid, Oisin reached in and lifted a turtle out of the box.

Mercy peered at the small reptile with the bright-orange neck and legs. "Is that a wood turtle?"

"Yep. Not good." Troy sighed. "Your Druids are out of line."

"Looks like poaching to me," said Gil.

They all watched as Oisin held the turtle up by the sides of his carapace.

"*Turtar,*" he intoned.

"*Turtar,*" repeated the rest of the Druids.

"Symbol of longevity, wisdom, protection, persistence, and endurance," pronounced Oisin. "The Cosmic Turtle."

"Braden Miller didn't poach a wood turtle for his own memorial service." Mercy felt compelled to defend the murder victim.

"Maybe not, but we don't know that they poached the turtle specifically for this service," Gil pointed out. "For all we know, they use the Cosmic Turtle in all their rituals. Which means everyone here is complicit."

"Or Braden and his partner—Quaid or Boswell or some unknown party—captured the turtle and Braden had second thoughts," said Troy. "Maybe he wanted to give it to the Druids. They fell out, and his partner killed him. Murder among thieves."

"Maybe." Mercy was not quite ready to give up on her mistaken-scarecrow-identity theory of Braden's murder quite yet. But there was no denying the poaching, no matter how spiritual the aim. The wood turtle population had declined more than 50 percent over the past thirty years—and many of the surviving wood turtles were old, as the younger specimens were the prime targets of poachers.

"That wood turtle is all the proof we need," argued Gil "I say we go in."

"Wait a minute." Mercy nudged her husband's shoulder. "Third Druid from the left of Oisin."

"That's Varden Lind."

"The poisoned Druid?" asked Gil. "I thought he was in the hospital. What's he doing here?"

"I don't know," said Mercy. "But I'd like to find out."

"We'll go for the turtle," Troy told Gil. "Mercy and Elvis can keep an eye on Lind."

"Roger that." Gil strode into the middle of the crescent, his park ranger campaign hat tilted at a rakish angle. "Park Ranger Gil Guerrette. You are in possession of a threatened species and in violation of both state and federal law."

Troy and Susie Bear flanked Gil. Mercy and Elvis stayed put, trying to keep track of Lind and the proceedings at the same time.

The Druids all stared at Gil for a minute, and then started moving toward Oisin. The Arch-Druid raised his palm up, and they all fell back. "We are only borrowing the wood turtle, Ranger Guerrette, for our service."

"'Borrowing' is not a legal term." Gil glared at him. "The legal term is 'unlawful possession.'"

"We are celebrating his god-hood."

"God-hood?"

Mercy smiled at that. She hadn't believed he'd meant to hurt the wood turtle. Not that that was any excuse. Wildlife belonged in the wild.

"His spirit, if you will." Oisin held the wood turtle out to Gil. "You can have him back now, if you'd like."

"His name is Poseidon. You turned off his GPS."

"We will switch it back on. We always intended to switch it back on and return the turtle to his preferred habitat."

Gil stood with his legs apart and rocked on his heels. "Did you know that wood turtles are among the most illegally trafficked group of vertebrates in the world? Thanks to people like you, we've lost half the wood turtle population over the past thirty years."

"We would never do anything to damage such a beautiful and sacred creature. We believe in living in harmony with the natural world."

"Place the turtle in the tub," ordered Gil.

"The tub?"

Gil pointed to the tub on wheels next to Quaid Miller. "I'm taking possession of the animal you have poached."

"We are happy to return the turtle." Oisin placed the wood turtle carefully inside the tub.

Gil reached for the handle of the tub on wheels. "You know, I could arrest you."

The Druids all started talking at once. Milling about and streaming toward Gil and Oisin. The dogs barked. Mercy lost sight of Lind in the shuffle. Again, Oisin raised his hand, and they fell back.

"I could arrest all of you." Gil seemed unimpressed by the objections. "But instead I'm issuing you a verbal warning. Leave the wood turtles alone."

Mercy glanced Lind's way; he was gone.

"Thank you." Oisin gave a short bow.

"We'll be watching you." Gil swept his eyes around the circle. "All of you. If we catch you anywhere near a wood turtle or any other endangered wildlife, you're going to jail. That's a promise."

"Understood," Oisin told Gil, then addressed Troy. "Two things, Warden Warner, if I may."

Don't push your luck, thought Mercy. She suspected that both Troy and Gil had had their fill of Druids for the day. But all her husband said was, "Sure."

The Arch-Druid leaned in toward Troy. "One, you will find none of us had anything to do with poor Braden's murder. Two, *turtar*—the turtle—is your spirit animal. You are a protector of home and hearth and habitat."

"Right."

You don't need to be a Druid to know that, thought Mercy.

Oisin gave Troy a grave look. "Three, your own home may be in need of protection. Be vigilant."

The Druids dispersed, and she and Elvis made their way back to the trailhead with Troy and Susie Bear while Gil took Poseidon back to his creek hideaway.

Becker was waiting for them.

"You're wanted at the estate," he told Mercy. "Thrasher's down there, with your uncle and Feinberg. There's some kind of protest going on."

Mercy would have to visit Willa Strong's grave another time.

CHAPTER THIRTY-TWO

When you're safe at home you wish you were
having an adventure; when you're having an
adventure you wish you were safe at home.
—THORNTON WILDER

BECKER TURNED TO TROY. "WE NEED TO GET DOWN TO THE station. Harrington has asked me to bring you and Susie Bear in for a search. Missing dementia patient at Pine Tree House. You can drop Mercy and Elvis off and meet us at the station."

"Okay." Troy bundled Mercy and the dogs into the truck and carted them off to their new old house, which wasn't that far away if you were a grackle, but by vehicle it was nearly a twenty-minute ride.

They could hear all the people before they saw them. Chanting, singing, drumming, a mêlée of sound and fury. Signifying something, Mercy just wasn't sure what yet.

Troy parked the truck and got out. "I'm going with you."

"You need to find that patient." She knew he felt torn. "I've got Elvis. And Thrasher's here with Feinberg and his bodyguards, no doubt."

"I'll walk you in." Troy placed his large hand at the small of her back.

Between Troy and the dogs and her walking stick, it was a fairly easy stroll through the protesters to the entrance of the limestone manor. *Soon to be officially* our *house,* she thought. All the protesters in the world wouldn't change that.

The trespassers were mostly familiar to her. She recognized a few of the Druids (who must have come directly from the memorial at the ruins) among the treasure hunters and the poets, although all wore civilian clothes now. That is, the usual Vermonter costume of flannel shirts and Dockers and barn coats, sweaters and jeans and parkas. Some carried signs that read THE WORLD NEEDS MORE POETS! and THE ARTS MATTER! and SAVE GRACKLE TREE FARM!

The colonel and the billionaire stood to Jillian's right with Dr. Saint-Yves. Mercy had met her briefly at the reception last night, but she had been so surrounded with admirers they hadn't had a chance to talk. Thrasher and Troy stepped forward together, projecting an unassailable authority between their uniforms and commanding presence. Behind them were two tough-looking guys in suits that Mercy recognized as Feinberg's bodyguards, whom she only knew as Lewis and Clark.

"This is private property," the captain called out to the crowd. "I'm going to have to ask you to leave. Don't make me throw you all in jail."

"Power to the Poets!" a few chanted.

"Long live Grackle Tree Farm!" bellowed one of the Druids.

"We'll be back," yelled one of the treasure hunters.

They all griped and groaned and grumbled, but slowly they began to disperse.

"What's going on here?" Mercy and Elvis joined Thrasher, the shepherd in herding mode, ready to escort the interlopers off the property. He stood on point, hackles up, lips curled, ears back, a posture that seemed to convince most of the stragglers to head for the parking lot.

"Word's gotten out about the key, and the possibility of more treasure. That's brought out all kinds—the exploiters as well as the protectors."

"How did they find out about it?"

"Someone leaked it. We're looking into it." The captain wore an expression of such fierce determination Mercy almost felt sorry for the leaker.

Feinberg's bodyguards Lewis and Clark advanced slowly, and the last of the estate camp followers disappeared behind the stand of juniper trees. Lewis raised his arm to the left, and Clark ambled in that direction, no doubt checking the perimeter, while Lewis took up his wide-legged stance in front of the house. Elvis cocked his ears.

"Stay," she ordered, knowing that a search of the perimeter was one of the shepherd's very favorite missions. But she needed Elvis here with her.

"We should get back to the station," Thrasher told Troy.

"I'm not alone, Troy," Mercy said. "And we've got Elvis and Lewis and Clark for protection. We'll be fine."

"We've got Russo in custody," Thrasher reminded them. "That should mitigate any threat. But I'll talk to Harrington about putting a uniform up here at least through Halloween, to keep the riffraff out if nothing else."

"Go save that dementia patient." Mercy smiled at her husband.

He smiled back. "Okay."

"I'm off, too." Jillian handed Mercy the keys. "Have fun."

Thrasher, Troy, and Susie Bear ushered Jillian out of the garden. As soon as they disappeared from view, Uncle Hugo spoke. "Now we must talk. Let's go inside." He pushed open the front door, but Mercy ignored him.

"I'm Mercy Carr." She offered her hand to Dr. Saint-Yves, who'd been silent all this time. "We met last night."

"I remember. Thank you so much for this opportunity to visit. I understand it will soon be your home."

"Yes, we're very excited about it."

The French woman put out a fist for Elvis to sniff, and he obliged. "Is this Malinois your dog?"

"Yes, this is Elvis."

"Elvis the King. *Très beau*."

"Thank you." Mercy smiled as Elvis allowed the newcomer to pet the soft fur on his long elegant neck. "He likes you. Believe me, he doesn't like just anybody."

"Dr. Saint-Yves is here to examine the letters you found," said Feinberg. "She wanted to see where you discovered them."

"Of course. I suppose it's very different from the home Euphemia Whitney-Jones shared with Leontine Bonnet."

"Yes. Very different. But it is charming in its own way. Although it is a little neglected."

"Unlike *L'Heure Bleu*."

Dr. Saint-Yves raised her eyebrows. "Leontine Bonnet was my great-grandmother. When Euphemia Whitney-Jones died, she left her home in Provence in trust to our family, to preserve as a testament to the love they shared. My grandmother oversaw the establishment of the museum, which now welcomes nearly two hundred thousand visitors a year. Almost as many as *Fondation Maeght*, the modern art museum in Saint-Paul-de-Vence."

"Your grandmother sounds like a force to be reckoned with."

"Yes. Her name was Sandrine Samara Bonnet. I'm named after her."

"Let's continue this conversation in the house, shall we?" Feinberg ushered them inside, and they all filed into the hallway of the old grande dame Mercy and Troy would soon call their own. Mercy left her walking stick by the door. She didn't need it anymore.

Elvis disappeared, doing his usual security detail while Mercy took the group on a tour of the first floor. For the benefit of her visitor from France, she shared what she knew of the history of the house, starting with the Strongs, who'd built the house in 1866.

"I feel like I have been here before, I've heard so much about it. It is nice to be able to see it now."

"Euphemia Whitney-Jones's family bought the house in 1918, and they've owned it ever since." Mercy changed the subject. "So your grandmother never brought you here."

"No, I was born long after Euphemia died. Since her death, our family has focused on the property in France."

"But you must know Euphemia's poetry."

Elvis returned to accompany them on the rest of Mercy's tour of the first floor. He shadowed Saint-Yves, as if she were his new best friend. Maybe she was. If Elvis liked her, she must be a good person. The shepherd was an excellent judge of character.

"My grandmother gave me the illustrated book of children's poetry when I was a child. She'd read a poem to me, and then I'd read a poem to her. It helped me with my English."

"Well, it worked. You speak very good English."

"My favorite was 'The Ghost Witch of Grackle Tree.'"

"Mine, too. And 'All the Unnamed Women.'"

"Let's go upstairs to the library," said Uncle Hugo. "We thought we'd show Miss Saint-Yves the secretary where you found the letters."

"Of course." Mercy led the group upstairs to the second floor. Elvis raced ahead, heading straight for the library, but she showed them the rest of the rooms on that floor first, saving the best for last. Elvis was waiting for them by the escritoire.

"What a collection of books!"

"You'll see all the classics, but there's more here that you might appreciate." Mercy showed the young woman the many bookshelves in Euphemia

Whitney-Jones's library stocked with books about witchcraft and ghosts and the occult.

"Have you ever seen her?"

"I'm not sure what you mean."

"The witch. My grandmother believed she was real. Her mother told her that she'd seen her here late at night."

Mercy told her about the time she spent the night there on a dare, and the wailing woman in white. She didn't say anything about Levi Beecher.

"My grandmother told me that many people have seen her. On hot summer nights when the moon was full, they'd see her leave the house, roam the grounds, and disappear into the woods."

"You're talking about the people who came to Euphemia and Leontine's literary salon here in the summer."

"Yes."

"They were poets."

Dr. Saint-Yves laughed, a sound as elegant as her French accent. "You do not like poets?"

"I love poets. But they have overactive imaginations. They like to tell stories. Play with words. And they love secrets. At least, Euphemia did." Mercy showed them the escritoire and the hidden compartment. Elvis nudged her hand with his nose, and she petted him.

"Incredible." The young woman traced the secret drawer with a slender finger.

"Have you read the letters?"

"Yes."

"And you're not worried about the reaction of the public? Euphemia and Leontine's devotees?"

"Daniel showed me the memorial of the American pilot. He was Euphemia's fiancé, but he married the sister. Maude."

"Yes. But the letters reveal that Euphemia loved Robillard."

"And so she did. For a time." She gave a little Gallic shrug. "He seduced her sister. Euphemia moved to France. She met my great-grandmother. The pilot went to war. He died. The sister married again. She moved to California. Such is life. Such is love."

"Right." Mercy supposed this was a very European attitude toward love and life. She couldn't help but think it was all more complicated than that.

Dr. Saint-Yves raised a smoothly shaped eyebrow at her. "Have you taken only one lover in your life?"

Mercy didn't answer that, but she thought about it. She had truly loved only three men in her romantic life. Her first sweetheart, who broke her heart when he betrayed her. Martinez, who broke her heart when he died. And now Troy. If or when or how he might break her heart remained to be seen.

Elvis raced out of the library, teeth bared.

Mercy called for the shepherd, but he did not return. She excused herself and left the room. On the landing she saw Elvis poised at the top of the stairs, still as stone, eyes focused on the window that graced the opposite wall. His way of telling her that there was something out there. Something dangerous. The fact that he was not barking scared her more than if he were howling like a cat on fire.

Mercy moved quickly back into the library. "Move away from the windows."

They all stared at her.

"Elvis is alerting. I don't know why, but a man died in this room three days ago. We can't be too careful."

The colonel nodded just as the sound of breaking glass startled them all.

"I think that came from the back of the house." Mercy flattened herself against the wall, and the others followed suit. The colonel pulled a Glock from his waistband, placed it on the floor, and slid it across the hardwood floor to Mercy. She slid downward, back to the wall, squatting down and catching the weapon with her fingers.

"Downstairs somewhere." Uncle Hugo slipped a Sig Sauer P365 out of the ankle holster on the inside of his left ankle.

"You have another gun."

"Of course I do."

How ironic that it was the octogenarian in the room who was the most well-armed and well-prepared. Or maybe "ironic" was not the right word. Maybe the right word was "inevitable."

"Thrasher's out there with Amy and the baby and Jillian." Mercy was worried about them.

"Surely they're gone by now," said Feinberg.

"I hope so. Where are Lewis and Clark?"

"I'll find out." Feinberg texted his bodyguards.

"*Qu'est ce que se passe?*" In her fright, the young French woman had reverted to her native tongue.

"I don't know. But better safe than sorry. Stay down. Stay put. Do what the colonel tells you to do."

With a terrible sense of déjà vu, Mercy ran for the library door, flattening herself against the wall of the landing. Elvis was still there, at the top of the staircase. Still focused on the bottom of the stairs. He acknowledged her presence with a twitch of his triangular ears and sank into his Sphinx pose.

The sound of more breaking glass drew her attention back to the library. The shepherd leapt down the stairs. "Elvis," she shouted after him, but he did not return. She raced back to the room, gun drawn.

"Is everyone all right?" She saw the colonel on the floor, holding his head.

"I've been hit by flying glass. Flesh wound, I think."

"Someone threw something through the window." Feinberg pointed to the center of the room, where a silver canister rolled toward the door.

"Is it a bomb?" asked the French girl.

"Tear gas," said Mercy. "Everybody out!"

But she was too late. She heard the door slam behind her as the canister exploded. No escape.

She dropped to the floor. "Get down. Cover your face with your shirt." Smoke filled the room, and everyone was overcome. Mercy's eyes and nose and throat burned. She could hear the French girl and Feinberg and the colonel coughing. Temporarily blinded, she sensed rather than saw the men enter the room and drag the sobbing young woman away. She screamed as they carried her off.

There was nothing Mercy could do. She couldn't shoot what she couldn't see.

She crawled over to the door, reached up blindly for the latch, and pushed the door open. She stumbled out into the relatively fresh air of the landing. She pulled out her cell and struggled to call 911. But she couldn't see anything. Her eyes were still too raw, too tearful.

She'd learned about tear gas in the military and she knew how dangerous it could be. She had to get her uncle Hugo and Feinberg out of the library. Not to mention her own pregnant self. She took off her coat and the Henley shirt she wore under it and wrapped her shirt around her face, then slipped her coat back on.

She commando crawled back into the room toward the corner where she'd last seen the colonel. The air was a little clearer now, between the broken window and the open door, but not by much.

The colonel was on the floor, doubled over, gasping for breath and disoriented. He couldn't speak. She grabbed him under his armpits and hauled him out of the room and across the landing into the nearest bathroom. She propped him up by the tub, turned on the water, and splashed his face and eyes with water. He seemed better, but she couldn't be sure.

Mercy left him there and went back for Feinberg. She was disoriented, too, and racked with nausea. It took her longer to find the billionaire than it had to find her great-uncle.

Feinberg was in better shape than the colonel, but not by much. He'd been the closest to the canister when it blew, so his relative youth and fitness level were only so relevant. He tried to say something but coughed severely from the effort.

"Don't talk," she told him through her Henley. She helped him up to his hands and knees. "Can you move?"

"Yes," he managed to say in between coughing fits. Together they walked on all fours to the landing. Feinberg collapsed about halfway to the bathroom, so Mercy had to drag him the rest of the way.

She propped him up next to the colonel, and washed his eyes and face, too. Now that she didn't have to go back into that library—and thank goodness, the thought that all those books were contaminated now was heartbreaking—she unwrapped her shirt from her face and flushed her own eyes and cheeks with water.

She could see a little better now, at least well enough to call 911.

Her mouth burned and speaking was very difficult. Her conversation with the 911 dispatcher was very brief, given the pain she was in, but she knew they'd get here as soon as they could. She tried texting Troy, but it didn't go through. She was so tired. It hurt to talk, it hurt to move, it hurt to see, it hurt to breathe.

She knew she needed to get them all out of the house. Tear gas vapors rose, so they were only protected in this bathroom on the second floor for so long. They had to get down the stairs and out into the garden, into the fresh air. She had to find the girl. And Elvis. And Lewis and Clark.

"Mercy." Feinberg's voice was just a faint rasp.

"We need to get out. Can you get down the stairs on your own?"

The billionaire nodded.

"Okay. I'll take Uncle Hugo."

Feinberg nodded again.

"Go."

Feinberg used the side of the tub to draw himself up, and stumbled out of the bathroom. She could hear him navigate the stairs, awkwardly, as she grabbed the colonel and heaved him up and over her shoulder. Lucky for her the colonel was a slender man, although more muscular than she expected. Heavier.

Mercy used the toilet to steady herself as she straightened up. It felt like her whole body was on fire. The pain radiated from her blistering skin through her muscles and fascia and deep into her very bones.

Uncle Hugo was a dead weight, dragging her down. She bent her knees and grasped the railing of the staircase with one hand and palmed the wall with the other to help keep herself upright as she staggered to the stairs.

She looked down the steps to the first floor. It seemed an eternity. An endless stairway to heaven, or a short flight to hell. She didn't know how she'd manage it.

Feinberg had managed it, though; the front door was open, and with any luck, he was outside right now, using the glorious autumn breeze to cleanse his lungs of the toxic mist of tear gas.

She heard an ominous *whoosh* behind her. She held on to her elderly great-uncle and twisted her neck to look behind herself. A crackle and a burst of light nearly blinded her again.

Flames.

The grand old Victorian—the house meant to be hers—was on fire.

LEVI BEECHER STOOD A hundred yards north of the massive old sugar maple behind the old barn, taking stock of the old vegetable garden and the greenhouse. He figured Mercy Carr and Troy Warner might want to bring the garden back to life. The raised beds were overgrown with weeds, and most of the glass in the greenhouse needed replacing, but he knew that young people liked to grow their own food; maybe they would, too.

Years ago, he and Adah had worked in this very garden each summer, along with everyone else at Effie's literary salon. Effie believed that all poets should get their hands dirty before they sat down to write. She expected everyone who came to pitch in on the creation of all meals. They prepared the soil, planted seeds and seedlings, watered and weeded, harvested and scrubbed and cooked and laid out the food on the long tables set behind the house.

Effie had believed in growing gardens and walking in the woods and sleeping under the stars. From what he knew of her successors, they'd believed in those things as well. Ever since Effie died, he'd dreaded the time when the property changed hands. The more he got to know Mercy Carr and Troy Warner, the more comfortable he felt about their taking over the estate.

Levi would give them a head start on the garden. His gift to the new stewards of Grackle Tree Farm. He'd weed the beds, rebuild the greenhouse, fix the fencing. He made a list of the supplies he'd need and committed it to memory.

He would start tomorrow.

A fever of grackles swooped suddenly over his head, fleeing the old maple and filling the sky with a flurry of black wings and sharp trills before disappearing into the forest. Levi looked back down toward the manor house.

He saw the smoke and he ran.

CHAPTER THIRTY-THREE

We all live in a house on fire...
—TENNESSEE WILLIAMS

MERCY NEEDED TO GET THE COLONEL OUT OF THE HOUSE. The fire would spread fast, as it typically did in these old houses. The old Victorian limestone manor may have been tough enough to last more than 150 years, but in reality it was a tinderbox. A strong tinderbox, but a tinderbox, nonetheless.

And whoever started the fire knew that. The arsonists must have tossed in the tear gas to incapacitate them all, and then started the fire, with the relative certainty that none of them would make it out.

But Feinberg was out. Time for Uncle Hugo to join him. She stood at the top of the stairs, looking down again. She knew there was no way she could carry him down the entire flight.

"Uncle Hugo." She squatted down, grasping the volute handrail with one hand and holding on to the colonel with the other, and lowered herself to a sitting position on the top tread. He was on top of her now; she held him against her chest as if he were baby Helena.

He moaned, and tried to move. "Mercy."

"Quiet," she commanded. "Stay still." She knew he wasn't used to taking orders from anyone, but for once in his life—or at least, since he'd been the highest-ranking officer in the room—she needed him to do as he was told. She told him as much, her mouth burning with every word. "The house is on fire. We're going down this staircase. If you fight me, we both die."

The old man groaned.

"Just hold on. We'll take it step by step." Mercy pulled with her legs, and dropped down on her butt to the next tread. To his credit, the colonel held on. Down they went together, from riser to riser, Mercy hanging on to her great-uncle as if he were a sack of potatoes.

Every part of her body screamed with every jounce; she could only imagine how the colonel was feeling. He grunted with every bump and cursed once or twice, but otherwise he said nothing as she descended the stairs on her derriere as quickly as she dared. She could feel the heat of the fire as it gained force behind her. By the time she reached the bottom of the stairs, she was sweating with the effort, and the salt irritated her already stinging skin.

Mercy grabbed the baluster and pulled herself up, bringing the colonel with her. Her bad foot was throbbing again, and the extra weight nearly finished her. She hoisted him back onto her shoulder and trudged out the front door. She didn't look back until she'd deposited the octogenarian on the gravel path next to Feinberg. The fire had yet to reach the staircase, but she figured it wouldn't take long, and then the smoke from the tear gas would mix with the smoke from the fire. Double the peril.

The billionaire was on his back, propped up against an overgrown yew. "Cell," he said hoarsely. Mercy saw the phone in his lap, and snatched it up. He'd called 911, just as she had. Between the two of them, EMTs should be on the way.

"Fire department?" she asked him, and he nodded.

"Yes." He pointed toward the house and winced with pain as he squeezed out each syllable. "Lewis. Clark. Girl. Still. In. There."

"Elvis?"

Feinberg shook his head, leaning back and closing his eyes. The effort of updating her had exhausted him.

Mercy was pretty exhausted herself. She drew herself up and limped back into the house. She turned into the kitchen, where the fire had yet to establish itself, although she could see flames licking at the corners of one of the inside walls. It wouldn't be long before the world's ugliest kitchen was gone.

She grabbed a towel, doused it with water, and held it over her nose and mouth. She searched the kitchen but found nothing and no one. She hobbled to the living room, where she found Lewis and Clark tied up and gagged. She untied them with trembling, blistering fingers, and together they all ducked down and lurched out of the room and into the hallway and out the front door, where the bodyguards fell to the ground, flanking Feinberg.

The sound of sirens pealed through the trees, and Mercy nearly cried with relief. She still had not found Elvis. Or Leontine's great-granddaughter. She couldn't save them unless she knew where they were.

She looked up to the second floor and saw a man up there on the landing, wielding a fire extinguisher. It looked like Levi Beecher, although she couldn't be sure, as he wore a bandana over his mouth.

She tried calling to him, but she couldn't make a sound. She tried whistling for Elvis. Nothing came out but a tortured squeak. Her pack was upstairs somewhere in the blaze, but she did have her cell. She texted Troy as she squeaked Elvis's name over and over again. She dragged herself to her feet. She'd go around the outside of the house; maybe she'd see something by looking in rather than looking out. She tottered down the gravel path, cursing with every footfall, clapping for Elvis with her blistered hands. She heard the barking before she saw the shepherd come barreling out of the back garden.

"Elvis!" She fell to her knees to hug him, and he stopped long enough to lick her nose and then blazed past her toward the front of the house. She launched herself back upright and reeled after him. She saw him on the front step. He barked at her and then bounded into the house. The house on fire.

"Where are you going?" Mercy pulled the wet towel back over her face and went into the house. She glanced up the stairs, but Levi—or whoever—was gone.

"Elvis!" She could hear his high-pitched yelping. It was coming from the kitchen. She couldn't imagine what the dog was doing in there; she'd checked that room already.

Always trust your dog.

Mercy plunged into the kitchen. She looked around for Elvis, but she didn't see him.

"Elvis!" she tried to shout, but her weakened voice was swallowed by the smoke. The fire had reached the kitchen.

The barking had stopped. Among the whining and whooshing of the fire and the cracking and crackling of the kitchen under siege, she heard a terrible banging, and realized it was coming from the far corner of the room. The pantry. She stumbled over to the built-in closet. Elvis was there, lying at the foot of the pantry, whining. He lumbered to his feet. Mercy knew that he was suffering from smoke inhalation.

"Go!" she told him. But he only moved as far as her side.

Mercy reached up and unlocked the door. She opened it, and Dr. Saint-Yves fell into her arms.

"Go!" she told Elvis again, and this time he led the way. Mercy half carried the distraught woman out of the kitchen, into the foyer, and out of the entrance. She careened down the front steps and across the gravel path to the raised beds in the front garden, where she fell down on a patch of lavender, taking her visitor from the South of France with her.

Mercy held the woman against her chest as she sobbed. Elvis curled up at her hip, and she stroked his ash-streaked fur. Looking up, she saw Levi slip into the burning kitchen. It may have been the world's ugliest kitchen, but it was her kitchen.

And she cried.

CHAPTER THIRTY-FOUR

The ache for home lives in all of us, the safe place where
we can go as we are and not be questioned.
—MAYA ANGELOU

A N HOUR LATER, MERCY SAT IN A HARD PLASTIC CHAIR IN A
treatment room at the ER while Troy and Thrasher and Susie Bear
stood watch. Elvis was in the Nana Banana, her grandmother's mobile
veterinary clinic, being treated by Patience herself.

"I'm fine," she told Dr. Chen. "But what about the baby?"

"Typically, being exposed to tear gas in and of itself does not cause ad-
verse outcomes during pregnancy. Apparently you did not panic or suffer
any severe disorientation during the exposure, which can lead to subsequent injury. Well done."

"Hear, hear," said Thrasher.

"Are you sure?" Troy paced back and forth across the tiny room. "The
Taliban used tear gas. They still do. Terrible stuff."

"You served in Afghanistan?"

"We all did." Troy tipped his head toward Thrasher and Mercy.

"I served there, too. I know my way around tear gas. So believe me
when I tell you that the prognosis is good, for both baby and mother." Dr.
Chen frowned. "That said, exposure can lead to a host of other compli-
cations. You need to get out of those clothes and into the shower. Nurse
Tamara will help you."

"What about Uncle Hugo and Feinberg?"

"Daniel Feinberg and Colonel Fleury have been transferred to the third
floor, where they'll be well taken care of."

"What does that mean, exactly?"

"You all are suffering from smoke inhalation from the fire. You are young and strong, and that makes all the difference. Mr. Feinberg is also relatively young and strong."

Mercy was scared for the colonel. "Uncle Hugo is not young."

"No, he is not. But most people exposed to tear gas fully recover in time. I believe your uncle will, too. But it may take him a little longer."

Mercy knew that Feinberg's bodyguards had already been treated at the emergency room and released.

"And Dr. Saint-Yves?"

"The patient from France is doing well. Again, she is young and strong. She's being treated in another ER room, but she keeps asking for you. Take that shower now, and then you can go see her." Dr. Chen addressed Troy. "See that she gets that shower pronto."

"I will."

"Good." The physician's professional mask slipped a bit, and Mercy saw a glimpse of true kindness in Dr. Chen's face. "I know your dog was there at the fire. I hope he's all right."

"Thank you. He's with my grandmother now. She's the best veterinarian in the state."

"Good to hear." The mask was firmly back in place.

Dr. Chen headed for the door. "Nurse Tamara is here to help you." The doctor left the room, swapping places with a sweet-faced young woman with a no-nonsense attitude.

"Follow me," the nurse instructed Mercy.

"What about my clothes?"

"There's scrubs or the gift shop." Nurse Tamara placed her hands on her hips. "Up to you, but there are some nice sweat suits in the shop. Softer, and you're going to want soft."

"I'm on it," Troy told Mercy. "Do what Nurse Tamara says, and then we'll go talk to Saint-Yves. After that, straight home to the cabin. Deal?"

"Deal."

"We'll be in room 121," the nurse told him.

The shower was equal parts pain and pleasure. By the time she was out, Troy was back with a camouflage-patterned sweat suit with bright pink stripes down the sleeves and pants legs. Not that she cared. Despite the careful washing and the soothing antibiotic cream Nurse Tamara had slathered over her, Mercy's blistering skin was still sensitive to touch, especially her extremities. The softer the clothing, the better.

She slipped on her new outfit cautiously, trying not to wince. "Good to go."

"Are you all right?" Troy looked at Nurse Tamara, as if Mercy's answer to that question could not be trusted.

"Get her home as soon as you can," the nurse advised.

"Will do."

Troy helped Mercy walk to the ER room down the hall, Susie Bear on their heels.

"I'll need another walking stick," she teased.

"Not funny."

Mercy laughed. "You sound more and more like a husband every day."

Thrasher followed with Susie Bear on a leash, prancing happily. Mercy hoped that her poor Elvis would be in similar high spirits soon. The Nana Banana was parked right outside in the ER parking lot. She'd wanted to stay with Elvis, but Patience told her the best thing she could do for him was to trust her to treat him properly. "He'll sense your anxiety," Patience had said. Mercy knew she was right. She also knew that if anyone loved Elvis as much as she did, it was her grandmother. And Troy.

With Troy and Thrasher's help, Mercy hobbled into the young Frenchwoman's hospital room. Susie Bear ambled over to the bed, and the patient gave her a sweet petting.

"Dr. Saint-Yves, how are you feeling?" asked the captain.

"Okay now." She looked at Mercy. "How can I ever thank you?"

"No need." Mercy was glad to see that she looked relatively well, considering what she'd been through. At least physically. Emotionally—well, that could take longer. "We're just glad you're all right. That everyone is all right."

"And Elvis the King?"

"He's with my grandmother. The best veterinarian in Vermont." Mercy carefully lowered herself into another one of those hard plastic chairs. Her tailbone was still sore from that arduous trip down the stairs with the colonel. Not to mention her sensitive skin.

"And your beautiful house?"

"Yes, well, I suspect the kitchen is a total loss."

"I'm sorry."

"It's okay. It really was the world's ugliest kitchen. Levi Beecher saved the rest of the house." She turned to Troy. "It was Levi, correct?"

"Yes," confirmed Troy.

"And he's all right?"

"Fine," said Thrasher. "Treated and released."

"Levi Beecher is the caretaker of the estate. I recognize the name." Dr. Saint-Yves looked at Mercy with those gold-flecked hazel eyes. Susie Bear heard the anguish in her voice and pushed her big shaggy head onto the doctor's lap. "I still don't really understand what happened."

"Do you remember anything about the men who locked you in the closet, Dr. Saint-Yves?"

"Please call me Samara. All my friends call me Samara." She ran her fingers through her shiny brown hair. "To answer your question, *non*. They were all in black and they wore masks." She stroked the Newfie's silky ears absently.

"Gas masks."

She nodded. "My eyes were burning. I could not see anything. I thought I was going blind." She paused to compose herself, and Susie Bear nuzzled her elbow. "Why would anyone do such a thing?"

"We're just piecing it together ourselves," said Thrasher. "We're grateful everyone got out in time."

"Thanks to Mercy." She pronounced it *merci*, just like Gil Guerrette.

"Thanks to Mercy," repeated Troy. "And Levi Beecher."

They all fell quiet for a moment. Mercy gazed out the hospital window, past the parking lot and beyond, to the Green Mountains, which were not green this time of year, but red and orange and gold. Maples and beeches and birches, changing as they always did over the course of the seasons, in the never-ending cycle of life. Spreading their seeds and shedding their leaves, budding and bowering and bearing fruit, slipping into hibernation's sleep for the winter. And waking up and starting all over again come spring.

Spring, when she'd give birth herself. Just another tree bearing fruit.

Something tugged at the corner of her mind. Something important. Mercy knew she was missing something. She closed her eyes and tried to capture the idea playing at the edge of her subconscious.

The forest for the trees. Mercy stared at the young woman named for her beloved grandmother Sandrine Samara Bonnet. *Samara.*

Troy grinned at her. "You have a theory."

"Sort of."

"Let's hear this sort-of theory of yours." Thrasher favored her with one of his movie star smiles.

"I'm not sure what it means."

"We can help you figure it out. Keep talking."

"It's got to do with keys."

"You know what the brass key fits," guessed Thrasher.

"Maybe, maybe not."

"I don't follow," said the captain.

"Some keys unlock physical objects, but some unlock mysteries." Mercy paused. "Poets speak in metaphor. Symbols. Suppose Euphemia's brass key is just that: a symbol. After all, there are all kinds of keys."

Troy snapped his fingers. "Like musical keys."

"Map keys," threw out Thrasher.

"*Clé de ton coeur.* Key to your heart." Samara gave Susie Bear a sweet look.

"Encryption keys." Troy grinned like he'd just won *Jeopardy!*

"Island keys." The captain gave Troy a look that implied that he'd trumped him.

"You're on the right track."

Mercy turned to the lovely patient from Provence. "Do you know what your name means?"

"Saint-Yves is the patron saint of Brittany. Protector of the poor."

"And your given name?"

"Sandrine is a form of Alexandra. Which means protector of man."

"Yes. And Samara?"

"Protected by God." Samara smiled.

"That's a lot of protection," said Troy.

"It's served Samara well so far," Thrasher pointed out.

"True."

Mercy looked at the French woman, who even from a hospital bed maintained her chic. "Samara is an unusual name. Your grandmother's name."

"Yes."

"You don't hear it very often here in the U.S."

"Or in France."

"There's the jazz singer Samara Joy," said Thrasher. "And the city in Russia."

"Give us a hint," pleaded Troy with a fake whine in his voice.

Mercy waved her arm at the window, with its view of the forest. "Think tree."

"Tree?" asked Samara with a confused look.

"Tree." Mercy wiggled her eyebrows at her husband, knowing this would be a clue that the man who spent all his time among the trees of Vermont would understand.

Troy groaned. "Seed key."

"Of course." Thrasher also knew his trees. He reached out to high-five her husband. "Seed key."

"What is this seed key?" asked Samara.

"A seed key is one of those little whirligig seeds you find on certain trees," explained Mercy. "Like ash trees and elm trees and sugar maple trees." She made a little twirling motion with her index finger.

"*Graine d'hélicoptére.*"

"Helicopter seeds. Exactly. The botanical name being *samara*."

"And we're right back to Scary Tree again." Thrasher looked at Troy. "Your wife has a one-track mind."

"Remember the poem Effie sent to her sister Maude that started all this." Mercy recited it again:

> *Scary tree, scary tree*
> *Looming large over me*
> *Hiding stories long untold*
> *Of people and places long grown cold*
> *Treasure in seeds and roots bound tight*
> *'Til all her secrets come to light.*

"*Treasure in seeds,*" Mercy repeated. "Seed keys."

"You think they named my grandmother and me after a seed key?" Samara tipped her head, and her shiny brown hair fell in a curtain along her shoulder.

"It's just a theory. But hear me out." Mercy knew she had to tread carefully as she thought this theory through out loud. "I think Leontine gave your grandmother the name Samara at Euphemia's request."

"Why would she do that?"

"Because the word 'samara' meant something to Effie. It reminded her of home and the Scary Tree, which is a sugar maple. Maples have twinned helicopter seeds."

"But Vermont is full of sugar maples, is it not?" asked Samara.

"It is. But the Scary Tree is special. It's the tree that anchors the estate. And there's an old carving of a heart on the trunk with P + M in the middle of the heart."

"P + M?" asked Troy.

"Michael Robillard called Effie 'Pug' in the letters, remember?"

"I remember," said Samara, who'd read all the letters, too. "*Pug and Michael*. But I don't see what that has to do with anything. Maybe Leontine just liked the name, and my mother passed it on to me."

This is not going to be easy, thought Mercy. But she owed it to Effie and Samara to keep going. "Samara is a seed. A symbol of new life." She plunged ahead. "Hear me out: Effie and Michael Robillard are engaged. They spend a lot of time in the sugar shack."

"Their love nest," said Troy. "Robillard mentions it in one of his letters."

"Exactly," said Mercy. "But then he elopes with her sister Maude. Effie goes off to France in 1939, where she meets your great-grandmother Leontine Bonnet, a young widow who'd just lost her husband."

"My grandmother was born in 1939." Samara pushed her hair off her shoulder and stared at Mercy. "Are you saying what I think you're saying?"

"Are you?" asked Thrasher.

"I'm saying that it's possible that Effie was the one who was pregnant, and Leontine agreed to pass the baby off as her own."

"Let's say you're right," said Thrasher. "It would spare the child the disgrace of illegitimacy. And keep Effie from being disowned by her parents."

"And yet she and Leontine still named the child Samara."

"Maybe as a nod to the father Robillard. And to her own lineage."

"*Impossible!*" Samara crossed her arms across her chest.

"It's just a theory, and maybe a bad one," said Mercy. "But there's an easy way to dismiss it. Have you ever had a DNA test?"

"No," admitted Samara. "I have never had reason to." She gave herself a little hug, then uncrossed her arms, laying her hands in her lap. "I'm sorry. I guess it *is* possible. But it is a lot to take in."

"I know." Mercy smiled at her. "This has all been a shock to you, and I'm afraid the surprises may not be over. In the meantime, we need to keep you safe."

"You think I am in danger?"

"You're the only one the arsonists locked in a closet."

Samara paled.

"I'll call Harrington." Thrasher pulled out his cell. "And I'll stay with her until we can get some uniforms over here. You might put a bug in Daniel's ear. Your uncle, too."

"They're our next stop." She smiled again warmly at Samara. "You'll be fine. Just do whatever Captain Thrasher tells you to do. And think about that DNA test. I'll be back as soon as I can."

"We'll leave Susie Bear with you, if that's all right."

"Sure."

Mercy rose from the hard plastic chair, and although her tailbone thanked her, her injured foot did not. Troy noticed her discomfort, and swept her up into his arms.

"Not this again. And not too tight."

Troy loosened his grip. "Just until we get you that walking stick."

"We're in a hospital," said Thrasher dryly. "I'm sure we can get you a cane."

Feinberg was waiting for them by the time Mercy and Troy arrived at the colonel's hospital room on the third floor. He was holding an orthopedic cane.

She groaned at the sight of it.

Troy placed her down gently in another one of those hard plastic chairs at Uncle Hugo's bedside. She was tempted to steal one of the colonel's pillows for her butt but decided against it. Troy would just worry more.

"Think of Oisin." Feinberg handed her the cane. "It's a symbol of strength."

"Right."

Uncle Hugo was sitting up, looking almost chipper. Despite the hospital bed and the hospital gown and the tubes and machines, he appeared as in charge as always.

"I'm glad to see you looking so well, Uncle Hugo."

"It was the shower, getting all that blasted tear gas crap off me." He gave her a pointed look. "Didn't they give you one?"

"Yes."

"Then why aren't you in a hospital bed like me?"

"They said I could rest at home."

"Then go home," ordered the colonel.

"I have a few questions for you both first."

"Shoot."

"What do we really know about Maude's step-grandson Gerard Fergus?"

"He runs the Fergus family business," said Feinberg. "Subject to the approval of the trustee, he's due to become the beneficiary of the Whitney-Jones trust, as Maude's nearest next of kin. But you knew that." He paused. "We're running background checks. I'll speed that up."

"And we're sure Maude had no biological children of her own?"

"Not to our knowledge. What are you thinking?"

"I'm guessing that most of the money came from her side, not the Fergus side."

"No, her husband Wilfred Fergus was a wine merchant," said Feinberg. "Eventually built his own vineyards. Very wealthy in his own right. My understanding is that when he died, the grandson inherited the bulk of his fortune. Maude had her own money through the Whitney-Jones trust. Why do you ask?"

"The Whitney-Jones clan was very old-money. Big believers in family wealth. They kept the fortune in the family, always. And they specified the manor could not be sold as long as the sisters were alive. Even though they were estranged, and one lived in France and the other in California." Mercy leaned forward toward her great-uncle. "This all started with Max Vinke's murder. There's a reason Maude sent him here. She knew the terms of the trust, and she knew her parents set it up that way to keep the fortune in the family. Barring a blood heir, that meant the step-grandson, since Maude had no children of her own. But what if there *were* a blood relation?"

Feinberg frowned. "I believe the trustee would favor the blood relation, according to the terms of the trust. Of course, we'll have to ask Barlow to confirm."

"But there is no blood relation," said the colonel.

"I think there is. I believe that Effie had a baby, continuing her family line."

"So who is this heir?"

"Sandrine Samara Saint-Yves." Mercy explained her theory, including the meaning of the name Samara, the metaphor of the key, the clue in her poems.

"Poets," muttered the colonel.

"I think Euphemia sent Maude the 'Scary Tree' poem to lead her to the letters and to Samara. Effie wanted her daughter to come into her birthright. She was asking Maude to make that happen. Maude knew Effie was trying to tell her something, but she wasn't sure what."

"So she sent Max Vinke to figure it out."

"And he's poisoned," said Feinberg. "Let me call my friend Barlow and get to the bottom of this."

"I'll have my best investigator do a deeper dive on the step-grandson," said Uncle Hugo.

"I thought I was your best investigator," teased Mercy.

"She has you there, Hugo." Feinberg laughed.

"Very funny." The colonel frowned. "If Samara is the heir, we need to keep that young woman safe."

"She can stay at Nemeton. She'll be safe there."

Nemeton was Feinberg's mansion outside Northshire. The place was practically a fortress, with state-of-the-art security with which Mercy was very familiar. "Good plan."

"Whenever she leaves, I'll have Lewis and Clark accompany her."

"That should be sufficient." The colonel folded his hands across his lap and gazed off into a past only he could see. "You know, Samara does have something of Euphemia in her. A certain *je ne sais quoi*."

DAY FIVE
ALL HALLOWS' EVE

———

CHAPTER THIRTY-FIVE

*The cemetery is the home of those
who are not here, come in.*
—ITALO CALVINO

MERCY AND ELVIS SLEPT LATE. SHE'D HAD A RESTLESS NIGHT, dreaming of quarreling sisters and houses on fire and her and Troy with nowhere to live. The shepherd did not appear troubled by any such nightmares. Elvis was fine, thanks to her grandmother's ministrations. Patience had ordered bed rest for the shepherd, just as Dr. Chen had ordered it for Mercy. When she woke up, the sun was already high in the sky over the forest. Elvis was curled up in the bend of her knees. Usually he slept in his own bed, but he obviously thought she needed him very close. Maybe she did.

Mercy showered, washing the weariness from her bones. Her blistered skin was less sensitive today, the striking water tingling her sore pores but not torturing them, and for that she was grateful. She put on her usual uniform of cargo pants and Henley shirt and pulled her hair back off her face with a boho band.

Mercy could hear quiet voices in the living room. Her family, no doubt, here to ensure her well-being. "Come on, Elvis. Time to face the do-gooders."

Her mother Grace met her halfway down the hall. Elvis raced past them to the living room, where Mercy could see her father Duncan waiting. The shepherd adored her father.

"I had trouble sleeping," she told her mother. "I never have trouble sleeping. Is this a pregnancy thing?"

Grace placed her slender arm around her. "Sleep is a mother's best friend."

"Uncle Hugo says you can sleep when you're dead."

"That may work for war, but believe me, it doesn't work for motherhood. Smart mothers sleep whenever they can."

"Who says I'll be a smart mother?" Mercy stopped, biting back tears that seemed to come out of nowhere. "Who says I'll be a good mother at all?"

"Oh, darling girl, you'll be a splendid mother."

"How can you say that? I'm too stubborn, too single-minded, too controlling—"

"Stop right there." Grace squeezed Mercy's shoulders with her slim but surprisingly strong fingers. "Look at me."

Mercy did as she was told and was struck as always by her mother's pale blond beauty. And the fierceness that underlies that beauty.

"Now look at Elvis."

"What?"

"That dog of yours." She pointed down the hall, where her father was rubbing Elvis's belly. "You treat that dog better than many people treat their children."

She laughed. "Mom, come on."

"I'm serious." She pivoted Mercy toward the living room. "That dog is the luckiest dog in the world. And your child is the luckiest child in the world."

"If you say so."

"I do. And you know I'm always right."

They entered the living room, and her father stepped forward to give her a big hug.

"You have a long line of visitors waiting for an audience."

"I've made you a list." Amy sat at the farm table, pen and paper in front of her. "I'll let them know you're up."

"Thank you. Where's Helena?"

"Down for a nap." Amy grinned at her. "I hope she sleeps as long as you did. I don't want to miss anything."

"Sit down on the sofa," called her grandmother from the kitchen. "I've made you some scrambled eggs and toast. And café au lait."

"You need your protein," said her mother. "And it's best to start the day with bland food."

"Right." Mercy allowed her mother to lead her to the couch, where she sat between Troy and Elvis, her legs stretched out, feet resting on the coffee table. Susie Bear settled down next to Troy.

"Eat up." Her mother placed the breakfast plate onto Mercy's lap and handed her the café au lait her grandmother had made her. "Visitors can be exhausting. You're going to need your strength."

UNCLE HUGO AND FEINBERG were the first to arrive. They perched in the easy chairs across from the sofa.

"You were right." Feinberg leaned forward and smiled. "A DNA test has confirmed that Sandrine Samara Saint-Yves's great-grandmother was in fact Euphemia, not Leontine Bonnet."

"Wow." Amy sat on the floor with little Muse on her lap, the kitty purring as she stroked her fur.

"So she has a legitimate claim to the Whitney-Jones fortune." Troy gave Mercy a triumphant look. "Nice work, sweetheart."

"Did you tell her? How is she?" Mercy couldn't imagine what it was like to find out that you were not the person you thought you were—and neither was your family. "It's a lot to deal with."

"She's still trying to process all that had happened to her—including the sizable inheritance that could be hers."

"Including Grackle Tree Farm." Mercy hated to even say it out loud. Their dream house was going up in smoke, after all. She looked at Troy. "We have to prepare ourselves for the fact that Samara may choose to keep Grackle Tree Farm."

"Keep it?" squealed Amy, sending the kitten scurrying off her lap. "She can't do that."

"I think she could," said Mercy quietly.

"But you saved her life!"

"This is bigger than us," said Mercy. "Grackle Tree Farm is part of her heritage, and part of the literary heritage she and her French family have been working to support all their lives."

"It would be a logical extension of *L'Heure Bleu,*" said the colonel. "The American side of Effie's story."

"You're not helping, Uncle Hugo." Grace left the farm table, where they'd been listening to the proceedings, and Duncan followed. Her mother perched on the arm of the sofa next to Troy, and her father took the other arm by Elvis. "What does Barlow say?"

Leave it to the lawyers to ask about the lawyers, Mercy thought.

"I talked to Barlow," said Feinberg, "and he confirmed that the step-grandson was due to become the beneficiary of the trust but that a blood relation would most likely take precedence should one be found."

"And Vinke?" asked her father.

"Barlow admitted that Max Vinke had been sent here to investigate the possibility of a blood heir. He thought nothing would come of it—he thought it was just wishful thinking on the part of Maude—until the man turned up dead."

Grace reached over Troy to give Mercy's knee a squeeze. "Try not to worry about the house. We'll do everything in our power to see that you and Troy keep Grackle Tree Farm." She turned to the billionaire and the colonel. "Won't we, gentlemen?"

"It's tricky," said Feinberg. "If Samara is named the beneficiary—which odds are she will be—and she wants to keep the house, she could throw the proverbial wrench into the works. She may not prevail in the end, but it would slow things down."

"Winter is coming." Her father looked worried, and he was not a worrier.

"The baby's coming." Her mother was a worrier, and Mercy could tell she was worried now.

"If Samara wants Grackle Tree Farm, we have to step aside." Mercy sighed. The estate was the perfect place, where she'd imagined living ever since that Halloween night when she was just a kid so long ago. She and Troy had come so close to calling it their own. It was enough to break her heart. "She's Effie's great-granddaughter—and it's what Effie would have wanted."

"That's just not fair." Amy wiped tears from her heart-shaped face.

"We don't know what Effie would have wanted," said Troy quietly. "And we don't know what Samara will do. But whatever happens, we will make a beautiful home for our family. That's a promise."

"A promise we will all help you keep," said Uncle Hugo solemnly.

"That's more like it," said her mother.

Mercy changed the subject before she broke down and cried, too. "What have you found out about the step-grandson, Gerard Fergus?"

"I had my team look into it," said the colonel, "and Daniel persuaded Harrington to do some digging as well."

"More like Becker and Goodlove did some digging, in cooperation with law enforcement in California," said Thrasher.

The colonel ignored that. "Fergus has been running his father's wine business into the ground. He's broke. Apparently he has a gambling problem—and spends an inordinate amount of his time in Las Vegas."

Seems like the colonel is back to his normal self, thought Mercy with relief. Too tough for tear gas.

"Andrei Russo is from Vegas," Troy reminded them.

"The man who shot the captain," said Amy.

"Spider-Man." Mercy flashed on that terrible moment when she'd found a bleeding Thrasher on the ground. She looked at the captain.

Thrasher's jaw tightened slightly, then he went on. "Apparently Fergus is already under investigation for fraud. They're searching his emails, texts, and phone calls to try and link him to Russo."

"What about the guys who tear-gassed the house and locked Samara in the pantry?"

"We suspect Fergus hired them as well. He's the one with the strongest motive."

"What exactly was Maude worth?" asked Troy.

Everyone looked at Feinberg, the money man.

"Somewhere in the area of ten million. Of course, that does not take into account the recently discovered treasures."

Troy whistled. "That's a lot of motive."

"Especially when you owe money to the sort of people who don't take IOUs for an answer," said Thrasher.

"Have the Santa Barbara PD picked Fergus up for questioning?" This from her father Duncan.

"They tried." Thrasher shrugged. "But Fergus has disappeared."

"A runner. Why am I not surprised," said Troy.

"Barlow suspects he's sneaked over the border into Mexico," said Feinberg.

"And Braden?"

"Odds are Fergus was responsible for his death, too," said the colonel. "Occam's razor."

"Maybe not." Thrasher looked at Mercy and Troy. "We've learned that Quaid Miller was recently recruited by a poaching ring out of Maine known for the illegal taking of deer, bear, and wild turkey. Looks like they're expanding into turtles."

"Part of that network of suppliers, smugglers, and buyers Gil told us about."

"U.S. Fish and Wildlife have been working hard to dismantle that network." Thrasher smiled. "They're getting closer."

Mercy was glad to hear it.

"What about Boswell?" asked Troy.

"Nothing so far to indicate that he's involved with these poachers."

"What does Quaid have to say for himself?" asked the colonel.

"Quaid claims that Braden knew nothing about the poaching. He thought they were just using the turtle for Oisin's ceremony," said Thrasher.

"Which turned out to be his own memorial service." Feinberg pursed his lips. "Irony, thy name is Druid."

Thrasher smiled at Mercy. "Your pal the Arch-Druid has been very helpful. Thanks to his influence, Quaid is cooperating with police. But he insists he had nothing to do with his cousin's murder."

"Those Mainers play rough," said Troy. "If they thought Braden was a weak link, maybe they got rid of him."

"Poor Braden." Mercy remembered the last time she'd see him, a dead scarecrow in a corn maze. At least they'd managed to save Samara. But she wouldn't stop worrying about her until Fergus was behind bars. She started googling Gerard Fergus.

"We should be going." Feinberg rose to his feet. "It's a big day. HOWL-oween."

"Surely you can persuade Harrington to give Mercy a pass," said her mother.

"I tried, Grace. There was no budging him. He can be surprisingly stubborn when he wants to be. That's why I procured the bicycle taxi."

Mercy looked up from her cell long enough to catch Feinberg fingering the gold cuff links on his French-cuffed white shirt. She'd never seen the man so embarrassed before. She suspected it was not a feeling he felt often—or enjoyed when he did. "It's okay, Daniel. I want to go."

"*We* want to go," corrected Troy.

"Right. *We* want to go."

"What are you talking about?" asked Amy. "I thought you hated the idea."

"I do. *We* do. The last thing we want to do is don absurd costumes and parade down Main Street in a bicycle taxi with Elvis and Susie Bear and a couple hundred dogs and their humans. But I have a feeling something could go down tonight."

"Why do you say that?"

Mercy held up her phone.

"What is it?" asked the colonel, peering across the room.

"It's Gerard Fergus." She showed the image of the clean-shaven man to her husband.

Troy looked. "I don't recognize him."

"Add a thick handlebar mustache and lederhosen."

"Lederhosen?" asked the colonel.

Troy looked again. "It's the guy from the common. The one who helped us with Varden Lind."

"Marcus Renner," said Mercy. "Also known as Gerard Fergus."

CHAPTER THIRTY-SIX

*It's the Old Dark House again. If we don't
know what's in the dark and quiet place,
we fill it with bogeymen and demons.*
—DENNIS O'DONNELL

PATIENCE SHOOED EVERYONE BUT GRACE OUT OF THE HOUSE.
Even her father left—reluctantly, but he left. Troy and Susie Bear
were in the bedroom, napping and snoring together. Mercy and Elvis
were ensconced on the sofa in the living room, under the helicopter care
of her mother, her grandmother, and Amy.

Dr. Chen had agreed that Mercy could go to the parade, provided she
rode in the bicycle taxi and elevated her foot. Her foot was elevated now.
But that wasn't good enough for her mother.

"I don't think you should go to that ridiculous dog parade," said Grace.
"Not with that lunatic running around loose out there."

"We will be fine." Mercy was getting tired of making this same argument
over and over again. "There's an APB out on Fergus. They'll find him."

"He did hire that man to kill you," said Patience. "You're not safe until
they've caught him, too." Her late husband, Mercy's grandfather, was a
sheriff who'd died in the line of duty. She never forgot—and she wouldn't
let Mercy forget, either.

"Samara is the target now. And she's safe at Nemeton."

At this point, Mercy was ready to go anywhere to escape her mother
and grandmother's protective custody. There were still several hours to
go before they could leave for the festivities. She'd wanted to spend the
time thinking through all the conflicting aspects of the happenings of the
past week—from the poisoning of Max Vinke to Doug Smith's poems in
Effie's writing box. But her mother and her grandmother had seen to it

that she'd had no peace at all. She actually longed for visitors. Even Harrington would do.

A knock on the door answered her prayers. Elvis raised his handsome head but didn't move, as Grace was halfway to the door already. When it came to guard dogs, even Elvis couldn't compete with her mother.

Grace ushered in Feinberg and Uncle Hugo, followed by Lewis and Clark. The bodyguards carried bulging garment bags, which they hung over the backs of the dining room chairs as instructed by her mother and then left to search the perimeter.

Grace waved Feinberg and Uncle Hugo into the armchairs across from the sofa.

"You're back," said Mercy.

"You have fifteen minutes," warned her mother, and retreated to her sentinel post at the farm table, where she donned her reading glasses and took up her needlepoint and kept on eye on the proceedings at all times.

Mercy frowned. "I thought Lewis and Clark were with Samara."

"We've left two of my top agents on guard there." Uncle Hugo staffed his private security company with former special ops personnel.

"Right. What's in the big bags?"

"Your costumes."

"Confirming my worst fears. Just how over-the-top are these costumes?"

"Just do it," said the colonel. "Think of it as 'hearts and minds.'"

Mercy laughed. "Right." Although she wasn't altogether sure whose hearts and minds she was supposed to be winning over. But she didn't want to miss Gerard Fergus should he make an appearance. He didn't know where Samara was, and he might show up at the parade with his partner to find her.

"Community-building," said Feinberg approvingly.

"I'll try to look at it that way." She pointed to the garment bags. "Daniel, do I even want to know?"

"Maybe not."

"I helped choose the costumes," said her mother.

"Well, then at least I know they'll be well-cut."

"I'm sure they're wonderful." Troy entered the living room, Susie Bear charging ahead to beg some love from their visitors. Mercy made room for her husband on the couch.

"Any proof that Gerard Fergus was behind Braden Miller's murder?"

"Not yet," said Feinberg. "But it's a logical assumption."

"I wish we knew more." Mercy ticked them off on her blistered fingers. "We can assume that Gerard Fergus's people killed Max Vinke, and attacked me and Thrasher, and locked Samara in the pantry, and set the house on fire. But who poisoned Varden Lind?"

"Maybe that had nothing to do with all this," said Feinberg.

"Maybe." Mercy wasn't satisfied. She knew she was missing something. She stared at her visitors. "What about your treasure hunters?"

"As you know, we thought there might be more treasure to find." The colonel sighed.

"Those guys in the river vests and fedoras did, too," said Troy.

"Naturally, when you found the letters, our interest was piqued," said Feinberg. "And one thing led to another. But now that we know about Samara, we have to admit that we might have been wrong."

"We're glad you figured out who she was. Effie would be glad, too." The colonel frowned. "Even if it didn't lead us to any more treasure."

"Time's up," ordered Grace.

The colonel and the billionaire rose to their feet.

"See you at the parade, my queen." Feinberg bowed.

"Hearts and minds," the colonel reminded Mercy.

And they were gone.

THE FOG ROLLED IN right on cue on All Hallows' Eve. It was a thick fog, so impenetrable that advisories had been issued all over the state. Mercy and Troy were in the bedroom, staring at the open garment bags strewn across the four-poster bed. Any excitement she'd felt over any crime-solving opportunity the event might provide faded in the presence of the costume she was supposed to wear.

"Maybe they'll cancel on account of the weather. Northshire's supposed to be fogged in through tomorrow morning," said Troy.

"No such luck. No one cancels Halloween on account of the weather. Bad weather is expected. 'It was a dark and stormy night,' and all that." Mercy held up the King of Bark and Roll costume that her mother had chosen for Elvis. It was a dog version of Elvis Presley's famous white

jumpsuit, complete with faux gemstones and golden studs. And a bouf-
fant headdress and guitar necklace. "The Maligator is getting off easy."

"Your mother must like him."

"You know she only tolerates him. You're the one she likes. I mean,
Knight in Shining Armor? Seriously."

Troy slipped on his chain mail pants and tunic and attached the shiny
silver armor pieces. He tapped his plumed helmet and brandished his
sword. "M'lady."

"Unbelievable. Even Susie Bear has a better costume than I do." She
pulled out the dancing bear's pink tulle tutu and the slip-on beribboned
ballet shoes and the bear hat with the cute little bear ears and the bright
fuchsia hair bow. Susie Bear was going to be the belle of the ball in this
outfit.

"At least you're not Cinderella."

"I suppose it could be worse. But I don't see how." She stared at the
white gossamer corseted Victorian Gothic floor-length gown with the
white petticoats and the white netted cape with a hood.

"It's a very nice dress."

"This isn't a dress, it's architecture." She pulled on the petticoats and
the dress, and Troy tightened the corset for her.

"You look great."

"Why couldn't I be a pirate?"

"I bet you were always a pirate when you were a kid."

"Every year. Every year my mother got me some princess costume, and
every year I dressed up like a pirate. This must be her revenge."

"Come on. You know you love that wig." Troy handed her the waist-
length glow-in-the-dark silver-white wig.

"I do love the wig." She tucked her tangle of red hair under the wig
and straightened it, and draped the cloak around her shoulders. "For once,
my mother can't complain about my hair. How do I look?"

Troy smiled. "Like the most beautiful ghost witch in the world."

MERCY AND TROY AND the dogs arrived at the head of the parade route
early, as Harrington had instructed. Northshire was already in full
Fright Night mode as the last night of Fright Week was upon them.

Downtown shops and saloons and restaurants were open and doing a brisk business. The streets were full of ghosts and skeletons and vampires, clowns and cowboys and princesses and superheroes. And that was just the dogs.

It was still very foggy; the streetlamps cast long shadows in the gloom as the trick-or-treaters and Halloween bar hoppers and teenage gangs of Freddys and Rippers and Frankensteins crowded the sidewalks and flowed over into the streets. The police had put up barricades along the parade route, and uniforms were out in force. All were keeping an eye out for Gerard Fergus, aka Marcus Renner, aka Herr Lederhosen.

Harrington was waiting for them.

"Nice costumes." Of course the detective wore his usual costume of bespoke suit, his only concession to the occasion being that he was dressed all in black, from his silk shirt to his jacket and trousers to his handmade Italian loafers. "Congratulations. I'll leave you to it."

Mercy and Troy and Elvis and Susie Bear greeted their fellow dog lovers and their canine companions as they made their way past the Dali Doberman and the Hulk pit bull, the Cinderella Saluki and the firefighter dalmatian and the Rocky boxer, and an entire team of cheerleader Chihuahuas. Troy helped her into the gleaming black bicycle taxi, powered by one of Harrington's uniforms. The taxi stood right behind the Northshire Fife and Drum Corps, which would lead their procession.

Mercy was surprised when Oisin and *Elisabeth with an s* approached them. Oisin held two beautifully carved maple staffs, one in each hand. He held up the slightly shorter one to Mercy. "I heard you needed a new walking stick."

"Oh, I couldn't."

"We'd like you to have it," said Elisabeth.

"We?"

"Oisin is my husband."

"I see." Mercy wasn't sure what to say to that. "You make a lovely couple." And they did, in an unorthodox sort of way.

Elisabeth looked at her as if she wasn't sure if she was making fun of them or not.

"About Quaid Miller . . ." The Arch-Druid pulled at his long white beard. "I can't tell you how disappointed we are that Quaid lost his way for a time. But he is truly repentant. And he is helping to clear Braden's good name."

Maybe, thought Mercy, *but that doesn't explain who killed him—or why.*

"You should know that we have asked around about your Varden Lind. No one around here seems to know him."

"Adah Beecher didn't know him, either."

"Maybe he's one of the Massachusetts Druids, in town for the holiday."

"Maybe. Well, thank you for the walking stick. It's beautiful."

Oisin smiled. "Use it well."

"Congratulations," said Elisabeth.

Mercy and Troy watched them as they melted into the crowd of Halloween revelers.

"The perfect couple."

Troy took her arm. "Almost as perfect as us."

Elvis and Susie Bear pulled at their leashes. Between all the dogs and all the people, heeling while their handlers were in a bicycle taxi was an exercise in discipline that even their well-trained dogs were finding a challenge.

"There must be three hundred people here with their dogs." She'd never seen so many dogs in the same place at the same time.

"And thousands more in the crowd."

"Even if Fergus is here, we may never see him."

"We can leave right now. I'll even carry you."

Mercy raised her chin. "No, let's see this through."

The drumroll began. Troy took her hand. "And we're off."

The bicycle taxi moved forward after the corps, the dogs on either side, Susie Bear prancing in her dancing bear costume, Elvis stepping out as if he were born to rock and roll. The noise was deafening: yowls and growls and howls, barks and bawls and bellows, yaps and yelps, woofs and whines, snarls and sneers and snaps. People yelled and laughed, clapped and chanted, and generally just roared their pleasure at the pageantry of the town's most beloved pooches.

As they rolled down Main Street to the beat of the Northshire Fife and Drum Corps, Mercy thought about how much the town had changed since the Whitney-Jones family had lived here. Effie could never have imagined a HOWLoween Puppy Parade and Party for the townspeople and their dogs. But Mercy liked to believe that if she could, Effie would be right here in Northshire, with her pug Cherie, strolling along with her fellow poets and their dogs.

Mercy tried to keep her eye on the spectacle of which she was a part, but in truth she was scanning the crowds. She saw no one who reminded her of Marcus Renner or Gerard Fergus. Her mind wandered as they waltzed down Main Street, winding their way around the rotary and back up to the village green.

She waved at the crowds lining the streets, a mix of locals, children and their parents, and tourists and teenagers and leaf peepers. Her family and friends were there along the route to support her, or maybe just to take as many photos as possible to embarrass her later. Her mother Grace was dressed as—who else?—Coco Chanel, and her father was dressed as Doctor Who. The Three Musketeers were there: Amy and Helena and Brodie. Patience and Lillian would be waiting at the common, where they'd be persuading people to adopt a dog.

She also spotted Oisin and his Cosmic Ash Grove Druids, Horace Boswell and Elisabeth Bardin and their fellow poets. She thought of poetry and Euphemia Whitney-Jones. Maybe Euphemia wouldn't march in this parade, after all; maybe she would resent being known all these years later as the poet who wrote witchy rhymes for kids. Maybe that was part of the reason she turned the Sylvia Beach Shanty from a writing studio into a guesthouse with barracks; maybe she felt her best work was behind her. Maybe that's why she stopped writing altogether after Leontine died. Maybe the naysayers were right and Levi Beecher was wrong and she did kill herself.

At least Mercy had done her part to restore Effie's reputation; the discovery of her letters was bound to lead to a revival of all her work. Especially poems like "All the Unnamed Women."

The rest of the parade was a blur. When they reached the end of the route, the bicycle taxi brought them back to the common for the rest of the events.

With Elvis and Susie Bear at their side, Mercy and Troy shook hands and petted dogs and awarded prizes for best costumes. When the presentation was over, Troy led her to the side of the booth, where there were two folding chairs reserved for the king and queen. Their role as royals was minimal, as the dog lovers were lining up to get a photo with the true stars of the evening, Elvis and Susie Bear.

Adah Beecher found them sitting there. She had her Jack Russell terriers Yin and Yang with her, dressed as, well, Yin and Yang. She stood with Mercy and Troy to the side of the *Dark and Stormy Night* backdrop, watching the Newfie and the Malinois indulge their canine and human fans in a little selfie fun.

Adah was dressed as one of the auntie witches from Alice Hoffman's *Practical Magic*, complete with a pitcher of margaritas.

"I love that movie, but the book was better."

"Absolutely," agreed Adah. "Since you didn't come to the psychic fair for a tarot reading, I came to you." She slipped a gloved hand into the pocket of her voluminous black skirt and pulled out a small stack of cards, whipping them into a fan in her palm with the dexterity of a magician. "This is the deck of the Celtic Tree Oracle. Choose just one card. Carefully."

Mercy looked at Troy.

"Go ahead."

The backs of the cards were a deep forest green, graced by an intricate gold Celtic pattern—knots and shamrocks within crosses within circles. She could only imagine what lay on the other side. She hesitated. She didn't like tempting the fates.

Silly. It was just a card. It meant nothing.

Mercy reached out and pulled a card from the left end of the fan.

"Turn it over," said Adah.

Mercy flipped it over, and saw the illustration of a tree in the center, framed by Celtic borders. The corners were marked by the number 1.

"*Beith.*" Adah took the card from Mercy. "Birch."

"What does it mean?" Mercy loved birch trees, if only because they were among the easiest trees to identify. Even in the dead of winter in a wood of naked trees, you could name a birch by its striking bark.

"It means new journeys, new beginnings. Tonight is All Hallows' Eve, our New Year's Eve. Tomorrow begins the new year, and the first month of the Celtic new year is called *Beith.* Birch."

"I see."

"Birch trees stand out in the dark tangle of the forest. When you are lost in the woods, look for the shining silver bark of the birch."

Before Mercy could say anything, Adah whisked the cards back into her pocket.

"Happy New Year," she called as she swept away, Yin and Yang on her heels.

"I'm confused."

"Me, too. But I think that was the point."

"Okay, now I'm really confused."

Mercy watched as a middle-aged couple and their Great Dane, all dressed as Sherlock Holmes, with capes and deerstalker hats, flanked Susie Bear and Elvis and posed for a photograph. She wondered what Sherlock would have made of this case.

"I can see the wheels turning in that superior brain of yours."

"The wheels seem to be stuck." Mercy twirled a long silver-white strand of her wiggy hair. "There's still so much we don't know. And what we do know doesn't seem to fit together in any sensible way."

"You worked out that tricky Samara bit, I'm sure you can work out everything else. Want to talk through it?"

"Sure." Mercy smiled at him gratefully. She tucked the strand behind her ear. "Let's start at the very beginning with Willa Strong and her lost daughter. We don't know what happened to little Lottie." Now that she was expecting her own child—a child she already loved more than life itself—she was beginning to understand in a visceral way how devastated Willa must have been after Lottie disappeared. And how desperately she must have tried to find her. Effie had tried to find her, too. She'd lost her own child in a way; helping to raise her with Leontine but never able to claim her as her own. Although she'd left a clue to her daughter's biological parents when she named her Sandrine Samara.

"What else don't we know?"

"We don't know if Effie killed herself, or if she was murdered. We believe Fergus had Vinke killed, but we don't know who poisoned Lind, or who killed Braden. At least, not for sure. We don't even know if Braden or Levi was the real target."

"There are a lot of loose ends," admitted Troy. "But we'll figure it out. Or you will, with my backup."

"You're absolutely right. There are too many loose ends. I hate loose ends."

Troy put his knight's shield down and wrapped his armored arms around her. "That's one thing we have in common."

"Effie hated loose ends, too. She liked neat rhymes, anagrams, puzzles where the pieces all fit together perfectly."

"That's for sure. Even her daughter's name Samara was a clue. We're not doing that, are we?"

"Never." Mercy laughed. "Besides, clues are pointers to secrets. We have no secrets."

"Good." Troy kissed the top of her veiled head. "No weird names for our kids. No secrets between us."

"Are you talking names?" Her mother Grace appeared as if from nowhere with Mercy's father Duncan.

Mercy changed the subject. "Are you here for a selfie with Elvis and Newfie?"

"Certainly not." Grace smoothed her Coco Chanel pearls. "We're here to see how you're surviving this ordeal. And to make sure you're safe."

"We're fine. We were just talking about secrets."

"Secrets pay the bills at our house." Her father laughed. "A lawyer's life is one long confidence."

"Euphemia Whitney-Jones didn't like secrets, either. If she did, she would never have left any clues to anything. She wanted the truth to come out."

"Sounds like she needed a better attorney."

Mercy laughed at her father's little joke, but she wasn't really paying attention. She was thinking about Effie. She was a complicated woman. With Effie, nothing was simple, but nothing was forgotten, either. She was precise and pragmatic. Apart from her affair with Robillard, she'd led an orderly life. For Effie, life was a puzzle that she made fit. No matter how difficult the challenge, she put the pieces together and she made them work. No leftover pieces.

No loose ends.

Mercy had misjudged Effie. She would never have ended her own life with so many things yet undone: Robillard's letters, Samara's inheritance, Doug Smith's poems, her relationship with her sister, even little Lottie Strong's fate. Levi Beecher was right: Effie would never commit suicide.

A sudden barking caught their attention. A small terrier mix dressed like a bullfighter was facing off with Elvis and Susie Bear, yapping away in a very noisy fashion. Neither the Newfie nor the shepherd had responded in kind. Yet.

"Looks like the dogs need a break." Troy went to save Susie Bear and Elvis the humiliation of a dressing down by ten pounds of pooch.

"Thank you." Mercy pulled at the corset of her dress and readjusted her veil.

"What's wrong?" asked her mother. "Is it the costume? It's the costume. You hate it, right?"

"Actually, Mom, it's growing on me."

"But something's wrong." Her mother looked at Duncan. "What's wrong?"

"I don't know. Maybe she's tired."

"I'm right here, you know. I'm not tired. It's something else. I've been thinking."

"She thinks too much," said Grace to Duncan.

Her father leaned toward Mercy. "You may as well tell us. You know you want to."

"I've been blind to the real Euphemia Whitney-Jones. She played with her poems until she got them right. She may have gotten it wrong with Robillard at first, but she got it right, and then he died. She may have gotten it wrong with Leontine, too, but she got it right, and then Leontine died. She got it wrong with her sister Maude, and she set out to get it right. She played with her life until she got it right. She would never kill herself before she got it right."

"What are you saying?"

"I'm saying that Euphemia Whitney-Jones did not kill herself. I'm saying that Grackle Tree Farm has more secrets to tell. I'm saying that Fergus tried to burn down the wrong house."

CHAPTER THIRTY-SEVEN

Going to the woods is going home.
—JOHN MUIR

O N A DARK, FOGGY HALLOWEEN NIGHT, THE RIDE TO THE estate was scary in and of itself. As Troy wound his Ford F-150 around the hairpin turns on Skyline Drive, Mercy kept her eyes trained on the road. It was her job to watch out for the oblivious deer and other wildlife that might run out in front of the truck and Troy may not see in time.

"What are we going to do about the kitchen?" Mercy asked as Troy turned right onto Old Sheep Lane.

"My dad and my brothers are meeting with your cousin Ed tomorrow morning at the house. They'll let us know what kind of time frame and budget we're talking about."

Troy let the dogs out of the truck and came around to help Mercy down to the ground.

"I'm fine." She pointed her staff at him. "I have my walking stick."

"That was nice of the Arch-Druid."

"Don't forget the poet laureate."

"And the poet laureate." He switched on his flashlight, and they made their way through the mist, out of the gravel lot and down the path to the house. The dogs ran ahead, disappearing into the fog.

They approached the house, and saw Becker petting the dogs. "I'm on guard duty tonight."

"I thought they'd need you down in Northshire tonight," said Troy.

"I volunteered to come up here."

"I bet. A lot quieter up here—and no drunken trick-or-treaters."

"Poor Goodlove. She got the short straw." Becker grinned at them. "So you're really buying this place."

"Yep. We just came to take a look—and check out the guesthouse."

"Sure. I'll be walking the grounds." He wandered off around the house, Elvis and Susie Bear on his heels.

Troy and Mercy stared up at the battered grand old manor.

"Oisin said the house would need protection."

"He was right about that."

Troy moved the flashlight up to the roof and down, illuminating the manor floor by floor, finally settling on the damaged kitchen.

"It looks better in the dark," said Mercy.

Troy whistled for the dogs, and they barreled around from the back of the house. He shone the flashlight on the gravel path, and they walked past the other outbuildings, barely visible in the inky gloom of the foggy night. Somewhere, a barred owl hooted.

They approached the stand of aspens, beyond which stood the Sylvia Beach Shanty.

The wind picked up, blowing leaves around in the dark, like an autumn snow globe. Mercy could feel the leaves brush her face, and catch in the netting of her ghost cloak. "It's spooky."

"It's Halloween," said Troy. "It's supposed to be spooky."

"They say Halloween is the time when the line between this life and the next is lifted. When the veil that separates our world from the spirit world is the thinnest. If you want to commune with the dead, now's the time."

"You're the ghost witch. Commune away."

Mercy laughed. "If only I could. I'd have a lot of questions for Euphemia Whitney-Jones and Michael Emil Robillard."

They rounded the stand of aspens, coming at last to the guesthouse. Mercy fished the keys Jillian had given her out of her pocket, and Troy held the flashlight on the ring until she could find the right one. She opened the door and the dogs raced inside. Troy held the door for her, and she stepped into the large great room. She reached for the light switch, and then remembered that the power had been off throughout the farm since the fire.

"We're going to have to make do with the flashlight. You haven't seen the inside before, have you?"

"No, but it seems nice." He waved the flashlight around the large room to get a sense of its proportions. "Cool high ceilings."

"It's a great place. Perfect for Amy and Helena."

"And Brodie."

"And Brodie."

Troy gave her a quick kiss and then shone the light at the fireplace. "What are we looking for, exactly?"

"A hidden compartment."

"Like in the writing desk?"

"Only bigger."

"And why do you think it's here?"

"I just can't believe that we've discovered all of Effie's secrets yet. The clues are in her poems. I've been thinking about 'All the Unnamed Women.'" She recited the very last lines.

> *Loving men already untrue*
> *Until we die and are born again*
> *In a fire of naming*
> *Shadows no more*
> *We rise in the land of men.*
> *Who are we now?*

"I'm not sure I get it," said Troy.

"We know from his letter that this is where Euphemia and Michael met for their trysts. This sugar shack was their love shack."

"Love shack, baby."

"Love shack, baby," Mercy repeated. "I think that after Robillard betrayed her, Effie couldn't bear to look at it, so she built that new sugar shack over by the barn and converted this old sugar shack into a place that reflected her new writer's life with Leontine, and named it the Sylvia Beach Shanty."

"A fire of naming."

"That's right."

"Maybe she means the fireplace. But that wouldn't be safe for whatever it is you think might be hidden here."

"I'm not sure what we're looking for. But you're on the right track. I do think 'fire' must have something to do with it."

"There's a cupola on the roof, correct?"

"Yes. Why do you ask?"

"Maybe the fire refers to the fire they used to boil the sugar." He trained the flashlight on the middle of the ceiling. "See that patch up there? There used to be a stove in the middle of the room where they boiled the sap. A pipe ran up from the stove to a hole in the roof, often covered by a cupola. The steam would pour out of it."

"We rise in the land of men," she quoted. "Just like steam."

"Maybe it's up there hidden in the beams." Troy ran the light along the beams in the ceiling. "See anything?"

"No. Where would the stove have been?"

He dropped the light to the wide-planked floor, revealing a number of dusty area rugs. Susie Bear had curled up on one of them. Elvis was nowhere to be seen, but Mercy could hear his nails clicking on the floor as he checked out the other rooms in the house.

Troy focused the light on the middle of the room below the cupola, which just happened to shine on Susie Bear. The Newfie looked up as if to say, *Why are you ruining my nap?*

"You're going to have to move."

Susie Bear drew herself up and ambled over to another rug nearby.

"Good girl." Mercy rolled up the old rug, revealing the floor beneath. "There doesn't seem to be anything here."

Troy got down on his hands and knees, placing the flashlight on the floor. He drew his fingers along the seams of the maple planks. "Here we go. One of the shorter boards is slightly loose." He got out his penknife from his pocket and ran it under the plank. He jiggled it a bit and then pulled the plank out. Mercy shone the light in the open space. Troy reached in and felt around.

"If this were a horror movie, something terrible would get your hand." Mercy paused dramatically. "A rat, a zombie, a serial killer."

"Good thing this isn't a horror movie." He whooped, a triumphant shout of victory. "I got something. And it's not a rat."

"What?" She placed the flashlight back on the floor so she wouldn't blind him.

Troy pulled his hand out and held up a rusted metal cylindrical tube, the kind used to store rolled-up paintings. He bowed and offered it to Mercy.

"You really are my knight in shining armor."

"And this is the holy grail."

"Maybe." Mercy registered the faint sound of footsteps behind them just as Susie Bear rumbled to her feet.

"I'll take that."

Both Mercy and Troy turned and looked up at the man in black standing over them. A man wearing a Batman-style mask. With the flashlight on the floor shining the other way, it was dark—but not so dark that she couldn't see that he held a gun, ready to shoot.

"You don't even know what's in here," said Mercy, her voice high.

The man laughed. "If Mercy Carr found it, it must be good, right?"

There was something familiar about him, but Mercy couldn't quite figure out what that familiarity was. She tried to keep him talking. "I don't know about that."

"False modesty doesn't suit you." He turned to Troy. "Hand it over, or your wife dies first."

Susie Bear growled.

"Don't make me kill your dog. Speaking of dogs—"

"Okay," said Troy loudly. "It's all yours." He started to get up.

"Stop right there. Don't move. Just toss me the tube. Underhand."

"Okay." Troy paused and looked at Mercy. She smiled at him. As he raised his arm to throw the tube, Mercy pushed the flashlight into the hole, plunging the place into darkness.

"Attack!" she yelled, and Elvis lunged out of the darkness, clamping onto the man's dominant wrist. He dropped the gun and it went off, and the man went down, cursing. Troy tackled him and Mercy fished the flashlight out of the hole. She shone the light on Troy and the man. Elvis still had the man's arm in his grip, and Troy was on his legs. The guy couldn't move.

She retrieved the gun from the floor and pointed it at the man. "If you want that dog to let go of your wrist, nod your head."

He nodded his head.

"I'll call him off, and then Troy's going to roll you over and tie your hands behind your back. If at any time during this process you make an unfortunate move, I will blow your head off with your own gun. I am a very good shot. Do you understand?"

"Yes."

"Off, Elvis." The shepherd released the man's hand, and he groaned. Troy rolled the man over onto his stomach, pulled his arms behind him, and drew his hands together. She tucked the flashlight into her waistband and pulled the corded ribbon from her corset, weapon still aimed straight at the man's head. She gave the ribbon to Troy, holding the flashlight so her husband could see to secure the suspect.

"We're getting up now." Troy helped the man to his feet and pushed him toward the door. "Fetch," he told Susie Bear, and she trotted over to the metal tube and picked it up in her mouth. Together they all escorted the man back to the truck, where Troy called for backup. He locked real handcuffs on the guy, reading him his rights and cuffing him to the hitch on the back of the truck. Elvis and Susie Bear took up positions on either side of the suspect, watching his every move.

"Good dogs."

"Shall I?" Troy tapped the mask that covered the man's face. "Or do you want to tell me who it is first?"

"I'm thinking Varden Lind."

"I guess he lost that lame beard and mustache." Troy stared at the ersatz Batman and snapped off his mask. There he was, the man claiming to be Varden Lind, the man they'd found dying in the bushes. "We saved your life." Her husband's voice had the edge Mercy had come to recognize as the fiercest of warnings. "Ingrate."

"I like your new look," Mercy said lightly, hoping to defuse Troy. "Perfect for prison."

The man leered at her.

Read the room, moron, thought Mercy. She placed her hand on Troy's shoulder. "Don't do it." She knew he was itching to punch the guy. She wanted to punch the guy, too, but that wouldn't get them anywhere—and if Harrington found out, it could land Troy in hot water. "He's not worth it." She remembered what Adah had said about his phony-sounding name. "Odds are he's not even a real Druid."

She stepped back with Troy, and together they stood apart from the suspect while they all waited for backup to arrive. Elvis and Susie Bear remained by the phony Druid's side, canine sentinels who looked as eager to bite the man as Troy was to hit him.

"After we went to all that trouble to save him. I'm regretting that effort now." Troy pulled Mercy against his chest and wrapped his arms around her, folding his arms into hers at her waist. "Who do you think poisoned him?"

"I think he's one of the treasure hunters who came to town when we found the first letter. Maybe another treasure hunter poisoned him to get him out of the way."

"Or maybe whoever poisoned Max Vinke poisoned him, too. Unless he's the one who poisoned Max Vinke."

"Or maybe he poisoned himself to throw suspicion elsewhere."

Troy considered that. "He must have followed us here."

"Maybe he's been following us all along." Mercy sighed. "I don't know. There's so much that still doesn't make much sense. Maybe Goodlove will have news that will shed some light."

The sound of footsteps interrupted them. Troy removed his weapon from the lockbox in his truck. Mercy still had the perp's gun. They waited—and were relieved when Becker came into view, pushing a hand-cuffed man before him. Marcus Renner. Also known as Gerard Fergus.

"I heard the shot and found this guy trying to get away, so I figured I'd better detain him."

"Partners," Mercy said. "Of course. Lind and Fergus are partners."

"Good work," Troy told Becker. "You've just apprehended a murderer."

Fergus said nothing.

Becker put him inside the truck. He slammed the door. "It could be a while before backup gets here, given how busy law enforcement is on Halloween."

"I'm sure Feinberg and Uncle Hugo will hurry Harrington along. I texted them."

"Of course you did."

"They *are* the experts on art. Besides, I'm guessing that whatever is in this tube is what they've been looking for all along." She explained what they'd found to Becker.

"How did they know it was here?"

"During the Cold War, Uncle Hugo helped a lot of artists behind the Iron Curtain escape to the West. He'd often bring them to *L'Heure Bleu,* Euphemia's home in Provence, to stay until they could settle somewhere safely. Some of them must have thanked her the way artists always say thank you."

"With art," said Troy.

"With art. That art is what Uncle Hugo and Feinberg are looking for."

"Don't you want to open it first?"

"Not really. Although technically, the art could be ours."

"Finders keepers."

"It *is* our house." *At least for now,* Mercy thought.

Backup arrived in the form of a police car and a long black limousine. Becker and Goodlove took the suspects way. Feinberg and Uncle Hugo emerged from the limo. Both were looking amazingly well for two men who'd just recently been hospitalized.

What the prospect of treasure can do for a man, thought Mercy.

"Nice limo," said Troy.

"Halloween treat." Feinberg smiled. "You're welcome to join us."

"Maybe later."

Mercy held up the metal tube for her uncle and Feinberg to see. "We found this."

"What's in it?" asked Feinberg.

"We don't know. Whatever it is, it's been in the ground for more than fifty years."

"It looks like a drafting tube." Uncle Hugo gaped at her. "You haven't opened it?" He seemed stunned by that.

"I thought we should wait for the experts."

"Remarkable restraint," said Feinberg.

"I couldn't agree more." The colonel stretched out his arm, spreading his bony fingers and waiting for her to pass the tube to him.

Mercy laughed. "Here you go."

Feinberg stepped between Mercy and her uncle. "I think the honor of opening it should go to those who found it."

The colonel pursed his lips and let his arm fall to his side. "Agreed."

"Step into my limo," said Feinberg.

"Let me get you some gloves." Troy reached into the Ford F-150 and pulled out a pair of plastic gloves.

They all piled into the limo, sitting on the plush leather seats.

While she slipped on the gloves, Feinberg held the metal tube for her. Resting it in his open palms like a sacred relic, the billionaire presented it to her with a formality that she hoped would not prove unwarranted.

The limo driver switched on all the interior lights. Mercy knelt on the carpeted floor of the limo, and unscrewed the lid at the end of the long cylinder. It took a couple of times, as the threads were ringed with rust. She twisted harder, and the lid loosened. Smiling, she finished unscrewing the top and handed it to Troy.

Uncle Hugo smiled at her. "Moment of truth."

Mercy reached into the tube and felt carefully along the edge first. "There's something in there. Something rolled up in paper." Gingerly, she reached in, and pulled out the scrolled object.

"It looks like it could be a painting." Feinberg grinned. "Wrapped in glassine."

"Careful," warned the colonel as Mercy placed the scroll on the limo floor and slowly unrolled the painting. As she did so, the glassine fell away, revealing a scene of ballerinas rendered in pastel oils.

"It can't be," whispered Feinberg.

"It looks like a Degas," said Mercy.

"*Five Dancing Women,*" confirmed Uncle Hugo. "Stolen from Baron Mor Lipot Herzog's famous art collection by the Nazis, never to be seen again."

"Is it the real thing?" asked Troy.

"It looks like the real thing." Mercy was struck by its luminosity. Even in the uneven light, the ballerinas were breathtakingly beautiful, heartbreakingly so.

They all sat there for a moment in silence, studying the painting.

The colonel finally broke the spell. "It does indeed look real."

"How did it get here?" Troy stared at Mercy.

"Someone must have given it to Effie for safekeeping," mused Uncle Hugo.

"But who?"

"It could have been anyone," said the colonel. "Before the war, or after the war. Between the Nazis and the Soviets and the collaborators and the crooked collectors, there were plenty of thieves to go around."

"She must not have opened it." Mercy looked at her uncle. "Why not?"

"She wouldn't have," said the colonel. "She was a woman of integrity. If she knew it was stolen, she would have returned it."

Mercy thought of all the lives Effie had touched one way or another. "It could have been one of her visitors to the salon. Or a soldier she befriended. Apparently she wrote to many soldiers over the years. The Korean War. Vietnam. Not just World War II."

"That doesn't surprise me," said her uncle. "She was a generous person."

"And she had a soft spot for soldiers. You'll figure it out. And return the painting to its rightful owners." A statement, not a question.

"Or heirs," said the colonel.

Her uncle was right, Mercy thought. The original owners were probably long dead by now, even if they had survived the war. But at least their heirs might benefit from their sacrifice.

"You've done it again, Mercy." Feinberg clapped.

She slipped her arm though Troy's. "*We've* done it again."

"You're quite the couple," said Feinberg. "A Knight in Shining Armor and the Ghost Witch of Grackle Tree."

"Very appropriate costumes, as we knew they would be," said the colonel.

"We just didn't know how appropriate." Feinberg grinned. "What a night. But we should be on our way. We need to get this masterpiece to a safe place."

Mercy and Troy climbed out of the limousine and watched as the colonel and the billionaire drove off into the fog with their treasure.

She handed her husband the flashlight. "Let's take one more look around, shall we?"

"Sure."

They walked back to the house. Troy shone the light on the old grande dame. Even with a burnt-out ugly kitchen, she was a thing of beauty. Elvis barked. Susie Bear whined.

"Now what?'

Something caught Mercy's eye in the corner of what used to be the library. A glowing figure in white. Or maybe just a wisp of fog.

"What's that?" She pointed up to the second floor. "I saw something up there."

"Your ghost?"

"Our ghost."

"You know I always wanted to live in a haunted house."

"Be careful what you wish for."

Troy wrapped his arms around Mercy, and she raised her eyes to the library once again. And there she was, bright as a full moon. The Ghost Witch of Grackle Tree.

DAY SIX
ALL SAINTS' DAY

————

CHAPTER THIRTY-EIGHT

Home is wherever you leave everything you love and
never question that it will be there when you return.
—LEO CHRISTOPHER

T HE NEXT MORNING, MERCY AND TROY MET HIS DAD AND HIS
brothers at the grand old Victorian. The Warner men were all in
what was left of the kitchen, taking stock of the damage and planning a
renovation inspired by her grandmother Patience's kitchen, Mercy's favorite room on earth. Proceeding as if the place would indeed be theirs.

Mercy waited outside with Jillian, who'd brought by more papers for
them to sign, watching the dogs run around the garden. Elvis and Susie
Bear were going to love it here, if this morning's frenetic activity was any
indication. Brodie and his friend Joey Fyfe were there, too.

"What is that guy doing?" asked Jillian.

Joey was making his way around the perimeter of the old Colonial,
dressed in a field jacket whose pockets were full of techno-gadgets. He
wore a thermographic camera around his neck and carried what looked
like a Geiger counter in his hand.

"He's looking for ghosts, spirits, demons." Mercy watched Joey as he
waved the Geiger counter in front of him as he walked. Elvis and Susie
Bear followed him, convinced he was playing some sort of game. "You
know, the usual."

Jillian giggled. "Seriously?"

"Hey, we saw the witch last night."

The Realtor giggled again. "Well, of course you did. It was Halloween."

"What do you mean?"

"She always appears on Halloween. Every year, like clockwork."

"Really."

"Old Man Beecher makes sure of it. He dresses up as the witch to scare away all the trespassers."

"Levi." Mercy thought of the card Adah Beecher had given her, the one of the birch tree, shining in the woods and lighting the way. Levi had been the estate's birch all these years.

"Now that you'll be living in the house, Levi won't need to do that. The Ghost Witch of Grackle Tree will be no more," Jillian said dramatically.

Like we'd ever let that happen, thought Mercy. She and Troy loved the witch, and they loved Levi.

"Anything I can help you do?" Jillian checked her watch. "I've got a few minutes before I have to leave for the luncheon." She paused. "I'm surprised you're not going."

"Luncheons are more my mother's thing."

"But this is for Dr. Saint-Yves. Lillian Jenkins is throwing it for her. Kind of a last-minute celebration to make up for the tear gas and the fire and all that. So the poor woman won't think we Vermonters are total barbarians."

"The men responsible for that were not Vermonters." Mercy, for one, was glad that Fergus and Russo were now behind bars.

Jillian tapped Mercy's chest with a manicured hand. Red this time, to complement her Talbots navy-and-white suit. "That's right." She rolled her eyes. "Californians."

"Close enough."

"You really should come."

"Maybe I will." Mercy did like the idea of giving Samara a fitting send-off. She hadn't seen her since the hospital. Feinberg and Uncle Hugo said she was getting used to her new status as a Whitney-Jones, and that so far she had shown no interest in Grackle Tree Farm, but Mercy would like to see that for herself—and to say a proper goodbye.

"I'll text Lillian to reserve a seat for you."

"And Elvis."

Jillian laughed. "And Elvis."

"Could you drop us off at the cabin on the way? I'll need to change clothes."

"A very good reason to give you a ride."

"You sound like my mother."

Jillian sobered, saying solemnly, "I love your mother."

"Of course you do."

"I'll meet you at the car."

Mercy spent the next five minutes convincing Troy that he should stay and work with his father and his brothers on the plans for the house while she and Elvis attended the luncheon.

"What about your foot?"

"It's fine now; I can drive. No problem." She gave him a quick kiss. "You can't shadow me for the next six months, you know."

"I don't see why not." He kissed her goodbye. "As long as your mother's there."

"Don't remind me."

AT HOME, MERCY SLIPPED into one of her Grace-approved outfits: emerald-green sweater dress, low-heeled cognac-colored riding boots, and matching pouch belt. She pulled her red curls into a ponytail with a leather scrunchie and slathered on moisturizer. She applied just enough makeup to please her mother and called for Elvis. She grabbed a cropped leather jacket in case the temperature dropped and slipped into the Jeep with Elvis.

The shepherd seemed just as pleased to be back on the road as she was. He kept his head out of the window, nose up. The last of the fall color brightened the route as they sped along to Northshire. It was sunny but cool.

Mercy was happy to let her mind wander while she maneuvered the Jeep down the country roads and into town. Now that Halloween was behind them, Northshire settled into the temporary calm that would prevail until Thanksgiving, when the holidays and ski season drew droves of visitors. All the witchy decorations were gone, and the village was once again dressed in only its plain old New England charm. Even Jillian's cupcake Victorian office seemed subdued now—at least until the Christmas finery went up.

Mercy pulled into the parking lot of the Wild Turkey Inn. *Lillian must have pulled some serious strings to book an impromptu sit-down event here,* she thought. The inn was one of Northshire's oldest and most venerable eateries, run by the same family for two hundred years.

She snapped a leash on Elvis, and in they went. The maître d' escorted them both to the garden room in the newest section of the restaurant, "new" being a relative term, where a glassed wall looked out over the creek that ran along the back of the property. Several round white-skirted tables with centerpieces made of books and orchids faced a small stage with a podium. On the wall behind the podium was a gold-and-black banner that read NORTHSHIRE ALLIANCE OF POETS.

Mercy spotted Samara at the head table with Lillian, Boswell, Elisabeth, Adah, the mayor, and the head of the local arts council. The rest of the attendees appeared to be poets, artists, and ladies who lunch. She dropped by Samara's table to pay her respects and was relieved when the woman greeted her and the shepherd warmly.

Mercy pulled the young woman aside. "Grackle Tree Farm is yours, by all rights. Troy and I understand that. And if you—"

"Oh, *non*." Samara interrupted her. "The estate is yours. You and Troy will make it a happy place again, which is how it should be."

"If you're sure . . ."

"I am certain." She smiled at her. "Even if you did not save my life and discover my true heritage, I would still believe this. You are the new stewards of Grackle Tree Farm."

"Thank you." Mercy could feel her face flush. "I'll let you get back to your fans."

"Thank *you*," she whispered to Mercy, "for everything," before turning to her next well-wisher.

Giddy with relief, Mercy led Elvis to Grace and Patience, who were seated with Jillian at a table by the side exit. Always a good choice, to Mercy's mind. She and Elvis greeted them with air kisses and tail wags. They'd saved her a seat between her mother and her grandmother, for which she was grateful. Elvis sat on his haunches to her right by Patience, ears perked. Always on guard.

The luncheon proceeded as luncheons do, a mix of overly long introductions and interminable speeches, lame jokes and polite laughter, finger sandwiches and light salads and heavy desserts. The exception was Samara herself, who gave a delightful talk about the pleasures of poetry, Effie and Leontine's legacy, and the charms of Provence. She was the perfect ambassador for *L'Heure Bleu*—and concluded by inviting everyone to visit and experience it for themselves.

The servers brought dessert, and people began to mingle. Jillian and Patience got up to make the rounds; now only Mercy and her mother remained at the table. Her mother was busy texting someone, which still managed to astound her.

Mercy pulled a peanut butter dog biscuit from the belt on her pouch and slipped it to Elvis. While he chomped away, she pushed away the Boston cream pie and examined the centerpiece. The books were all by local authors, some of the same books she'd seen in the library at the manor house. The Northshire Alliance of Poets anthologies, Elisabeth S. Bardin's *The Shires*, Horace Boswell's *Song of Ares*.

Ares. God of war. Mercy slipped the volume from the tower of books and began to read. "I can't believe it." She took her cell phone out of her pocket and clicked to the photos she'd taken of Doug Smith's poems, the poems in the box Effie had given Levi for safekeeping.

Her mother looked up from her phone. "What are you up to now?"

She showed her one of the poems in Boswell's book.

"Good poem."

"But it wasn't written by Boswell. This is Doug Smith's poem."

"Who's Doug Smith?" She briefed her mother on the poems they'd found in Effie's writing box. She opened *Song of Ares* again and flipped to the copyright page. "1968. The poems we found in Effie's writing box were written earlier in the war."

"Boswell stole them?"

Mercy took photos of the poem in Boswell's book and the copyright page and texted them to Troy. "Levi told me Horace served in Vietnam, too. He must have known Doug Smith. I'm guessing Smith did not survive the war."

"And Boswell palmed off Smith's poems as his own."

"Looks like it." The texts didn't go through. Mercy cursed. The sooner they got high-speed internet up at the estate, the better.

Mercy scanned the room for Boswell. She caught sight of him just as he was leaving the garden room. She stood up. "If we're not back in five minutes, text Troy and tell him about Boswell. If you can't get through to Troy, try Thrasher."

"What are you going to do?" asked her mother.

"I'm just going to talk to him." She grabbed Elvis's leash and ran.

"Wait for backup," Mercy heard her mother yell after her.

BOSWELL WAS DRIVING OFF in his silver SUV when Mercy and Elvis caught up to him in the parking lot. They jumped into the Jeep and tailed the plagiarizing poet down Main Street and out of town. Elvis kept his eyes straight ahead, focused on the SUV. He knew they were on the job, and Mercy could tell he was as excited as she was. She tried sending the texts to Troy again, and they still didn't go through.

She followed Boswell south along Route 7a and then north onto Skyline Drive. He was going toward Grackle Tree Farm, speeding recklessly around the hairpin curves. Mercy stayed well behind him. About five miles past the turn onto Old Sheep Drive, Boswell took a sharp right onto a gravel drive-way marked only by a battered old mailbox bearing the number 124.

Mercy slowed down and pulled over to the shoulder. She checked her phone. No service. Elvis cocked his head at her as if to say, *What are we waiting for?*

"I know, boy, but it's just not us anymore."

Normally, she wouldn't even hesitate. She'd charge right in, Elvis by her side. But she had no backup and no gun and no signal and a baby on the way. And she was wearing a dress and riding boots. Not ideal for stealth work in the woods.

Boswell was a plagiarizer, but he could also be a poacher or a poisoner or both. On the plus side, by now her mother would have alerted not only Thrasher, but every arm of law enforcement in the state. She hoped they could find this place.

Elvis whined. He was ready to go.

"Okay, here's the plan. We go in on foot and surveil. See what we're up against before we make our move." Mercy slipped on her cropped leather jacket and clicked a long lead onto Elvis's collar, and they got out of the Jeep. She grabbed the shovel she always kept in the back for weather emergencies. Better than nothing.

She checked the mailbox. Empty except for a mailer addressed to "Resident."

She and Elvis crept along the edge of the gravel driveway, keeping to the maples and birches and beeches that lined the road. Out of the line of sight, from both Boswell and any security cameras, with any luck. The driveway was relatively free of brush and other debris but deeply rutted with thick tracks left by trucks, not SUVs.

"Interesting," she whispered to Elvis.

The driveway curved to the left, and as they rounded the bend, Mercy saw a large log cabin a quarter mile down the road. Elvis pivoted abruptly and pulled at the leash.

"Easy, boy."

"Stop right there." A man dressed in a coonskin cap stepped out from behind a large hemlock about ten feet away. It was Boswell, and he had a muzzleloader trained right on her. "Drop the shovel."

Mercy let go of the handle, and the shovel fell to the forest floor.

Elvis growled.

"Shut him up."

"Sure." Mercy slapped her thigh. "Come, Elvis."

The shepherd trotted over to her. He stood at her side, eyes and ears on Boswell. He was no longer snarling at him, but he looked ready to pounce. No doubt he was.

"You're trespassing."

"We just came to talk." If she could only keep him talking until the cavalry arrived.

Boswell laughed. "About what?"

"About poetry."

"Right."

"How did you come to write *Song of Ares*? They're very powerful poems."

"You've read them?"

"I was at the luncheon for Dr. Saint-Yves today. There was a copy on the table. Part of the centerpiece." Mercy smiled at him. "I got bored during the speeches. So I started to read."

"Why are you really here?"

"I wanted to talk to you about Euphemia Whitney-Jones. My husband and I just bought Grackle Tree Farm."

"So what?"

"We're interested in the history of the place. Especially the literary history. You know, the literary salons Euphemia ran. I know you were a part of them."

"She was my mentor."

"She must have been very upset when she realized that you stole Doug Smith's poems."

Boswell moved toward her, the muzzleloader aimed at her chest. "I did not steal his poems. I don't need to *steal* anyone's poems."

"We have proof of the plagiarism. Effie kept the poems that Doug Smith sent her from Vietnam. The ones you published under your own name after he died."

"There is no proof. It did not happen." He glared at her.

The man actually seemed to believe what he was saying.

Mercy studied him. "You've been lying so long, playing the part of the brilliant poet for so long that you've convinced yourself that's who you really are."

"I am a Pulitzer Prize–winning poet." Boswell was sweating now, despite the chill in the air. "Doug Smith was a terrible soldier and a terrible poet. That's why he died. That's why he died a nobody."

"He was a gifted poet."

"No one's ever heard of him."

"Effie'd heard of him. That's why you had to kill her."

"That is not true." He waved the muzzleloader at her to emphasize his point. "I loved Effie."

"She confronted you about the poems. Threatened to expose you. So you poisoned her and made it look like suicide."

"It *was* suicide. She was a very troubled woman."

"You've spent years looking over your shoulder, worried that the truth would come out. And now it has. It's over, Boswell."

"It's over for you, not me."

"The police are on their way. Don't make it worse for yourself."

"You think your fish-cop husband will come to save you? Well, looks like he's late." He nodded toward the house. "Walk. Stay to the middle of the road."

Mercy started toward the cabin, avoiding the worst of the potholes. She could hear Boswell behind her, his boots crunching on the gravel.

Elvis pushed ahead on his long lead, nose to the ground, angling closer to the shoulder by the trees. On the scent of something.

"Faster," he said.

As she picked up her pace, she let the leash slip from her hand. "Jeep," she said, just loudly enough for the shepherd to hear her.

Elvis veered into the woods.

Boswell stopped to fire the muzzleloader at the shepherd, but he missed. Elvis was long gone.

Troy was right, thought Mercy. He was not a very good shot. She knew he'd have to reload, and while he did, she could disappear into the woods just like Elvis.

She took off. She'd only gone a couple of yards when the heel of her riding boot caught the edge of a deep rut. She tripped and fell, but she caught herself, scraping her palms on the gravel.

Mercy struggled to her feet. A shadow fell over her. She sensed rather than saw the blow coming, and she tried to run. Pain rocked the back of her head, and she went down into the darkness.

THE FIRST THING MERCY felt was the cold. The second thing she felt was a terrible pounding at the back of her skull. She opened her eyes to a gloom so deep she could barely distinguish her surroundings. She tried to move, but she couldn't. Her feet and hands were tied with duct tape, and she was propped up against a wooden post on a dirt floor like a sack of salt.

The only source of light appeared to be two vents, one set high into the front wall on the right side of the door and one set low to the floor on the other side. As her eyes adjusted to the murk, she realized she was in what appeared to be a root cellar. Roughly made shelves held boxes of turnips, carrots, potatoes, onions. Apples and pears. There were jars of pickles and beets and dried herbs, too, and baskets full of bulbs and rhizomes.

She was shivering in the clammy cold of the cellar. She was still wearing her dress and jacket, but her boots were gone. Her stockinged feet were freezing. As were her hands. She wiggled her fingers and toes to generate some heat.

Mercy considered her options, which were few. She could wait for Troy to find her. Elvis would be waiting at the Jeep and would surely bring him to her once Troy arrived. Provided Troy even knew about this place. This was not Boswell's primary residence. Jillian had told her at the poetry reading that he had a mansion on Grand Avenue in town that he could barely afford.

She looked around for something that she could use to cut the tape. No tools anywhere, apart from some large metal scoops hanging on nails pounded into the wall by the shelves. She looked up, toward the low ceiling, and spotted two metal meat hooks. If she could get over to one of the spiky curls, maybe she could use it to rip the tape off her wrists.

First she had to get up. She pulled up her knees and fell over onto her side. Her head swimming, she paused a moment to catch her breath. She inhaled and exhaled, deep breathing until her head cleared. She sat up on her knees, closed her hands into fists, and used them as leverage as she straightened her legs into the most uncomfortable down dog of her life. She stopped again to breathe, and then scooted her tied ankles toward her wrists in little hops, thanking the yoga gods and goddesses for all those forward folds. Slowly, she uncurled her spine and stood upright. The room spun around her. Teetering, she stumbled over to the closest wall, and collapsed against the shelves. Still standing. She closed her eyes, breathing hard. She waited there until she could open her eyes without the gloom whirling around her.

Mercy set her sights on the closer of the two meat hooks. About six feet away. Not that far. She could make it. She jigged across the room, one tiny jump at a time. She stood under the meat hook and raised her wrists up and over the sharp edge, resting them in the curve of the hook. Exhausted, she hung on like a side of beef until she could move again. She counted to ten and then lifted her hands toward the point of the hook. Wrestling her wrists around the sharp steel, she felt the skin of her palm slice open. She ignored the blood; the pain seemed to steady her. The point now positioned on the tape in the small space between her wrists, she pulled down with her arms. The blessed *rip!* was music to her freezing ears.

She did it again. She could feel the tape giving. She tried to separate her wrists, and they broke free. She nearly cried with relief as she lowered her arms. She leaned over—another thank-you to forward folds—and tore the tape off her ankles. The skin on her wrists and ankles was smarting, but she barely noticed.

Mercy was now fully mobile. But she still couldn't go anywhere. The door was locked—from the outside. A combination lock on a latch, by the sound of the rattle when she shook the door from the inside. No way she could lockpick her way out of this one. She would have to break down the door.

Just the thought of throwing herself against that wooden door could make her sore head pound hard enough to take her breath away. She sat down to think about it, wondering if she'd ever have the strength to get up again. She glanced at her enemy, the locked door, and spied the vent, the one that ran close to the floor. It would be a tight squeeze, but she might be able to do it. She moved over to the vent, lifted her legs, and punched them at the metal. The metal crinkled a bit. Kicking her legs forward again, she powered them through the vent. It clanked to the ground outside the root cellar.

Mercy rolled onto her stomach, preparing to crawl through the hole. Just as she moved into position, a familiar face appeared in the opening.

Elvis.

The shepherd scurried through and rewarded her with a lick. She sat up, throwing her arms around him, holding on for dear life.

"Are you in there, Mercy?" called a deep, rough voice.

Not Troy. Not Thrasher. Not Lewis or Clark.

It was Levi Beecher.

"I'm here."

"Hold on." Within minutes Levi had picked the lock with his own Swiss Army knife and opened the door.

Elvis dashed by her. Mercy stumbled out into the sunlight, shading her eyes. Levi took her by the elbows to steady her.

"How did you find me?"

"Adah was at the luncheon. Your mother told her about Boswell, and she texted me. Told me the cops were on the way, but I'm just down the road. Thought I'd take a look."

"Thank you."

"Saw your truck and your dog. Elvis brought me here." He scratched the sweet spot between the shepherd's ears. "Smartest dog I've ever seen."

"Smartest dog in the world." She stepped back and gave Elvis a good scratching of her own. "And Boswell?"

"His SUV is gone. No one here, as far as I can tell. Figure he's on the run." Levi looked her over, his lean face lined with worry. "You need a doctor. Let's get you to the hospital."

Mercy knew Levi was right. She'd already put this baby through enough; now she might have to add a concussion to the list. She'd get checked out, follow doctor's orders, and then she'd go home to her couch and not move again until this baby was born.

The root cellar was built into a ridge that ran behind the cabin. They headed down past the house and toward the driveway. Elvis raced ahead, diverging from the gravel road and aiming for a large barn on the far edge of the clearing.

"Now what?"

"Call him back," said Levi. "We can check it out later."

Sirens sounded in the distance.

"Better yet, let the cops check it out."

Mercy relented, whistling for Elvis. The shepherd ignored her, continuing on to the barn without bothering to look back. When he reached the barn, he sank gracefully into the Sphinx position at the foot of the double doors.

"What's he doing?"

"He's alerting. There's something in the barn he thinks we should see."

Levi stuck his hands in the pockets of his jeans and leaned back on his heels. "I suppose you want to take a look."

"I do."

Levi sighed. "All right. But let me help."

He took her arm and guided her to the barn, where Elvis waited patiently. She stood aside while he swung open the double doors, and they went into the large space. The shepherd barreled past the bales of hay and farm machinery to the back of the structure, where he disappeared from sight.

They followed him. There appeared to be no one here but the birds chirping in the rafters and a farm cat sleeping in a patch of sun on one of the hay bales. Behind the farm machinery was a temporary plywood wall. And behind that wall were a number of plastic tubs with long handles and a couple of large open tanks of water.

Elvis was nosing one of the tubs.

"What do we have here, boy?" Mercy pulled the top off the tub. And she was not surprised by what she saw.

"It's a wood turtle."

CHAPTER THIRTY-NINE

Old houses, I thought, do not belong to people ever,
not really, people belong to them.
—GLADYS TABER

FORTY-EIGHT HOURS LATER, MERCY SAT IN A CAMP CHAIR BY the entrance of the grand old Victorian. Troy stood beside her. He hadn't left her side since he'd found her in Boswell's barn with Levi and Elvis and the wood turtles. She'd spent a night in the hospital, just for observation, thanks to the concussion she'd suffered at the hands of the deranged poet/poacher/poisoner. Dr. Chen told her she'd been extraordinarily lucky that both she and the baby appeared to be fine. But she also warned Mercy, in very strong language, that her luck was running out.

Mercy vowed to take it easy and Troy vowed to make that happen.

Which was why she was sitting in a camp chair watching the dogs run around the front garden. Troy's dad and brothers were inside with her cousin Ed, working on the kitchen. The sound of saws and hammering competed with the barking dogs and the chirping birds and the weird clicking of Joey Fyfe's ghostbusting equipment.

Mercy and Troy watched Susie Bear and Elvis trailing Joey and Brodie as they looked for supernatural creatures.

"I can't believe you're letting them do this," said Troy, laughing.

"It's Brodie's contribution to our future happiness." Mercy laughed along with him. "What I can't believe is all their paraphernalia. If there was any ectoplasm around, the dogs would have found it already."

It was good to laugh. It was good to sit here, safe and sound, with her new husband at their new home, with nothing but decor and gardens and baby names to think about. Boswell was in jail; Becker and Goodlove chased him down before he even managed to cross the county line. Thrasher and Troy rescued two dozen box turtles and another wood turtle from Boswell's barn, and thanks to their investigation, the U.S. Fish and Wildlife Service had infiltrated the Maine poaching gang and intercepted another three hundred turtles on their way to Asia. Russo and Fergus were making plea deals in the hopes of reducing their inevitable prison sentences.

Best of all, Samara was back home in France, ten million dollars and a priceless literary heritage richer. The museum director turned heiress kept the letters for *L'Heure Bleu* but donated a substantial sum to the new Euphemia Whitney-Jones Literary Salon here in Northshire, to be run by the Northshire Alliance of Poets. And Feinberg and Uncle Hugo were hot on the trail of the heirs to that Degas, which was in fact the real thing.

All's well that ends well.

Adah and Levi Beecher walked up the brick path. Levi carried Effie's writing box, which he handed to Mercy. Adah carried her trug covered with a blue-and-white-striped cloth.

Levi beamed at Mercy. "We knew you'd figure it out. Well, Adah knew you'd figure it out."

Mercy laid the box in her lap. "You didn't suspect him?"

Levi shook his head. "I knew Effie gave me that box for a reason. I knew Horace was a jerk. But I never imagined he was capable of this."

"It does explain why his early work was so superior to his later work," said Adah with a crooked smile. "Horace must have been holding his breath all these years since her death, hoping against hope that the truth would not come out."

"As long as Effie was dead and no one was in the house, he was safe," said Mercy. "But then Max Vinke showed up and started snooping around. And Varden Lind."

"You think he poisoned them, too?" asked Levi.

Troy shrugged. "Boswell's lawyered up. He's not talking. But they found a number of the same poisons in a locked medicine cabinet in his cabin. He's going to spend the rest of his life in prison." He crossed his arms and leaned against one of the manor's long windows. "I still think poison is an odd choice of weapon for a poacher."

Adah's smile faded. "The poet in him chose poison, not the poacher."

Mercy thought about that. *"It is the poison'd cup."*

"And Braden?" asked Adah.

"We're not sure," said Troy. "It could have been Boswell or the Maine poachers. Boswell because it finally occurred to him that if Effie had confided in anyone, it would have been Levi, and he mistook Braden for Levi. The poachers because Braden balked at handing over the Cosmic Turtle."

"My money's on Boswell." Levi looked at Mercy. "From what we saw in his barn, Boswell was deep into the poaching thing, too. So he had to kill the scarecrow, for one reason or another."

"That's three murders." Adah paled. "All for stolen glory."

"And almost Varden Lind, too." Mercy couldn't believe the nerve of the man.

"And very nearly you," pointed out Troy.

"I'm so glad you're all right. And the baby, too." Adah set the trug down at Mercy's feet. "I brought you some herbs and other organic goodies."

"Thank you. I was hoping that was for me."

Brodie and Joey Fyfe came running up to them, Elvis and Susie Bear on their heels.

"You definitely have ghosts," said Joey.

Levi looked the ghostbuster up and down. "I could have told you that."

Mercy bit back a laugh.

"Geiger counter went crazy." Brodie pointed to the side of the house. "Especially around the back porch."

"We'll want to come back after dark and take more thermal photos, if that's okay with you."

Mercy looked from Joey to Troy, who shrugged. "Sure."

It was just Mercy and Troy and Adah and Levi and the dogs in the front garden now. Troy turned to Levi. "We can't thank you enough for saving Mercy."

"And saving the house."

"Glad I was here to help."

Levi always seems to be around to help, thought Mercy. Like her husband, he always showed up when you needed him. When Effie needed him. When the estate needed him. "You're not the witch, you're the guardian angel."

"I wouldn't say that."

"I would." Adah smiled at her brother with affection. "He's been saving this place for years. Now it's your turn."

"We'll do our best," promised Troy.

"With your help." Mercy wasn't ready to say goodbye to their guardian angel quite yet.

"I'll be around."

Adah touched her brother's shoulder. "We need to get back to Beecher's Pasture."

Mercy and Troy watched as the Beecher siblings walked off, arm in arm.

Troy reached for Mercy's hand. "Are you up to a walk?"

"Sure." She waited while he called the captain about the writing box, scrutinizing the garden and dreaming of the planting she'd do come spring.

She'd barely plotted one raised bed before Troy finished his call. He handed her the walking stick Oisin had given her. "Come on, dogs."

They set off past the back garden and through the back gate, Elvis and Susie Bear racing ahead. They passed under the Scary Tree, and Mercy stopped just long enough to trace her fingers around the heart and initials carved into the trunk so long ago by Effie and Robillard.

From there, Troy led her through the forest, down an old trail marked by dead limbs and dead leaves and dead ferns. Winter was nearly here.

"Dad says he can have the house ready in three weeks. Well, at least the kitchen."

"That's great news." Mercy stepped over a fallen tree, using her stick for support. Her foot was nearly healed now, just the occasional twinge, but the last thing she—or the baby—needed was another fall. She didn't know this trail. "Where are we going?"

"You'll see."

They trudged on through the woods, under a canopy of hemlocks and white pine, red oaks and sugar maples, beech and birch trees. The only sound was the hammer of woodpeckers and the hoot of owls, the rustling of leaves along the forest floor, and the faint ripple of a creek somewhere to the south.

They stepped into a small clearing, and there was the copse of birch and the large red oak where Willa Strong was buried. Mercy could see the hulking shadow of the ruined castle's arches beyond the trees. Where Willa Strong had died grieving for her lost little girl.

Together they knelt by the bereft mother's gravestone. Elvis and Susie Bear disappeared into the understory.

Envy is a terrible thing, thought Mercy. It drove Augustus Strong to resent his own wife Willa and daughter Lottie. It drove Horace to plagiarism and murder. It drove Effie and Maude apart for most of their lives.

Unbridled envy led to greed and ultimately to theft. People trying to take what was not theirs and claiming them for their own—Horace taking Doug Smith's poems, Maude taking her sister's fiancé, Quaid Miller taking animals from the wilderness, Gerard Fergus taking Samara's inheritance.

"Lottie is probably here. There must be some evidence in these woods somewhere."

"We'll find it."

"Effie and Levi spent years looking." Mercy didn't see how they could find her now.

Troy leaned over and kissed her forehead. "They didn't have you."

Mercy kissed him back. "Or you."

"Or the dogs." Troy stood up and helped her to her feet. He passed her the walking stick and whistled for Elvis and Susie Bear.

The Malinois and the Newfie crashed through the brush to join them once again. Together they hiked back toward the house. When they reached the huge old sugar maple that towered over the old Victorian, a loud cawing stopped them cold. Even the dogs stopped to watch the flock of grackles burst from Scary Tree's thick branches, soaring into the sky, wheeling through the air. A cacophony of grackles.

As the last of the blackbirds disappeared from sight, Mercy and Troy made their way along the gravel path around the grand limestone manor they would soon call home. Troy's dad and brothers and Mercy's cousin Ed had all gone home for the day.

When they reached the front entrance, Troy uncurled her fingers from the knob of her walking stick and set the stick against the doorframe. "Looks like we're finally alone."

"I thought they'd never leave."

He gathered Mercy into his arms and pushed open the door with his foot.

Elvis and Susie Bear bolted past them into the house.

Mercy flung her arms around her husband's neck. "Welcome home."

She knew that there are many places we can call home, and the longer we live, the more places we will call home. But as her husband carried her over the threshold, Mercy could only hope that she'd be calling this place home for a very, very long time.

ACKNOWLEDGMENTS

I'VE ALWAYS WANTED TO SET A STORY DURING HALLOWEEN. AUTUMN in New England is spectacular and spine-tingling. Think of the witches of Salem. The spectral soldiers of Union Cemetery. The daemons of Waterbury. *Home at Night* was the perfect opportunity to weave all manner of mysterious goings-on into Mercy and Elvis's next adventure.

Needless to say, I got carried away—and it took my grounded genius of an editor, the incomparable Pete Wolverton, to drag me and my story out of revision hell and into your hands, dear reader. So thank you, Pete, once again, for saving me from myself. And thank you to the entire team at Minotaur/St. Martin's Press: George Witte, Andy Martin, Kelley Ragland, Allison Ziegler and Kayla Janas, Claire Cheek, Ben Allen, Kiffin Steurer, NaNá Stoelzle, Rowen Davis, David Baldeosingh Rotstein, and Jonathan Bennett.

I also need to acknowledge the wonderful folks of the University of New Hampshire's Natural Resources Steward Program. I had the honor and pleasure of taking this course while I was writing *Home at Night,* and much of what I learned there about environmental issues, conservation and sustainability, and the flora and fauna of New England informs the story. Thanks to the knowledge, wisdom, and heart of Mary Tebo Davis, Lauren Chase-Rowell, Rebecca Dube, and all the wildlife biologists, foresters, soil scientists, entomologists, and other specialists who shared their time and expertise, I am now a certified Natural Resources Steward—and proud of it. A special shout-out to my fellow Stewards, especially the Class of 2022.

And I'd be remiss if I failed to mention Lauren's Jack Russell terriers, who inspired Yin and Yang, as Lauren herself inspired the wonderful Adah Beecher.

My heartfelt love and gratitude to those who keep me on track: my Career Author family—Hank Phillippi Ryan, Dana Isaacson, Brian Andrews, and Jessica Strawser—who talk me down off the ledge through every draft; my agent, friend, and personal Yoda, Gina Panettieri; all my fellow Talcott Notch peeps—Amy Collins, Saba Sulaiman, Dennis Schleicher, and Nadia Lynch—and of course, my Stone Cold Crime Writers and my Scribe Tribe.

The crime-writing community is unfailingly generous, and I am lucky to be a part of this literary family. I'm lucky to be a part of the Lee/Munier/ Bergman family as well: my love and appreciation always and forever to Alexis, Greg, and Mikey; Trisha and Chris; Elektra, Calypso, and Demelza; my mother and my husband, Michael, who assured me more than once that I would finish this book just like I'd finished the first four.

Finally, to you, dear reader. Without you, there is no Mercy Carr, no Troy Warner, no Elvis or Susie Bear. Thank you for allowing me to spend time with these characters, and with you. Until next time . . .